"So who is this vampire hunter?"
"The undertaker. Mr. Toomes."
Bob scratched his head.
"The undertaker."
Paltruck nodded.
"Is a vampire hunter."
"Uh-huh."
"And his name is Toomes."
"Yes."
Bob said: "Are you putting me on?"

This is a work of fiction. The people, events, locales, and circumstances depicted are fictitious or used fictitiously and are the product of the author's imagination. Any resemblance to any actual events, locales, organizations, or persons, whether living or dead, is entirely coincidental.

TELEVISION MAN

a novel

by James V. Viscosi

PROLOGUE

The Diner

REMEMBER THE SIX of us as we were, before everything went crazy?

We sit in a corner booth at the Raincoat Cafe in Old Forge, where we have just finished a lunch of salads and soup, cheeseburgers and club sandwiches, French fries and apple pie: Extravagant, compared to the food we get now, but unremarkable at the time, ordinary. The dishes have been cleared away. Chuck's map is spread across the top of the table—so archaic, a paper map; but then, Chuck always was a late adopter—showing the Adirondack Park, the vast mountain preserve of northern New York, where the wild things still lived then. Where they live even now.

Chuck traces his finger along the red line of Route 28. His plan is to follow it to Blue Mountain Lake, then head north to Tupper Lake, Saranac Lake, Lake Placid, and beyond. We would make a circle through the enormous park and head south on I-87, also known as the Northway, and return home via I-90, also known as the Thruway. South on the Northway, and not through on the Thruway, that was his plan. Is it any surprise things didn't work out the way he expected?

"Blue Mountain Lake," Chuck says, tapping a spot on the map. "We'll stop at the Adirondack Museum—"

Chuck's wife, Gwen, makes the crucial interruption. "A museum? You want to spend a beautiful day like this cooped up in a museum?"

"You didn't complain about the museum when we were planning this trip."

"You mean when you were planning it," she says. "I don't remember being asked for my opinion."

"It's a starred attraction," Chuck says.

"So?"

"So it's really good."

"Says who?"

Chuck holds up a thick little book. He points at the logo on the cover. "Says the auto club."

Gwen rolls her eyes extravagantly.

"Okay. What do you want to do instead?"

"Take a side road. Drive into the wilderness. See what's really out there. The auto club doesn't have everything in the world mapped out, you know."

"Everything worth doing," Chuck says, his voice bordering on a mumble.

"She's got a point," Kyle says. "It might be fun to do some exploring."

"See? I'm not the only one." She looks at the rest of us. "What do you say?"

Before any of us answers, Chuck waggles the book at her. "We've got the whole trip laid out right in here. It—hey!"

Gwen, quick as a ferret, has snatched it away from him and is already sliding out of the booth. Seated on the outside, she gets a head start on Chuck, who has to squeeze his belly around the table. By the time he is on his feet, she is out the door and into the morning sun.

The diner stood—still does stand, under a different name—on the eastern bank of the Moose River. It has a wooden pavilion that sticks out over the water, striding on pilings above the cool black current. Gwen runs to the railing of the deck. Customers sit eating at plastic tables beneath patio umbrellas. They were watching the river flow past, hoping to spot herons, ducks, an otter, perhaps even the moose that gives the river its name; now they're watching Gwen. She stands at the edge, holding the book by the spine. Waiting.

Chuck comes out of the restaurant and spies her. The rest of us are right behind him. "Quit fooling around," he says. "Give that back. Our whole itinerary is in there."

"I'm sick of doing what this thing says to do." Gwen shakes the guidebook over the water. "It's predictable. It's safe. It's boring."

"You're acting like a spoiled brat," Chuck says. "If you want to plan the trip next time, just say so."

"I don't want to plan anything. I want to drive away and be surprised. I want to have an adventure!"

"Okay, well, there's white-water rafting places in there. That's an adventure. There's horseback riding places in there. That's—what are you doing?" She has turned to face the water. She flings the guidebook away. It spins through the air, white pages flashing; then it splashes into the river and begins to drift away in the languid current. Some of the other diners are scowling at Gwen, at all of us. We are ruffians and litterbugs. We are noisy. We argue. We throw things in the river.

"Oh, that's terrific," Chuck says.

Gwen turns, smiles, and walks away from the railing.

"That was very mature," Chuck says. "What are you going to do for an encore, drive the van into a lake so we'll have to travel on foot?"

"No," she says. "You're going to drive. We're going to go exploring."

So that's what we did; and as often happens when you travel with neither map nor destination, we found things we weren't looking for. When that turns out well, you might call it serendipity.

Let's call this something else.

A DAY IN THE MOUNTAINS

Exploring

CHUCK COULDN'T BELIEVE Gwen had thrown away the guidebook. How were they supposed to know where to stop without a list of restaurants and attractions? He knew some of the others had brought their smartphones, and could maybe use those to look things up, but reception was spotty out here in the big wide park. Paper never let you down. She'd pitched it good and far, though; nothing he could do except hook his thumbs into his belt and watch the book get thick and swollen as the river carried his travel plans away.

When he went back around front, Gwen stood with Kyle next to the van—she laughed at something he said, and touched him on the arm—while Robin stood off to the side, arms folded, squinting at the sky like she was trying to figure out if it might rain. Kyle and Robin were Gwen's friends, a couple she'd met at the gym she'd recently begun using. Chuck was pretty sure that Kyle, a glad-handing twit in his opinion, just wanted to fuck Gwen; Robin was kind of quiet, a moody type, with an expression that suggested a stone in her shoe was poking her in the foot. Chuck suspected the stone was named Kyle. When Gwen had floated the idea of inviting them, he'd told her he would think about it, and it had never been mentioned again; but after they'd picked up Bob and Myra this morning, Gwen had reminded him that they also needed to pick up Kyle and Robin, who, it turned out, lived just around the corner. And then what was he supposed to do? Say no, and have to explain why?

Kyle saw Chuck approaching and flashed that salesman's smile of his and said, "So, we're going to do some exploring?"

Yeah, Chuck knew what kind of exploring Kyle was interested in. "I guess," he said. "We'll drive a big loop and hope something interesting comes along. I'll take the turns nice and fast. It'll be a thrill a minute." He circled the van and climbed into the driver's seat. Gwen wordlessly took her place next to him, while the others filled up the two benches in the back. Behind the last bench, Chuck could just see the tops of their bags, piled up in the cargo area. During the week, and on a lot of weekends, the van was one of Chuck's small fleet of vehicles-on-call, transporting seniors, children, and, occasionally, dogs, but for this outing it had been repurposed into a hiker-hauler for coolers and day-trip bags. Kyle and Robin had even brought serious-looking backcountry packs, like they were planning to walk the Appalachian Trail all the way to Maine. He wondered if Kyle had condoms stashed in his. You know, just in case.

Once the last door was shut and everyone was buckled in, Chuck started the engine and they pulled out of the parking lot. He made a left onto Route 28, heading north out of Old Forge. He had only been kidding about taking the turns fast; the road was narrow and curvy, rising and falling and bending and twisting with the fractured terrain. The villages of Eagle Bay and Inlet came and went, slowing them down with speed zones as they passed homey restaurants and quaint shops and amusements for children and sandy driveways running off to tree-shrouded camps. Beyond Inlet the forest grew thick and dark and close, and the road became even more tortuous, like an enormous go-cart track. If they were going to find someplace remote and uncivilized to walk, the stretch of wilderness between Inlet and Blue Mountain Lake, which hosted the museum that Gwen had declared unacceptable and boring, was a good place to look. Chuck began keeping an eye out for desolate spurs, preferably unpaved. There were plenty of access routes leading to lakes and fishing areas, trailheads around every bend, no shortage of places where you could pull off onto a sandy bulge in the shoulder, get out, and walk along the road under the watchful glare of signs threatening you with arrest for taking a step into the unknown; but Gwen wanted to go *exploring*. Labeled parking lots and common trails and roadside turnouts would not do.

At some point, well after Inlet and well before Blue Mountain Lake, just after they rounded a tight turn, Chuck spotted a narrow, unmarked dirt road that branched off to the right and vanished around a rocky outcropping. No warning signs, no *Private Road*, no gate, no chain. Perfect. He stepped on the brake and veered off the blacktop. The vehicle lurched and wobbled as it left the pavement and bounced across a washed-out shoulder; then they were rumbling along a narrow, rutted path, pines and encroaching underbrush waggling with their passage, leaving a cloud of dust that obscured the view from the rear window.

"Chuck?" Gwen said, clutching the armrest. "What the hell?"

"We're exploring," he said. He didn't look at her; he was too busy keeping the van out of the woods. He hadn't anticipated that the road would be quite so unkempt. The ruts held the van wheels tightly enough to make it difficult to control, but not tightly enough to prevent it from jumping them in the turns.

"A lot of these little roads lead to private camps," Robin said. "We might be trespassing." So, the buzzkill from the back bench had a voice after all. Chuck hadn't seen any signs, so he didn't worry about it. The road banked sharply to the right and began to climb. The trees to the left fell away, revealing a steep, rocky slope rolling down to a shallow river. Coffee-colored foam flecked the black surface of the water where the current broke over the rubble-strewn bed. Someone was fishing in the creek, standing in hip boots near a heap of boulders, the water not much past his knees. The yellow pole in his hand flashed back and forth, whipping a thin line—it was barely visible against the black water, fine as spider's silk—into a delicate pattern before letting it fly. The fisherman glanced up for a look at who was rumbling through his wilderness, but from this angle Chuck couldn't see his face, just his maroon shirt, glistening black waders, and grey hat festooned with colorful lures, like tufts of decorative frosting on a red velvet cupcake.

"Chuck!"

He reflexively stomped on the brake, and as he turned saw why Gwen had shrieked: A young buck stood in the road only a few yards ahead, staring at them with stupidly vacant deer eyes, soft black deer nose twitching, stubby deer antlers still fuzzy with fresh deer velvet.

"Jesus Christ, Chuck." Gwen relaxed back into her seat. "If you're going to drive like a maniac, at least look at the damn road."

The others remained conspicuously silent. Embarrassed, Chuck thumped the horn. The deer recoiled from the noise; its ears swiveled, and its eyes narrowed in an almost human expression of annoyance. It bounded off the edge of the road, skittering down the rocky hillside toward the water. He watched it go, its tail straight up, white as a flag of surrender. The animal splashed across the river and vanished into the woods on the other side. The fisherman was gone, too; he must've moved downstream, out of view behind the boulders, away from the intruders and their noisy vehicle.

Chuck stepped on the gas. They started moving again. Chastened, he drove more slowly, and he looked at the damn road. After a little while it bent to the left, then plunged steeply down to the riverbank. Chuck stopped at the top of the slope, eyeing their future route, if they continued onward. It ran along the top of a rough berm between the wide, shallow current on the left and a swampy, soft-looking meadow on the right. Mountains ringed the flood plain, bare rock crowns thrusting blue-grey from the tops of spiny pine sheaths. Thin clouds crossed the sky like white scrapes, or scars. He eyed the sharply angled descent. Maybe this was far enough. They could leave the van here and proceed on foot.

Kyle leaned forward to pat Chuck on the shoulder. "Think you can get this jalopy down the hill without tipping it over?"

"We could just park up here and walk down," Gwen said.

"Nah, we haven't gotten anywhere yet," Kyle said. "Hey, Chuck, let me drive. I can handle her."

Asshole. "We'll be fine," Chuck said. He stepped on the gas.

They rumbled down the slope toward the meadow. The van shook and bounced; the speedometer needle crept upward, ten, twenty, thirty. Chuck touched the brake, but the van didn't slow much; he heard dirt grinding beneath the tires as they skidded along in a mini-landslide of sand and loose soil. The wheel twisted under his hands as they started to turn sideways. He wrenched the wheel back the other way, overcorrected, then finally got it straightened out. They stopped at the bottom of the hill, angled across the road, with only a few feet of space between their right front bumper and a sign that was so overgrown with brambles that it was unreadable. After a moment, Bob said: "Well, that was an adventure all right."

Chuck heard the back door slide open and looked over his shoulder. Kyle and Robin were getting out. He watched Kyle close his eyes and inhale deeply of nature's bounty. He wondered if he'd get in trouble for driving away and leaving Mr. Wonderful out in his element.

"Will we be able to get back to the top?" Gwen said, leaning over to peer up the gravelly hill.

"I think so," Chuck said, although he was sort of wishing he had brought one of the SUVs instead of the van. Gwen made a dubious noise as she opened the glove compartment and removed the Adirondack map. Chuck watched her struggle to unfold it properly in the small space available. "I thought we weren't using maps anymore," he said. "I thought you wanted to explore."

"Explore, yes. Get stuck in the wilderness, no."

"We won't get stuck. If we can't make it up the hill, we'll call the auto club."

"There's no cell service out here."

"Someone can walk out and flag down a car, then. Here, give me that." He took the map out of her hands, then opened the door and exited the vehicle. The river rushed by a few yards in front of him. Chuck went and tossed the map in. It was immediately swept away. Maybe it would meet up with the guidebook someday in some far-off, stagnant eddy. Reunited and it feels so good.

Kyle's voice floated over from the other side of the van: "Hey, look at this!" Peering through the window, Chuck saw that he was using a stick to hold the thorny creepers away from the front of the sign, which was made of wood and said, in faded yellow letters, *Village of Blackberry Hollow 3 miles*. An arrow pointed in the direction they were going.

"*Blackberry Hollow*," Robin said. "That sounds pretty."

"Why's the sign so overgrown?" Bob said. He sat on the ledge created by the open sliding door. Myra was behind him, leaning on his shoulders, surveying their surroundings.

"Maybe the village is abandoned," Kyle said. "Ski resort closed down, everyone moved away. We can do some urbex."

"What?" Chuck said. "Some what?"

"Urbex. You know. Urban exploration?"

"It doesn't get much less *urban* than an abandoned village at the end of a dirt road in the middle of the Adirondacks," Myra said, to Chuck's surprise. She'd been peering up at the mountains and he didn't think she'd been following the conversation.

"Details," Kyle said. "I vote we check it out. Who's up for it?" He cast about for support. "Show of hands?"

"We don't need to vote," Gwen said. "We're down here already. Let's go."

"Great! So it's settled. We won't run out of gas on the way, will we, Chuck?"

"Of course not." He knew how to monitor a gas gauge, for Christ's sake. So evidently they were going to Blackberry Hollow. How had that happened?

Bob and Myra made way for Kyle and Robin as they climbed back into the van, then returned to their seats. Chuck got in the driver's seat and put the car into drive, and they moved out. After its initial climb and subsequent descent into the valley, the road stayed near the river, hemmed in by low, rocky, round-topped mountains. Coniferous and deciduous trees formed a patchwork in shades of green clinging to the sides of the peaks. To their left, the river splashed and bounded in the looming shadow of thick forest; to their right, high grass and shrubs, thorny creepers, and low, twisted trees spread under the shadow of a particularly craggy peak. Chuck didn't see any blackberries in the bramble. Maybe they weren't in season yet.

Eventually, the road veered away from the river and climbed a gentle, grassy slope, then split into three separate routes. The right fork, which vanished into the forest, was blocked by a wooden gate bearing a sign that said *Blackberry Mountain Retreat*, and below that, *PRIVATE*. The left fork ran at a slight downward angle along the top of the ridge, then bent right and disappeared from view behind an outcropping of weathered grey stone. Straight ahead, the road widened and curved around the trees. A weathered marker showing a stick-figure hiker pointed at the middle fork, so Chuck went that way, skirting the edge of the forest. They hadn't gotten far before Chuck heard a grunt from the back seat, and then Bob's voice: "Myra?"

"Just a headache coming on," she said.

"Just a headache? Not a migraine?" Chuck didn't catch Myra's response, but obviously Bob did. "You want a couple?" he asked.

"Yeah, all right. Thanks."

Chuck wondered: A couple what? Then he heard Bob rummaging through their packs, and a moment later, the plastic rattle of tablets in a container. In the rearview mirror he saw Bob handing his wife a water bottle and a couple of light blue pills. She downed them with a practiced motion, then took a big swig from the bottle. "Do we need to turn around?"

"I don't think so," Bob said. "We'll let you know."

"Okay," Chuck said. He'd known Myra suffered from migraines, but had never been around for one. Maybe it had been brought on by Kyle's stinky cologne. Chuck couldn't decide if it would repel bears and scavengers, or attract them.

They drove on until the road widened and ended in a badly eroded gravel parking lot. No other vehicles were present. Chuck stopped the van. A clear path ran into the woods to the right, with a large brown sign next to it that said, in carved letters with faded yellow paint, *Blackberry Mountain Trail, 2 miles*.

Chuck twisted in his seat to look back at the passengers. "Are you up for this? Myra, Bob?"

"I'll stay here," Myra said.

"Me too," Bob said.

"No, go ahead." Myra's voice was unsteady. "I'll be fine by myself."

"Don't be silly." Myra didn't reply, and after a moment Bob said: "The rest of you go. We'll stay here."

"But—"

"We came out here to hike and be outside," Bob said. "Go do it. If Myra feels better, we'll meet you at the top."

Kyle nodded, and said: "Well? Robin? Gwen? Chuck?"

Chuck was pretty sure he had heard a slight, denigrating delay between his name and the other two. He eyed the path. It looked fairly level, but who knew what happened deeper in the woods? It could go straight up the side of the mountain. He didn't relish the thought of hanging from a cliff by his fingers and toes. "Sure," he said. "Sure, I'm up for it."

"Attaboy."

Kyle was already on his way out to join Robin at the rear door, and didn't see the glare Chuck aimed at him, which was probably just as well. Robin was getting their backpacks out of the pile. Why those two thought they needed to carry all that crap for a two-mile hike was beyond him, but whatever. Chuck grunted and started to exit the vehicle, but Gwen put her hand on his elbow. "Chuck. Wait. Leave the key for Bob."

"What?"

"Leave the key so they can run the air conditioner if it gets too hot inside."

"But somebody might steal the van."

Gwen gestured at the surrounding wilderness. "We're in the middle of nowhere, Chuck. Who's going to steal the van? A bear? Bob, are you going to let a bear steal the van?"

"Uh, no," Bob said. Then: "Look, you really don't have to—"

"Yes, we do. Chuck. Leave the key."

Chuck pressed his lips together. Gwen didn't get it. This was a company car, not his personal vehicle, and Bob didn't even *want* the damn key, but Gwen had decided it must be left in the van, and if he refused she'd just add it to his list of violations. This supposed getaway was turning out just like any other day spent bickering about where to shop, what to watch on television, what to have for dinner. "Fine," he said. He put the key back in the ignition, then got out, slamming the door shut behind him.

Kyle jumped, apparently startled by the sharp noise, so that was a little bit gratifying, at least; but then Robin, not looking up, said: "Let's all try to keep it down so we don't make Myra's headache worse, okay?"

Chuck felt his face redden. Nothing like a gentle rebuke from someone you barely knew to make you feel subhuman. "Sorry. I wasn't thinking." She did look at him then, and surprised him by smiling a little before turning away and slipping on her backpack. It occurred to him that she probably never heard an apology from Kyle, for anything, ever.

Not having his own pack to retrieve, he went around to gently close the rear door, then followed Gwen, Kyle, and Robin up the path and into the woods.

~~~~

As the others disappeared up the trail, Bob moved to the front passenger seat, giving Myra room to stretch out on the middle bench. She'd gobbled a couple more of the tablets while the others got ready to go, but they didn't seem to be helping. Now she lay flat on her back with her right arm folded across her eyes, looking miserable. Low seventies, sunshine, light breeze: It was a beautiful day, but she couldn't enjoy it, and neither could he. Bob had been looking forward to spending some time outside. He supposed sitting parked in the shade with the windows down sort of qualified as being outdoors, but so far, this excursion had been anything but relaxing. What was up with Chuck and Gwen today? They'd been bickering even more than usual, one awkward scene after another. No wonder Myra had developed a migraine. All the posturing and squabbling gave him a headache, too.

Maybe it was something to do with having Kyle and Robin along. He knew them by sight from around the neighborhood, had exchanged greetings with them once in a while when they'd met on the sidewalk. They'd always seemed pleasant enough during those brief encounters, but now that he'd spent some time with those two, he wouldn't be in any hurry to take them on another road trip. Kyle had turned out to be a needler, and while his snark was mostly directed at Chuck, Bob wouldn't want to be on the receiving end of it.

He reclined in the seat a little, closed his eyes, listened to the gentle sounds around them: The burble of the distant creek, the rustling of tree leaves, the melodic calls of the ... Well, there weren't any bird calls at the moment. Which was, yeah, a little bit odd, all the birds taking a lunch break at once. No insect noises either. Why was it so quiet? It wasn't quite natural. Maybe the noisy van and its occupants had silenced them.

Suddenly Myra shrieked, shattering the stillness. Bob nearly fell out of the van. He twisted in his seat to look at her. She was propped up on one elbow, eyes wide open and unfocused, staring at the ceiling. Her face glistened with sweat. Her mouth still hung wide open, but she had stopped shrieking. The noise she emitted instead was a high thin whine that was, somehow, worse. As he goggled at her, she flipped over onto her stomach and buried her head beneath her arms. She started screaming again. Her voice was muffled by the fact that she was pressing her face into the seat, but it sounded like she was making words, or trying to. Or was it just grunting? Jesus Christ. Then she fell silent, and that was even worse.

Bob said: "Myra?"

She lifted her head, looked at him without seeing him, and lowered it again, pressing her face into the upholstery. Bob had no idea what the fuck was going on, but knew he needed to take her back to town, find an urgent care or something. He scanned the woods. No sign of the others. They could be hundreds of yards away by now. Should he go after them, tell them to come back? Myra screamed again. Her voice trailed off into an incoherent gurgle. No, he didn't have time to find the others. For all he knew she was having a stroke or an aneurysm or her brain was exploding.

He climbed over the center console to the driver's seat and started the engine. Now he was glad Gwen had insisted on leaving the keys. "Hang on," he said over his shoulder. "This is going to be a bumpy ride." She didn't answer. He didn't know if she even heard him. She certainly wasn't in any shape to hang on to anything. Bob turned the van around and they rumbled up the access road, back the way they had come. The van bounced along the rough road, raising a huge cloud of dust. He was going too fast. When they started skidding on loose soil and rocks he eased back so they wouldn't end up in the river. Finally, the slope they had careered down came into view, absurdly steep as it loomed through the windshield. It hadn't seemed that tall on the way in.

He revved the engine and roared up the hill, but they'd only gotten halfway before the van stopped. The speedometer needle crept up as the wheels spun faster, but the van just sat there, digging itself four holes. Bob finally took his foot off the gas and the speedometer dropped to zero. Looking over his shoulder, he threw the vehicle into reverse, stepped cautiously on the gas. The wheels spun, but the van only moved a little. Deciding to treat the sandy gravel like snow, Bob put the van in drive and stepped on the gas. It nudged forward. He immediately threw it into reverse again and gunned it, then back into drive, then back into reverse. Finally the big vehicle hauled itself out of its ruts and tottered backwards down the hill, coming to a stop at the bottom, near the sign for the village again.

Bob looked back at Myra. She lay very still now, not screaming, not moving. He couldn't tell if she was even breathing. "Myra?" he said. "Still with me?"

No response.

Damn it all. Why had Chuck picked *this* road to wander down? They couldn't get up the hill. There wasn't any cell reception. There wasn't a ranger station. What was he supposed to do? Abandon the van and walk out to the road and hope the signal came back or that some passerby would stop? No. He couldn't leave Myra alone for however long that might take. He decided to turn the van around and head for that Blackberry Hollow place. Maybe there would be a doctor there, or a cell tower, or at least someone with a land line to call for help.

And if Blackberry Hollow was deserted? What then?

Well, he would worry about that when he got there.

Because, really, he didn't have anywhere else to go.

~~~~

The trail up Blackberry Mountain wasn't difficult at first; it started out wide, flat, and smooth, the ground a ruddy tan from years of fallen leaves and pine needles, not unlike the jogging paths in the park near their house. Gwen almost expected to see a flock of brightly colored all-terrain-stroller-pushing mommy-joggers go by. Soon, though, the going got rougher. The trees, full and green, pressed closer to the trail. They passed huge, solitary boulders. Fallen trunks became common, evidencing their age by the extent to which moss covered them. The mommy-joggers never materialized.

Some distance further on, they reached a section where the trees had been flattened. All of them pointed in the same direction, as if they'd been steamrollered. Rich dirt still clung to the exposed roots, thick and black as a mountain man's beard. They must have been blown down by a storm, she figured, though it seemed weird that a storm strong enough to knock trees down would have left their leaves attached. She thought they might turn around, but Kyle and Robin clambered into the tangle of limbs and trunks and slippery foliage and kept right on going. Chuck glanced at Gwen, then at the rustling barrier, and then plunged in as well, leaving her standing there alone.

Gwen sighed and started picking her way through the downed trees, trying not to let her white shorts—hardly the best choice for the woods, she now realized—get too messed up. Branches plucked and grabbed as if trying to pull her back. She had to be careful to avoid getting her legs scraped by the rough-skinned branches; it took her a good ten minutes to get to the other side, where Chuck was waiting, looking flushed and somewhat impatient. She brushed herself off in a slow, deliberate fashion, and then they continued up the mountain. The others had not waited; they seemed to be pretty far ahead, audible but not visible, their voices occasionally echoing down from above as the path became steeper and rockier.

They eventually found Kyle and Robin waiting for them at the bottom of a barren stretch of rock. "This part's a scramble," Kyle said, pointing. "We just wanted to hang out and make sure you were up to tackling it before we went up."

Chuck peered at him, then at the slope, then brushed past and started picking his way up. "Try not to slow me down," he said over his shoulder.

Kyle grinned and winked at Gwen; she thought she caught an eye-roll from Robin. The two of them moved out and, after a moment, she did, too.

At the top of the scramble the soil grew thinner, bringing the tree roots closer to the surface, bulging from the earth like knotted veins. The spine of the mountain began to show through the skin of dirt, grey rock that was patchy at first but grew more and more prominent. The visual distinction between the trail and the surrounding wilderness was lost, and they had to rely on faded red markers nailed to tree trunks to guide them. Chuck started to drop back again. He tried to keep up, to pretend that he could surge up the mountain just as fast as Kyle and Robin, but his body couldn't meet the demands of his ego. Soon he was breathing hard, pausing to take mini-rests up against trees; the rests got longer as they climbed higher. Kyle and Robin pulled farther ahead. Gwen tried to keep up with them for a little while, but it was hard on her feet, moving that fast. She went back to find Chuck. He was sitting on a small boulder, leaning forward, hands on his knees, face tipped toward the ground, wheezing.

"You okay?" she said.

He nodded.

"You don't look okay."

"Fine," he said.

"It's fine that you don't look okay?"

He squinted up at her; the sun was over her shoulder, making his sweaty face seem very red. "Just need to rest a minute."

"You don't get enough exercise to be pushing yourself like this."

"Don't need exercise," he said. "Got a car."

"Uh-huh."

"Everything all right?" Kyle called. He was some distance up the slope, standing on one leg, with the other bent at the knee on a triangular outcropping. He looked like an explorer who had sacrificed a limb on a daring survey expedition, or maybe a mad prophet. Robin was not in evidence.

She waved to him. "We're just resting!" she shouted.

"Okay!" Kyle unfolded himself from his perch and disappeared.

Chuck stood up. His face was flushed again, angry-looking. "Do you want to go back down?" Gwen said.

"I'll make it."

"Are you—"

"I said I'll make it."

After a moment Gwen said: "Don't kill yourself trying to prove some stupid man thing."

He didn't answer her; he just started trudging up the path. She stood there for a minute, then followed.

Overhead, the sun continued creeping across the sky, as if it, too, had something to prove.

~~~~

A few miles up the left branch of the road, Bob came to what was, he supposed, Blackberry Hollow. It didn't amount to much, not even a wide spot in the road. Whereas Old Forge had all the trappings of civilization, such as restaurants, gas stations, sidewalks, and paved roads, Blackberry Hollow consisted of a hard-packed dirt street surrounded by houses in varying states of disrepair. They didn't look deserted, exactly—they weren't falling down, they didn't have trees growing through their roofs—but a few of the places had broken windows or smashed-in doors, and none gave the impression of being permanently, or even currently, occupied. He drove slowly up the main drag. Uprooted trees lay everywhere, all pointing the same way that the van was traveling, their leaves still green and not yet wilted. The town was wired for electricity but the poles were down. The wires doodled along the ground like errant pencil scribblings. Apparently they'd recently had a bad storm and the damage hadn't been fixed yet.

Where were all the people?

The buildings slowly scrolled by. Entering what must be the business district, he passed a shuttered tavern that catered to snowmobilers and a small, dark mini-market. The stump of a pay phone stood on its front porch, next to an ancient-looking ice machine. Silver wires protruded from the shorn-off post. He wouldn't be calling for help from there. A short distance past the store, he came to a large house with a sign in its yard. The sign had somehow survived whatever disaster had befallen the trees and the utility poles, and stood in the afternoon sunshine advertising the offices of one Harry Zane, M.D. Bob stopped the van and leaned over, peering at the place through the passenger-side window. It didn't look as deserted as some of the others; the yard was mowed, the shrubs were trimmed, an Adirondack chair on the porch was free of leaves and crap. What a place like this would be doing out here in a tumbledown settlement at the end of a dirt road in the middle of nowhere, he had no idea. Maybe he treated snowmobilers who spent too much time at the tavern and then crashed on their way out of town.

Bob glanced at Myra. She lay on her back, eyes closed, face twisted into a grimace. He could see the shallow rise and fall of her chest. Speaking softly, he said: "We're at a doctor's office. I'm going to see if it's open." He didn't wait for her to answer; she rarely spoke when suffering from a migraine. She never, ever screamed. Until today.

He hurried to what appeared to be the office, an addition on the side with a wooden door bearing the doctor's name. No bell. He gave the door a few solid raps, waited a moment, then cut across the yard to the big front porch. This door had a bell. It bonged thunderously when he rang it, so this place, at least, still had power. Maybe the doctor ran a generator. Bob waited a few minutes, then reached for the bell again, but before he pressed it the door opened to reveal a tall man in late middle age. He had apparently been gardening recently; lines of black dirt shadowed the fingernails of the hand he'd used to open the door, and he wore work clothes with old, laundered grass stains at the knees and elbows.

The man said: "Can I help you?"

Wondering if this might be the doctor's landscaper, Bob said: "Is Dr. Zane in?"

"Yes, he is."

"Is he, uh, is he seeing patients today?"

The man raised a bushy eyebrow. "I could," he said. "Do you need to *be* a patient today?"

"Oh. Sorry. Not me. My wife. She's in the van." He pointed at the vehicle, as if Dr. Zane couldn't see it parked right there in front of his house. "She gets migraines. She had one in the car, a bad one, she screamed, and now she's just lying there, like, unconscious. I'm afraid she might be having a stroke or something."

The doctor nodded gravely. "I understand your concern, but please, try not to worry yourself. It's quite unlikely your wife has had a stroke. When did the headache start?"

"About twenty minutes ago. We were going to climb Blackberry Mountain, but when we got to the lot, she——"

"All right," Dr. Zane said. "I'll help you bring her into my office. Wait here a moment." The doctor stepped back and closed the door. It opened again shortly and he emerged, now wearing a long white coat and a stethoscope around his neck, which evidently he kept in the front hall for just such an emergency. Groundskeeper to medical-show stalwart in ten seconds flat.

Well, whatever. If he could help Myra, Bob didn't care if he did a quick-change into a red sequined dress.

~~~~

The trail offered a decent workout, gradually steepening until it was obvious that you weren't just climbing a hill, you were on your way up a mountain. But Chuck. Good God. The pace he set, you would think he was scaling the Himalayas. Kyle had never once seen Chuck at the gym with Gwen, and now he knew why: The exertion of climbing the stairs to the equipment room would have killed him.

Kyle had been that out of shape once, but he'd had a reason: He'd almost lost his leg in a motorcycle accident, had spent weeks immobilized in the hospital because of that, and months immobilized on the sofa in front of the television, just because. That period of sluggishness had ended the day he'd gotten out of breath going down the hall to the toilet. Looking in the mirror, he'd promised himself he was going to change, gimpy leg be damned. He was going to get back in shape. He was going to get back to the way he'd been before. And he had done it.

So what was Chuck's excuse?

Normally Kyle would have just left him behind, but Gwen was hanging back, too, letting him drag her down. Kyle figured highlighting Chuck's inadequacies might motivate the big blob to move a little faster, so he adopted a pattern of brisk climbing, followed by waiting for them to almost catch up, followed by more brisk climbing that left them behind again. Robin, being Robin, moved at her own pace, pausing occasionally to look back, frown a little, and continue climbing. He passed her when she was sitting out in the sun at the edge of an outcropping, looking at the valley. Off in her own little world, no doubt, with its own little sky and a sun the color of a California poppy.

The forest fell away as the trail rose higher, allowing a panoramic view of the valley and surrounding mountains. He stopped a few times to take pictures with his phone. The region seemed uninhabited, except for a small cluster of buildings on the valley floor off to his right. There was no sign of other hikers. They were completely alone out here. If Chuck and Gwen weren't around, he'd be tempted to take Robin off the path and fool around a little. Or if just Chuck weren't around, he'd take Robin and Gwen off the path and fool around with both of them. Not that Robin would ever go for that, of course.

"They're way far behind." Robin's voice came from above, startling him. She was perched on a large boulder alongside the trail, crouched on all fours. How had she gotten up there? She hadn't passed him; she must scrambled up the near-vertical slope from where she had been sitting.

"Yeah," Kyle said. "Should we wait for them to catch up?"

"Probably."

Kyle sighed and looked back down the trail. Chuck and Gwen had yet to crest a steep stretch of bare splintery rock that he had scaled ten minutes earlier, though he thought he could hear them scuffling along it. It was the first and, until this boulder, only, stretch where he'd had to use both his hands and feet to climb; fortunately the broad stone face was heavily weathered, with lots of crags for fingers and toes. "He's so slow." Kyle idly started picking bits of bark off a nearby tree, flicking the pieces down the path. "He should've waited in the car with Bob so the rest of us could get to the top while it's still daylight."

"At least he's trying."

"Trying." Kyle shook his head. "He'd rather be home with a beer watching golf."

"*You* drink beer and watch golf."

"That's different."

"Mmm," Robin said. "Of course."

Eventually, Gwen came into view. She looked up at them and waved. Kyle waved back. Then Chuck appeared and Kyle waved at him, too. Chuck just grimaced and kept climbing.

"I don't think Chuck likes you much," Robin said.

"I intimidate him," Kyle said.

"Oh, is that the problem?"

"Uh-huh."

Robin looked like she might have something else to say, but she didn't say it. Instead she sat down at the edge of the boulder and stretched her legs as they waited in silence for Chuck and Gwen to catch up.

Climbing

BOB PERCHED ON a chair in the examination room as Zane checked out his wife. She remained unresponsive as the doctor did all the usual doctor stuff: Shined a light in her eyes, thumped her knee with a little rubber hammer, inflated an old-style manual blood pressure cuff on her arm and then scowled at the dial as if he found it balky. He seemed a little out of practice. Bob wondered how long it had been since he'd given someone a checkup. Maybe he was coming out of retirement just for Myra.

Finally Dr. Zane packed up his stuff and told Bob, "Let's talk outside."

Oh God. There was something so horribly wrong that he couldn't say it in front of Myra, even though she was practically unconscious. Bob got up and followed Zane into the waiting room, then into a small storeroom. As the doctor unlocked a metal cabinet on the wall, he said: "I think it's just a very severe migraine. Does suffer from hay fever, by any chance?"

"Hay fever? No."

"Hmm. Still, all the pollen in the air could be provoking an allergic response. We had a big storm not long ago that stirred everything up."

"But the way she's just lying there ..." Bob trailed off, unwilling to complete the thought, to say that he was afraid Myra had checked out of her body and wasn't coming back.

Dr. Zane cocked his head, listening intently, waiting for him to finish, though if Bob didn't know better he'd have sworn the doctor was listening to someone talking in his ear. After a silence that went on a moment too long, Zane said: "In rare cases catatonia can be associated with migraines, especially in women your wife's age who take certain medications to prevent the headache—specifically, the pills you showed me." He turned and stuck his head in the cabinet, rummaging for something.

"Oh," Bob said. "Catatonia? That's bad, right?" Then, when no answer came: "Sorry, what are you looking for?"

"Something to help her wake up sooner than she might otherwise. Ah, here it is." He straightened up, holding a little bottle and a plastic-wrapped syringe.

"What's that?"

The doctor squinted at the bottle, then showed it to Bob.

"*Lorazepam*," Bob said, reading the small print.

"Yes," Zane said, sounding pleased, as if Bob were a clever pupil. "Lorazepam." It almost seemed like he hadn't known what it was. Maybe he wasn't sure how to pronounce it. They returned to the waiting room together. "You may have a seat here. The chairs are more comfortable. Unless you would like to watch me administer the injection?"

"Um, no, that's fine. I'll wait." Bob plopped into a cushy seat along the outside wall, near a window. A full length mirror on the wall to his left showed him a reflection up the hallway as the doctor went up it and entered the examination room, leaving Bob alone. Spying a stack of magazines on a table under the window, Bob riffled through them. The address labels had all been peeled off, lest the doctor should attract stalkers and identity thieves. There were lots of outdoorsy titles, a few about cars, one about showbiz. He remembered the film on the cover of the entertainment mag; it had made a pile of money and swept the awards shows. Four years ago. He put that aside and picked up an automotive magazine instead. He leafed through it—three-year-old pictures of sports cars were still, after all, pictures of sports cars—until the doctor returned. He was carrying a steaming cup of coffee, perhaps obtained from a quick-brewing pod machine hidden in the back somewhere.

Bob put the magazine down and gave the doctor an expectant look.

"I'm afraid we must be patient a little while longer," Dr. Zane said. "If the injection is going to work, it should do so within half an hour."

"Oh," Bob said. It hadn't occurred to him that not working was an option. "What if it doesn't? Should we call, like, a helicopter or something now? So it can be on its way if we need it?"

"It won't come to that. In all likelihood she will soon be fine. An unnecessary air ambulance call would cost you thousands of dollars."

"Um. Okay. If you're sure?"

The doctor appeared to consider this before saying, "Quite. Yes, quite sure."

"Okay. Great. Thanks. Thanks a lot." Bob stood up and took out his wallet. "What do we owe you? I didn't think to ask if you take our insurance."

Dr. Zane waved his hand, as if to say money was of no consequence here in the paradisiacal garden that was Blackberry Hollow.

"There must at least be a copay."

"No, no. Really. Put that away." Bob looked up. Dr. Zane smiled at him. His teeth were very even and very white. "I have no need of payment from you."

Bob thought he detected a subtle emphasis on the *you*, and for a moment thought the physician was going to name a price, denominated in something other than dollars, to be paid by someone else—Myra, maybe—but he didn't; he just stood there with a slightly-too-wide smile on his face that made Bob oddly uncomfortable. He returned the wallet to his pocket and said: "So, ah, she'll be okay in half an hour, then?"

"Probably," the doctor said. "Everyone reacts differently, of course." He offered the cup to Bob. "You look like you could use a little caffeine."

"Oh. Yeah, I could. Thanks." He took the cup and had a sip. The brew was hot, strong, and fresh, but a little more bitter than Bob was used to. He wondered how many pods had gone into making it.

"Now that the crisis is averted," Dr. Zane said, "I wonder if I might ask you to move your van around to the rear of the house? There's a small parking lot back there."

"Um, sure, I guess, but why——"

"I would hate for you to get a ticket." Dr. Zane pointed out the front window, and Bob realized he had parked right in front of a fire hydrant. He hadn't even noticed it there when he'd pulled up, though that wasn't much of a surprise, he'd been in such a flustered hurry.

Who expected to find a fire hydrant in a place like this, anyway? He was surprised they even had a village water system. While the doctor beamed at him, so thrilled was he to have been of service, Bob headed for the front door, fishing the keys out of his pocket. He went out onto the front step of the office. The door clicked shut behind him. He went down the stairs to the yard, then stopped.

There wasn't a fire hydrant next to the van. There was just a sandy verge with a few bedraggled flowers.

Puzzled, he scratched the back of his head for a moment, then went to the road, looked up and down it. No hydrants anywhere, on either side. He went back to the office and tried to open the door, but found it locked. What? He rattled the handle, then pounded on the glass a few times, garnering no response to his muted thumps. What kind of game was Dr. Zane playing here? He put the coffee cup down next to the steps, then backed off a few paces and charged at the door, putting his shoulder into it like they did in the movies. To his own surprise, this worked; the door burst inward and he stumbled into the office, ending up sprawled on the carpet. He picked himself up and looked around. Dr. Zane wasn't there. No one was. He went to the examination room where Myra had been. She was gone, as if she had never been there. The big pad on the cot looked undisturbed. He left the examination room and searched the place, opening every door, peering into every room. There weren't many, and he had already seen all of them except the bathroom and Zane's small office, with its old school wooden desk and uncomfortable-looking wooden chair and stacks of patient binders. A telephone sat on the desk, but it had no dial tone. There was no computer. Bob ended up back in the waiting room. He noticed something gleaming on the floor in front of the wall mirror. He knelt down and picked it up: A nice, clean syringe, the shiny hypodermic needle uncapped, plunger fully depressed. This was the medication Zane had injected Myra with, wasn't it? What was it doing out here?

Bob stared at the syringe for a moment, then put it down on the table next to the magazines. He looked around again. There had to be another way out of here. Zane and Myra were gone, and they didn't just vanish. So the other way out must be hidden. What the fuck kind of doctor's office had a secret door? Was Zane some kind of mad scientist?

He went out and did a quick circuit of the entire place. The house itself had a back door, leading to a small patio surrounded by a garden full of weird flowers, but the office addition had no exterior door other than the one in front. Bob was pretty sure you weren't allowed to have a workplace with just one exit, not even in the middle of nowhere, so he figured there must be some way to get from the office to the house. He just hadn't found it. He cut through the garden to the back door, deliberately tramping through Zane's flowerbed. The door was locked and sturdy. No one responded to his pounding. He went to a nearby window and peered through it into a kitchen. It was dim, illuminated by light coming in through an archway from the front of the house, where the sun was, and looked like the sort of kitchen you might find in a museum house, as an exhibit of how people cooked forty or fifty years ago, but not a place where anyone actually prepared food. Through the archway he could see a dining room that looked similarly disused, with a table set with old flatware, like for a tea party that had never happened.

He took a step back and cast about for something he could use to break a window. The patio and garden and surrounding yard seemed conspicuously short on things like rocks or bricks or heavy pots. Maybe Chuck had a tire iron in the van. Bob returned to the vehicle by completing his circuit of the house. None of the rooms he could see through the windows appeared to be any more lived-in than the kitchen or the dining room. It was almost as if he were casing a giant dollhouse.

Back at the van, he found the tire iron in a compartment in the rear cargo area. He hefted it, gave it a swing. Yeah, that would work. He took it up to the front door, which he pounded a few more times, shouting for Zane to open up or face forcible entry. Again, there was no response. All right then. Bob moved to the tall window that flanked the door, raised the tire iron, and swung. The window shattered into a million little pieces, like the fake glass in a movie. Inside, the house was empty, literally. It was just a shell, with nothing inside. No rooms, no walls. He could see all the way across to the back wall, could see the fake kitchen and dining room, reversed, on the window he had looked through. Even from here the level of detail was astounding, the fake 3D effect almost convincing him that he was looking through into a room on the other side. There was no actual door next to the window. Evidently it was a fake, mounted on the outside of the house.

Bob backed off, then—still clutching the tire iron—returned to Zane's office and went inside. He just wanted to make sure it was really there. It existed, but was as deserted as it had been when he left it. He turned in a slow circle in the examination room, baffled, and stopped when facing the mirror. For a second it showed, not himself, but what looked like a tower room in a black castle, big and dark, with huge ornate furniture and a massive fireplace. He could see a wide, fur-covered bed, on which Myra lay, evidently asleep.

The tire iron slipped from his fingers and thunked to the floor, half-rolled and half-bounced under a nearby chair. He took a step forward, but even as he did, the image in the mirror fluttered and faded and returned to showing Bob, staring at himself, looking stunned and confused. He touched the mirror with his fingers. Hard and cold, like a mirror should be. It was made of highly polished metal, not glass. It didn't move when he tugged on it.

What the *actual* fuck was going on here?

~~~~

From the top of the mountain, the destruction they had crawled through at the start of the path was even more obvious, and stranger: A swath of fallen trees, all pointing in the same direction, came into view from the left, curved around the edge of Blackberry Mountain, and sliced straight through the forest below. The trail of smashed trees continued on until it entered the cleared area around a few buildings off to the right. Robin, eyeing it, said: "What do you think? Tornado?"

"No, they're all pointing the same way," Kyle said. "A tornado would've tossed them all over the place."

"Microburst?"

"Too narrow for a microburst," Kyle said. "It must have been a machine."

"I didn't see any tracks. Anyway, they wouldn't just flatten down the trees and leave them like that."

"Maybe it was a giant boulder from space," Kyle said. This absurd suggestion signified that he had lost interest in the matter. Robin favored him with an *mmm* and moved away down the rounded summit, coming to the edge of a palisade. She could see the road they'd driven down, and the river beside it; the mountains were higher in that direction, blocking the view of the rest of the park. In fact, they were totally boxed in by taller peaks. She could only see the surrounding marshy meadow, nothing beyond, none of the other nearby lakes or villages or even the main road. She felt strangely let down. The little valley was pretty enough, but you expected a sense of distance from the top of a mountain. Instead, she felt ringed in. Enclosed. Trapped, even.

She heard footsteps and panting from behind her. Chuck and

Gwen had finally arrived. Because she was off the summit and away from the path, they passed by without noticing her, which was fine. Not that Chuck was a bad guy, really: A little stick-in-the-muddy, maybe, set in his just-so ways, probably heading towards a curmudgeonly middle age, but not *bad*. And if he didn't like Kyle very much, well, she couldn't really blame him for that, could she? A lot of the time, she didn't like Kyle very much either. Then there was Gwen who, Robin thought, liked Kyle more than she should. Ha. Just wait until you get to know him better, sweetheart.

Robin lay down and stretched out on the rock. It was warm from the sunshine, felt good against her skin. The surface was highly splintered here, broken into hundreds of tiny chunks. She idly pried one loose, a little piece maybe the size of a playing card, turned it over in her hand. This fragment had been part of the mountain for a billion years, and she had dislodged it. The side that had faced the sky was blank and weathered; the other had an odd wavy-line pattern where some sort of moss or root or lichen had once grown beneath it, loosening it so that Robin could come along and pop it free. "I think maybe it's time to move on," she whispered to the chip. "Don't you?"

The sliver of rock didn't answer, but Robin knew it agreed.

She flicked it off the edge of the cliff and it fell to the tops of the trees on the next highest level of the mountain. She heard it slice through the foliage, whisking as it pierced the leaves. She didn't hear it hit the ground. Maybe it never did; maybe it somehow caught the wind and kept going like a little wing. She knew it was happy to be somewhere else. It had been stuck on the mountain, detached but not free, for far too long.

Robin closed her eyes and pretended that she was part of the mountain, too. The sun shone on her just like on the rest of the grey stone, lulling her. She thought she might fall asleep, and maybe she did, but then something started making noise at the bottom of the cliff and disturbed her. She cracked one eye, then the other, then rolled over and crept to the edge of the precipice. The trees were so thick she couldn't see through the canopy of leaves, but she could hear something moving around down there, something big and kind of clumsy. It crunched through the fallen leaves, crashed through the brambles. The movement sounds drew closer and closer, then stopped; one of the trees directly beneath her position began to shake. The thing was climbing it, she thought, or using it as a backscratcher. A black bear, maybe? Didn't they rub up against trees to soothe their itchy butts, and use them as giant scratching posts to mark their territory or sharpen their claws?

She felt a hand on the small of her back. Kyle crouched down next to her. "What're you looking at?" he asked.

"I don't know. Some big animal."

"What kind of animal?"

"I couldn't see it."

"Then how do you know it was big?"

"I could hear it. And it was shaking that tree." But the tree had stopped quivering now; whatever it was had found its perch and or assuaged its itch, and had moved on.

Kyle looked at it for a second, just long enough to pretend to be interested, then said: "We found something. Up at the summit."

"What?"

"An old cabin." He stood and offered a hand to help her up. "Come take a look."

~~~~

Kyle led Robin up the slope toward the rounded peak. To the right, the crumbled stone gave way to soil and scrub where the mountain turned downward; ahead of them, the trees bulged outward, taking advantage of a wide cleft in the cracked summit where dirt and humus had accumulated, sufficient to support a soul patch of pine on the peak's otherwise barren chin. It was in this wooded pocket that he and Gwen had found the cabin. It had been an exciting discovery, not least because Chuck had stayed behind to catch his breath, leaving the two of them alone in the little shack. Kyle had made a suggestion about trying out the bed, and been rewarded with an encouraging giggle. That had led to his arm around her waist and a few other suggestions, more specific this time, that had prompted a nervous grin and a blush and a question about where Robin was, which had, somehow, led to his getting sent to find his wife. He wondered if—

"Is there anything interesting in this cabin?"

He looked at Robin. "Huh?"

"Is there anything interesting in there?"

"Oh, yeah. Lots of stuff. It'll take a couple trips to get it all back to the van."

"What?"

"I said it'll take a—"

"You're kidding."

He stopped. They were right at the edge of the copse. He could just barely see the tumbledown old shack through the trees. As far as he knew, Gwen was still poking around inside. "Well, I mean, it's abandoned. It doesn't belong to anybody."

"It's protected. Everything here is. It belongs to the state."

"Robin. The door is a blanket. The roof has a hole in it. The windows are broken. Nobody lives there. Nobody uses it. Why should we just leave everything in there to rot?"

"Oh for fuck's sake. What are you planning to do, try to sell pieces on the Internet?"

"Of course not! But that museum Chuck was talking about, they might want it."

"They would want you to tell them about it so they could send people to look at it in place, not pack it up and bring it to them. You want to show them what you found? Take a picture."

"They might think a picture was fake."

"Seriously? You're so full of shit. You're just trying to convince yourself it's okay to clean the place out." She pulled her hand out of his and turned around. "Do whatever you want. I'm going back to lie in the sun."

~~~~

Gwen looked up as the blanket was thrust aside and Kyle stalked into the cabin. She had been investigating the contents of a peeling birch chest at the foot of the bed, which seemed to contain nothing but shabby old hand-stitched clothes and a stained pair of crude leather boots. "I thought you were getting Robin," she said.

Kyle shrugged. "She disapproves."

"She doesn't want us to take anything?"

"She doesn't even want us to *touch* anything. Says it's all protected. She thinks we should just tell the museum about it."

"Oh," Gwen said. "Well, maybe she's right."

"Yeah," Kyle said. "Maybe." He moved over to stand next to her, their hips touching. "Most of this stuff is junk anyway."

"Yeah."

"I guess maybe I'll take a few pictures and call the museum, like Robin said." He got out his smartphone, tapped the screen, and took a couple of snapshots. "How about a few of you? For scale? You can unbutton the top couple of—"

"Kyle, what are we doing?"

After a moment, he said: "Documenting our find."

Gwen shook her head. "No we're not." She headed for the filthy blanket door, lifted it with her fingers, and stepped outside. She felt vaguely guilty, even though she hadn't really done anything but flirt; and anyway, was it really her fault? Kyle had been the one who started talking to her at the gym, not the other way around. And if she hadn't exactly discouraged him, well, maybe that had more to do with her and Chuck than with Kyle or Robin or anything else. She walked away, her feet sinking into the soft black earth beneath the trees. Before long she was back on the warm grey rock of the mountaintop. Chuck stood on an outcropping twenty yards farther up, looking out over the valley. Robin was nearly the same distance away, but straight ahead, also gazing down from the mountain.

She heard movement in the woods behind her. Must be Kyle coming out of the cabin. She headed toward Chuck, scuffing along the ancient, weathered stone. He didn't notice her approaching until she was nearly there, and even then he didn't talk, he just glanced at her and looked away.

"Listen, Chuck—"

"I think I can see the village from here," he said. "Blackberry Hollow, I guess."

"I want to—"

"It's over there." He pointed at a distant spot, nothing more than a large clearing in the trees, really, where a number of dark things that might have been rooftops poked up from the surrounding vegetation. The line of downed trees connected with it like a left hook.

"Chuck, listen, I'm sorry I threw your book in the river, okay?"

"Okay," he said. "Sure."

Gwen let the silence stretch out to nearly a minute before speaking again. "That's all you're going to say?"

"Is there something else you want to hear?"

She sat down on the rock and pulled her knees up to her chest, locking her arms around them. The wind rustled the trees below the drop-off, making their leaves shiver. "Forget it," she said. She scratched her nails on the mountain. A spreading cloud of dust arose from the left side of the clearing. For some reason she thought of Bob and Myra and Chuck's van. "Is that a car?"

"Must be," Chuck said.

"It's going fast." Then: "I hope Myra's okay."

"She'll be fine. Migraines aren't fatal. Why, do you think that's them?"

"Maybe."

"No way." Chuck shook his head. "Not Bob. He would never drive that fast on a road that bad."

~~~~

The van raced up the road, bouncing and creaking and raising a tremendous cloud of dust. Bob replayed the whole crazy scene in his head as he drove: Myra screaming and then going catatonic; Dr. Zane with his dirty fingernails and his perfectly white teeth; the disappearing fire hydrant, disappearing doctor, disappearing *wife*; the house with nothing inside; the mirror that didn't reflect the room. None of it made any sense. It wasn't possible. Maybe there were magic mushrooms sprinkled in the coffee Zane had given him. Who knew? But he needed help. He had to find the others.

He slowed as he reached the intersection where the three roads met. He swung left, heading back toward the trailhead and the parking lot. He bounced to a halt in the shadow of the trees. The path beckoned, a dark opening in the forest wall. He got out of the van, stood a moment in the sunlight. He checked his phone. Still no reception. No surprise there; it wasn't like new towers had sprouted up since earlier in the day. He got out of the van, peered at the path, got back in the van, and leaned on the horn. A big vehicle like this, he'd expected a long, loud blast, but what came out was a feeble toot. Jesus. What was the deal with horns these days? He tried again a few times anyway, Morse code style, *honk honk honk* pause *honnnk honnnk honnnk* pause *honk honk honk*. The woods just ate the sounds up. If you send out an SOS in the forest and no one hears it, did you really send out an SOS?

Fuck. He was going to have to climb the mountain.

Bob left the van and went to the trail. It was cooler under the trees. Smelled like wood, leaves, earth, rain. He heard movement noises from up ahead, but couldn't tell where they were coming from or what was making them. It could have been something small and close, like a rabbit, or large and distant, like his friends. He thought it was small and close. As he went further along the trail the air became very still, heavy and expectant, almost like before a thunderstorm, but that had to be his imagination running away with him; the sky was clear and blue. No storms would be coming any time soon.

The path snaked back and forth and eventually stopped at a swath of destruction that sliced through the forest. The trees had been flattened, all pointing in the same direction. He remembered the damage in the village. Had the same storm done this here? He heard movement again behind him, small, stealthy sounds of something little creeping through the brush. He imagined small animals gathering in a circle to stare at the big clumsy human, waiting for him to move on; but then someone tapped him on the shoulder.

Surprised, he whirled, and backed up against the fallen trees. The thing that had touched him wasn't a person; it was a vine, a small, thorny vine, the offshoot of a big thorny vine, itself the offshoot of a simply massive thorny vine, that bobbed in a breeze so faint he didn't feel it—at least, he hoped it was being moved by a breeze rather than moving under its own power—and had poked him like an attention-seeking finger.

Thorny vines? What the hell? Where was the forest he had walked through? Instead of trees, great lumpy tendrils grew from the ground, each festooned with hundreds of crimson thorns. They ranged from tiny saw teeth to spikes the size of daggers. The thick vines curled and curved and twisted around the trail, embracing it with rough green arms. He could scarcely see the sky through them. Vines like that didn't grow in the Adirondacks. As far as he knew they didn't grow *anywhere*, outside of fairy tales.

He shut his eyes, shook his head, pinched his nose. "Not there, not there, none of this is there," he said, and opened his eyes again.

The bramble wall was still there. If anything, it had grown thicker and tighter in the few seconds when he hadn't been looking at it. As he stared, a small creeper sprouted from the ground only a few feet away from his feet, poking and threading its way through its larger fellows, sprouting new thorns as it snaked higher. Its smooth bark scraped against the thick, rough hides of the previous growth, producing a faint scratchy sound, like a small animal. The whole thing was absurd. There was no such plant. It must be a flashback from whatever Dr. Zane had given him, the stuff reaching into his brain to fuck with his perceptions some more. Maybe he should close his eyes again and just walk right through it.

"There, not there," a reedy voice said from behind him. "What's the difference? Either way, if you try to walk through it, you'll be spit full of holes in no time flat. Those aren't blackberries, you know."

Bob turned around. He didn't see anyone behind him among the fallen trees. "Who said that?"

"Nobody here but us pigeons," the voice said.

He still couldn't quite tell where the voice was coming from. "What are you, a mind reader?"

"A mind reader? Nope. Not *me*." The foliage of a fallen sapling in front of him rustled. "Maybe you're just not very subtle."

Bob reached out and parted the leaves, revealing a little person standing behind it. Or maybe not a person. More like a gnome, one of those jolly little gaudily-painted concrete statues people liked put in their gardens, only not made of concrete and not gaudily painted, and not really all that jolly-looking. He was maybe two feet tall, dressed in a green tunic that looked like it had been stitched together out of leaves and moss. He had big bare dirty feet sporting four toes each, grubby four-fingered hands, and a brown beard in which twigs and bits of bark clung, as if he had recently been dining on branches. A hat woven of fern fronds sat on his head.

"Oh," the gnome said, stepping out through the opening Bob had created. "Hi."

Bob goggled at him.

"Paltruck's my name."

Bob goggled some more.

"Staring is rude. What's the matter, never seen a sprite before?"

"I don't think so." Then: "Except for the soda."

Paltruck rolled his eyes. "They didn't invent that name, you know," he said, in a slightly aggrieved tone that suggested this was a joke he had heard before and never found funny.

"Um, okay. What are you doing out here, hiding in the trees?"

"Just waiting for somebody to come along and talk to me."

"I was looking for my friends. They should have come through here an hour or two ago. Did you talk to them?"

"No, I just got here a little while ago. So lucky you, you're the one who gets to save the Princess."

"What princess?"

"Princess Myra."

After a moment, Bob said: "Princess who now?"

"Princess M—"

"Myra? *My* Myra?"

"*Your* Myra? Not for much longer. Not unless you get a move on."

"A move on to where?"

"To the Count's castle. His helper put a sleeping spell on her so she won't wake up until later, and brought her there. It's all part of the Count's plan to become the Prince."

"How is Myra part of this plan?"

"Come nightfall the Count will marry Princess Myra, and then—"

"What? He can't marry Myra. Myra's already married to me."

"Uh-huh. 'Til death do you part? Nice little loophole there, right? When the Count marries her, she'll be dead. Get it?"

Bob shook his head. "No."

Paltruck sighed, making him feel like an obtuse student who kept getting one plus one wrong. "Look, it's very simple. The Count bites Princess Myra. Princess Myra dies and comes back as a vampire. The

Count marries her, and together they rule the kingdom forever."

"The Count is a vampire?"

"What else would someone called the Count be?"

Bob drew a deep breath, held it, let it out. "Okay. I'll play along. Which way should I go to find her?"

"To rescue a Princess, you have to go through a wall of thorns." The sprite pointed at a small gap in the brambles. Bob bent over to examine the opening. He would have to crawl to get in, but it opened up a bit after that. Like a tunnel, or a throat, it ran back into a dim twilight; the vines twisted so tightly that they formed a tube, blocking out the sky. Vermilion thorns, some the size of his arms, poked inward in all directions. He would have to slouch along in the dark, hunched over, trying not to get impaled. What fun.

"By the way," Paltruck said, "you might want to get your hands on a wooden stake."

"Where am I supposed to find a wooden stake out here?"

Paltruck didn't answer.

Bob turned around. "How far away is——"

He broke off, because Paltruck was gone.

Bob looked around, but saw and heard nothing. The woods had gone completely quiet. "Paltruck?"

Silence.

Louder: "Hey, Paltruck!"

More silence. The little guy had bailed on him, and evidently there was a timetable for this rescue operation. He couldn't stand around all afternoon hollering, hoping his new leprechaun friend would come back.

Bob slithered through the opening and began picking his way through the tangle of spines towards his date with the Count.

Ghosts

KYLE PACED AROUND the cabin for a little while, wondering what had gone wrong with Gwen. Maybe he'd been a little too forward, suggested a little too explicitly what they might do here in the cabin while Chuck and Robin were off on their own. It probably didn't help that the cabin was so old and dingy, and had what appeared to be a dead opossum in the corner with four pink feet sticking up in the air, and smelled kind of fusty, like the locker room at the end of a long day when the showers weren't working.

He exited through the blanket door and went out among the trees. Gwen was visible some distance off to the right—the pines blocked the sunlight that would support underbrush and had few lower branches, so he could see some distance through them, as if through a forest of telephone poles—heading back towards the barren summit. He would let her go, give her time to think it over and realize just how attractive his offer was; then he would tease her a little more, and try again somewhere under other circumstances, in a place that didn't stink. He looked around, and spotted a low wall to the left, deeper into the stand of pines. What might that be? An old foundation? He wandered in that direction and soon came upon a decrepit burial ground, four rounded heaps of rock surrounded by a slumping border of stacked flat stones. Each cairn was marked with a weathered slab that looked to have been chipped out of the mountaintop and braced upright, though most were now quite tilted. Circling the plot, he could make out the remains of lettering on the tombstones, but couldn't read the inscriptions. He thought he might make one up. *Here lies Mountain John, once was here, now is gone.* Yeah, that was pretty good, he thought. Very Boot Hill.

Surely this was a find that even Chuck would appreciate; they probably had all kinds of displays like it at the museum up the road that he'd been so hot to visit. There, though, they would probably have a tall fence around the graveyard, and Plexiglas over the doors and windows of the cabin, so you could look but not touch. This was better, right? Nothing between you and history. You could walk right into the past and poke around. He turned back toward the summit and hollered, "Hey, guys! Come and check this out!" His voice echoed through the trees and died away. He waited a little while, but nobody answered and nobody came. Were they ignoring him? He peered toward the summit, but despite the lack of underbrush, the profusion of tree trunks kept him from seeing the bare mountaintop where the others were. The little stand of pines wasn't so little after all. He headed back the way he'd come, intending to fetch the others, but stopped when he heard rocks shifting and clattering behind him. Thinking he might have inadvertently destabilized something, Kyle looked behind him. The walls and the four piles of stones didn't seem to have changed. He watched them for a little while, but nothing happened. Maybe there had been a rockfall nearby. With a shrug, he turned away and kept going.

On the way out, he passed the little cabin. He heard noises from inside, like someone was scuffling around in there. Maybe Gwen had come back. Kyle pushed the blanket aside and entered. Someone was there, all right, but it wasn't Gwen. It wasn't Chuck or Robin, either. It was a man, kneeling in front of the bed, rummaging through the old birch chest at its foot. His clothes appeared to made of deer hide, stitched crudely together. He wore a cap that had once been a small animal, gutted and inverted and stretched into a hat, with four pink little feet and a snout sticking up into the air. Wait ... that was the thing Kyle had spotted in the corner of the hut, which he'd assumed had crawled into the cabin and died there. He never would've guessed it was headgear, or that the cabin was still occupied. Thank God Gwen had gotten cold feet and taken off. Kyle couldn't imagine this guy would take kindly to strangers fornicating in his hovel.

As Kyle tried to withdraw before being noticed, a water bottle in the side pocket of his pack somehow caught its neck on a knothole in the wooden wall, pulled free, and fell to the floor with a dull *thunk*. Kyle froze as the man slowly turned to look at him. Underneath the cap was a mottled, blotchy face with egg-white eyes and a grey-lipped mouth. Kyle noticed that the hands that had been pawing through the contents of the chest were likewise purplish-black with patches of yellowish-white showing through. What the fuck? Did this guy have a case of flesh-eating bacteria? Was he some kind of leper? Is that why he lived out here?

The man said something unintelligible in an angry, garbled voice. Kyle caught a whiff of rot that made him want to gag. He felt momentarily dizzy, as if the room were spinning around him. He needed to get out of here. Hastily backing up towards the door, his foot came down on the water bottle. It shot out from under him and he fell on his ass just as the cretinous mountain reached behind the chest and retrieved an ancient-looking rifle, barely two steps up the evolutionary chain from a flintlock. The fucker brought the long gun around, sighted down the barrel with a milky eye, and fired. The shot thunked into the floor near Kyle's feet, throwing up a little spray of dirt that pattered against the soles of his boots. He scrambled up and stumbled through the blanket. It clung and scratched as he passed through, and then he was out in the forest, in the clean mountain air. He raced to the nearest big pine tree and ducked behind it, staying very still, waiting to see if Deadly Crockett would come out after him or would be satisfied to have run him off. Maybe he would get lucky and one of the others would come looking for him and attract the guy's attention.

His heartbeat slowly settled. He didn't hear anyone moving around, but the ground was soft, no leaf litter, few branches to crunch. The guy could be stalking him silently, following his tracks, rifle slung over one shoulder, rusty knife at the ready. He could be on the opposite side of the trunk, getting ready to thrust around it and stab him in the kidney. He could be thrusting it forward *right now*!

Kyle lurched away, suddenly convinced that he was about to get slashed from behind. He spun around and flattened himself against another tree, looking back toward the cabin. No one was visible. Kyle darted off and scurried in a wide loop to crouch beside the cabin, slowly rising until he could peek through a window. It stood empty, which meant Daniel Bone must be out here, in the woods, with him. Right? But the chest was closed, and from this angle, Kyle could see the butt of the ancient rifle lying on the dirt floor in the narrow space between it and the foot of the bed. The floor had no bullet gouge. It was as if nothing had happened, except for two things: His water bottle still lay near the door, partially crumpled by his stepping on it; and the noisome animal-skin hat now hung on a peg near the door.

Kyle looked left, looked right, looked deep into the trees, and saw nothing out of the ordinary. He listened, and heard nothing except the wind. He slowly crept back to the door, lifted the blanket. The interior was completely deserted, untouched, exactly as he had left it the first time, and as he had just seen it through the window. The chest wasn't open. The divot in the floor wasn't there. The hat hung nearby. Its pointy little face seemed to be sneering at him.

He snatched up his water bottle, let the blanket drop, and ran to find the others.

~~~~

Robin had gotten bored with lying in the sun, and had decided to climb a tree instead.

Although it had been years since she last done it, she'd spent quite a big portion of her childhood up in the branches; there was something about being high off the ground, surrounded by cool, fragrant foliage, that used to make her terrestrial, usually peer-related, problems disappear for a while. Maybe she'd once had a little more monkey in her than the average girl. Maybe she still did.

After wandering around reviewing trees for suitability—up here it was mostly pines, and she didn't want to climb a pine; she would get pitch and needles all over skin and clothes—she found herself a nice maple that grew a little way down from the summit, at the edge of the broad rocky patch where the evergreens began to dominate. It was fairly distant from where Kyle and the others were hanging out, which was fine with her. She didn't want to deal with them right now, with their bickering and sniping and dirty sideways looks. With all that high school behavior, no wonder she was reverting to her arboreal ways.

Robin studied the layout of the maple's branches for a little while, then grabbed a low, strong-looking limb and swung up, catching it under her knees so that she was hanging upside-down. She hauled herself into a sitting position, and rested a moment—this had been easier when she was twelve—before she started climbing. Soon she was ensconced in secure leafy comfort in the crook of a limb maybe a third of the way up, hidden away from the world inside a green bubble. She leaned back against the trunk and closed her eyes. It was very quiet up here on the mountain; the only sound was the leaves rustling in the breeze. The white noise was very soothing, though she knew better than to let it lull her to sleep. She had learned from experience that if you fell asleep in a tree and you weren't properly secured, you would fall out.

She hadn't been there long before the tree quivered a little; she felt the slight vibrations passing from the trunk into her spine and the back of her skull. Robin cracked one eye, then the other, then shifted a little so she could peer downward. The foliage beneath her was so thick that it obscured the ground completely. She couldn't remember ever having been in a tree where she was unable to see all the way down; branches that were big enough to hold a person, even a smallish person such as herself, tended to be rather sparsely furred near the trunk. Reaching up to the branch above her, she pulled herself to her feet and rearranged herself a little, trying to find an angle where she could see the ground, without success. It was as if the tree had explosively leafed out since she climbed it. Somebody had really poured on the Miracle-Gro.

The tree vibrated again, with a little more oomph this time, reminding her of how much that one at the bottom of the cliff had shaken earlier. What might make a tree do that? A bear? She didn't think so. Two bears? A maniac with a big axe? A dinosaur? A herd of dinosaurs? Yeah, sure, that was it. A herd of dinosaurs was on the loose, roaming the Adirondacks, knocking over trees. Wouldn't that be funny?

Suddenly the maple lurched and snapped like someone had crashed a bulldozer into it.

Arms windmilling, Robin fell out of the tree.

~~~~

Chuck wasn't sure what had motivated Gwen to come and apologize for the tour book incident, and he didn't really know how to respond. Part of him wanted to withhold forgiveness, at least for a little while, but that would make him kind of a selfish asshole. Was he one of those? Maybe. Maybe he was. Anyway he couldn't figure out what to say, so he just sat down on the edge of the cliff and patted the rock next to him. After a few seconds she sat down beside him. Together they looked off across the valley, at the roofs in Blackberry Hollow, at the lush green treetops, at the silver stream that glittered in the sunlight. Before he knew what he was doing, Chuck had put his arm around Gwen, and she leaned against him, and it was almost like the old days, for a few minutes anyway. At least until Kyle came running up behind them. Perfect timing from Mr. Wonderful.

"Hey," Kyle said, panting.

They both peered up at him. Gwen said, "Hey." Chuck said nothing.

"Didn't you guys hear me calling you?"

"No," Gwen said.

"Chuck?"

"I didn't either."

"I was yelling really loud."

"Well, we didn't hear you," Chuck said.

Kyle was silent for a moment, as if mulling this over, then said: "You guys didn't see somebody come out of the woods before me, did you?"

"We weren't looking at the woods," Gwen said.

Chuck said: "Are you talking about Robin?"

"No, no, not Robin. Somebody else." He rocked back and forth for a minute, his eyes scanning the mountaintop. Chuck had no idea what he expected to see. Finally Kyle said, "Where *is* Robin, anyway?"

"Last I saw she was down that way." Chuck indicated the lower part of the summit, where a few maples stood, holding off the advancing pine army. "Looked like she was inspecting the trees."

"Okay." Kyle turned, put his hands around his mouth, and bellowed for his wife. Her name echoed down the mountain and faded. Robin didn't answer. "I think she's pissed at me," Kyle said, apparently to himself.

Chuck couldn't imagine why on earth Robin might be pissed at Kyle.

Gwen said, "Who did you think we would see coming out of the woods, if it wasn't Robin?"

"What? Uh, nobody. Never mind. Listen, I found something."

"Yeah, a cabin," Chuck said. "We know."

"No, something else. An old graveyard."

"A graveyard?" Gwen said. "Up here?"

"Uh-huh."

"How'd they dig holes deep enough to bury people?"

"They didn't. They used piles of stones. I thought we could stop at your museum after we leave and, you know, tell them what I found. They'd like to know about it, wouldn't they?"

"Probably," Chuck said. Kyle seemed to anticipate some kind of credit or recognition. Maybe he figured they would name the trail after him, or even the whole mountain. They could call it Dickhead Peak.

"So? Want to come look? It's not far."

"Yeah, sure," Gwen said. She stood, swatted grey stone dust off her the back of her white shorts.

Chuck noticed Kyle's gaze flick to her vibrating fanny. No way was he letting Kyle get any more alone time with Gwen than he'd already had. He stood too. "What about Robin?"

"What about her?"

"What if she comes back and can't find us?"

"She'll be fine. Robin doesn't quite inhabit the same reality as the rest of us, you know?" Kyle turned away. "Besides, we'll be back before she even notices we're gone."

~~~~

Myra could tell she was dreaming because, in real life, she would never have climbed, naked, to the top of a high-jump diving board in an arena full of spectators. The fact that the spectators were tiny red creatures, like bipedal fire ants, was another clue.

Evidently this was going to be some sort of dream of Olympic glory. She had once read somewhere that the original Olympic athletes competed in the nude, so perhaps that explained her lack of attire. She doubted that the set of events included the high dive, but whatever. It was her turn to go, so she didn't have time to think about things like that. She spread her arms, jumped into the air, landed. The platform, which she had supposed to be made of rigid concrete, instead bowed beneath her and then snapped up, launching her into the sky. She shot high into the air, hundreds of feet above the mountaintop, pausing at the apex of her jump with the scenery laid out beneath her; she could see it all in exquisite detail, as if by intruding upon the domain of the eagle, she had become one herself. Directly below, the mountain that the others had climbed humped upward. She could see Chuck and Gwen on the barren rock summit, tiny from this height, sitting together at the edge of the cliff. Kyle approached them, and they talked, and then the three of them headed towards a stand of pines not far away. She couldn't see Robin; maybe she was already in the woods. She couldn't see Bob, either, which made sense, since he wasn't there.

That mountain stood alongside another one, slightly taller, more jagged, and rather more menacing; its lower slopes were choked by what looked like giant thorn bushes with crimson spines.A dark castle squatted on top of it, brooding over its slopes, like a black angel with barbed-wire wings. Myra didn't care for that mountain at all. She had the impression that it was just waiting for the right moment to stand up and unfold those wings and spread its massive shadow across the ground.

She turned away, looking across the flood plain toward the village, Blackberry Hollow, that stood some distance away. The homes and businesses looked like models from here, fake little worse-for-wear plastic things arranged among trees that were green-dyed cotton tufts stuck on twigs. She could see some kind of storm damage in the village, could trace it back to a line of downed trees that carved a path through the lowland forest. She followed the line of destruction back up the valley toward another, bigger, broader mountain that stood between the one they had climbed and its castle-crowned cousin. The third mountain wore a large, institutional building like a battered hat atop a thatch of browning, overlong grass. Together, the three peaks dominated the pan-shaped depression, with this last one dominating the dominators. Everything beyond the circular valley was obscured by clouds; she might as well have been at the top of a world locked inside a frosted glass globe, only able to see what lay within the sphere.

And then the dream turned unpleasant, as dreams often did; her magically extended hang time came to an end. Not an eagle after all, Myra fell back to earth. She picked up speed, plunging faster and faster. She looked below her, and instead of the arena and the pool, she found she was falling directly into the black castle. The roof came rushing up at her. It had a spike on top, like a lightning rod. She was going to land right on it. Just before that happened, she opened her eyes and sat up, her own shriek of terror echoing in her ears.

Myra rubbed her temples, then took a look around. She was in a room with a fireplace, a four-poster bed, a couple of furry rugs, and two large doors on facing walls, one of iron-bound wood and the other of glass. So obviously she was still dreaming, the Olympic scenario replaced by something else, a room in the black castle she had fallen into. It was round, like one of those plush tower prisons that movie villains liked to use for storing important captives. She'd been upgraded from athlete to Princess, apparently. At least she had clothes on again.

The bed beneath her was soft and slightly prickly, as if stuffed with large, stiff feathers. It stood directly opposite the mammoth, ash-filled hearth. She got out of bed and did a quick circuit of the chamber. Other than the bed, a cloth-shrouded object near the fireplace, and thick furs that lay scattered about—she avoided stepping on them; they emitted vaguely unpleasant aromas, as if they'd been rather inexpertly separated from their original owners—the room was largely devoid of furniture or decoration. She stopped at the massive wooden door. She tried it. Locked. Next, she visited the object on the far side of the fireplace. The fabric that covered it was black velvet, thick and soft. Pulling it off, she discovered an oval mirror taller and wider than her, set into a frame that allowed it to spin on a vertical axis. She rotated it. The backside was a mirror, too, but the reflection was wrong in a disturbing way, like a funhouse mirror with bad intentions. She gave it a little spin, then moved on to the glass door. This proved to be unlocked. She pushed it open and went out onto a small stone balcony.

Holy shit. She really *was* in a tower prison.

Did that make her a Princess?

~~~~

The trail through the briars, if it could even be called a trail, nothing like the one Bob remembered following before he got to the fallen trees and met Paltruck. This one never ran straight; it twisted and turned in unexpected ways, through terrain that was much more broken and folded than it should have been, and the knotted, overarching vines cast the passage in a perpetual twilight. He picked his way through the gloom, bending and contorting to avoid the wicked thorns, scarcely noticing the ground softening from stony soil to earth to mud, until it started sucking at his boots, each step making an almost comical suctioning noise as he took it. He would have been relieved when the tunnel finally expanded into something he could stand upright and walk comfortably in, except that at the same time the footing degraded into a morass of slick, viscous muck, glistening black, the gelatinous surface pocked with small, odious ponds on which misshapen insects skated. Beetles crawled in and out of holes bored into the woody creepers, huge hard-shelled things vaguely similar to what you might expect to see creeping out from behind the refrigerator in a city tenement, if the city stood in a radioactive wasteland. When he disturbed them the insects kicked up an incredible racket, their carapaces popping open to reveal smudgy wings that thrummed like discordant guitars, creating an ungodly din.

Bob suddenly felt a sharp, burning pain in his right thigh. He yelped and fell down in the mud; gunk squirted every which-way with a sodden farting sound. His leg burned as if it had been stabbed with a knitting needle. He quickly discovered that some sort of new weird insect had attached itself to him and jabbed its proboscis through his jeans and into his flesh. Its big eyes glittered like hot rubies against an exoskeleton the color of cold coals as it clung to his leg, its body thrumming like a pump as it siphoned blood. What kind of hell-mosquito was this?

He reached to grab it and it took off, but he somehow managed to catch its wings before it escaped. Jesus Christ. The thing was as big around as a half-dollar. It wriggled and buzzed in his fingers, spiny legs jerking, swordlike nose slashing, trying to get him to let go. He crushed it against the heel of his other hand, taking care to avoid that dagger nose. It made a crunching sound, like an eggshell breaking. Reddish goo oozed from the crumpled exoskeleton. Disgusted, Bob tossed it away and wiped his hands through the mud to get the blood and bug juice off them, then stood. His clothes were caked with clammy muck, thick gobs of it clinging to his legs, his back, his arms. It felt freezing, even though the air temperature wasn't particularly low.

He started moving again, shaking off the mud, trying to regain some of the body heat it had sucked out of him, but it didn't really work; there was no sun to warm him, and he was ankle-deep in sludge, and he couldn't get up enough speed to really exert himself, generate some muscle warmth. It didn't help at all that part of the chill he felt was fear, coming from the slowly creeping realization that *this wasn't going away*. He wasn't waking up in Dr. Zane's office. He wasn't seeing this thorny wasteland fade back into the forest that it should have been. He had to stop walking for a few moments as a sudden panic threatened to overwhelm him. What if he *never* woke up? What if things stayed like this forever, him alone in a world of slime and brambles and ferocious bugs?

No. No. No meltdowns. He could do this. He could handle it. He could get to the castle and rescue Myra. He had to.

Bob reached out to the nearest creeper, touched it, verified its solidity. He ran his fingers along the knotty brown bark, its surface somewhat hairy but thick and hard like a coconut shell. The plant rippled where the thorns grew, reminding him of the base of an animal's horn. He grasped one of the needle-tipped shafts, noticing that the crimson was marbled with veins of green, fading to a pallid yellow at the root. The thorn was about as long as his forearm. It felt smooth, cool, and waxy, and seemed to be slightly loose. He gave it a twist and it came off in his hand, leaving the tiniest trace of a stalk in the middle of the blunt end, which was several inches in diameter. Crimson sap oozed from the pale green socket where the thorn had been. He tested the point with his thumb, drawing a pinprick of blood. Damn, that was sharp. Despite the ease with which he'd detached it from the vine, the thorn itself seemed quite sturdy. Maybe it contained seeds, so that when an animal impaled itself and wriggled away to die, the thorn would go with it and make a new bush somewhere else.

Bob stepped away from the tendril, turning his prize over and over in his hand.

Well, at least now he knew where to find a stake.

Separation

As she followed Kyle into the wooded area below the mountain's summit, Gwen became aware of a scent she hadn't noticed before, a vague, rotten, dead-animal smell lurking under the pines. The odor was faint but noticeable, and it grew stronger the deeper they went under the trees. Kyle had said bodies were buried under the stones he had found. How did he know that? Was he guessing, or had he dug one up? Surely a corpse that old wouldn't still smell, would it?

They passed the cabin, sad and sorry and half falling down. The stench became overpowering as they passed the little building, as if there were an entire zoo rotting under the old dirt floor, which was ridiculous, because she had stood inside it a little while ago and hadn't smelled a thing. Gwen slipped away from Chuck and stopped at the blanketed door. He paused, looking back at her. "This is the cabin you told me about?" he said.

Gwen nodded, running her hand along the heavy fabric that hung limp and tattered, weathered by its years exposed to the elements in the open doorway. She pushed it aside and peered into the cabin. Dim light seeped through the broken ceiling and the shuttered, glassless windows. Everything was as she remembered: The decaying wood-frame bed, the moldering birch-bark locker, the rusted tools, the moth-eaten skins nailed like macabre posters to the wall. Although she didn't remember the ridiculous animal-hide hat, head and feet and all, that hung near the door. Maybe Kyle had found it and put it there? She couldn't really imagine him handling such a thing. Maybe she just hadn't noticed it before. The odor inside the cabin was appalling. She definitely would have noticed *that*. What could have generated such a stench in the short time since she'd been in here with Kyle? If something had crawled in and died, it wouldn't reek this much yet.

"We've already been in the cabin," Kyle said. She glanced back at him; he stood some distance away, near a tree, and looked ready to duck behind it and hide if she decided to throw something at him. "Come on, let's go to the graveyard."

"In a minute," Chuck said, his voice coming from around the side. Now that they had dragged him here, he must be going around, giving the place the once-over. Couldn't he smell the stink? It was enough to make her gag. She was about to withdraw when she noticed that a little spot of earth had started to move, midway between the door and the bed. The dirt seemed to have loosened and shifted, like something was burrowing its way up from below. Expecting to see a gopher or a chipmunk or something, she was startled when a filthy finger broke the surface instead. At first she took it for a fat white worm, until she noted the black-rimmed, purple-blue nail at the end of it. This was followed by another finger, then another, until an entire handful of them had pushed their way up, pallid and grimy, with dirt ground into the lines of the skin. The fingers wriggled like grubs as the hand beneath them moved from side to side, working itself free. The dirt gave way around it until she could see a bony wrist; then an entire forearm tore itself free in a shower of brown soil. Suddenly she noticed that one of the fingers was wearing a ring. It looked familiar. She glanced down at her own hand, where the same ring was on the same finger. Her grandmother had given her that ring. The only difference was that the one she wore wasn't dull and pitted and caked with dirt.

Now the arm from the ground bent at the elbow and the hand started digging vigorously in the soil, uncovering a layer of matted hair that was of a color not naturally found on human heads. Despite the filth, Gwen recognized that hue. She had a bottle of it in her medicine cabinet.

When the fingers twined themselves into the hair and started to pull, threatening to tear the scalp free of the bone beneath, Gwen tried to retreat, but she had gotten tangled up in the blanket, or it was stuck to her somehow, clinging and holding her fast like a spider's web. She began to struggle against it, trying to break free. The thick, rank fabric had wrapped itself around her head. She couldn't breathe. With a shriek she wrenched herself backwards and the blanket tore free from whatever held it in place. She fell down hard on the ground, blanket clutched in both hands, looking up at the sky.

Chuck poked his head from around the corner of the cabin, looking concerned. "Gwen? You okay?"

"Yeah," she said, staring at the door of the cabin. Nothing inside but decrepit furnishings, of course. No arm, no hand, no head, no hair.

"Why did you scream?"

She looked at him.

"Spider," she said.

~~~~

Kyle had been leaning against a pine, ready to bolt if any rifle-toting zombie mountain men showed, but trying to project an air of insouciant boredom, while Gwen went to the door of the cabin and Chuck wandered around examining it like a structural engineer conducting a pre-buy inspection. Gwen moved the crummy blanket aside and then just stopped moving, sort of freezing in place, as if she had spotted something riveting that had captured her entire attention; a moment later she screamed and fell backwards, still clutching at the fabric, pulling it down with her. Chuck poked his head around to see what had happened, and Gwen gave him some bullshit about a spider.

Really? A spider? Kyle didn't believe it. He approached the cabin warily, giving Chuck and Gwen a wide berth. He flattened himself against the outside wall next to the door and took a quick peek inside. Nothing. Emboldened, he entered the doorway, standing on the warped plank lintel, looking all around. There was that ridiculous hat again, with those beady little eyes and toothy snout. He could swear it was snarling at him. He would have taken it off its peg and thrown it under the bed, but it was gross and he didn't want to touch it.

Someone tapped him on the shoulder, startling him, but it was only Chuck. "We're going back down to the van," he said.

Kyle looked around. Gwen had retreated to a nearby pine tree, the same one he had been hiding behind earlier, Kyle though. "What?" he said. "Why?"

"Gwen wants to leave."

"But you haven't been to the graveyard yet."

"Yeah," Chuck said. "I don't think we're doing that."

"Come on." He pointed. "You can see it from here."

Chuck, peering in the direction Kyle indicated, said: "Where? I don't see it."

"It's right over ..." Kyle trailed off, because he *couldn't* see it from here. All he saw was uneven mountaintop ground strewn with brown needles and small branches and decaying leaves that had blown in from God knew where.

Chuck made a great show of shading his eyes and squinting.

"It was there. I swear it was there."

"Sure," Chuck said. "Anyway, we're done up here. Are you coming with us, or are you moving into the cabin?"

"Ha ha. Tell you what. You guys find Robin and I'll meet you at the top of the trail, all right?"

"*You* find Robin. You're the one who's married to her."

"I'm going to find the graveyard."

"The one you can see from here, except you can't?" Chuck shook his head, then tipped it toward the sunlit rocky slope. "Fine, you go look for your invisible graveyard. We'll look for your invisible wife."

They went in opposite directions, Kyle into the gloom of the woods, the other two toward the open summit. That asshole Chuck thought he was crazy, but he knew what he had seen. He *knew*. It had been *right here*. He looked back over his shoulder just in time to see them exit the stand of pines. Simultaneously, he stumbled over a low stone wall and nearly fell on his face. Mother *fucker*. There it was, just like he remembered, and just *where* he remembered. He set his backpack down on the wall and dug his phone out of it. He couldn't make a call from up here, but he could take photos. He would show it off to the others, prove the burial ground was here, and who's the asshole now, huh, Chuck? You are.

Kyle circled the graveyard, getting careless shots from different directions. Sometimes the flash went off and sometimes it didn't. He stepped over the wall, one foot on either side of it, bending over for a close-up of one of the flat stone markers. He forced the flash, thinking maybe the angle would create shadows and make the inscription readable. He took the shot, then checked the display to see what he'd gotten.

It had worked. The scrawl was legible now. It said *Kyle Peterson*.

What the hell?

He slowly lowered the phone, staring at the gravestone. Weathered as it was, coated with slimy lichen and crawling forest gunk, he couldn't make out the letters. He looked at the picture again. The marker still had his name on it. He moved the picture to the trash, took another one. There was his name again. Kyle set the phone down in a bed of moss on top of the wall and picked up the slab of rock, holding it carefully by the edges so as not to smear the schmutz. Worms and grubs and millipedes, suddenly exposed, ran away like civilians fleeing a giant monster. He cradled the stone, tilted it this way and that. His name was definitely not written on it. Whatever was scratched into the stone underneath the layers of lichen and moss and bird shit remained unreadable. So why did it show up in the picture?

Suddenly it hit him.

Robin.

Yes, that had to be it. Robin had loaded some kind of app on his phone to let her doctor the pictures it took. She must have remote control over it. She had probably followed him, after saying she wasn't interested in the cabin, and come to look at the graveyard after he went back—which would explain why no one knew where she was—and was now hiding out nearby, activating her program, messing with his head. She was out there among the trees, watching, listening, trying to keep from giggling. It would hardly be the first mean prank she had played on him. Remember the time she found his secret address book and had called all the numbers in it, telling everyone he had herpes? Or the time she had keyed his car in the parking lot of that girl's apartment complex? Or the time she had replaced the condom in his wallet with a lollipop head with the stick snipped off? Of course, she always denied she was responsible for things like that, but who else would have done them? If she were here, he would be tempted to break the weatherbeaten slate over her little blonde head.

But no. Mustn't damage the find. He carefully returned the headstone to where it had originally been, levering it back into its original slot. Unfortunately it fell over when he let go of it, hitting a jagged rock on the ground and cracking across the middle. At the same time, the screen of his phone split in two, and in exactly the same way. The snap as it fractured sounded like a gunshot. Kyle reflexively hit the dirt, thinking the mountain man had come back and was shooting at him. After a moment, feeling stupid and reactive, he rose to his knees. His phone lay right in front of him. It was still on, but the display had turned a flickering, milky blue-white. It was ruined, his pictures lost. He'd never heard of a phone spontaneously cracking before, and certainly not in sympathy with an ancient hunk of slate. So what the fuck?

A thick brown fluid began to ooze out of the crack in the phone. Battery fluid? The stuff flowed off the screen and formed a little puddle that soaked into the moss, staining it black. Where the dappled sunlight struck, though, the fluid's true color was revealed. Crimson. His phone was bleeding.

Now how had his crafty bitch of a wife managed to make it do that?

~~~~

This, Myra thought, could well have been the most boring afternoon ever.

After some considerable time spent fiddling with the latch, she had given up on opening the massive wooden door; she'd hoped to get out and explore the halls of the sombre castle, but it seemed that was beyond the parameters of this dream. Admitting defeat, she had then flitted between bed and balcony, with one side trip to the fireplace, where she had crawled in over the cold ashes to see if she could maybe climb up the chimney and get out onto the roof. No dice. The black throat of the shaft was blocked by iron bars, and anyway, she couldn't see any light up it. Whatever route smoke took on its way out, it wasn't direct, and the last thing she needed was to get jammed up in the flue like a Santa whose luck and magic had both run out.

So now she sat on the edge of the fluffy bed, staring at the ashes in the fireplace, wondering when she was going to wake up. What had happened to her imagination? Usually her dreams could be counted on to provide at least *some* entertainment value; they might be weird or unpleasant or even apocalyptic, but at least stuff happened. This was the first and, she hoped, the last time she dreamed herself to be a tower-bound princess. Those fairy tales of imprisoned maidens never mentioned how crashingly *dull* it was to be the damsel. No wonder they always threw themselves at the first prince who came along.

Speaking of princes, wasn't it about time for one to show up?

Myra went out onto the balcony again. She couldn't possibly get down from there except by way of gravity, and given the tower's height and the hard surfaces below it, such an escape attempt wouldn't end well for her. The sun had descended near the mountains, sunk low beneath the high, smoky clouds, haze-blurred into an enraged crimson smear, as if it found the atmosphere an infuriating personal affront. Everything was cast in a dully bitter red; even the black castle had soaked up some ruddy undertones. The air had a nasty metallic bite, as if someone nearby was forging armor and weapons to equip a legion. Maybe the iron fog was exhaust from that operation.

She climbed up onto the railing, swung her legs around, and sat on the balustrade for a little while, swinging her feet. She looked between her shoes at the ground far below. This being a dream, she could push off and fall and she'd wake up before she hit, right? Or maybe a pair of wings would pop out of her back and she could flutter off like a bird or a butterfly and land safely somewhere outside the castle walls.

Or maybe she'd go *splat*.

Bored, careless, and dreaming, Myra climbed up onto the railing and balanced there, her feet rocking back and forth on the curved lip of stone. The valley stretched out below her, matted with thorny vines, hemmed in by stony mountains with stubbly forest beards and hard grey summits. If this were the real world, which one would be Blackberry Mountain, where the others had gone climbing? Hers, where the castle stood, with its impenetrable tangle of spines? Or the one straight ahead, low and flat and crumbling, with a crown of barren rock and scrubby pines? Or the one to the left, where the top had been cleared of trees to form a vast yard around a big, institutional-looking building? What *was* that building, anyway? One of those old Adirondack sanitariums?

She suddenly felt someone watching her. If she raised her eyes, if she looked in the right direction, she thought she might meet a stranger's gaze; except there was no one here to be gazing at her. She was alone. Wasn't she?

Myra slid off the railing and landed hard on the balcony. She leaned forward against the balustrade to keep herself upright. A faint pain began to spread out from her temples, low and dull, like lengthening shadows stretching across her brain. "Who's there?" she said. Her voice sounded small and faint in her ears, the way it often did in dreams, when you were crying for help and no one could hear you, because sound had gone on strike and refused to travel. But somebody heard her this time. It just wasn't anyone who was interested in helping her. She felt a breezy gust from the thorn forest, a hot, fetid, iron-laden puff of air, a heavy breath that hit her in the space between between her lungs. She pushed herself away from the railing, turned, pressed into it with the small of her back. The sun's reflection was a bloody glob spread across the thick-paned glass of the doors, the sky a grey and oily canvas behind it. On the other side, she could make out someone standing in the tower room she had abandoned, way back in the shadows, where the red light of the waning day didn't reach. She couldn't see his face, but she knew he was looking out at her, and she knew he was smiling.

She could tell by the clean white line of his sharp, sharp teeth.

~~~~

When Kyle finally appeared from the trees, Gwen thought he seemed shaken; his face looked pale beneath his tan, and he walked like he thought he was being followed but didn't want to give his suspicions away. He'd been acting funny the last time he came out of the woods, too, asking them if they had spotted anyone else, someone who wasn't Robin. What was that all about? What had he seen? She thought about the fingers and hair in the dirt of the cabin, realized she was twirling her own hair in her own fingers, and stopped, not wanting to be reminded of any stuff like that.

"I'm all set," he said as he approached. "Let's get the hell out of here. Did you find Robin?"

"Nope," Chuck said. He stood. Gwen allowed him to pull her to her feet. "Get your pictures?"

"Yeah. But I, uh, dropped my phone and it broke." His gaze kept flicking from side to side, as if at any moment, from any direction, a wildlife stampede might appear and require evasive maneuvers.

"You okay?" Chuck said.

"Yeah. Fine. Pissed about the phone, you know? Where's Robin?"

"We haven't found her in the ten seconds since you asked the first time," Chuck said.

"She's not here," Gwen said. "Maybe she went back to the parking lot."

Kyle shook his head. "Robin's not an idiot. She wouldn't just leave and walk down the mountain by herself without telling anyone."

"So what are we supposed to do, then? Sit around until she decides to come back from wherever she went?"

"Yeah, Chuckles, that's exactly what we'll do. Good thinking. We'll set up camp here and wait for her. We'll light a fire, tell some ghost stories, eat some bark. It'll be fucking awesome."

"Kyle, calm down," Gwen said.

"I *am* calm," Kyle said. "I'm calm and I'm in control and I want to know where the fuck my wife went. Come on, help me look for her."

He moved off down the mountain. Gwen looked at Chuck, who shrugged. The three of them scraped and scuffed along the barren stone, Kyle hollering for Robin every few minutes. He sounded royally pissed off. Gwen wouldn't have been surprised if he started punctuating his calls with *you bitch* and other choice phrases. They wandered around most of the accessible parts of the summit, eventually returning to the tree line where the bald crown of the mountain broke out of its skin of dirt. The trail to the parking lot beckoned, gloomier than she remembered, though that probably just reflected her state of mind more than the state of the light. She and Chuck stood silently by as Kyle stomped back and forth along the edge of the forest, shouting his wife's name and telling her that he didn't think this was funny. Gwen didn't think it was funny either. She thought Kyle might be cracking up a little.

Chuck said: "Maybe Gwen's right. Maybe she went back already."

"Yeah? Then why don't you go down and check? You can send us up a smoke signal if you find her."

"Can we stop bickering? Please? It's not helpful."

"Sorry. Yeah. I know. Sorry." Kyle closed his eyes, drew a breath, visibly willing himself to relax. "All right."

"Look," Chuck said, "there's plenty of daylight left. We can all go down, and come back up if she's not there. Okay?"

"Okay. Let's do that." Then: "Sorry. I'm just worried about her, is all."

Chuck nodded, but Gwen wasn't convinced. Kyle didn't seem worried to her. He seemed enraged, and she didn't understand why. But if she were Robin, and she'd heard him yelling for her like that, she might not have answered him either.

~~~~

Bob stood at a fork in the thorn tunnel, up to his ankles in a soupy puddle, beetles buzzing noisily around his head. Which way went to the castle? The path had twisted and turned so much that he wasn't even sure which direction he was facing anymore, let alone which direction would take him where he needed to go; and without the sun to guide him, he couldn't even guess. Maybe he should flip a coin. Too bad he didn't have one.

An insect the size of a hummingbird landed on his arm, hooking his skin with its barbed little legs. They had done this a lot as he'd slogged through the muck, frequently scoring with their needle-sharp probosces, until he gradually became hypervigilant enough to thwart their attacks before they could do him injury. As this one prepared to stab him, he pinned it in place with his thumb, pressing it against his flesh so that it couldn't properly deploy its puncturing apparatus. This wasn't sufficient to squash it, but kept it from escaping while he spun his thorn and stabbed the bug laterally through its thorax. Its legs spasmed and scratched at his skin before it became still. With a flick of the thorn, the dead bug sailed off and vanished into the murk. Just call him Bob the Bug Slayer.

Another one started buzzing him, and then another. He could

keep killing them, but they were getting bolder, like buzzards who had decided maybe that cow really *was* dead and not just faking it. He had to pick a direction. He was so turned around by now that he had no idea where he was in relation to the castle, and Paltruck, that dispenser of incomplete instructions, hadn't mentioned that he would be coming to an intersection.

So, fuck it. He went right.

Before long the muck finally began to thin out, becoming more watery with a hidden surface, spongy but solid, beneath. Soon an old, narrow plank road emerged from the mire like the skeleton of some ancient, gigantic bog-snake. Pleased that his decision had led him to better footing, he picked up the pace. Myra was as good as rescued, you bet. He followed the road as it curved off to the left through what was effectively a throat lined with needles. He thought of those carnivorous plants that lured insects in with tender aromas, then trapped them with sharp, inward-pointing hairs that prevented egress and dissolved them for nutrients. He hoped the good road wasn't just a lure, that he wasn't playing the role of a fly heading for a sweet vat of digestive nectar.

He still had that disquieting thought in mind when he rounded the bend and came to the concave shore of a broad oxbow lake. It was a hundred feet across if it was a yard. He couldn't tell how long it was; it curved out of sight behind him in both directions, vanishing into the field of jagged creepers. He supposed it could be a very slow-moving river, but given its stillness and its faint scent of decay, he didn't think this water—if it *was* water—had any current to it. The planking continued across it in the form of an age-blackened bridge. Moss and mushrooms sprouted from the shaded spots, strange weeds from the sunlit ones. Gaps in the flooring winked with the erratic regularity of the black keys on a piano. At the other end of the bridge, a dark opening beckoned from the far bank. His destination, a black and barren mountain, loomed just beyond. A castle perched on top of it, tall and narrow and massive-looking. It seemed to have been chiseled directly out of the summit. He could see a road leading to its outer wall, switchbacking up the slope like a shoelace. At least he wouldn't have to scale a cliff to get there.

But first, he had to cross the water. Was this bridge the final part of the lure? Was he the ant after all? Did he have any choice but to find out?

Resigned to the possibility of falling in and being digested, Bob started picking his way across the bridge.

Lost

THE FIRST TIME Robin woke up, it was because her cheek scraped across something sharp, and the fresh pain dragged her back to consciousness.

Her eyes fluttered open. It took her a moment to realize that she was sliding through the forest, plowing a furrow through the fallen leaves and the ferns and the soft baby pines. This was because someone—or something; the hulking shadow ahead of her didn't seem quite person-shaped—had hold of her ankles and was dragging her by the legs. Was this the thing that had shaken her out of the tree? She remembered how she'd fallen, hit a few branches, and blacked out. Her body ached in any number of places, as one would expect after becoming a human pachinko ball, but not as badly as it would if she had broken something. At least, she didn't think so. So that was good. Unless she was just in shock, with dulled senses. That seemed like a possibility. She did feel light-headed. Light-headed and foggy and, oh, rather sleepy. Feeling sleepy after you banged your head ... Didn't that mean something?

Yeah. It meant you should take a nap.

Robin closed her eyes, and dropped back into the darkness.

The second time she woke up, it was because someone was shaking her. Robin grunted and pushed whoever it was away, but he came right back, hand on her shoulder. Shake shake shake.

"Go away, Kyle," she said. "I'm sleeping."

The hands went away.

But wait a minute. She wasn't in bed; she was on a mountain. And she had recently fallen out of a tree and been dragged through the woods. And whoever was bothering her had stopped when she told them to. All of those factors, taken together, made it unlikely that the person who'd been trying to wake her up was Kyle, didn't it?

She forced her eyes open, and discovered that she was locked in a cage.

It was made of tree limbs, some as thick as her arms, others as thick as her legs. They were splintered and twisted at the edges, as if they'd been wrenched off rather than chopped or sawed, and were lashed together with braided strips of some kind of pinkish hide that she didn't want to examine too closely. Crosspieces connected the opposite corners, meeting in the middle, forming an X-shaped roof that stabilized the structure. It was maybe fifteen feet on a side, big enough to hold quite a few captives, although at the moment it seemed rather empty.

She sat up. Considering the fall she had taken and her subsequent dimly-remembered excursion along the forest floor, she didn't feel too bad: Sore in the back, bruised on both sides, scraped along the face, an ache at the base of her skull—she touched herself there gingerly, felt a tender lump the size of a small egg—but nothing that hurt badly enough to be broken. She decided to call herself lucky to still be breathing. She looked around for fellow-prisoners, figuring that whoever had been trying to wake her was probably in here with her; it might have been someone outside poking her with a stick, but she didn't think so. It had felt like a hand. She quickly spotted the likely suspect, a figure crouched in the opposite corner, clutching a knobby bar with one hand, facing away at the darkening forest. Robin saw the back of a long, filthy, tattered white coat, as if this were a doctor who had wandered outside for a smoke break and gotten lost in the woods for a few years.

Robin shifted around, trying to get a better look at her fellow prisoner without being too obvious about it, but her movement did not go undetected. She stifled a gasp as the other captive turned and crossed the cage in an instant. If this *was* a doctor, she hadn't gone out for a smoke break; it looked like she had fled the scene after butchering a patient. The front of her coat was stained with crusty brown blood, spreading from the neck, splashing down the coat like a dried-up crimson waterfall. Her cheeks, lips, and chin were a smeared mess of flaking gore. Her long black hair hung clumped and matted and tangled. Within that grotesque mask, her dark eyes burned with a desperate intensity. She grabbed Robin's sleeve with one hand, imploring her with squeaks and throaty grunts.

"Shhh," Robin said. "It's okay. Relax." The absurdity of telling a feral ghoul to relax while they were both locked in a cage in the deep forest was not lost on her. It also didn't work. If anything, at the sound of Robin's voice, her new friend became even more frantic with her tugging and distressed vocalizations. Was she some sort of mute? Raised by wolves? "Sorry. I don't understand. Can't you talk?"

The woman paused at that, then let go of Robin's clothes, backed off, and raised her left arm, which, Robin finally noticed, ended well short of her wrist. The stump was inexpertly wrapped in bloodied hospital gauze held together with dirty strips of surgical tape; the skin just before the bandage was charred and crinkled, like parchment paper that had been in a hot oven. The woman pointed at her missing hand with her remaining one, then opened her mouth and pointed there, showing Robin an empty cavity where a tongue should have been. As Robin goggled, aghast, the woman swiped at her coat, trying to scrape mud and gore and forest gunk away from a name patch sewn into the fabric. Through the stains Robin could see that the patch said *Dr. Margaret*. So she *was* a doctor. Office hours were clearly over.

Margaret—Robin decided to consider it a first name—scuttled to the opposite side of the cage, jabbing with her remaining hand at a tree across the clearing. Robin joined her, trying to interpret the squawks and gestures. She quickly realized that the woman wasn't indicating the tree itself, but rather, a structure built up against it. At first glance it was just a pile of tree limbs, but closer inspection revealed it to be a crude hovel of wood and brush, with walls made of branches and a roof of leaves and thatch. It seemed to be some sort of dwelling. Kyle had mentioned finding a cabin on the mountaintop; was this it? She didn't think so; she wasn't on the summit anymore. If she were, she could scream and the others would hear her and come to rescue her. Wouldn't that be nice? To be rescued? Maybe she should go back to sleep until—

Margaret grabbed Robin's shoulder and shook her, bringing back to awareness. The doctor pointed at the tumbledown hut, then at the cage, then at the hut again. Evidently the person who had captured them lived there. Robin eyed the structure. There were no windows to reveal anything about its interior, but she could make out a section of the front wall that seemed like it might be a door. Judging by the size of it, the person who went in and out that way was either enormous, or overcompensating for something. She thought of the hulk that had dragged her through the forest. She had only been semiconscious and never got a good look at him, but she thought that might be a door he would be comfortable with.

Robin turned to the doctor, who mimicked a chopping motion at her hand severed arm, then mimed eating it. Robin stared at her mutilated companion as she repeated the gesture again, then again, then again. Finally she said: "Are you trying to tell me somebody *ate your arm?*"

Vigorous nods.

"And then they bandaged you up?"

Another nod.

Well, fuck.

Robin settled back on her haunches to think for a second. So. Okay. Whoever lived in that sorry excuse for a house had hacked off one of Margaret's major body parts for dinner, then given her enough medical attention to keep her alive. What for?

So he could make another meal out of her, of course.

Eyeing the crude cabin, Robin no longer needed to wonder why she had been brought here; the cut-and-cauterize approach to keeping one's food alive and fresh would only work for so long. Robin really didn't want to hang around until it was her turn on the menu. She set out on a circuit of the cage, testing the bars one at a time. Margaret followed close behind as she went from bar to bar, watching as she gave each one a firm shake, or tried to, anyway; although a few barely wiggled, like teeth that needed some attention but weren't prepared to fall out, most wouldn't budge. She had hoped to find a spot that was a little weaker than the rest—a piece of wood that had cracked or grown soft, a binding that was loose, a knot she could unravel—but, no, whoever had built this little prison had done a pretty good job with the materials at hand. She pictured a giant with a cartoon hammer pile-driving branches into the ground, *bam bam bam.*

Her grand tour of the cage soon brought her back to the door, which wasn't a promising escape vector either. Its hinges were thicker versions of the leathery swatches that held the bars together, and its constituent branches, while smaller than those that formed the walls, were jammed and twisted like the work of a powerful and demented basket weaver. And what the hell was that on the latch? A *padlock?* She reached through the bars and hefted it in her palm to make sure it was real, this shiny silver thing with a bright red knob. It looked fresh from the hardware store and belonged on a locker at the gym, not out here on a gnarled pen in the woods. That was just too much. That really took the prize. She glanced at Margaret, wishing the woman could talk, could tell her something about the freak who'd dragged her here, could explain why this primitive, jungle-movie-reject cage would be secured by such a thing. Where had it come from? Maybe the same place as the gauze and surgical tape?

Robin let the padlock drop and withdrew to the center of the enclosure. She wasn't going to be able to rip her way out of here with her bare hands. Not a chance. She couldn't dismantle the walls or the door, she couldn't slip between the bars, she couldn't reach the diagonal crosspieces that connected the corners and held the thing together. If she still had her small knife then she might be able to cut through the bindings, but it was in her pack, and her pack was gone, lost somewhere between here and the mountain where she'd been captured.

The mountain. Kyle and the others must be looking for her up there, right? They would've figured out by now that she wasn't just asleep in a nook somewhere. What would they do when they realized she was no longer on the summit? They would fan out into the woods, she hoped. Maybe they would find the trail where she had been dragged through the leaf litter, find her pack, find the clearing, find *her.* She crouched down, silent, listening, willing herself to hear someone coming to save her, but there was no sound except the rustling of the leaves, Margaret's snuffly breathing, and her own beating heart. So quiet.

She could scream for help. She *should* scream for help. She opened her mouth, closed it, glanced at the hovel. No, she didn't think she was going to do any screaming. That would bring their captor out, and he would shut her right up. Margaret had probably screamed for help, too, and how had that turned out for her?

Not well.

No, not well at all.

~~~~

Chuck didn't recognize this stretch of trail.

Kyle had taken the lead, of course, but the way he was looking around, muttering, and frequently hollering for Robin, Chuck wasn't sure he was paying any attention to whether or not they were going the right way, especially after the path veered left, entered a deep gully with a sharp turn in the middle, and emerged into an area of low, densely-foliated trees and gigantic ferns that crowded the path, their mammoth fronds dripping with moisture. Had there been a rainstorm? Chuck didn't remember one. The trees were weird, too. They had ash-grey bark mottled with splotchy mildew-black stains, thin, brittle branches, and grey-green leaves the size and shape of plastic food-service gloves. He had no idea what species they were. Nothing he was familiar with. He stopped and turned in a slow circle. On the way up, the route had been marked by little circles nailed up at regular intervals. Any idiot could have followed them. It had obviously been a long while since the park service had been up here replacing them—the once-red disks had weathered to a pale, irregular pink, rendering the white writing on them all but unreadable—but still, they'd been there. There weren't any along this narrow deer path.

They hadn't come this way. This wasn't the right trail.

Kyle had continued plodding along, either not noticing or not caring that Chuck had stopped, and was now some distance ahead. Gwen was in between them, looking back at him. "Chuck," she said. "Come on."

"No. Hold up. We're in the wrong place." Kyle kept going, so Chuck said it louder. "Hold up!"

Kyle paused and glanced his way. "What's the matter, Chuckles?"

"You tell me. Where are we?"

Kyle peered at him, then at their surroundings, as if noticing for the first time that they were out in the woods and not in a shopping mall. He checked his wrist compass, the way he'd been doing periodically the whole time, like Dick Tracy wondering why no one ever called him on his watch anymore. "This is the right direction," Kyle said.

"I didn't ask what *direction* we're going," Chuck said, "I asked where we *are*." He grasped a fern frond between his thumb and forefinger and pulled it down. Cold water ran off in rivulets. "Do you remember anything like this on the way up? Because I don't."

"Well, no, but—"

"No, of course you don't remember them, because we never saw them before," Chuck said. He let go of the fern, turned to Gwen, spread his arms. "We're lost."

Kyle rubbed the back of his head.

"*Are* we lost, Kyle?" Gwen said.

"We're not lost," he said at last. "Okay, fine, we didn't come up this way, but we're going in the right direction. This trail probably runs parallel to the one we were on before. At worst we'll end up at the road and have to walk to the parking lot."

"At worst," Chuck said, "we'll fall off a cliff. I think we should go back up and find the right path."

"That's a waste of time," Kyle said. He had his hands on his hips now, looking impatient. "This one will take us down."

"How the fuck do you know that? You've got no idea. It could end in a swamp."

"A swamp." Kyle snorted. "We're on a mountain. There's no swamp up here, man."

"I don't know," Gwen said. "Maybe we *should* turn around."

"Fine. You two go on back, then. We'll see who gets to the parking lot first."

"This isn't a race to the parking lot, Kyle," she said. "We're looking for Robin. Right? If she did start down, if she's waiting somewhere, we won't find her along this path, will we?"

Kyle looked like he was going to say something else, but then he closed his mouth—first time ever!—and came back to join them. "Okay," he said. "You win. Let's go."

And so they turned around and headed back up the slope, Chuck in the lead this time. Stone sides rose around them as they followed the path into the curve of the deep, narrow gully. They rounded the hairpin turn. The trail should have climbed out of it, as Chuck recalled, but instead it stayed more or less level, and when they came out the other side they were looking at what seemed to be the same trail they had just left. Chuck thought he even spotted the fern he had tugged on, with a spattering of dark soil underneath where the water had fallen.

What the fuck?

Chuck glanced back at the others. Gwen was peering around him at the path ahead; Kyle stood behind her, looking over her shoulder. Their faces wore similar expressions of bafflement. "It's the same trail," he told them.

"It can't be," Kyle said.

"I know," Chuck said, "but look."

"Hang on." Kyle levered a flat, roughly triangular rock out of the wall of the gully and tossed it out onto the trail. It thudded into the dirt, grey against the reddish loam.

"What are you doing?"

"Wait here." Kyle turned around and walked back up the gully.

Gwen started after him. "Kyle, where—"

He showed her his palm, telling her to stop. She did. He

disappeared around the bend. Gwen looked at Chuck, who shrugged. He had no idea what the fuck Kyle was up to either. Maybe they would get lucky and Kyle was going to ditch them, but, no, back he came. Only now he was carrying a rock, turning it over and over in his hands. It looked like the same one he had thrown out onto the trail. But it couldn't be, because that one was still there. Kyle brushed between Gwen and Chuck and went out to retrieve it. He brought both rocks back and showed them off, one in each hand. They were identical, down to the flecks in the stone, the pattern of scratches and dirt.

"How is that possible?" Gwen said.

"Fuck if I know, babe," Kyle said, "but I'm pretty sure going back to the summit is no longer an option."

~~~~

The bridge across the oxbow lake was theatrically rickety; as Bob moved gingerly from plank to plank, each vertical piling would shift left or right, forward or back, threatening to spill him into the drink with every step. The sodden, decrepit boards bent beneath his feet, sometimes making softly ominous cracking sounds. He avoided the ones that looked the most rotten, and took long, careful steps over the gaps where the wooden flooring had already fallen away. The lake looked black and endlessly deep when viewed through those shadowed openings; he half-expected some suckered tentacle to reach up through one and yank him down into the depths.

As he got farther out over the water, the entire span began to sink, sway, and buck in time with his movements. Icy water sloshed over the sides, further darkening the waterlogged surface. Bob paused, waiting for the motion to subside, and realized that he had crossed some boundary onto a section that was supported by flotation rather than pilings. It had been unstable enough when it was a bridge, and now it was a raft that couldn't go anywhere. He glanced behind him and could see the spot where the transition occurred: The first third of the bridge, anchored to the shore, rose a good foot or two above the portion where he now stood, which was attached by sliding iron bracelets to a pair of vertical poles on the stationary section. Looking ahead, he saw a similar set of poles near the far shore, which demarcated where the final span began and ran back to solid ground. The rings were rusted and badly pitted, leaving ruddy streaks along the black wood as they moved. He was surprised they hadn't fallen apart yet.

Bob was pretty sure the floating middle span was going to sink even farther as he continued towards the middle. What if it went all the way under? He wouldn't be able to see the gaps, many of which were big enough to fall through. He didn't know if he could swim in jeans and hiking boots. He wished he had a walking stick he could use to probe in front of him, looking for holes. If this were a normal forest he would go back ashore and find himself a branch, but here, there was nothing but creepers and spines. Even if he could cut one down, which he couldn't, it would be like trying to navigate using a thorny garden hose. So he hung where he was, studying the way ahead, trying to memorize the layout, where the pitfalls were, large and small. Then he started forward.

As he'd expected, the bridge submerged as he moved out and the angle of the rings changed, reducing the friction. Lake water intruded from both sides and welled up from the holes like black blood from an infected wound. It splashed around his ankles, then his calves. It got into his boots, freezing his feet. His socks immediately started to chafe. He hadn't expected to need waders on this trip. He slowed down, trying as best he could to superimpose the remembered pattern of holes on the blank surface ahead. It was harder than he'd thought it would be; he kept anticipating holes that weren't there, probing ahead with his toe before committing himself to each step. His water-filled boots felt like they weighed twenty pounds each. His toes were going numb. He wondered if——

The board Bob was standing gave way beneath him.

He had one leg extended toward his next step, and he was leaning slightly back to counterbalance it, so he toppled backwards. The sky wheeled overhead as he fell, splashing down into the foot or two of water that covered the bridge. Jesus God it was cold. For a second he thought the shock might send him into cardiac arrest. Gasping, he sat up. Glacial runoff sluiced from his body. He had let go of the thorn when he fell and now it bobbed some distance away, riding low in the water, like a submarine that had surfaced to admire the havoc wrought by its torpedoes. It was out of reach and he wasn't about to swim after it. He stood, his limbs stiff from the chill. If his lips and skin weren't blue already, they soon would be. At least now his feet had company in their sodden misery.

He started forward again, trying to keep his weight split between boards, moving with a sort of shoes-on-the-ground shuffle, the way you might inch barefoot through a dark, unfamiliar room where hostile dogs were sleeping. In this way he made slow, zigzagging progress across the floating section, until, with a wet, wooden *pop*, the far end of it detached from the stationary span and began to sink.

Well, fuck.

Bob half-scrambled, half-swam forward, boots only occasionally finding the solid surface below, shoving it a little further down each time he managed to kick off it. The icy water reached to his waist, then his ribcage, then his shoulders. A final lunge brought him to the third section. He encircled the piling on the right with the sort of hug normally reserved for a long-lost relative, his numb hands grasping each other on the other side. His boots kicked against the submerged section, looking for purchase on the slick, spongy surface. Finally his toes caught the iron ring. It had gotten stuck on an irregularity in the pole. It wasn't much of a hold, but it was enough to let him drag himself up out of the water and onto what had once been the final span of the bridge. Now it looked like a dock. He lay there panting, frigid water seeping from his clothes. After a little while he sat up and reached for his shoes. He fumbled with the laces, his shivering fingers barely able to hold on. He finally succeeded in untying them and pulled his boots off, decanting them into the lake; then he took off his socks and wrung them out. The sodden planks didn't absorb any of the water, it just puddled on top and dripped through the cracks. His feet and toes were a lovely shade of purple. He massaged some feeling back into them before putting his footwear back on. Meanwhile, the submerged section of bridge slowly resurfaced, like a crocodile getting ready to attack. By the time he was ready to go, it was nearly back to its original position, just offset a little, as it no longer had the cuffs on this side to keep it perfectly aligned.

Bob stood and gave the bridge both middle fingers and said, "Fuck y—"

The boards broke beneath him and he once again plunged into the lake.

~~~~

Robin had decided to try digging her way out of the cage; by the time she finally gave up, her once-glossy nails had been reduced to splintered, bleeding, black-lined stubs. Why had she sacrificed he fingertips in a gesture she'd known from the start would be futile? Kyle would probably have said it was because she was such a damn contrary bitch, but she preferred to think of herself as determined. Unfortunately determination wasn't enough to burrow through firm, rocky ground shot with stones and gnarled roots. Determination and a pickaxe, now, that might have gotten her somewhere.

Margaret's interest in her escape attempt had waned, but once it ended, the doctor crept over to offer a clinical diagnosis. She crouched down and inspected the disturbed earth, poked at it with her remaining hand, then looked at Robin and shook her head.

"Yeah," Robin said, "right. Thanks."

Suddenly a loud thud from the hovel made them both jump. It sounded like something big had just hit the ground. Margaret made a distressed noise and fled to the far corner; Robin slowly stood and turned to face the lean-to. Something was crashing around inside now, doing God-knew-what. Rearranging furniture? Then the door opened and their captor shambled out to where she could see him, and, Jesus Christ, he was an ogre. *Literally* an ogre. He stood about eight feet tall, a hulking, shambling pile of hair and muscle. His massive, shaggy head rested on top of an enormous hirsute body as if it had been dropped there by a retreating ice sheet. Incongruously, he wore the tattered remnants of a coat with a similar cut as Margaret's, although his was blue, and even filthier than hers, badly stained with brown splotches that might have been forest grime but were probably blood. Margaret's blood, maybe.

The monster scratched himself vigorously about the crotch, perhaps taking care of some pesky fleas, then shuffled over to the cage and peered inside. Robin took a good long look at his face. It was human, almost, but distended and lumpy, like skin stretched over a quantity of ball bearings. He had a nasty case of under-bite; the lower jaw protruded several inches farther than the upper, revealing large, sharp, chisel-shaped teeth. Robin scanned the coat, looking for a name tag. There it was. Only partially intact, its remaining letters said *xte*. What name had an *xte* in the middle of it? All she could think of was *Dexter*. Dexter the Ogre. Sounded like a series of bad children's books.

Dexter looked at the cage for a long moment, perhaps wondering who had built a stockade in his front yard; then, apparently remembering that oh, yeah, *he* had built it, he leaned forward and started working on the padlock. He seemed to be having trouble remembering the combination. Robin wondered if maybe she should call out numbers and confuse him even more. No, that would probably make him mad. Instead, she retreated to the far side of the cage, joining Margaret in her corner. The other woman kept trying to hide behind her. Dexter finally got the code right, popped the lock off the door, and swung it open. He crouched down and peered inside at them. His hot, gusty breath stank of meat and infection. She could see little tatters of dark skin stuck between several of his thumb-shaped teeth. Gross. He didn't move for a little while, maybe trying to decide if he was in the mood for leftovers or wanted something fresher, while Robin and Margaret jostled each other to see who could get an extra inch or two away from him. Pointless, really. Once Dexter made up his mind, he just reached right in with a long knotty arm, shoved Robin out of the way, grabbed Margaret's hair, and pulled. Easy as grabbing a bunch of carrots out of the crisper, except *these* carrots shrieked and clutched and twisted in a fruitless campaign not to be dragged off. Robin, cowering against the back wall, squirmed away from the questing fingers of her one remaining hand. Then Dexter grabbed Margaret's arm and wrenched it backwards with a thick, sticky snap. Margaret screeched and went limp. Mumbling, the ogre carried her out of the cage. He paused to slap the lock back together, then carried his prize off to his lair.

Robin slid slowly to the earth, trembling, heart hammering. Margaret had begged for help, and Robin had slapped her back. Not that anything she could have done would have made a difference; if he'd wanted to, Dexter could have broken her in half with the arm that wasn't carrying Margaret.

But now she knew how she'd react when death's scythe was in motion and she was in its path, didn't she?

~~~~

Myra had been on the balcony for what felt like hours, watching shadows gather in the bedroom. The figure inside never moved, never took a step, not once; it just stood there in uncanny stillness, hands behind its back, watching her. And yet it somehow stayed at the advancing edge of the darkness, drawing ever closer to the glass doors, as if the shadows were pulling it along. She could see its eyes now, in addition to its teeth; they were reddish-green, like in a photograph taken dead-on with a flash. They never blinked, those eyes, never turned to look anywhere but at her. The creature never spoke, and she hadn't addressed it for fear of what might happen, that talking to it would be construed as an invitation. You weren't supposed to issue invitations to things like this.

She became aware of faint scuffling sounds from far below. At first she took it for animal noises and paid little attention, but then she heard a few errant curses and she knew it was a person. She spun and peered at the bramble wall, and spotted movement in a spot that might have been an opening for a path. A rescuer? Had the prince finally arrived? Yes, he had: Bob came stumbling out of the creepers, clutching what looked like a gigantic toothpick. Even from here she thought he looked bloody and bedraggled, his clothes hanging strangely on his frame. She called his name. Her voice sounded flat and muted, as if the air itself was against her, unwilling to carry her words to where they needed to go. She called him again, as loud as she could, and this time he heard her; he backed away from the wall, peered left and right and, finally, up, spotted her, and returned her frantic waves. "Myra!" he shouted. "Listen, this is going to sound crazy, but there might be a vampire in there with you!"

"Yeah, I know! He's right behind me!"

"Stay away from him!"

Yeah, no shit. Did he really think he needed to tell her that? "I don't have a lot of options here, Bob!"

"I'll find you!" Bob gestured along the wall with the toothpick-thing. It was nearly as long as his arm. "How do I get in? Where's the door? *Is* there a door?"

Good question. Finding a door in the outer wall, which she couldn't get to, hadn't been a priority. Now she followed it with her eyes until she located a gate. A tangle of creepers had grown over it, obscuring it from easy view, but it seemed to be ajar, maybe partially off its hinges. It opened onto a muddy courtyard, separated by a wall from the one directly beneath her balcony, and mostly obscured by the outward curve of the lower part of the castle; she could only see the part of it near the exterior, flagstones and muck and small, grass-topped splotches of solid ground, an archipelago in the sludge. "I see it! Go left!" she yelled. "No, *your* left! Your left when you're *facing* me, Bob!" She gesticulated until he got himself pointed in the right direction. "Look for a bunch of dead ivy just in front of a ravine—there's a gate behind it!"

"Okay! Hang in there!"

Hang in there. As if she had a choice. She glanced over her shoulder. The spreading angular shadows had nearly reached the doors, and there was the figure, watching her, waiting, still and silent, pallid visage gleaming, teeth and eyes aglow, and although the face was blank she sensed its eagerness, its desire. It wanted her. It wanted to sink those teeth into her and drink her in. Oh yes.

If she was still on this balcony when the sun went down, she decided, then she was going to find out what happened when you jumped from a great height and went *splat* in a dream.

~~~~

Kyle led the others along the path—which was, apparently, the *only* path—still hoping that it would take them where they needed to go; but as the day wore on he knew something had gone badly wrong. Not that he needed more evidence of that beyond the mirrored stones. The thing was, they were going in the correct direction; he'd been watching the compass. They'd been heading south when they went up, and coming down, they were heading north. So where was the road? Did it even exist anymore? They hadn't really talked about the amazingly weird, fucked-up phenomenon of a gully where the entrance and the exit were the same thing. What was there to say?

He held up his wrist. The needle was steady, just a shade to the right of north. Gwen sidled up to him and peered at it. "North," she said.

"Yeah."

"North is the right way?"

"Uh-huh. But we should have reached the road by now."

Chuck leaned back against a tree, obviously grateful for the rest break. "Hey, Kyle, you got anything to eat in that pack?"

"Not really," Kyle said. "Just a couple energy bars."

"Yeah? I'm surprised you haven't got a whole pantry and camp kitchen in there."

"Well, I would, if we were camping," Kyle said, "but we were supposed to be eating in restaurants."

"It wasn't *my* idea to turn this trip into a back-road adventure," Chuck said.

"Let's all just settle down, okay?" Gwen said.

"I'll settle down once we're at the van instead of lost in the goddamn wilderness."

"We're not lost."

"We're not? Then where's the trail we were *supposed* to be on? Where's the road? Where's the parking lot?"

"Look, we'll get there, okay?" Kyle said, turning toward Chuck. "We just have to keep going north, and …"

He trailed off, because his compass needle hadn't moved, even though he'd just rotated three-quarters of the way around. It still said north. He shook his wrist hard, looked at the compass, shook his wrist again.

Still north. *Fuck.*

"What's the matter?" Gwen said.

"Nothing." Kyle flicked the dial with his finger. The pointer didn't budge. He hit it again, harder this time, with his knuckles. Finally the needle bobbed, spun, and rocked back and forth before coming to rest in a different place.

"If nothing's the matter, why are you beating up on your Boy Scout watch?" Chuck said.

"I don't fucking believe this. The compass needle was stuck." He looked at the others. "We're going west."

Gwen said: "What?"

Chuck stood up. "Are you saying we just spent *three hours* going in the wrong direction?"

How had he failed to notice this? Chuck's fault. How was he supposed to concentrate on anything with that fat asshole needling him all the time? "I don't know how long it's been. It depends when the needle stopped moving."

"It had to be when we went through that ravine," Gwen said.

"Yeah." Chuck nodded. "Everything has been fucked up since then. Bob and Myra must be freaking out waiting for us. And Robin! Who knows where *she* is." Then, shaking his head: "Who knows where *we* are."

"Just shut up for a minute and let me think." Kyle assessed their surroundings. The large ferns had thinned out a while back, when they had entered a heavily forested area, terrain that was in line with what you would expect to find on the lower slopes of an Adirondack mountain. The underbrush was minimal; it would be easy enough to set off in a northeasterly direction. That should get them back where they needed to go, though God knew how long it would take to get there. Or they could keep going west and hope to run into Route 28. He looked north, looked west. What to do?

Gwen said: "Kyle?"

"Okay. Look. Let's cut through the forest. Now that my compass is working again, we can head back to——"

"Wait. Wait. You want to leave the trail?" Gwen's tone of voice made it sound like Kyle had suggested they go swimming with sharks, or eat some broken glass. "I don't want to walk through the woods."

"We probably already are," Kyle said. "This probably isn't a human path."

"What? What does *that* mean?"

"He just means it's probably a deer path," Chuck said. "Right, Kyle?"

"Right," he said.

"I don't know, though. If it's a deer path, it probably goes down to the river. But if we cut through the woods we might come to a cliff."

Oh, sure, *now* Chuck wanted to keep to the path, just because Kyle had suggested they leave it. He was almost as contrary as Robin. "We're off the peak, so I doubt we'll hit a cliff. But if we do, we'll just follow it until we find a way down."

"I can't climb down a cliff," Gwen said.

"These are not the Himalayas, babe. They're not even the High Peaks. You won't have to climb down a cliff. I swear. Okay?"

Neither one of them answered.

"Okay? Through the woods?"

"You'll watch the compass this time?"

"Yes, Chuck. I'll watch the compass this time."

"You're sure this'll get us back to the parking lot?"

"I'm not sure of anything after what happened back there," Kyle said, "but it's better than any other direction. Okay?"

Chuck and Gwen looked at each other. Chuck sighed. "Okay. Seems like we don't have much choice anyhow. Before we move out, can we split one of those energy bar things?"

"Sure." Kyle slipped off his small backpack and reached inside.

A skeletal hand closed around his wrist. Fingers, thin and dry and bony, locked onto him. He felt the joints directly against his skin, pinching his flesh. He yelped and yanked his hand back and out it came, easy as anything. Nothing was holding onto him. Nothing had grabbed him. Or had it?

Chuck was staring at him.

Gwen said, "Kyle?"

Kyle shook his head. Slowly, he opened the pack, looked inside. It looked the same as it ever had. He rearranged the contents. There were the energy bars, settled to the bottom. He carefully reached in, took one out, and tossed it to Chuck.

"Thanks," Chuck said, tearing it open.

Still staring into the backpack, Kyle said: "Don't mention it."

Dusk

BOB WALKED AS quickly as he could along the castle wall, heading in the direction Myra had indicated. The outer rampart rose up to his right, a rough patchwork of black stones with no mortar visible between them. Towering over this was the castle itself, tall and narrow, dark walls pierced by darker windows. It, like everything else around here—the thorns, the sky, the stench in the air—just radiated gloom, despair, death.

Maybe Chuck had crashed the van, driven it into the river. Maybe they were all dead and this was the afterlife, in which case the afterlife sucked.

He shook his head. No, he was being ridiculous. They weren't dead. He was dreaming, that was all. His imagination had conspired with his subconscious to dredge up this castle with Myra in it, and the brambles and the bugs and the lake and the bridge, and an inscrutable know-it-all, Paltruck, to sort-of tell him what to do. Too bad he hadn't dreamed himself up a helicopter gunship. Then he could have just flown here and blown the shit out of the place, instead of slogging through that nightmare bramble swamp, getting soaked in that nearly-frozen lake—*twice!*—and, after hauling himself out a second time, following a trail that turned into a tunnel that turned into a tube through the brambles that eventually narrowed down to about the size of a badger. At that point he'd only kept going because the forward-pointing thorns made it impossible to turn around, or even to back up.

Busy feeling sorry for himself, Bob nearly missed the patch of dead vines Myra had told him about, only realizing he'd passed it when he nearly fell into the eroded ravine just beyond it. Ivy hung over the wall like a lanky, unwashed forelock. He went over to examine it. He couldn't see a gate, but Myra had said it was there, so he started gathering up the rustling tendrils and pulling them aside, revealing the edge of a broken wooden door. He gave it a tug, but it wouldn't move; it was partially embedded in a dried mud flow. Apparently water drained through this aperture when it rained, hence the ravine that started at its edge.

Maybe he could squeeze through the opening. As he positioned himself to do so, he felt something drop onto his ear and start tickling his cheek. He brushed it away, hoping it was a dead leaf. But no. It was a black and yellow spider with a body as big around as a quarter, and now it was on the back of his hand. He shrieked and shook it off, and that, apparently, encouraged all the other fucking spiders in the ivy to come after him. *Come on, girls, we've got a live one here!* He dropped the vines and stumbled back, jerking his body like a dancer in the groove, swatting and brushing himself all over. Colorful arachnids pattered to the ground like fat raindrops. One of them bit him near the wrist. Mother *fucker*! It felt like being stabbed with a hot kebab fork. A fiery warmth spread up his arm. He didn't look at the bite; if he saw a couple of big spider-fang holes in his flesh, he thought he might just pass out, and then the little bastards would swarm all over him, shooting him up with their venom before sucking out all his delectable juices.

Get a grip, Bob. Get a fucking grip.

The ivy had, like a curtain, fallen back to cover the gate, and the spiders he hadn't squashed were scuttling back to its shadowed safety. He glared at the dry vegetation, wishing for a flamethrower. Bob thought for a second, then scrambled down the rocky slope to the edge of the bramble forest to pluck himself a second thorn. Getting back up to the castle wall was a little harder than going down had been, but he made it. Holding one thorn in each hand, he pinched the ivy between them and pulled it aside. A fresh set of spiders came swarming out in response to the movement, but he was far enough back this time that they didn't land on his head. They seemed to have some trouble holding on to the waxy surface of the thorns, and many fell off. He squeezed through the opening as fast as he could. On the other side he stumbled and spun and scraped the thorns against each other, sending the angry, many-legged attackers flying, but in his whirling haste he tripped over some debris and fell flat on his face on a rough, uneven surface of caked earth, stones, and rubble. He rolled away from the door and pulled his knees in and looked at the gate, fearful of being smothered under a carpet of spiders, but they were once again retreating towards their tangled lair.

Bob sat up. From this side he could see the big doors, so decrepit that he didn't think they would ever close again; the iron binding was dull and pitted, and the vertical wooden boards had become fat and spongy, and riddled with distended insect holes. He imagined the spiders—already, in his mind, inflated to the size of silver dollars instead of quarters—lying in wait for the termites or whatever lived in those holes to poke their little heads out. They probably feasted on the beetles from the bramble forest, too, and on mice and small birds and unwary travelers who camped outside the walls. Fuckers. He finally looked at the bite on his arm. The spot had begun to swell, and, yes, there were two small puncture wounds in the middle of it, oozing some clear, thick fluid. He didn't throw up, but he wanted to.

He picked himself up and turned towards the castle. Beyond the dry flagstoned strip where he stood, he saw a wide courtyard full of viscous mud. Another damn quagmire. A series of small grassy knots poked up through the mud, forming an archipelago across the courtyard that led to a brick skirt around the entrance to the castle proper. They were too far apart for stepping, but he thought he could jump from one to the next. Not that he wanted to. The invitation was so obvious that it simply *had* to be a trap. But what else was he supposed to do? Slog through the mud? He had no idea how deep it might be. He looked around. There were a few dead trees in here that had taken root, grown for a while, and then perished. He managed to snap a branch off of one of them, which he brought back over and pushed into the muck, hoping to find a solid surface a few inches down, maybe a foot. Nope. After three feet, he ran out of branch. Another foot or so and he ran out of arm, too. At least the mud soothed the pain from the spider bite.

He left the branch to its fate and pulled his arm out of the sucking muck, scraping it off with the back of his other hand. Then, like a platform-game hero, he positioned himself in front of the nearest knoll, steadied himself, and hopped for it. He half-expected it to sink or tilt underneath his weight—it had been that sort of afternoon—but no, it was solid and steady. From here, he had a couple of options for his next target. He studied them and decided to go for the larger one, although it was a little farther away. He made that jump, and the next one, and the next one, and had just landed on the next-to-last one when the sun dipped below the level of the walls and went out like a candle snuffed by a shovelful of dirt. Darkness poured in with the force of a physical flood. It overwhelmed and unbalanced him. He instinctively clawed at the gloom, as if he could catch hold of it and tear it aside and reveal the daylight beneath.

The wild, reflexive motion unbalanced him, and he toppled over into the cold, gooey mud.

~~~~

Myra watched Bob's progress, such as it was, leaning way out over the railing to keep an eye on him. He seemed to be having some trouble with the door, flailing and swatting as if being swarmed by insects, then he paused to test the depth of the mud, and all the while she felt the presence of that *thing* behind her, impinging on her back. She shouted at Bob a few times, yelling for him to hurry, but it seemed the castle had figured out how to muffle even her loudest screams; he never gave any sign that he had heard her. Finally, *finally*, with the sun much lower than she would have liked it to be, he started moving forward, jumping like a grasshopper to the first little island, then the next. At that point the wall blocked him from view, no matter how far she leaned, so she turned around to see how close the creature—the vampire—had gotten.

Too close. Oh, so much too close.

While her back was turned, the glass doors had been silently flung wide. Her captor loomed at the threshold, only four or five feet away from her, at the very edge of the light. His green-red eyes stared at her. His teeth gleamed. The stench of hot iron enveloped her. But it wasn't really iron she smelled, was it? It was blood. It had always been blood, and it was coming from him.

The sun still hung above the mountains, but its angle left the tower almost entirely draped in darkness. Bob's courtyard was completely enshrouded. Myra's little patch of sunlight was all that still escaped the dusk. She had nowhere to go. She jumped up and sat on the balustrade, facing the vampire, looking into its vast unblinking eyes. She found it difficult to break the eye contact, but managed to drop her gaze. She turned her head to the side, swung her feet up and around so that they dangled over open space. She could push herself off and fall before he caught her. She raised her eyes to check the sun, and realized that other peak—the one with the building on top—was casting an overlong shadow in the wrong direction, pointing *towards* the sun like a jabbing, accusatory finger, like a beacon that projected darkness instead of light. She half expected the ebon cone to start rotating, a beacon calling all the creates of the night home.

As soon as she thought that, the projected shadow swung itself around and stopped to point directly at her.

Something from the mountain slammed into her, some powerful force, a spectral wind that lifted her off the balustrade and blew her backwards toward the tower room and what waited within. Powerful, claw-like fingers grabbed onto her shoulders, catching her in an icy grip that sent chills up her neck, along her scalp, down her spine. The vampire swung her around and hurled her at the bed. She landed on her back in a tangle of pillows and blankets, staring at her pallid assailant. He smiled and opened his cavernous mouth. She saw two rows of sharklike teeth running all the way around its bluish gums. He moved forward in a flash, sliding across the floor, hands once again locking on her shoulders. He hauled her roughly to her feet. She squirmed, but couldn't break his grip. His filthy mouth closed on her neck. The stench of blood became nauseous and overpowering as the rows of teeth dug in, sawing through her flesh as he shook his head like a dog with a squirrel. She felt her artery burst, spewing blood across the vampire's face, into his hungry mouth.

And then she felt nothing at all.

~~~~

Kyle had been right about cutting through the woods; the slope was downward and gentle, with little underbrush to get in their way and slow them down. He kept checking his compass, showing it to Gwen and Chuck from time to time just to prove that the needle wasn't stuck, that they were going in the right direction. Gwen figured this was mostly for her benefit, because she hadn't wanted to leave the deer path, though Chuck seemed to think he was being needled. But then, Chuck usually thought that.

Eventually, the ground leveled out and the trees started to thin, dusky blue sky becoming visible through them ahead. Kyle, looking cheerful, glanced back and gave them the thumbs up. They must be coming to the bottom, finally. Her feet were killing her. She was looking forward to getting back in the van and sitting down for a while on a nice, soft seat, then finding a restaurant for dinner. But when they emerged from the tree line, Kyle stopped dead, bringing them all up short. They weren't at the river bank or on the roadside; they were on a strip of rock about a dozen yards wide, ending in a cliff that was, somehow, taller than the one at the summit where they had started.

Kyle said: "What the fuck?"

That was just what Gwen had been thinking. How could they possibly be this far above the valley floor, after spending all that time going downhill? It made about as much sense as hiking through a cleft in the rocks and discovering that the way out was the way in, and vice-versa.

This was too much. She simply couldn't keep going. She was exhausted and her feet were killing her. As Kyle moved forward and then scurried back and forth along the edge of the cliff like an ant whose scent trail had been interrupted by a stream of bug spray, Gwen went to a nearby large rock and sat down, staring at the carpet of trees below. There was the road, or at least, *a* road, running alongside the river, or at least, *a* river. Gwen didn't even know where she was anymore. It wasn't the Adirondacks. It was some bizarro-world of haunted cabins and trails that didn't go anywhere and landscapes that rearranged themselves when you weren't looking. She pulled her aching feet out of her tennis shoes, took off her ankle-high socks. They smelled awful. Look, blisters. And she hadn't even noticed all the little scratches on her calves and shins from scuffing through spindly branches. She let her head fall into her hands. This wasn't at all the sort of exploring she'd had in mind.

Chuck and Kyle started arguing again. Of course. She wanted to stick her fingers in her ears and shout at them both to shut the hell up, but when she lifted her head and saw the sun, she completely forgot what she was going to say. The sun. The *fucking* sun. Its bottom edge was now touching the tops of the mountains across the valley. How could it possibly have gotten that low? How long had they been walking?

She said, "What time is it?" But her voice came out a squeak, and the others didn't hear her over their squabbling.

The second time she asked the question, she screamed it.

They stopped talking over each other and stared at her. Kyle flipped down the watch face of his compass, peered at it, and said, "A little after three."

That was about what she'd expected; so why was the darkness rising so quickly in the valley beneath them, as if someone had dammed a river of ink to create a black reservoir?

It seemed Chuck had noticed it too. "You sure, sport?" he said. "Maybe your watch hands stopped, too. That's not a three-o'clock sun."

"My watch is working fine."

"Oh, I guess the sun is broken then?"

"I think it is," Gwen said. "I think the sun is broken."

That shut them both up for a minute. Then Chuck said, "The sun's not broken, Gwen. We've just been lost for a——"

"We're not lost," Kyle said. "Look, there's the road. All we have to do is get down the cliff and we can make it in an hour or two, tops."

"Yeah? How do we get down the cliff? You going to carve us some stairs? Got a hundred-foot ladder in your pack?"

"Fuck you, Chuck," Kyle said.

"Fuck *me*? I'm not the one who brought us here. You are. So fuck *you*."

Kyle shook his head and said something under his breath.

"Sorry, what was that?" Chuck said. "I didn't catch it."

"Nothing. Forget it."

"*I* caught it," Gwen said. "It was something about Robin."

"Robin is probably at the van with Bob and Myra, wondering where the fuck we are," Chuck said, helpfully.

"Robin's not at the van, asshole," Kyle said. "She's——" He broke off and turned away.

Gwen and Chuck exchanged a glance.

"Kyle," Gwen said, "where do you think Robin is?"

"I have no fucking clue."

"Then how do you know she's not at the van?"

He turned back to them. "Because she would want to follow me and have a good laugh at her little jokes."

"What jokes?"

"Hacking my phone. Making my compass needle stick. Playing that trick with the ravine."

"Have you completely lost your shit?" Chuck said. "Okay, it's not inconceivable that she could hack your phone, that she could fuck with your compass. But that thing with the ravine? Whatever the fuck that was? How can you *possibly* blame that on Robin?"

"You'd be surprised what Robin can do when she puts her mind to it."

"Jesus, Kyle," Gwen said. "You're making her sound like some kind of witch."

"Maybe she is. Maybe she is a witch."

"Well, good," Chuck said. "Maybe she can load us all on her broom and fly us off this crazy fucking mountain."

~~~~

Robin was startled awake by the clinking of the padlock. She sat up, wary, but it didn't appear that her captor had any immediate interest in her; he carried Margaret over his shoulder, and tossed her roughly to the ground. She lay like a discarded rag doll as the ogre slapped the lock closed, then shambled back into his hovel. After he was gone, Robin crept to Margaret's side. The woman reeked of burnt flesh. Fighting not to choke on the stench, Robin rolled her over. The ogre had wrenched off Margaret's right arm at the elbow, crudely cauterizing the stump until it was scorched black, leaving her alive to provide one more fresh meal. The bandaging job was even more slapdash this time than last, just a few strips of tape and scraps of cloth. He was getting careless with her, probably understanding that she didn't have much longer to live anyway before blood loss, shock, or infection killed her. Besides, he knew where his next meal was coming from.

After making sure Margaret was breathing, Robin retreated to the other side of the cage, trying to get away from the stink of burned meat. It didn't work; she could still smell it no matter where she went. She rocked back and forth, watching her fellow-captive, waiting to see some spark of consciousness. Eventually Margaret's eyes flickered open and she stared up into the night sky, though Robin didn't think she was really seeing anything, at least at first. After a while she tried to sit up. Robin went over and helped her get vertical, stayed close as Margaret hunched over and began to sob and shake. Robin stroked the woman's filthy hair. The gesture of useless sympathy seemed to go unnoticed.

Leaving Margaret to her sobs, Robin crept back to her corner and closed her eyes and tried to sleep. She didn't have much luck; she kept remembering the ogre dragging Margaret away, and herself doing everything she could to avoid being the one taken. At some point she became aware that something was stealthily creeping around Margaret's side of the cage. Robin cracked an eye and looked in that direction. She thought she saw a small dark shape just outside the bars where her fellow-prisoner lay. It was bigger than a skunk but smaller than a wolf, and seemed to have its arms stuck between the opening, its little hands moving over Margaret's injured shoulder. A raccoon, trying to snag a tasty morsel for itself from the ogre's pantry? Robin sat up sharply and the hands withdrew, the shape behind them melting into the darkness. A moment later the door of the cage began to rattle. She slowly turned her head, her gaze moving along the gnarled bars toward the opening. The fussing with the lock stopped. She heard it pop open. A moment later it landed softly in the loam. The door creaked open at the hands of a stumpy creature with bark-like skin, wearing a ratty outfit made of foliage.

"Hi," he whispered. "I'm Paltruck."

"What on earth—"

The being raised a stubby finger to his lips. "Shh. Indoor voice. So as not to wake Lumpy." He stepped back and motioned her forward. "Come on."

Robin didn't move. "Why would I go anywhere with you?"

"Because I'm the helpful one."

"Yeah, I'll need a better reason than that."

"Okay. How about this? If you're not far, far away when old lunkhead gets hungry again, you're his next meal."

That was a good reason. Robin checked on Margaret; the woman was asleep, or maybe passed out. She reached out to give her a little shake.

"Uh-uh," Paltruck said. "Bad idea. She'll slow you down and get you caught."

She shot a glance at him. "I'm not leaving her here."

"You should."

"I'm not." Then: "I thought you said you were the helpful one."

"I am! I healed her up so she wouldn't die."

"So what? He's going to *eat* her."

"He already ate a lot of her anyway."

"Well, he's not going to eat the rest." Robin gently touched the other woman's shoulder. "Wake—"

Margaret sat up screaming.

Robin immediately clapped a hand over the woman's mouth, muffling her cries. She looked at the hovel. The ogre had surely heard that, but maybe he would just think the screaming was because Margaret had bumped her latest injury and it hurt. He couldn't be expected to know a lawn gnome had come to let his prisoners out, right?

Right?

"Have you done this before?" she whispered. Then, when Paltruck didn't answer: "Let people out, I mean?"

Still no answer. The little guy was gone, melted back into the woods or the ground or wherever he had sprung up from. Apparently being the helpful one didn't extend to getting caught with his hand in the cookie jar, freeing the snickerdoodles. At least he had left the door open.

Margaret squeaked a question into Robin's palm. "Yes," Robin whispered. "Get up. We're going." She pointed at the entrance. "The cage is open and we're going. Quietly. Can you stand up?" After a moment, Margaret nodded. "Okay. Good." Robin helped Margaret to her feet. She seemed unsteady, but managed not to fall over as they exited the cage. Robin wondered how difficult it was to balance when you suddenly didn't have any arms. She hoped never to find out.

Outside of the cage, Robin stood around for a few seconds, befuddled by her sudden options. Which way to go? How to find the others? She had no idea where this clearing was in relation to the mountain or the parking lot; she had no way to judge their location, nothing to guide her but the stars. Unfortunately she'd left her sextant in her other jeans.

Margaret gave her a gentle kick in the shin to get her attention, then gestured with her head, indicating a spot in the surrounding forest. Robin thought she saw a faint path there, or at least a thin spot in the brush.

"That way?" she said.

Margaret nodded.

At least one of them had a clue. "Okay," Robin said. "Let's go."

They went.

~~~~

When Bob landed in the mire, torches flared into life around the walls, lending a fitful, flickering illumination to the courtyard. He didn't know if he had triggered them by falling, or if this was a regular occurrence, like streetlights coming on every evening. He had a bad feeling it was the former, that he had tripped some sort of alarm system, and that his circumstances were about to become even more wretched. He managed to pull his arm loose, but his legs were in deep. There was a solid bottom down there—the tips of his toes were touching it—and although it kept him from sinking any further, it didn't offer a platform he could use to push his way out, either.

He had managed to hang on to both of his thorns. Reaching as far as he could towards the nearest island, he plunged them into the soft earth with all the force he could manage. Using them as anchors, he slowly dragged himself forward, pushing and flexing and inching his way up out of the muck until he was finally free of it. He collapsed on the stiff grass, waiting for the weakness in his arms and legs to go away. Had he ever been this filthy and exhausted before? He didn't think so. Not since college, for sure.

When he thought he could manage it, he got up, steadied himself, and made a few more jumps. He paused on the final grassy platform before the apron of stone at the base of the keep. A tall, narrow archway beckoned in the wall ahead, opening onto a dark hallway that disappeared into the depths of the castle. One last, tottering leap brought him to solid ground, but he landed badly, stumbled, and fell forward, landing on his stomach with his hands and the upper part of his body just inside the opening. One of the thorns broke beneath him with a waxy *snap*, but that sound was quickly lost in the buzzing whir of a horizontal blade that slashed out and swished by just over his head. A thin crop of his hair settled to the floor around him, scythed away like wheat.

Jesus Christ.

Keeping as low as he possibly could, with one eye on the wall—now that he knew it was there, he could just barely see the slot from which the blade had slashed out—Bob scuttled forward. Ahead was a black, echoing chamber. He stopped before reaching it; thresholds seemed like dangerous places around here. He coiled himself up, braced his feet as best he could, and launched himself forward like a speed swimmer starting with a shallow dive. As he did, there was a metallic *click* followed by the screeching rattle of a chain unrolling fast. He felt a sharp pain in his ankle, coincident with the clang of metal on stone and an abrupt check on his forward motion. Something had pinned his foot. Bob rolled over as best he could, looked back at his foot. A heavy iron grate had fallen when his weight left the hallway floor, catching his right ankle between its bottom bar and the floor. Jagged spear-points rested in a series of bite-like depressions in the stone, but these had missed him. The points created a few inches of space below the bottom crossbar. That plus the padded high-top of his hiking boot were the only reasons his ankle hadn't been crushed into talcum powder.

Bob squirmed briefly, trying to work himself free. No dice. He was about to untie his boot and see if he could slip his foot out of it when he heard an unseen winch start up. The hidden chains went *clack-clack-clack* as the grate retracted into the ceiling. He rolled away, curled up, and felt his injured foot. He didn't think it was broken, but he was going to have one hell of a bruise. He stood and tested his weight on it. It hurt, but it held, and he thought he could walk it off. He gave the grate an unfriendly look as it disappeared into its slot. He hoped that was the last trap in the gauntlet.

Turning away, he looked around, wondering which way the stairs to Myra's tower might be. From the courtyard, facing the front of the castle, her tower would have been off to the right; he didn't have any reason to think the stairs wouldn't be that way. Of course, he didn't have any reason to think they *would* be, either, but no better option was on tap, so he limped off in that direction, keeping close to the outside wall. He sensed that he was at the edge of a large room, but he couldn't see anything beyond his immediate vicinity. In here, no torches burned. Well, there was one, just inside the killer hallway, but he had no intention of touching a fucking thing in this nightmare hellhole unless he absolutely had to. Not a brick, not a stone, not a fixture.

As he left the torchlit hallway behind, he became aware of a pallid yellow light emanating from his person. He quickly sourced this back to the thorn, which was, evidently, luminescent in true darkness. It had the feeble intensity of a just-about-used-up chemical glow stick. Its purpose was probably to attract insects for night pollination or big dumb animals for self-impalement, but it was so astonishingly serendipitous that Bob stopped for a second just to look at it and contemplate his good fortune. As his eyes adjusted, he spotted a nearby flight of stairs, going up into what looked like a tower. It was the right spot. If these weren't the steps that led to Myra, Bob would eat his thorn, pointy side first.

He started moving again, picking up the pace, holding the thorn out in front of himself, a lucky trick-or-treater approaching the best house in the neighborhood. He half-hobbled, half-ran up the stairs, ignoring the pain in his ankle, leaving behind a trail of flaking mud. The stairs went round and round and round, clinging to the outer wall, rough stone to his right and an abyss to his left. There was no railing to prevent a slip, a tumble, and a bone-breaking drop to the floor, but he didn't slow down. Something was here, and it wanted to take Myra away from him, and he had to get there before it could do that.

Finally the stairway ended at a landing, where a thick wooden door stood open a crack, inviting him to peek inside. He scrambled up the last few steps, closed the last few yards. The door was right in front of him, grey in the dimness. He heard wet noises from inside, soft mushy tearing sounds. It reminded him of one of those hideous nature documentaries where they would zoom right in on predators eating a carcass.

Bob hesitated outside the door. He shifted his grip on the thorn, squeezed it tight, as if that would make it sharper, make it glow brighter.

A low, husky, feminine moan drifted through the opening. What was happening in there? He put his hand on the door, pushed it gently. Abruptly, the sounds stopped. Raising the thorn, he shoved the door open and hurled himself into the room. He was just in time to see the backside of a wraithlike shadow, the pallid glimmer of its barren skull a small bean-shaped moon. It was fleeing, Myra slung over its shoulder, leaving a trail of blood that hung in the air and pattered to the floor like a thin rain. As Bob goggled, the shadow leaped into what appeared to be a mirror on the opposite side of the room. He heard a sound like an air-filled bag popping, and then Mya and her abductor were gone. The mirror spun and spun like a rotating sign in the wind, or one of those toys that simulated motion by having a different picture on each side. What Bob saw reflected in the twirling mirror was not the dim tower room but a brightly lit corridor in some kind of facility. It dimmed as the mirror's rotation slowed and stopped.

Before he had time to think about what he was doing, Bob charged the mirror and jumped into it. If the shadow could go through it, then so could he. He reflexively closed his eyes before he hit the surface, expecting a crash, but instead he felt a faint resistance and then he landed on carpeting.

Bob opened his eyes.

He had not passed through into the corridor; he was back in Dr. Zane's waiting room, on the floor in front of the wall mirror. Neat and sterile, functional, empty, it looked like any other doctor's office after hours, when the patients and the nurses and the doctor had all gone home, leaving the place deserted.

Wait. No. Not deserted. Up the hall, directly in front of him, something glinted with reflected light.

Something sharp, held in the grip of a shadow.

~~~~

Myra opened her eyes.

She was lying on her back on a hard, narrow cot. The vampire—that hairless, smooth-skinned monster who had chewed apart her neck on that enormous bed in her tower prison—was not present. She remembered the hot rush of her blood, then everything going black, as if she had fallen into a deep sleep. How had she ended up here?

A dream. It must have been a dream, brought on by that terrible headache, which, thank God, was just as gone as the vampire. She sat up, her whole body trembling with the aftermath of the migraine or the nightmare or both. Her neck hurt, right in the spot where she'd dreamed of being bitten, but it was probably just stiff from lying on the uncomfortable cot. Just to be sure, she ran her fingers all over it. No ragged bloody holes, no scars. She climbed down. Her sneakers were on the floor near the chair, but otherwise she was fully dressed. She put her shoes on, then went to the window on the wall to her right. Pale light came through the closed Venetian blinds, providing the only illumination. She parted the slats with her fingers and peered through. It was dark outside; night had fallen while she'd been sleeping. A few stars glittered, washed out by the moon, full and floodlight-bright.

She went to the door, opened it, and peered out into a corridor, antiseptic and harshly-lit. It looked like she was in a large facility; as far as she could tell, the corridor went on forever, lined by an endless series of closed, blank doors on each side. After the twilight of the examination room, the startling fluorescent glare was pretty close to blinding. The door directly opposite hers was open, though. A variety of sounds and voices came out of it, with the tinny quality of a small television speaker. With no better idea of what to do, she crossed the hallway—she didn't like being out in it, felt exposed to unseen eyes—and entered the other room, where she stopped dead. It was large and dome-shaped, and contained a single piece of furniture, a red vinyl couch sitting on a large raised platform. The platform slowly rotated, so that if you sat on it and looked straight ahead your gaze would eventually complete a circuit of your surroundings. The interior of the dome was lined with dozens, maybe hundreds, of small, curved television screens, laid edge-to-edge like bricks. Except for a single black panel, each one displayed something different. It was like the control room for a mad surveillance network. What *was* this place?

Somebody was sitting on the couch, which was currently facing away from her, so all she saw was the back of his head. She stood there as it rotated around until it was facing her, at which point the platform's motion stopped. The person on the sofa was a young man. "Hi," he said. "I'm Patrick."

She goggled at him.

Patrick said: "Are you the type who doesn't talk?"

"The type of what?"

"Oh," he said. "I guess not." He eyed her. "You're not dressed like a patient. Are you a visitor?"

"A visitor?"

"Did you come here to see someone?"

"No. I'm not even sure where I am."

"Really." He cocked his head at her. "Are you sure you're not a patient?"

"Yes. Did you say your name was Patrick?" He nodded, grinning, as if pleased she remembered. "Are *you* a patient?"

"Yep! I live here." He looked around with his eyes as he spoke, as if he still couldn't quite believe he had ended up in such a swank place as this. Then he added, a little darkly: "For now."

"Are you planning to leave?"

"Well, I'm not planning to stay. I guess that's the same thing. Do you like TV?"

"What?"

"TV. Television. You like it?"

"Um, sure, I guess," Myra said.

Patrick patted the sofa. "Sit down and watch it with me, then."

She shook her head. "I'm okay here."

"Come on," Patrick said. "This is the *special* TV lounge. Not everyone gets to see it. Most people have to make do with the regular one."

"I'm sure I'm honored," she said, "but I, uh, I have to get going soon."

He shrugged. "Suit yourself." The platform started rotating again. Myra, curious, moved forward to take a closer look at the screens. She turned in a slow circle, unconsciously mimicking the motion of the platform; she saw slice-of-life surveillance video, game shows, shaky-cams, movie monsters small and large, an evil doctor, sitcoms, alien invaders … Wait a minute. She turned back to the evil doctor. He was menacing a man who knelt on the floor of a waiting room, near a large mirror.

The man on the floor? Bob.

"What's this?" she said, maybe a little more sharply than she'd intended.

Patrick peeked at her from over the top of the sofa; while she'd been looking around, he had rotated away from her again. "What's what?"

"This! The one with my husband!"

"Which one is that?"

"Right there! The one with the doctor!"

"Which doctor?"

"*This* one!" She smacked the screen with her hand.

"Yeah?" Patrick said. The sofa's slow rotation suddenly accelerated and in a moment it was facing the television that showed Bob. "Looks like he's in trouble. Come sit down and we'll watch."

"Watch? No! We have to help!"

Patrick picked up a remote that lay next to him. He clicked a button on it and all the televisions froze at once. "Help? We can't help. It's a show. They're all shows."

Myra stared at him. "A show?"

"Of course," Patrick said. "You're actors, and this is a show. Or maybe a movie. Sometimes it's hard to tell the difference."

She tapped her finger on the screen that showed Bob. He was reaching for something under a chair, something Myra couldn't see, as the doctor—more madman than physician, his eyes maniacal, his face a sneer—rushed at him with the scalpel. She turned back to Patrick. "Are you doing this?"

"I don't understand what you mean."

"These *shows*. Are you making them happen?"

"Oh. No, of course not. I'm just watching them."

"What about that?" She pointed at the remote.

"This?" He looked at the device. "It can pause and fast-forward and rewind and skip, but it can't change what happens in a show. Haven't you ever used one?"

"I don't think I have." She held out her hand. "Can I try it?"

"Nuh-uh." The remote disappeared, as if by sleight of hand. "It's mine."

"Okay." She took a breath, held it, let it out. "Okay. So you're not producing these shows. Then who is?"

"Well, you just said it. The producer is producing them."

"And who's that?"

Patrick shrugged. "Beats me. It would be in the credits, but I always skip over those. Come on, let's see what happens next." He raised his hand—the remote was back in it, materialized out of nothing—and pointed it at the screen that showed Bob.

She said: "No!"

He gave her a sidelong look. "I thought you said you liked television."

His voice had taken on a different tone, one she didn't care for. "I do. I do like television," she said. "But I don't like the way that show is going."

"You don't get to decide how the show goes."

"But what if I could find the producer? Have a talk with him about his programming choices? Then maybe he would change it."

Her new friend seemed dubious. "Yeah. Maybe. But you'll have to go look for him."

"How do I get outside?"

Patrick nodded at the wall behind him and a door appeared there, wooden and nondescript, incongruous with the televisions that surrounded it. It was up a short flight of stairs, inset into the curve of the dome. She hurried over to it and up the steps, then paused, hand on the knob. Patrick wasn't even looking at her anymore, he was watching the screens. The entire half of the dome opposite her was now devoted to Bob and the doctor, their image spread across all the sets, so that each of them appeared to be eight feet tall; the doctor loomed over Bob like a giant.

"Patrick?" she said.

"Mmm?"

"You can come with me, you know. You don't have to stay here."

"Yes I do," he said. "I——"

"Yeah," she said. "Right. You just watch."

She opened the door and stepped through it into darkness.

A NIGHT IN THE

MOUNTAINS

Monsters

KYLE FOUND A tree a little bit away from the others, its gnarled roots chewing into the rock near the edge of the cliff. He settled into the hollow of its knees. The bark was rough against his back, the trunk thick and solid, wide enough to conceal him from somebody sneaking up from behind. Like Robin. She was responsible for all this. She had to be. He wasn't surprised that the others didn't believe him. They didn't know her like he did, didn't have to live with her day in and day out. She was always so smart, always knew what was going on, even when she didn't seem to be paying attention; and now, not only had she somehow done all that crazy shit back at the cabin, but she had also run ahead along the trail and rearranged the landmarks—trees, rocks, trail markers—so he would get lost and take a wrong turn down the gully, which she had then somehow bent around on itself so that the way you went in was the way you came out, even though they were in different places. And somewhere along the way she had found the time to drag the sun across the sky faster than it was supposed to go. Pretty fucking impressive, when you thought about it.

Yeah, Chuck had nailed it. Robin was clearly some sort of witch. If only Kyle had known that when he married her.

He picked absently at a nearby root. It crawled over a fold in the mountainside, skinny and twisted like an ancient, arthritic limb. The bark was rough, flaky; it peeled off easily, and before long he'd gotten pitch all over his fingers. He scraped it off on the bark and then shifted around so he wouldn't get more of the sticky ooze on him. He sniffed his fingers. They smelled nice, like he'd just finished handling air fresheners. He was pretty sure you could eat pine bark if you cooked it right, but of course he hadn't brought any camping gear, since this was supposed to have been a day hike. No little propane stove, no tent, not much food, not nearly enough water. They were going to be hungry and thirsty if they were still out here at the end of the day tomorrow. But that wouldn't happen. He would find the road in the morning. He would climb down the cliff, and if Chuck and Gwen didn't want to come with him they could stay up here and try to flag down a passing helicopter.

Kyle snuggled back into the tree and curled in on himself against the light chill. He had started to drowse off when a monstrous howl shredded the night, louder and deeper than any dog he had ever heard, more like an angry, phlegmy foghorn than an animal. *That* woke him right back up again. The sound went on and on, seeming to come from all around, finally trailing away into a series of yips and chirpy grunts before falling silent.

Chuck said: "What in the name of God was that?"

In a small voice, Gwen said: "A coyote?"

Kyle hugged his knees. Could he make himself any smaller, any less visible? Could he actually climb *inside* the tree?

The howl rose again, a deep, throaty roar this time, with an almost human undertone of frustration. Kyle thought it was coming from somewhere down below, in the forest. It wasn't on the mountain. Maybe it was in the parking lot. Maybe it was Robin playing a recording through a bullhorn.

Chuck said, "Maybe we should take turns staying awake, in case whatever that is comes this—"

Another roar cut him off. This one was much closer, and briefer, and ended with a satisfied chuff, as if the beast behind the sound had detected something pleasing. Kyle discovered that he had become one with the tree. As he peeled himself off the bark, he noticed that Gwen had moved to the edge of the cliff to peer over the side. Her sharp intake of breath told him she saw something, even before she motioned for them to join her. Kyle hesitated, then crept forward to find out what she wanted them to see: A dark shape, scaling the cliff wall.

"What the hell is that?" Chuck whispered.

"I don't know," Gwen said.

"Jesus," Kyle said. "I've never seen anything like it."

Too big to be a man, it was roughly the size of a bear, though no bear could have climbed straight up a precipice like this thing did. The arms and legs seemed almost human, but impossibly massive, a comic book exaggeration of a man twisted to monstrous proportions. It wasn't moving fast, but it was moving steadily. It was coming for them with its muscles and its teeth and its gut-wrenching roar.

Gwen stood up, hugged herself. "We need to leave."

She was right. They needed to run. Kyle knew he could easily outpace the two of them, but the best way to make sure he didn't get caught was to make sure that thing came all the way to the top.

And if that meant shoving Gwen over the cliff before he took off into the woods, well, that was survival of the fittest, wasn't it?

~~~~

Exiting from Patrick's special television lounge had somehow deposited Myra on the front porch of a doctor's office. The door hung partway open; beyond it was a waiting room that looked like the one from the show. She sidled through and crept inside. Yes, this was definitely the same waiting room. The place was quiet, the lighting dim. Bob wasn't there. She heard a dripping noise from somewhere nearby. She followed the sound up a hallway, toward a mostly-closed door that blocked her view into what was probably an examination room. Light emanated from within, filtering around the edges, faintly illuminating that end of the hall. She had to pass a darkened lavatory to reach it; she flattened herself against the opposite wall, watching the black opening and the space beyond as she went by. Somebody quick and ruthless and competent with a scalpel could easily have lunged out of there to gut her as she passed, but didn't. The carpet began to squish under her feet as she neared the door. She crouched and pressed her fingers into the fibers, then held them up to her face. Blood. The carpet was soaked with it. She could smell the iron tang. But maybe it was something else, not really blood. She had to be sure. She licked it off her fingertips.

She'd been right. It was salty, delicious blood. But whose was it?

The intriguing taste still strong on her tongue, she stood and pushed the door open with the butt of her palm. It swung inward easily, revealing the scene beyond. Moonlight streamed through the window, unnaturally bright. A man lay supine on the examination table, his head on the footrest, his feet on the pad that passed for a pillow. His arms and legs were spread wide, hanging over each side of the platform. His throat had been cut on a jagged diagonal, letting his head tip at an unnatural angle; blood drooled from the slash, and although it was only a trickle now it must have been a gusher at first, judging by the enormous stain spreading across the carpet and out to where she stood. His skull was caved in, his face barely recognizable as a face, but she could tell one thing for sure: The dead man wasn't Bob.

Myra sagged against the wall as relief took the stiffness out of her body. He wasn't Bob. When the floor had gotten soggy with blood she knew there would be some kind of carnage on the other side of the door, and had been sure it would be Bob in there, dead, eviscerated maybe, his intestines strung from the fixtures like grotesque tinsel.

A floorboard creaked behind her and she turned.

Bob stood at the other end of the hallway, where it opened to the waiting room; he was looking at her with an odd expression on his face. Her first urge instinct to fly up the corridor and into his arms, but something about the way he carried himself gave her pause. He carried a bloodied tire iron, clenched in his fist, the way a small child might clutch a pencil.

"Myra?" he said. "Is that you?"

"Yeah. It's me."

He took a step forward. He was covered in lacy splashes of blood, some of it the doctor's, she supposed, and some of it his own; he was pretty cut up along his arms, bleeding from multiple ragged slashes.

"Are you all right?" Bob said.

"I'm fine," she said. "Are you——"

"You're lying. The vampire got you. I was too late. I saw him carry you away."

How did he know about her dream? Unthinkingly, she reached up and ran her fingers along her neck. No marks; not even a scratch. "I'm all right. That was only a dream." He just stared at her. She took a step toward him and he almost fell over himself in a panicky retreat. "Bob, you have to trust me."

"Don't come any closer."

She stopped.

He stopped.

They looked at each other.

"Look, I'm perfectly fine. I'll prove it. Come and see." She stepped into the bathroom. There had to be a mirror in there, right? Bob thought she was a vampire, but she wasn't; once he saw her reflection, he would calm down.

Myra heard him coming up the hallway, but didn't make any move toward him. The last thing she wanted was to panic him now. She waited until he appeared in the doorway behind her, then flicked on the bathroom light. Nothing happened. There wasn't any electricity.

Bob moved away and came back carrying one of those examination lights, the kind a doctor might stick in your ear. He turned it on and pointed it into the room. It was hardly as bright as a candle, but was sufficient to illuminate the mirror, which hung on the wall directly opposite the door.

It showed Bob, alone, peering into an empty room, despite the fact that Myra was standing in front of him. As far as the mirror was concerned she wasn't even there.

Bob made a strangled noise and was gone in an instant, fleeing up the corridor, abandoning the tire iron and the little light; he was out of sight almost before they hit the ground. She heard the front door bang shut behind him. She thought about going after him, but didn't; that would only make things worse, he would think she was chasing him, looking for a meal.

Instead, she just stared at the mirror, where her reflection should have been, but wasn't.

~~~~

Gwen was falling.

Funny how long it seemed to be taking for her to hit the ground, as if she were plunging through water instead of air. She had heard how time seemed to stretch out in such situations, had seen it depicted in a hundred movies—car crashes, explosions, gunfights, something that took only a second or two of real life stretched out and dramatized in slow-motion—but Gwen had never thought to experience it for herself. Yet here she was, watching the cliff scroll by a few feet away, grey and jagged, tufted with grass and scrub. It seemed like she was moving so slowly that she should be able to catch hold of something, but nothing projected far enough for her to grab: No ledges, no big branches, no crevices she could jam her fingers into; and anyway wasn't it ridiculous when a plummeting hero seized some nonexistent handhold and checked his fall using nothing but his willpower and his fingertips? Wouldn't he just break all the bones in his hands and keep right on going? Of course he would. But now she found herself thinking that the magical safety grab wasn't such a bad cliche after all. Now she was totally in favor of the concept.

She heard Chuck shouting, but couldn't make out the words. She felt a burst of irrational anger that he didn't come down here and help her, instead of just yelling, but what was he supposed to do? Fly down and catch her, or snag her ankle with a web? He wasn't a superhero.

He couldn't save her from going *splat* on the bottom. Nobody could.

Until, unexpectedly, somebody did.

A large body smacked into her and took charge of her descent. She felt herself change direction, moving laterally now, away from the cliff. It took her a second to realize what it was: The climbing beast had sprung off the wall to catch her in a *very* solid grip. They fell together, Gwen cradled in a set of massive arms. They hit the ground with enough force to crack the bedrock, but the thing took the brunt of the impact in its legs and knees, protecting her from the worst of the impact. Her innards got a pretty good rattling, but that was it. The monster itself seemed unfazed after slamming a pair of footprints into solid stone; it held her up to its face, sniffed and snuffled and snorted all around her body as if it were some kind of giant dog and she had been rolled in hamburger. Its hot breath stunk like rank meat that had been left out in the sun for a couple of days, and its mouth looked big enough to bite her head off. It poked and prodded and squeezed her with its big fingers, a discerning shopper checking out a cantaloupe in the produce section before putting it in the basket. Apparently she passed muster, because the monstrous thing flung her over its shoulder and bounded off into the forest. She wondered where it was taking her.

Probably not back to the van.

~~~~

Robin and Margaret had gotten some distance into the woods when a horrible roar filled the night, echoing from the darkness behind them. Margaret froze, cringing. Robin had never heard a howl quite like that before, but she knew who must be making it. Robin got in front of her companion, looked her right in her ruined face, and said: "The *last* thing you want to do right now is stop moving. Right?" Eyes wide, Margaret nodded. They started walking again, side by side, making poorer time than Robin could have done on her own—Paltruck had not been wrong about that—but she could tell by the set of her companion's jaw that they were moving with a purpose, and in a situation like this, that wasn't nothing.

Before long, the path grew steeper; fortunately the footing was solid and craggy, because without any arms, Margaret had trouble keeping her balance. Robin wished she knew where they were going. Why *up* the mountain rather than *down*? What if they got trapped on the summit with that thing snuffling around below them, just like when he had first snared her? If he caught them again he would probably just kill them and eat them and not worry about his next meal until he was hungry again a week or two later.

Some time later—Robin had no idea how long it had been since their escape; she didn't wear a watch, and her phone had been in her lost pack—Margaret stopped suddenly. She cocked her head as if listening to something. "What is it?" Robin whispered, but a second later she heard it too: Something was crashing through the trees from higher up the mountain, something big, coming their way. Margaret looked around wildly, obviously about to bolt. Robin caught her and hung onto her. "No," she said. "No. We can't run. He'll catch us." She pointed to one of the many boulders strewn about the mountainside. "Hide. Over there, okay? Can you do that? I have an idea."

Margaret looked at her for a long moment, then nodded and went to the big rock she had indicated. Robin didn't go with her. She was pretty sure the ogre would be able to sniff them out, and he was certainly faster than they were, given that he had already managed to get ahead of them. No, running wasn't the way to escape. Neither was hiding. They had to fight. And Robin sure as hell wasn't planning to fight fair.

She picked up the biggest rock she could carry, one about the size and shape of a bowling ball, and staggered over to a nearby spine of grey bedrock with a worn, flattish top. It was nearly as tall as she was. She managed to work the big rock up on top of it, added a few smaller rocks for good measure, then scaled it herself. Climbing that tree had been a good warm-up for this evening's activities. Hiding on top of the boulder, waiting, she prayed that the ogre's head wasn't as thick as it looked, even though it probably was.

Before long, he came lumbering into view. He wasn't heading directly toward them, but at an angle, down the slope and away. Maybe he would pass them by completely and she wouldn't have to jump him. But then she realized he had something slung over his shoulder. It wasn't laundry. Robin saw arms hanging down, over his back, and longish hair. A woman. He seemed preoccupied with his latest catch. If she just laid low, maybe he would keep going, and then she and Margaret could be on their way. After all, it wasn't Robin's responsibility to rescue everybody, was it? That little guy, Paltruck, he would probably come around again and let the new victim out, right?

Right?

Shit.

Robin whistled, just loudly enough to get the ogre's attention. The creature paused and looked around, sniffed the air with his bulbous nose. She whistled again. This time he oriented on the boulder and lumbered toward her, peering suspiciously into the darkness, sweeping the forest with his gaze. Robin flattened herself as far as she could so he wouldn't see her as he approached. He didn't seem to know where she was, exactly. Maybe his sense of smell wasn't as acute as she'd supposed. She threw one of the smaller stones off to the side, making noises in the brush. The ogre spun, looking in that direction.

Robin picked up the big rock and jumped. The stone struck the monster's skull with the satisfying sound of a pumpkin being whacked with a mallet. Caught by surprise, the ogre toppled over, ending up face-down in the dirt. He had brute strength, but he was top-heavy, especially when carrying a victim. Robin landed on top of him, bashing his head again and again. Pounding acorns into meal, baby! Even after the ogre stopped twitching she kept at it, smashing, smashing, smashing, until finally it dawned on her that she could stop; she had done as much damage as she was going to do with the strength and material she had available. Panting, she dropped the rock. Her hands were scraped and bleeding. She wiped them on her clothes, then looked for the captive. She lay some distance to the side, having gone sprawling when Robin attacked. She rolled the woman onto her back. It was Gwen. Where had he picked *her* up?

"Hey. Gwen. Wake up."

She didn't wake up. Robin felt Gwen's wrist. Her pulse was strong and steady.

"Come on, wake up." She lightly slapped Gwen's cheek. Her eyelids fluttered, then opened.

"Robin?"

"Yeah."

"Robin, there's this thing—" Suddenly she looked over Robin's shoulder, her eyes widening.

Anticipating a scream, Robin pasted her hand over Gwen's mouth and glanced backwards. It was only Margaret. "It's okay," she said. "That's Margaret. She's with me. We know all about the thing. We took care of it. Okay?"

Gwen nodded and Robin let go of her. She heard some noises from behind her. Margaret had gone to the fallen ogre and was kicking him in the side of the head, but then she lost her balance and fell over. What a bunch of marauders they were. Evil beware.

Robin helped Margaret to her feet. Gwen was up as well, leaning against a nearby tree. "Can you walk?" Robin said.

"Screw walking," Gwen said. "My feet are rested now. I can run."

~~~~

Alone and unencumbered by whining fat-asses or delicate flowers in improper footwear, Kyle moved fast down the mountain, nursing two scraped elbows, a twisted ankle, and a bruised knee, all of which he had acquired in the first few panicked minutes of his flight. He was starting to feel safer, now that he had put some distance between himself and the cliff; unfortunately, he was also totally lost, the compass needle having long since given up any pretense of stability. It just pointed wherever the hell it felt like pointing. A vast full moon that had appeared in the sky while he was fleeing, and while he was thankful for the illumination it provided, he had to wonder what it was doing up there, because there had been a quarter-moon yesterday night. He had no idea what the fuck was going on. He was in the Adirondacks, not the fucking Bermuda Triangle. Graveyards were not supposed to appear and disappear at whim. Compasses were not supposed to spin like roulette wheels. The phases of the moon were supposed to follow an orderly progression.

Monsters were not supposed to exist.

Things started to look up when he stumbled across a pretty good path: Wide, clear, trending downward. It reminded him of the lower part of the trail from the parking lot, so he followed it. After some time trudging through the darkened woods, it led him into a glade. He stayed at the periphery while his eyes adjusted to the too-bright moonlight streaming into it. This didn't appear to be a natural break in the trees; it looked to have been cleared, the bushes and small trees uprooted, the larger trees pushed over and dragged away. A crude shelter leaned against the trunk of a large maple that had been left standing near the center of the space. He waited a while, listening, until he was sure no one else was moving around in the vicinity. Then he approached the shack. He could smell a doused fire, and something else, a cooking odor, but not a pleasant one. Maybe whoever lived here had burnt a rabbit or something. Kyle circled the shack until he found the door, which was made of more saplings, all lashed together with some kind of leather. Directly in front of it, a ring of large blackened rocks formed a bonfire pit, the ashes cold. Beyond that, a gnarled cage stood, like an animal pen, though right now its door hung open, its occupants fled. He wondered what sort of livestock it was for. Goats? Dogs? White-tailed deer? Maybe whoever lived here was out looking for them. Maybe the place was abandoned. Either way he might be able to spend the night there in safety from whatever was roaming these woods.

Keeping his back to the door, Kyle grasped the rough handle, which seemed to be made of bone. It wasn't a knob; there was nothing to turn. That meant there was nothing to lock. He hoped to find a bolt or a bar on the inside that he could use to barricade himself away from all the insanity.

"I wouldn't go in there."

The unexpected voice startled him. He jumped away from the door and looked around, but saw no one.

"Up here."

He looked above him, into the night sky.

"On top of the shack, silly, not flying around. I'm no vampire."

He lowered his gaze and saw a dwarfish shadow sitting on the roof of the hovel, dangling its stubby legs over the edge. "What are *you* supposed to be?" Kyle said.

"I'm supposed to be a sprite." The thing jumped off the roof, landing in front of him. It looked as if someone had taken a garden gnome, dressed it in ratty clothes, and animated it. "The name's Paltruck. I live around these parts."

"This is your … uh, place?"

"This dump? No."

"Then what were you doing on the roof?"

"Waiting for someone. But I don't think they're coming back. I was just getting ready to leave." The sprite gave him a narrow look. "You should leave too."

"Yeah? Why?"

Paltruck gestured at the shack. "The owner's not too hospitable."

"As far as I can see, the owner's not around."

"He'll be back."

"Well, I need a place to spend the night."

Paltruck snorted. "Trust me, you don't want to spend the night here."

"I'll decide that for myself, thanks."

Kyle started forward, pushing the gnome aside. Paltruck offered no resistance, but said, "I'm warning you, don't go in there. You'll be sorry."

"Why do you care?"

"I'm just trying to help."

"Yeah, sure. Out of the goodness of your heart?"

"Uh-huh. It's what I do. I'm the helpful one."

"You are?"

"Yes."

Kyle was insulted. What kind of sucker did Robin take him for, sending a midget to try to lead him away from the only shelter he'd found all night? He turned, lunged, and picked Paltruck up. The little guy weighed nothing at all, as if he were made of leaves and air. He struggled and squirmed like a puppy trying to get back to the ground. "Hey! Let go!"

"I don't need help from a lawn ornament," Kyle told him. Then he drop-kicked Paltruck into the forest. His foot connected with a good, solid, satisfying *thump*. The midget sailed away into the darkness. After a long moment of silence, he could hear the little runt crashing down through the leaves some distance away. Field goal. Three points for Team Kyle!

That done, he turned back to the door, pulled it open, and stepped through, into a huge cloud of flies. The sound of their wings thrummed in his ears. Disgusted, he waved his arms, clearing them away. This revealed the *reason* for the huge cloud of flies: They had been feasting on the remains of a half-eaten human arm, which lay on a crude wooden table to his immediate left. Insects crawled under and over and all around the severed limb, nibbling on the spots where flesh had been torn off in strips, buzzing contentedly. Others, squirming along the tabletop, fed off scraps and bloodstains and bits of gristle. Denuded bone stuck out from near where the shoulder would have been, cracked and gnawed and hollow, all the tasty marrow sucked out.

Kyle stared at the arm. It was like looking at the remnants of a giant chicken wing. The flies that he'd disturbed when he barged in began settling down on it again, the racket of their wings diminishing. He turned away from the table and tried to puke, but his stomach was basically empty and nothing much came of his efforts. Finally he straightened up.

Paltruck hadn't been lying. He couldn't stay here. It wasn't safe, not at all. Kyle turned to go, but found the doorway blocked. From the shape of the shadow he recognized the ogre from the cliff, empty-handed and angry-looking. Its face was bruised and scraped, and blood flowed from one side of its nose, which appeared to have been recently broken. It stepped inside and pulled the door shut behind it.

As the monster advanced on him, Kyle found himself wondering what it had done with Gwen.

~~~~

Myra stepped out of the doctor's house and stood for a few moments on the front step. The night air was cool and fresh, smelling of pines and rain, but with a hint of acrid smokiness, as if, somewhere, a large greasy fire burned.

She found that she could see pretty well in the darkness. Her eyes seemed to gather up the moonlight and wring out everything it knew about the night, all that transpired beneath its pale glow. It told her Bob had turned left upon fleeing the office; she could sense his passage, could almost see his fading footprints on the grass. She followed his trail just far enough to get beyond the house. Then she stopped, her gaze sweeping upward, away from his traces, away from the town, toward the horizon. The three peaks dominated the landscape, two adjacent and a third behind and between the others. The black castle topped the mountain on the left. She could see the twisty brambles growing up its slopes, stopping near the top where the towers spiked upward. The vampire who had bitten her was still there; his home radiated a deathly chill that reached out and enfolded her in a cold embrace.

She turned her gaze away from the castle, not ready to become a player in that dark carnival. She turned to the next mountain, the smallest of the three, and the only one without a large structure, its summit a tonsure of rock. The moonlight told her someone was up there; she thought it might be Chuck, and she thought he was alone. Why would that be? Where were the others?

Myra turned to the largest mountain, the one that loomed behind the two nearer peaks. The moonlight showed her a building near the summit, long walls and black-eyed windows and erratically spaced chimneys. Her remote gaze roamed over grounds wild and overgrown with summer grass, over a sunken graveyard strangled by the weeds, out past a chain-link fence and a heavy iron gate that kept wandering things out, or in. Or maybe both.

And then, abruptly, she was sitting on her butt in the grass, nursing a headache. Something had noticed her wandering eyes, and given her a big old kick right between them. She stood, felt briefly dizzy, and leaned against the wall of Zane's office. Not such a good idea to go probing at the big mountain, then. Not right now anyway. Maybe later, when she was stronger.

Bob's trail had gone cold but she could still tell which direction he had gone, and could certainly catch up to him easily enough. But did she want to? He was in quite a state; he would probably freak out if she showed up right now. He might even try to kill her. Still, she needed somebody to come with her, a companion, a helper, a sidekick, somebody who could buffer her interactions with Bob and the others when she found them again. And because she didn't know where any of the others were, she decided to recruit Chuck.

She had no sooner thought about going up to where Chuck was than she began to feel light on her feet; and then she was levitating a few inches off the ground. Seconds later she was outright flying, like in a dream, laughing—not quite like a madwoman—as she soared through the darkness toward the barren mountaintop.

~~~~

Chuck had been too slow to react when Kyle shoved Gwen over the edge; he'd stood there like the fat, stupid clown Kyle thought he was, watching Gwen plummet, barely noticing when Kyle ran away, and, finally, when the monster sprang off the wall like some kind of deranged superhero to snatch Gwen out of mid-air, falling to his hands and knees like a man who'd dropped a dollar down a sewer grate. Feeling clumsy and useless and stupid, Chuck had watched the thing carry his wife off into the woods; and then he'd had the bright idea of climbing down the cliff and going after her. Climbing down had to be easier than climbing up, right?

Wrong. Oh so very wrong.

He had barely gotten ten or fifteen feet before stalling out above a concave spot where the rock had sloughed away. Now he couldn't find a way to continue downward, and he wasn't strong enough to pull himself back up; and so he had been stuck there for he didn't know how long, clinging to the rock, fingers jammed into narrow cracks, feet twisted sideways and precariously planted on ledges that were basically just uneven spots in the wall. His ankles were way past aching and felt like they were about to pop; his fingers were so raw from hanging onto the stone that he thought they must be worn down to nubs, like overused crayons. He didn't know how much longer he could hang on, and when he fell, there wasn't going to be any leaping hulk to catch him. He would be taking a one-way trip to the bottom, but maybe, if he were lucky, Kyle would happen to be walking by below and he would land on the motherfucker's head.

One of his feet slipped. He managed to catch it before it slid completely off its little ripple of stone, but now he was caught at an even worse angle. His back groaned and crackled. Chuck stretched out his right hand towards a blemish in the rock that was nearly out of reach but promised a better handhold, and maybe a chance to make a little progress, if only he could catch it. Finally he did; unfortunately, the dark spot he had taken to be a lipped pocket turned out to be nothing but a patch of black moss that came right off under his fingers like a poorly secured toupee. Chuck screamed as he pitched over backwards. The forest spun crazily beneath him, treetops grey in the moonlight, a hundred feet below. Fortunately for his mental health, he passed out before he hit the ground.

When he woke up, he was back on top of the cliff, lying on stone that was still a little bit warm from the sun. He didn't seem to be dead. He sat up, rubbing his sore ankles with his sore fingers, and looked around to see what the hell had happened. He noticed a human shape that stood nearby, looking off into the darkness. It stood in the shadow of a boulder, out of the direct moonlight, but he could see a set of pallid hands clasped behind its back. Had it saved him? It was much too slim to be the monster, so Chuck said, experimentally, "Hello?"

The shape turned and stepped closer. It was Myra. "Hello, Chuck," she said.

Strange that he had never noticed before what a voice she had: Smoky, sexy, but powerful. Her voice made you hope she would tell you to do things, just so you could obey her. Her skin, pale as alabaster, seemed to glow in the moonlight. She was beautiful, too, Chuck suddenly realized, flawless really, her face and features perfect as a sculpture. "You … you're … how's your head?" Chuck said, stumbling over words like a teenager trying to make small talk at a dance. He felt a strange urge to crawl over and kiss her shoes. He shook his head. Why was he thinking things like this?

A flicker passed across her expression and she turned away. "Fine. My head's fine. Thanks for asking."

"How, um, how did you get up here?"

"I found a shortcut up the mountain," she said.

"Oh." Then: "How did *I* get up here?"

"You fell. I caught you."

Silence.

"You … How, um, how did you …"

He trailed off as she looked at him over her shoulder. Her crimson lips were slightly open; he could see too-white, too-sharp teeth between them. "Best if we don't get into that just yet, maybe," she said.

She turned away again. He watched her for what seemed like a long time, though it was certainly only a few seconds. She looked like Myra—mostly—and she sounded like Myra—mostly—but how the hell would *Myra* have been able to catch him as he fell off a cliff? He noticed she had the tire iron from his van tucked under her belt. What was *that* about? And what was up with her voice? Why was he sort of hoping she might ask him to jump off the cliff so she could catch him again?

"I can see you've got some stuff to work out in your head," Myra said, still not looking at him, "but I need you to decide pretty fast if you're going to trust me or not. There's no time to waste. I'm sort of on a quest."

"A what?"

"A quest. I need to find someone. Someone who can get us out of this mess. I think." Pause. "And I need to get it done before dawn."

He started to ask her what would happen at dawn; but then he thought of what he had seen and heard and felt—her skin, her lips, her teeth, her voice—and asked something else instead. "Why me? Why not Bob? Where *is* Bob, anyway? Wasn't he with you?"

She stiffened, but said nothing.

"Myra?"

"Bob ran off. I'm not sure where he is."

"Why would he ... Did you—"

"I didn't do anything to him. He had a lot to deal with in a really short time and he got, uh, rattled." Her voice hardened into something with an edge that could cut meat. "Maybe *you* should tell *me* where everyone *else* is."

Inordinately pleased that she had asked something of him, Chuck said: "Well, Robin disappeared a couple of hours ago. We couldn't find her. I thought maybe she went back to the parking lot. The rest of us tried to get down but Kyle got us lost and we stopped here for the night, but then this monster thing started climbing up the wall like it was coming to get us. Kyle threw Gwen off the cliff and ran. I tried to—"

He stopped speaking the instant she turned around, looking astonished, and much more like herself, at least for that moment. "Kyle did *what* to *who?*"

Chuck was a little disappointed—he had been hoping she might order him to crawl over and grovel at her feet—but thinking about Kyle raised the temperature on his anger to the point that it temporarily burned off his desire to carry out whatever absurd command Myra might deign to issue. "He threw Gwen off the cliff. I think he thought it might make the monster leave. It worked, too. That thing jumped off the cliff and caught her and carried her away."

"And you, what, tried to climb down and go after it?"

"Yeah, but I got stuck partway. That was why I fell."

"If you *didn't* get stuck," she said, "what would you have done when you caught up with it?"

"I, uh ... I don't know. I didn't think that far ahead, I guess."

"Maybe it's a good thing you didn't make it to the bottom."

"Yeah," he said. "Maybe. Thanks, by the way. For, um, catching me."

"Don't mention it."

He wanted to ask if they might look for Gwen, but it was pretty obvious that Myra had other intentions. She was no longer looking at the section of woods down below where the monster had disappeared; instead, she had turned towards one of the other mountains, the tallest one, a black silhouette against the moonlit sky. What was she seeing up there? Something he could not, no doubt. Something big and important. And she wanted him to go with her. Was there any doubt that he would?

Of course not.

"So, this quest?" he said. "Who are we looking for, exactly?"

"I'm not sure," she said, "but he's up there. And we'll know him when we find him."

Quest

TAKING DOWN THE demented, scalpel-wielding Dr. Zane had shown Bob that he might have what it took to survive here, that he might be more than raw meat for the monsters. It had also served as a valuable, if painful, lesson that he couldn't trust anyone, least of all his own wife. That was just what they were counting on. The Count had sent Myra to trick him, get him to let his guard down and kill him, but he was too wary and hadn't been fooled. Bob didn't blame Myra for her actions; the Count had made her this way, and if he were killed, she might get better. That was what happened in the movies, anyway. A vampire chomped the girl—it was always the girl—and then the heroes had to race against time to save her before the change became permanent. Except in this case there were no heroes, no band of vampire killers. There was only him. Could he handle it on his own?

"Back already? You must have taken a shortcut from the castle."

Bob whirled, but it was just Paltruck, black and grey in the moonlight at the edge of the forest. Bob's unthinking flight from Myra had brought him back to the little guy's territory at the edge of town, where the houses met the woods; the little guy was hanging out under the trees, not venturing into the village. Because of the rules, Bob supposed. He wondered who had laid those rules down, and if they could be broken, and what the consequences might be if they were.

Paltruck motioned him forward. Bob ambled over to join him at the scrub line.

"So," Paltruck said, with a studied casualness, "the rescue didn't go so well, huh?"

"No," Bob said. "Thanks for nothing on that."

"Thanks for nothing? Really? You guys! I stick my neck out to help, and what do I get? Attitude from you, and kicked into the forest by that other jerk."

"Somebody kicked you? Are you all right?"

"I'm fine. It'll take more than a boot in the rear to hurt me." Paltruck made a face. "I don't know why I even bothered trying. I could tell he wasn't worth the effort."

"Did you get this jerk's name? It might be somebody I came here with. Maybe he can help."

"Sorry. I put it out of my mind already. Anyway, I wouldn't expect any help from him. He won't be kicking anybody else with that foot in the future, I can tell you."

"Why? Did you do something to him?"

"Me? No. I just gave him good advice, which he ignored." Paltruck clapped his hands. "Anyway, enough about him! Let's talk about you. What happened? Lose an argument with the thorn bushes?"

"Huh?"

"You're cut up all over."

"Oh. Right." Bob had forgotten about the slashes on his hands, his arms, even his face. They didn't really sting that much anymore, as if the nerves had gotten tired of complaining and had given up. "I got these from Dr. Zane. When he tried to kill me. After I, uh, went through the mirror in the castle."

The little guy's stone-colored eyes widened. "Zane tried to kill you?"

"Yeah. With a scalpel."

"And you got out alive?"

"Obviously."

"How?"

Bob shrugged a little. "A tire iron is bigger than a scalpel."

"Wow." Paltruck eyed him, possibly admiringly, then took a step forward. "Nice job. But you can't run around here with all those open wounds. You'll get infected. Things will smell the blood and start following you." He cast his gaze around the darkened town. "They probably are already."

Interesting choice of words, Bob thought: *He*, not the wounds, would get infected. He didn't want to ask what might infect him, or what sort of *things* might already be following him around. "Yeah, well, unfortunately, I'm out of bandages."

"You don't need bandages. You've got me. Just crouch down and hold still."

Bob did as instructed. Paltruck stepped up to him and moved his chubby hands an inch or so above his injuries. They started to itch, then scabbed over; then the scabs flaked off, revealing thin white scars beneath. It was like watching a time-lapse video of cuts healing. Bob ran his fingers over his face, feeling little lines of smooth skin where the wounds had been. He looked at Paltruck and said: "How did you do that?"

Paltruck shrugged. "I didn't do much, really. Your body did the work of healing. I just speeded things up."

"Can you heal Myra if we find her?"

"What she's got wrong with her is not something I can fix," Paltruck said.

Bob had been afraid he would say that. "Okay. What if I kill the Count? Then she'll go back to normal, right?"

"Are you kidding?" Paltruck eyed him. "No, I see you're not. Well, I don't know. But the question is moot anyway."

"Because why?"

"Because you'll never kill the Count. Not at night. He's way too strong. Your only shot was to get Myra away from him during daylight and then go to ground. Now it's too late. You want my advice, you should lie low until dawn. But it stays dark for so long this time of year."

"This time of year? It's summertime. Days are long. Nights are short."

Paltruck gave him an inscrutable look. "Are they?" he said.

For some reason, those two little words—and the flat tone in which the sprite uttered them—unnerved Bob more than just about anything else that had happened so far.

"So," Paltruck said, "shall I make some suggestions as to hiding places? There's this cabin—"

"No," Bob said. "I'm going to kill the Count. And you're going to help me."

"Say what?"

"You heard me."

Sounding panicky, the little man raised his little hands. "Now, now,

I've never gone in for that action hero stuff. Besides, what could I do against a vampire? Look at me, I'm only a foot tall."

"You're two feet tall."

"One foot, two feet, I'll still be useful as a mushroom when you go up against old bat-face."

"Look, I'm not asking you to help me fight him. Just come with me. You can be my guide, and if I get hurt, you can do that thing again."

Paltruck shook his head. "You need a vampire hunter, not a sprite."

"Yeah, well, vampire hunters are in short supply."

"There's one back in town," Paltruck said.

After a moment, Bob said: "What?"

"There's a vampire hunter back in tow—"

"Why didn't you tell me that before?" Bob jumped to his feet. "Don't you think that information might've come in handy?"

"There wasn't time, you had to hurry to rescue Princess Myra! But since you botched that up, you have all the time in the world."

The squirt had a point, although Bob could've done without the dig at his failed effort to save Myra from the Count. "So who is this vampire hunter?"

"The undertaker. Mr. Toomes."

Bob scratched his head.

"The undertaker."

Paltruck nodded.

"Is a vampire hunter."

"Uh-huh."

"And his name is Toomes."

"Yes."

Bob said: "Are you putting me on?"

"No."

"All right, take me to him."

"I can't," Paltruck said. "Against the rules."

"Rules? What rules?"

"The rules that say I can't go into town."

"But—"

"Just like a vampire can't enter your house without permission, I have to stay in the woods. It's just the way things are."

"If you can't go into town, how do you know Toomes?"

"Duh. *He* can come into the *forest*."

"What, does he visit you in your hollow tree to eat pine cones and moss cake and sip rainwater tea?"

Paltruck pouted. "That was uncalled for."

"Sorry."

"Apology accepted. Look, you're wasting time badgering me. I can't go with you. End of story. Just look for the big black house with the caskets out in front. You can't miss it."

"Caskets?"

"They have night-blooming flowers in them. Toomes says they keep the undead away."

"I think I would've noticed a black house with caskets full of flowers out in front of it."

"Well, you were pretty distracted."

Bob sighed. "Okay. Fine. I'll go back to town and track down this vampire hunter. But if I can't find him or he's not home or he doesn't feel like helping me, I'm going after the Count on my own."

"Don't worry, he'll be home. He doesn't go out at night unless he's on a job." Bob grunted and turned away, but Paltruck said: "Hey, Bob."

He stopped. "Yeah?"

"Make sure you tell Toomes that you killed Zane."

"Okay. Why?"

"Trust me. He'll want to know."

~~~~

After they had been walking uphill for what seemed like miles, Gwen sidled over to Robin and said: "Thanks. For what you did back there."

"It was nothing."

"It wasn't nothing. You might have saved my life. I don't know what that thing was going to do with me, but——"

"He was going to eat you," Robin said.

After a moment, Gwen said: "Yeah?"

"Yeah. See Margaret?" Robin gestured toward their mutilated companion, who was still leading the way up the trail. "Notice the *Venus de Milo* look? He was keeping her in a cage and eating her one piece at a time."

Gwen eyed the other woman. "One piece at a time?"

"Uh-huh."

"How ... uh, how do you know that?"

"When I met her, she still had one of her arms."

Gwen felt sick. Kyle had thrown her to that thing. He had thrown her to be cut up and eaten. She was still debating whether or not to tell Robin what Kyle had done; she was afraid Robin would get mad at her and accuse her of lying, or maybe abandon her out here, leave her alone in the dark with the monsters. *Alone* was the last thing she wanted to be right now. "I'm glad he's dead."

Robin glanced at her, raised an eyebrow.

Gwen said: "He *is* dead, isn't he?"

"I think it'd take more than me and a big rock to kill that thing," Robin said. Then she pointed out Margaret's ratty, filthy jacket. "Did you notice she's wearing like a lab coat?"

"So?"

"It's got a name tag stitched onto it. It says *Dr. Margaret.*"

"A doctor with no arms and no tongue isn't going to be much help if we get hurt."

"I'm not looking for an exam. I'm wondering what she's doing out here. A doctor wouldn't wear her lab coat out for a hike in the woods, right? So she must work somewhere nearby."

"I don't know. I guess. Does it matter?"

"It might. Maybe she's taking us back to her office, or whatever."

"Maybe? You mean you don't know where she's going?"

"Nope. Not a clue."

"Why are you following her, then?"

"Because *she* seems to know where she's going."

Suddenly Margaret squeaked loudly, making Gwen jump. Robin turned and hurried to join the other woman. Gwen followed more slowly, picking her way among the rocks and roots, wondering how a nice little hike had turned into a nightmarish trek through the black wilderness, in the company of a mute, armless doctor and the wife of a guy who had wanted to fuck her until he decided he'd rather push her off a cliff. Talk about things not going the way you planned.

She caught up with the others. They had reached a chain link fence topped with tangled razor wire. The trees and brush had been cleared about ten feet back from the fence, giving them an open area in which to stand; beyond the barrier was an unkempt, weedy lawn. Boulders strewn across the grounds cast misshapen moon-shadows, but the biggest shadow by far came from the decrepit building at the top of the mountain. It looked institutional, forbidding, a place you would put people when you wanted the world to forget they existed. Although numerous windows winked from the high walls, all were dark; its dozen or so chimneys were cold and inert, except for one that oozed a thick, noxious smoke, oily black against the starry sky. Gwen didn't know what you might burn to get smoke like that, but it couldn't be anything wholesome. The place sported an odd little dome on top, like a miniature planetarium. Maybe it was a science center, or a museum.

Robin looked at Margaret. "This is where you wanted to go?"

The doctor nodded.

Liking this plan less and less, Gwen went to the fence, curled her fingers through it, and stared up at the distant structure. "What is it?"

"Some kind of hospital maybe?" Robin said. "Margaret, did you work here?"

The armless woman nodded, but then shook her head.

"I don't understand. Did you work here or didn't you?"

Margaret made a sighing sound and nodded.

"Why do we have to go in there?" Gwen said. "I don't like it."

"Yeah, well, I don't like anything that's been happening lately," Robin said. "If you have a different suggestion, let's hear it."

"Anywhere is better than here. I mean, *look* at this place! Who knows what's waiting for us inside?"

The mute doctor made a frustrated sound and stamped her foot. Robin glanced at her, then back at Gwen. "We're here. Margaret brought us for a reason. Let's at least check it out."

Gwen sighed. "Okay. Fine. How are we supposed to get in? Margaret can't climb the fence, and look at that barbed wire on top."

"I think that's razor wire. But, yeah. So. There must be a gate. We'll go along the fence until we find it. Margaret, which way?"

The armless woman hesitated a moment, then started moving. Robin followed. Gwen watched them go until it became obvious they weren't going to stop. Shit. She pulled away from the fence and hurried to catch up. Before long, they reached a hard-packed dirt road that ran up the mountain to a wrought iron double gate. A thick, ancient chain secured with a rust-scabbed padlock was draped from one half of the gate to the other, binding them together but leaving a narrow open space between. Two stone columns flanked the entrance, anchoring the fence at either side. An arched banner consisting of two parallel iron tubes swooped between them. Big metal letters connected the bottom tube with the top, spelling out *Blackberry Mountain Retreat*. It looked as if the letters had once been painted white, but most of the color had faded, leaving the words rusty-red and smeary. The columns had begun to crumble, the mortar dry and flaking, letting some of the big, flat rocks fall out to lie in the dirt around them, like chalky droppings.

"*Retreat*," Gwen said, looking at it. "What kind of retreat has a razor wire fence?"

"Well, not the spa kind of retreat, I guess," Robin said.

Gwen snorted. "Obviously."

"Margaret, when I asked you before if you worked here and you said yes and no … Did you *used* to work here?"

Margaret bobbed her head in the affirmative.

"And did it change? Did it get … weird?"

Margaret nodded, much more vigorously this time.

"So you were working here then? When it happened?"

The woman nodded and squeaked.

Gwen said: "You think it used to be a normal, uh, whatever it was, and then, *poof*, now it's a crazy haunted insane asylum?"

"Yep. That's what I think."

"Abracadabra."

"Pretty much. But here's what I really want to know. What happened to everyone else who was inside? Staff. Patients. Visitors. Where are they? Where did they go? Margaret, any ideas?"

Margaret shook her head, shrugged.

"That monster. He was wearing a coat like yours. Part of one anyway. Did he work here too? Did he change into a monster when the building changed?"

Margaret squeaked, nodded.

"Shit," Gwen said, lowering her voice a whisper. "That means there might be more things like that inside."

"Yeah, there might be. But I have a feeling there's not. And we *know* there are things like that out here."

A feeling. Great. Just what Gwen wanted to trust her life to. "Seriously? You want to go in there?"

"I seriously don't, actually," Robin said, "but I'm going to do it anyway."

~~~~

Kyle awakened slowly from blackness into a gauzy fog of pain. He lay still for a little while, trying to remember where he was and what had happened to him, then trying to forget it once he did. It was no surprise that his head hurt; considering the size, velocity, and hardness of the fist that had connected with his face, he supposed he was lucky that he woke up at all. He had tried to fight his way out of the hovel, but it had been a pretty short scuffle. He had landed a shot or two, but it was like punching a tree trunk. Then one hit from that thing, that *monster*, and out he went.

He pushed himself upright and a bolt of pain shot from his right thigh, nearly making his head explode. He must have popped his kneecap, maybe even broken his leg. He ground his teeth together and squeezed his eyes shut, trying not to cry out. He didn't want to attract the beast's attention. When the agony subsided to a tolerable level he opened his eyes again. His cheeks felt hot and wet and he realized he'd been crying. His mouth throbbed. He probed around with his tongue and discovered that several teeth were missing on the right side. The monster must've knocked them out. Among all his other pains, he hadn't even noticed that small ache until he had clenched his jaws. He wondered where the teeth were. Maybe he had swallowed them.

Kyle tried to stand, and immediately realized he couldn't. His entire body felt unbalanced. His left leg couldn't bear his weight, not because it was broken, but because it was *gone*, terminated at the knee, which was, bizarrely enough, wrapped in a layer of cleanish gauze. The flesh just above the gauze looked blackened, hot and crusty, like a nicely done rotisserie chicken. What the fuck? Where was the rest of his leg? Hanging from a hook in the monster's hovel? Sitting on that fly infested table, half eaten, the bone broken open and the marrow sucked out? He remembered the arm he'd seen, cooked up like a piece of rotisserie chicken. Damn. He wouldn't be drop-kicking any more midgets into the forest, or footballs, for that matter. Not without a leg to stand on.

A leg to stand on. Kyle startled to giggle, heard the crazy noise in his own ears, and stopped. He sounded like *that guy*, you know, the guy in the movie who snapped and lost it and fell to pieces when things went south. He needed to keep his shit together and not become *that guy*, because *that guy* always ended up getting wasted.

He looked around, really looked, seeing his surroundings for the first time. He wasn't in the woods. He was in the pen he had seen earlier, before entering the hovel. He dragged himself over to what appeared to be the door. Like the rest of this prison, it was made of thick tree limbs lashed together with some sort of cord. The stump of his leg throbbed as it scraped across the ground. He could imagine the severed artery, its enormous pressure sealed only by a layer of charred flesh and bandages. If he dislodged the burned tissue, if the bandage got caught on a stick and tore off, he might be dead in moments. The thought frightened him and he stopped dragging himself along the ground. He turned his back against the side of the cage and sat there, looking at the door. Something silver glimmered in the moonlight. He craned his neck for a better look.

It was a shiny new padlock. In fact, he thought he had the same one in his gym bag.

He heard the crazy giggling again, and this time he just went with it.

~~~~

Chuck was overweight, and not a small guy to begin with, but he was no heavier than a sack of feathers in her arms as Myra carried him through the night. She knew from movies and television that vampires were supposed to be hugely stronger than the people they once were, but to actually *be* one, to have such strength at her disposal … Well, with the flying and the heightened senses, it was almost like she was a superhero. Almost. Chuck didn't seem to be relishing the role of sidekick though. He had his eyes squeezed shut, and his hands clenched her arms in a death grip. Maybe he was afraid she would drop him; maybe he was afraid that she would bite him. Or maybe he was *hoping* she would.

Bite him … Yeah, she could bite him. Nobody knew what she had become, except for Bob, and where was he? Nowhere. He had run off and abandoned her. Why should she care what he thought? Why should she care what *any* of them thought? It would be easy, so easy, to shift Chuck a little, rip into his throat, drink deep, and drop him into the forest for the animals to find. Maybe that would fix the sick hunger that had begun to grow inside her.

No one would know.

No one would ever find out.

And so what if they did?

She must have actually shifted him closer to a biting position before checking herself, because he suddenly said: "What's wrong? Don't drop me!"

She recoiled. What had she been about to do? Luckily he hadn't opened his eyes, or he might have seen her teeth heading for his throat. "Nothing's wrong," she said, hoping her voice wasn't shaking. "I won't drop you. We're just getting close to the top is all."

"Okay. Sorry. Just panicked a little. First time flying without an airplane, you know?"

Ha. He would *really* panic if he realized what she had almost just done. She needed to put him down before she really *did* absent-mindedly take a chunk out of him. Fortunately they were nearing the top of the big mountain—that hadn't been a lie—and she had spotted a road snaking up the mountainside. She decided to set down there. They could walk the rest of the way. If he wasn't *right there* in front of her nose, she might not be so inclined to gobble him up like a nice juicy slider. Besides, she wasn't sure she wanted to fly right up to that big building; whatever lived in it might see her coming and shoot her down with psychic antiaircraft fire. So she landed not far from the top, touching down on the dusty surface of the dirt track. Chuck tumbled away from her and lay flat on his back for a moment, staring up at the sky, looking so relieved to be back on the ground that she wondered how he had managed not to soil his pants during the flight. She stepped over to help him up. He started to reach for her hand, then faltered, his eyes widening.

Myra said: "What?"

"Your face. It looks … wrong."

It *felt* wrong, too, she suddenly realized, the skin tight and stretched. Her lips felt too narrow, her mouth too large, her teeth *much* too sharp. She remembered the thing that had feasted on her, the way his jaws had unhinged, the rows of razor fangs. If she looked at herself in a mirror, what would she see? Would she see that?

No. She would see nothing.

"Myra?" Chuck said. He scuttled back a few yards. Any second now he would bolt, and she would either have to go after him or continue on alone. Or maybe she just would hunt him down and kill him and eat him like the predator she was.

But she didn't want to do any of those things. She wanted to fix her face, keep pretending to be a person. It shouldn't be too difficult. You didn't need to know exactly how it worked when you moved your arm or smiled or tapped your foot, you just did it. So she could do this. She just had to think about it the right way and her old face would come back. She figured she had succeeded when Chuck leaned forward, then stood, and then, finally, came closer, like a rabbit approaching a hawk that had just turned into a carrot.

Myra said, "Better?"

"Yeah," he said. "What was that all about?"

"I guess that was just … what's inside me now. Poking its head up." She turned away, gave him a sidelong glance back. "I'll understand if you want to stay here instead of coming with me."

"Stay here?" Chuck looked around. She could see him weighing his options. Be abandoned on a deserted mountain road in a forest full of unknown monsters, or keep going with a monster he already knew? "Um. No, I don't think I want to stay here. Just … don't let that thing poke its head up again, okay?"

Myra smiled, relieved. "Okay." Having him around was, she thought, helping her stay mostly human.

Mostly.

For now.

~~~~

Once they squeezed through the opening between the gates of the asylum, Robin felt a change in the atmosphere. The easy night breeze died away, as if smothered by the high chain-link fence; the air grew clammy, sucking warmth out through her pores. She shivered, wishing she had something to wrap around herself, but her pullover was lost along with the rest of the contents of her pack, back on the mountain somewhere, or in the ogre's hut. She didn't think she would be seeing it again. Ever.

Now that they were on the grounds, the Retreat itself seemed very far away. The driveway snaked and twisted on its way to the parking lot; of course, they could just cut across the yard, pushing through the waist-high grass. Gwen, evidently thinking along the same lines, said: "Should we go straight to the entrance?"

Robin considered the question. Flatten the hills and straighten the curves; that was what Kyle liked to say when he was driving too fast on a country road. But this wasn't a Sunday drive, and there could be things hiding here that were much worse than state troopers behind billboards waiting to hand out speeding tickets. "I don't think so," she said. "There could be stuff in the weeds."

"What kinds of stuff?"

"All kinds of stuff. Let's stick to the driveway."

And so they stuck to the driveway, following its meandering path. The way it weaved brought them sometimes closer to the Retreat, sometimes farther away, making slow progress forward. They passed a big tractor, which looked to have been abandoned in the middle of mowing; a trail of shorter—but still long—grass ran behind it like the fading wake of a boat. A baseball cap sat, saucily askew, on some kind of shifter. The word *Zane* was embroidered on the front of the hat. Someone's name? A key was stuck in the ignition, with a penknife dangling off it from a beaded metal chain. Robin stopped, and the others stopped with her. She turned to look at them. "Wait here a sec," she said, pushing into the tall grass, bulling her way to the tractor. It wasn't far, but even so, she ended up with a few lightly bleeding scratches from the rough grass. She climbed up into the tractor seat. Now that she was closer, she could see that the knife shell also said *Zane*, the text burned into the plastic case. That must have been the guy who operated the tractor. Robin wondered what had happened to him. She tested the key. It would neither turn nor come out, but she wanted that knife. Robin backed up and plopped herself on the tractor's seat to think for a minute.

That was when she noticed the cemetery.

She hadn't spotted it from the road, but from her new perch she had the elevation to see it over the grass. It wasn't far off, a largish stockaded island choked with weeds growing up and over the spiked black iron fence, nearly obscuring it. Inside the perimeter, a jumble of oblong shapes jutted crookedly from the ground, draped with dead vegetation. Tombstones. It was difficult to tell how many there were; Robin guessed maybe two dozen, including a big one right in the middle with a giant cross on top.

Not looking away from the cemetery, Robin said: "Margaret."

The doctor squeaked in response.

"What's the deal with the graveyard?"

Another squeak, uncertain. Margaret didn't know what the deal was.

Gwen said: "Graveyard?"

"Yeah. Graveyard." On closer inspection, Robin realized that not all the shapes inside the fence were tombstones. They weren't all stationary, either. "Shit. Things are moving around in there."

"*Things?*"

She could hear movement in the tall grass, like large snakes writhing through it. Creatures that were lying still had begun to stir. "Yeah. Things. Time to go." Finding some new reserve of strength, she ripped the knife off the chain, then hopped off the tractor and hurried to rejoin the others. Back on the driveway, Robin turned in a slow circle, surveying the overgrown lawn. The grass shivered on all sides, the rippling movements coming closer. The air had taken on a rank, fetid odor, as if they had wandered onto a damp, rotting shore. She caught glimpses of pale, rotten faces, when the vegetation shifted in just the right way to reveal what was coming, before closing curtain-like to hide them again.

"Time to go," she said, pulling Gwen into a run, Margaret tottering along behind, following the swoop of the driveway toward the gates. They didn't get far. The tall grass was infested with animated corpses, squirming, crawling, staggering onto the driveway, cutting off their escape. All roads led to gnashing teeth and clutching fingers. She and Gwen and Margaret stopped running and pressed themselves together, back to back to back, the living surrounded by the hungry dead, bodies with rotten faces barely clinging to their heads, skin hanging loose in wattles. Some were bloated by internal gases, others little more than stick-figure skeletons, flesh shrink-wrapped onto bone.

Robin had always had kind of a problem with zombie flicks. How did cadavers move around? How did wasted muscles impel, milky eyes see, jellied brains process even the most rudimentary information? But now that a horde of shambling predators actually surrounded them, those questions seemed kind of academic.   One that remained relevant: How do you kill things that are already dead?

She unfolded the knife blade and prepared to find out.

~~~~

Kyle opened his eyes suddenly.   Despite the pain in his leg——or maybe because of it——he had lost consciousness. He didn't think he had slept. If he had slept, he would feel at least a little bit refreshed. If anything, he felt worse than before, sore and cold and stiff. And, of course, terrified. And now someone was watching him. He knew it, he could sense it, hungry eyes on him, and not because he looked good in hiking shorts. Kyle peered left, peered right. Nothing. Nobody. The little clearing was deserted, silent.

Then he heard the cage creaking above him, and looked up.

Something hovered above him, hanging on to the crosspieces where they met in the middle. X marked the spot. Kyle could see long, pallid fingers wrapped around the gnarled branches, and eyes that glowed a soft, dusky red behind them.   Then the apparition vanished, rising away from the cage and disappearing into the night sky, as if reeled in on a line.   The branches never moved.   Maybe nothing had ever been there at all.   At night, in the forest, hurt and alone, your imagination could really run away with you.   Yeah, and your imagination might get really nervy and run away with your leg. Kyle heard himself doing that crazy giggle again, and tried to stifle it. He was only partly successful.

A few seconds later something appeared at the door of the cage. It stood there staring at him, clutching the bars with hands the color of baby powder. Kyle scuttled to the far corner of his prison. Whatever this strange figure was, being near it made Kyle's flesh crawl. By the time he got to the other side of the enclosure, the visitor was gone. As Kyle shifted around for a better look, fingers clamped down on his right shoulder, five sharp nails piercing his shirt and digging into his flesh.

"I am *looking*," a voice said into his ear, the sibilant whisper so soft that he barely understood the words, "for a *man*."

Not to respond seemed inconceivable.   "What … What man?" Kyle said.

"A *man* who took *something* of *mine*."

"What makes you think I know——"

The fingers squeezed, choking off Kyle's voice. "I *smell him* on your *clothes*. You *know* him. Where *is* he?"

"But I don't know who you're talking about."

The nails bit deeper, touched bone. Icy cold spread throughout Kyle's body. His skeleton had become a refrigerator coil.

"Think *harder*," the creature said.

Kyle thought harder. He had to say something to make this monster go away, or he'd be killed before the other monster got a chance to finish eating him. Would that be a better fate? He wasn't sure. "It couldn't have been Chuck, I was with Chuck all day. And it's not me. Right? Not me? So it must Bob."

"*Bob.*" The name came out like a mouthful of spoiled food. "*Where* can I *find* this ... *Bob*?"

"I don't know. We got separated. His wife had a headache and they stayed in the car. I haven't seen him in hours." Squeeze. "That's all I know, I swear!"

The hand released him suddenly. His shoulder felt hot and wet. "His *wife*. Give me her *name*."

Mustering up what little courage he had left, Kyle said: "I'm not telling you anything else."

"*You* will tell *me* anything I *ask* you."

"No I won't."

After a moment, the thing began to make strange gulping noises. It took Kyle a few seconds to realize he was laughing. Suddenly, stupidly angry, Kyle said: "I'm not afraid of you!"

"No?" The hand grabbed him around the throat, squeezed sharply, and then the voice said: "Ah, you have *urinated* to show your *contempt* for me, then?"

Kyle's bladder had indeed emptied involuntarily; he expected his colon to do the same at any moment. He wanted to say something defiant, but couldn't. It felt like this creature had plunged its fingers into his brain instead of his shoulder, was using those long nails to shred it into so much grey gelatin. He heard himself say, "Myra! Her name's Myra!"

"*Myra.*" The thing stretched her name out like a particularly delicious piece of taffy. The fingers released his shoulder. The cold retreated from Kyle's extremities back toward the wounds in his shoulder, but didn't leave completely. He had a feeling it never would.

"I told you what you wanted," he said. "Now go away and leave me alone."

Brittle laughter clawed at Kyle's ears. "No," it said.

Kyle heard branches splintering behind him as the thing tore the cage apart. Bits of broken wood pattered down on Kyle's head. He wanted to crawl away but it seemed all he could do was gibber. The entity reached in and hauled him out through the opening it had made, then lifted him and turned him around so he finally got a look at this new tormenter. Now he could name the creature: Vampire. The pallid skin, the eyes, the narrow lips around jagged fangs, the eyes, the smooth bald cranium, the eyes, the eyes, *the eyes*!

Suddenly a roar split through the night, deep and rumbly as thunder. The vampire paused, holding Kyle up with one hand, leaving his toes just scraping against the ground. Kyle couldn't see what was roaring, but it could only be one thing: That *other* monster, the first one, who had taken his leg. It must have caught on that someone was raiding the pantry. The vampire glanced sidelong at the shack, then looked back at Kyle. "My *friend* there in his *hovel* thinks you will serve as his *dinner*. But I *like* you. You are *pliable* as *putty*. I will *mold* you, and you will serve *me* in a *different*, better way. But *first*, I must use my *powers* of *persuasion* so that we are not *harried* and *pursued*."

The vampire casually flung Kyle aside. He sailed across the clearing and hit the ground hard on the other side, near the trees, tumbling and rolling to a stop. For a few seconds he couldn't see anything beyond the haze of lights bursting in his head. When it cleared and his vision returned, he saw the two monsters squaring off like wrestlers about to go a few rounds in the moonlight. It looked like a total mismatch, a nine-foot hulk versus a toothpick wrapped in black crepe. Kyle had no idea who to root for. He didn't want to get eaten like a brisket, but he didn't want to get molded like pliable putty, either. Whatever the fuck *that* meant.

He waited until they started fighting—the ogre threw the first punch—then began surreptitiously crawling away. The painful stump of his leg and his unwillingness to look away from the contestants meant he made very poor time. None of the big monster's blows connected. Those enormous fists probably packed enough force to knock down a medium-sized tree with one blow, but the intended target jumped or ducked or cartwheeled out of the way. And the vampire, the *fucking* vampire, kept looking at Kyle, pinning him in place with those red eyes, letting him go, pinning him again. No. *No*, God damn it. Kyle closed his eyes, turned away, scuttling like a beetle. He felt shivers in the ground as the ogre stomped around, trying to fight an opponent that was too fast, too sharp.

Then the shivering stopped.

Kyle couldn't help but pause and look back. The fanged victor strode toward him, black blood dripping from its long, clawed fingers. In the background, the ogre was still upright, hands pressed to its throat as dark fluid oozed from beneath its palms. As he watched, the giant tipped over backwards, crashed to the forest floor, and lay there twitching. And then the vampire loomed over Kyle, looking down at him with hot red eyes. It raised its hand. The long, slender fingers were stained dark; it thrust them into its mouth, pulled them out clean, and then spat. "*Ogre's* blood. So *flat*. So *bitter*." It cocked its head at an angle that should have been impossible. "You will *come* to me, that I may *drink*."

Kyle opened his mouth to say he would do nothing of the sort, but in fact he was already moving, dragging himself forward. This time he had no thoughts of escape; there was only the need to obey the command. As he pulled himself along, a broken jag of wood caught the bandage on his severed leg and unraveled it, pulling free the cauterized flesh at the end of the stump. Blood spurted out, hot and strong. Kyle didn't care. He just kept going. He was bitterly disappointed when he didn't make it. Numbness had begun to spread across his body. He had lost so much blood. His vision grew spotty, his hands cold. He raised his head to look at the vampire. The red eyes were aimed directly at his. "I said *come*."

Kyle didn't move, but only because he couldn't. The hydraulic system was low on fluid. The engine was out of gas.

So his new master came to him instead, floating along just above the ground. The black cloak rippled as it trailed along the grass. Freed from the gaze for a moment, Kyle tried to turn to the side, to crawl away, but he hadn't gone more than a foot when a cold hand closed on the back of his neck. It lifted him easily off the ground, held him up facing the forest. Another hand cupped the stump of his leg, gathering the blood that flowed from it. The vampire turned him so they were face to face. "You are a *dog*," he said. "A *worm*. See how you *crawl*, with your *belly* on the *earth*?"

Its jaws opened wide as its eyes drew Kyle in.

He fell into them, like falling into a grave.

~~~~

Bob stood at the edge of the undertaker's yard. How the hell had he missed it the first time he came through town?

Toomes lived in a home attached to a funeral parlor, set well back from the road in a large, manicured yard, enclosed by a black wrought iron fence topped with spikes. Both buildings were painted dark grey; each sported a black slate roof. The house boasted a high widow's-walk tower that looked like it should have a bell in it. The coffins Paltruck had mentioned—there were two, flanking the gravel walk—did indeed support some kind of night-blooming plant. It grew in a thick vine over a trellis between the two caskets, drooping enormous white trumpet-shaped flowers that Paltruck could have worn as a hat. Bob went to the gate, stood under the large horn-shaped flowers for a few moments. They had a sweet smell, sort of like honeysuckle; he imagined them listening to the sounds of the night, relaying information through their roots to the vampire hunter in a subterranean control room in the house. Was that a crazy thought? Was *any* thought crazy anymore?

The gate was latched but not locked. He opened it and pushed through. It didn't squeal the way such gates always did in the movies; it moved silently, obviously well oiled and cared for. The gravel crunched under his feet as he walked up the path. He wondered how far the sound carried, if the Count could hear it, wherever he was. The porch steps creaked as he ascended; the boards groaned as he crossed to the massive front door. The wooden surface was ornately carved in patterns and figures that he found vaguely disturbing. Maybe they were magical symbols, things to keep monsters at bay. Maybe he should consider getting some of those done on himself. Tattoos or something. He could scratch them into his skin with a thorn. *Then* how hardcore would he be? Oh yeah.

There was no doorbell, just a flat knob sticking out of a tarnished brass plate the middle of the door. He eyed it for a minute, decided he was supposed to turn it, and did so. The response was a grinding, semi-musical tone from the other side. He waited a few minutes, then turned the knob again. More grinding music; still no answer. Disappointed, Bob turned away from the door.

Someone was standing at the foot of the porch stairs, pointing a crossbow up at him. "Jesus Christ!"

"Not hardly," the guy said.

Bob knew he was goggling, but couldn't get his face back under control.

The fellow's trigger finger looked a little twitchy. "Got nothing else to say?"

"Are you, uh, are you Mr. Toomes?"

"Yep. Robert Toomes. That's me. Everybody just calls me Toomes. And you would be … ?"

Although Toomes kept his gaze fixed on him, Bob could tell that he was also continually scanning the night around him, as if expecting to be attacked from above, below, front, back, left, and right, at any moment, by any number of foes. "My name's Bob. Bob Sinclair."

"You shouldn't be out alone in the dark, Bob Sinclair. Here, catch."

Toomes tossed something at him. Bob caught it, fumbled it, and caught it again. A crucifix. He looked down at it, then at Toomes. "Is this some kind of test?"

"Yep."

"Did I pass?"

"That one." Toomes fired the crossbow.

Bob felt a stinging pain in his cheek. He yelped and recoiled, his hand automatically going to the wound. His cheek felt sticky. "What the fuck? Are you trying to kill me?"

"Are you dead?"

After a moment, Bob said: "No."

"Well then." Toomes raised an eyebrow. "Show me."

"What?"

"Show me." Toomes tapped his cheek. Getting the idea, Bob turned his head so the man could see the shallow cut on his face. "Huh," the vampire hunter said. "You're a bleeder."

"Are we finished?"

"Yeah, we're finished. Come on inside." Bob turned back to the ornate entrance, but Toomes said: "Not that way. That's not really a door. It's just there to fool the stupid ones." He led Bob around the side of the house, to a featureless steel panel tucked behind some shrubbery. Toomes lifted a metal plate that was almost invisible in the dim light, revealing a hole beneath. He produced an enormous key, inserted it into the hole, turned it, and used it as a handle to slide the panel to the right. It didn't make a sound. He ushered Bob through, reclaimed the key, slid the door shut—the inside had a handle and a deadbolt—then led the way into a small, rather cozy living room. The furnishings were dark and ornate, in keeping with the front door; most of them looked quite old. Aside from this room, which Bob decided might be called a parlor, the house was dark, archways to other areas showing only the vaguest outlines of what was in them.

Toomes leaned the crossbow up against the side of a high-backed chair, then settled in. A half-empty martini and olive rested on a coaster on a nearby end table. "Have a seat," he said, motioning toward a couch opposite the chair.

Bob sat.

"I saw you looking around at the merchandise. You see something you like, make me an offer. I get most of this stuff out of their dens. They live a long time—I use the term *live* loosely—so they tend to have a lot of antique furniture, jewelry, stuff like that. At least the ones who aren't living in culverts or old railroad tunnels or such."

"You mean vampires?"

Toomes looked at him like he was an idiot.

"You *rob* them?"

"Finders keepers. Hey, I have expenses. It's not like anybody pays me to kill the bastards." Toomes picked up his drink and gave it a little swirl. The olive rolled around inside like an eyeball that still couldn't quite believe it had been impaled on a little plastic cutlass. He held the glass up for inspection. "Want one?"

Bob said: "No thanks."

His host shrugged and put the glass down.

"So, uh, my issue is pretty urgent."

"Aren't they all," Toomes said. He plucked out the olive and ate it, then aimed the tiny sword at Bob. "Go ahead, sadden me."

So he told Toomes the whole story, from Dr. Zane to Paltruck to the castle to Dr. Zane again, and how he met up with Myra in the office after she had become a vampire. Toomes appeared to listen carefully, watching Bob the whole time, occasionally taking tiny sips from his martini glass. Bob finished up with his last encounter with Paltruck, when the little man had sent him in search of Toomes. The vampire hunter looked at him for a moment, then knocked back the rest of the martini and put the glass down on the table.

"So, um, what do you think?" Bob said.

"I think you got a problem, son."

"Well, yeah, but—"

"It sounds like your wife hasn't accepted what she's become. That's good; it means the Count hasn't solidified his hold on her yet. Once she gives in to his will, though, it's game over; she's one of them. And it's just a matter of time until that happens."

"How long?"

"Depends how strong she is. Most people buckle right away; some hold out for a whole night. None of them make it past dawn, though."

"Which is how far away?"

Toomes pulled a watch from his shirt pocket, consulted it, frowned, shook it, consulted it again, and then put it back. "Well, you got a while yet," he said.

"How long is *a while?*"

"It depends. Now, you mentioned you've got friends up there on the mountain?"

"Yes. I'm not sure where they—"

"You might as well forget about them. They're probably dead by now."

"What?"

Toomes picked up the empty martini glass, stared darkly at the remains of his drink. "You heard me."

"Why—"

"On account of because." Toomes sighed. "Okay, look. The Count lives on top of the eastern mountain, right? He's always got some minion or other running around causing trouble. The—"

"But—"

"Hush, son, I'm telling stories. Now, then, the western mountain—the one your friends climbed—that's just a goddamn menagerie. Pioneer ghosts, ogres, giant spiders, don't even get me started. And then there's the Retreat That's on top of the southern mountain. Word is that place is shot with secret passages and full of zombies and goblins and gods, oh my."

Bob wondered who Toomes had gotten that information from, given that he seemed to be the only person around here who wasn't undead or deranged, and Bob was just taking the *not deranged* part on faith. "Zombies and goblins and gods? Do you believe that?"

"Maybe. Maybe not. What goes on up at the Retreat is somebody else's problem."

"What kind of attitude is that?"

Toomes tapped himself on the chest. "*Vampire* hunter," he said. "I can't take on every weird thing that hangs around these parts."

Bob leaned forward. "Can I ask you a question?"

Toomes tipped the empty glass toward him.

"Why do you live here?"

Toomes looked puzzled. "I don't follow."

"This place is insane! Ogres? Zombies? Goblins? *Giant spiders?* Come *on.*"

"Oh. Well, you know how it is. You come to visit a place, you fall in love with it, you never leave."

"No. No, I *don't* know how it is. I don't think I would fall in love with a place that was crawling with all that kind of stuff."

Toomes shrugged. "There are a thousand things that can come out of the blue and kill you. You could go out for the paper and get creamed by a runaway truck. A meteor could crash through the roof of your house. It's no different here."

"Of course it's different here! *Vampires?* They aren't supposed to exist!"

"Oh. They aren't? Guess I'll just have another martini instead of worrying about your wife problem, then."

Bob couldn't think of a good response to that.

"Look, I thought you were in a hurry. Quit arguing about my life choices and tell me what you need." Then: "You want me to kill her for you, is that it?"

"What?" Bob was aghast. "No! I want you to come with me to the Count's castle. To kill *him*. Not *her*."

Toomes stared at him for a moment, then started laughing.

"What's so funny?"

"Sorry." With an obvious effort, the vampire hunter composed himself. "You want me to help you kill the Count?"

"Uh-huh."

"In his own castle?"

"Uh-huh."

"At night?"

"Uh, yeah."

"*That*, son," Toomes said, "is not going to happen."

"How come?"

Toomes looked at him critically. "The Count knows every square inch of his castle. It's chock full of booby-traps and dead ends and spider-holes. We would never even see him before he killed us."

"But, all your stuff." Bob gestured around him at the antiques and tchotchkes.

"What about it?"

"You said you take it from their lairs."

"Those are just regular vampires. Their lairs are houses and stores and crypts, not *castles*, and I'm certainly not stupid enough to go creeping around in them at night while the bastards are awake. So let's forget about bearding this particular lion in his den, okay?"

After a moment, Bob said: "Okay."

"Good." Toomes got up, went to an antique sideboard that must have belonged to a vampire with especially baroque tastes, and started mixing himself another drink. "You sure I can't get you one?" he asked, not turning around.

"I'm good."

Toomes brought his now-full glass back to his chair, sat, and took a sip. "Now, you say you killed Zane?"

"Yes."

The vampire hunter emitted a disapproving grunt.

"What? Was I supposed to let him remove my appendix?"

"No," Toomes said. "No, of course not. But the Count won't be happy about it."

"He'll get over it."

Toomes chuckled. "Son, you're in way over your head, but damned if you aren't swimming like hell." He saluted Bob with his drink, took a sip, and said: "And seeing as how you've gone and started a land war in Asia, well, we might as well fight it. And we do have one thing going for us."

Bob waited to hear this one thing; then, realizing he was being cued, he said: "What's that?"

"Well, see, the Count gave Zane some of his own blood, to make him more than a normal human. Or less, depending on your point of view. But either way, Zane was a little stronger, a little faster, a little quicker to heal, and a whole lot crazier than you and me. Now he's gone, the Count will want a new servant as fast as he can get one." Toomes looked thoughtful. "I'll bet he wants *you*, but you're here, so he'll have to find one elsewhere. Making a new servant means he'll need to share his blood again. He'll be a hair weakened. And maybe, just maybe, we can take him out before he recovers."

"Great! Let's go."

"Whoa, down boy! We need to get you kitted up first. If we're going out hunting, you've got to be able to pull your weight."

"Oh. Okay." Then: "Speaking of going out hunting, should you really be drinking so many martinis right now?"

"It's not a problem."

"Said every drunk driver ever."

The undertaker grinned and handed him the glass. "Have a sip."

Bob did. Water with a twist of lemon.

"You've got to stay hydrated when you're hunting vampires," Toomes said. "And what can I say? I like olives."

In The Dark

CHUCK AND MYRA followed the road until it came to a black iron gate that stood between two columns of decaying river rock. An arched sign across the top of the gate said, in rusted, fading lettering, *Blackberry Mountain Retreat*. Beyond the fence the mountain had been shaved clean of trees; what should have been a rocky summit was instead the grounds of some sprawling institution. Chuck wondered why anyone would build such a large facility right on top of a peak like this one. It must be virtually cut off from the rest of the world in the wintertime. He eyed the opening between the two sections of the gate. He didn't think he could fit through there. Myra did, though, easily. She paused on the other side to give him an *aren't-you-coming?* look. Feeling even schlubbier than usual, he gestured at the gap, then at his belly.

"Ah," Myra said. She gave the chain a little rattle, tugged the lock. "Rusted shut."

"Can you break it?"

"Probably. But … I don't think I should. We'll just hop over it."

Chuck started to express his preference for staying on the ground, but she was already there, picking him up and jumping over the gate, easy as stepping over a curb. She deposited him on the other side, but she seemed distracted, peering up at the darkened yard. "Something's going on farther in," she told him. "When we were up in the air, I saw people."

"Our people?"

"Not sure. Maybe. But it's not just them. There are some other things too. Not human."

"Not human? What are they, then?"

"I can't tell. The moonlight isn't saying."

"The moonlight?"

"Never mind." She glanced back at him. "I think the others are in trouble. I have to go, see if I can help. Catch up when you can, all right? Stay on the driveway. The grass isn't safe."

"Why can't I come with—"

"Sorry, Chuck. Not this time." She slid the tire iron out of her belt, held it by the curved end, like a sword or a shotgun. "You'll just get in the way."

Without waiting for him to respond, Myra vanished into the sky.

After a moment, Chuck—placed in the sad category of people who would just get in the way, and needed to be left behind—started trudging up the long, curving driveway.

~~~~

The zombies had completely surrounded them, and were tightening the circle, moving in slowly. Gwen knew how this worked. The mindless dead didn't have speed or smarts or strength; they overwhelmed you with numbers and persistence. You couldn't stop them. You couldn't reason with them. For every mob you escaped, there was another, bigger mob beyond, waiting for its turn to wriggle their fingers into your soft parts. Eventually you ran out of space, time, and luck. As the ring of shuffling dead closed in, Gwen found herself wondering if they would be like the ones in that movie where they ripped you apart and ate you in pieces, or like the ones in that other movie where they just opened your skull like a beer can and ate your brain. She supposed it didn't make a lot of difference. Look at Margaret. Talk about getting eaten in pieces? She had already lost her arms and her tongue. She must smell like an open buffet. No wonder the carnivores had come out.

Maybe they could use Margaret as a diversion, Gwen thought. Push her forward and escape while the zombies were feasting. She tried to push the idea away. Wasn't that just what Kyle had been thinking when he threw her to the ogre? And now she was thinking about doing it to someone else? How low was that?

But they were going to eat her!

Suddenly a dark shape landed in front of Gwen, dropping out of the sky as if lowered on a string. Another monster? It took her a moment to realize it was Myra; it looked like her from behind, anyway. But how would Myra be flying? And why would she be carrying a tire iron? The new arrival glanced at Gwen over her shoulder. It *was* Myra, barely; her eyes glowed red in the moonlight, her face was pinched and puckered, her wide mouth brimmed with rows of shark-like teeth. Good God. What had happened to her?

"Stand back," Myra said, as if they had anywhere to stand back to. "This is going to be messy." Then she turned away and waded into the crowd, wielding the tire iron like a boss, smashing and bashing and stabbing skulls. Black fluids splashed; splinters of bone and gobbets of rotten flesh flew; scabrous bodies burst and ruptured and disgorged their decaying contents all over the driveway; the atrocious stench became ever more overpowering. And the mindless, voracious creatures kept shambling into the meat grinder that was Myra. They had no sense of self-preservation, no ability to recognize a threat. But Gwen did, and for all she knew, this thing that looked like Myra was taking out the dead because she wanted the living all to herself.

Robin bumped up against her. She was still clutching the penknife she had taken from the tractor, its little blade black with zombie blood. It had snapped off a third of the way up. Robin looked at it, then at Myra, then tossed the useless weapon over her shoulder. "I shouldn't have brought a knife to a tire iron fight," she said.

"How can you be making *jokes*?"

"It beats going crazy."

Gwen was going to suggest that maybe it was a *symptom* of going crazy, but then Margaret squealed and went down; a stump-legged zombie had wormed its way in unnoticed through the grass and gotten hold her ankle. As it struggled to drag her off into the brush, or at least haul her close enough to take a chunk out of her calf, Robin caught her under the stumps of shoulders and fought to pull her back. More crawling squirmed forward, reaching with blackened hands and filthy nails.

"Gwen! Help me!" Robin shouted.

Gwen backed off, unsteady on her feet. She didn't want to help. She wanted to vomit. Where was the Myra-thing? The Myra-thing was supposed to be handling this. Gwen looked around frantically and saw that Myra was otherwise occupied, surrounded by a scrum of zombies, like a quarterback in one of Chuck's football games who was about to be sacked. They clawed and bit and were rewarded by getting their heads smashed with the heavy chain, getting their faces ripped off by her clawed fingers. Gobbets of putrid zombie flesh flew every which-way. Her wicked face seemed gleeful to be inflicting such carnage. She was *enjoying* it, so much that she didn't notice Margaret's predicament. Or maybe she just didn't care.

Margaret's mutilated face was even more twisted than usual; she keened in horror as her legs disappeared into the tall grass. Robin leaned back, tried to brace herself. Her feet had scoured ditches through the gravel. Gwen realized that she herself had retreated almost to the edge of the driveway. She started moving towards the others, but gasped and stumbled away as more putrid hands emerged from the tall grass to clutch at Margaret's calves and dig at her lab coat trying to get at her belly. Sightless faces came into view, with withered lips and boiled pearl onion eyes that nearly glowed. Gwen couldn't help Margaret. She couldn't help anybody. She could only—

Cold, sticky hands grabbed Gwen from behind, closing on her bare legs, her hips. They yanked her off balance and she toppled over into the damp grass. It slid against her backside as they pulled her away from the drive. She twisted and kicked but more hands were on her now, catching her flailing limbs. She tried to scream, but only a squeak came out. The grass scratched at her exposed skin. A dead thing crawled on top of her as others moved in, impatient diners lining up at a buffet. The fetid mouths came down. She beat and punched and hammered with her fists. Disgusting fluids splashed from the impacts, but she barely slowed them down, and then one of them caught her hand in its jaws and started chewing and tearing, trying to separate her wrist from her arm. Jagged teeth headed for her throat. Gwen finally managed to scream, but it only lasted a second before it turned into a strange, whistling wheeze.

The last thing she saw before it all went black was one of the dead, chewing on her extracted windpipe, contented as a dog with a bone.

~~~~

Myra's tire iron smashed through the last zombie's chest, shattering its ribcage. When she ripped it free, what remained of its heart and lungs came with it, briefly clinging to the metal before detaching and splattering to the ground. Obviously the thing didn't need those parts; it kept snapping its teeth at her, kept trying to grab her with its only remaining arm. She bashed it over the head, swinging the tire iron with both hands, hitting so hard that she split it nearly to its navel. The dead thing collapsed into two noisome, twitching halves of oozing parts and half-rotted entrails.

She looked around. She had cleared the driveway, but she could still hear noises in the tall grass; some were still out there, hidden from the moonlight by the overgrowth, invisible to whatever special vision she had that so unerringly let her find her human prey.

"Help!"

Myra whirled. Robin was struggling to keep another person from being pulled into the grass. Myra leaped into the air, did a little flip over Robin's head, and landed feet-first on a small clutch of crawling zombies that had hold of the other woman's legs. Their torsos collapsed in a most satisfying manner, and when one of them tried to get up again, she crushed its head between her ankles. The brittle skull caved in like an empty soda can. Robin fell backwards, pulling her companion with her. They quickly scuttled away from the grass, not incidentally putting some space between themselves and Myra. She inspected the two of them. Robin didn't seem to be seriously injured, but the other one looked little better off than the dead; her hair was matted and filthy, her face was a mask of crusted gore.

"Are you all right?" Myra said. When the woman didn't answer, she turned to Robin. "Did they do that to her?"

"No," Robin said. "That was somebody else."

Myra nodded, then absently put her blood-covered fingers to her lips and licked them. She recoiled at the flat, sour taste and spat into the driveway. What the hell was she doing? Robin stared at her, looking appalled. In the momentary silence, Myra detected a crunching sound from the tall grass on the other side of the driveway. Obviously Robin heard it too; her eyes widened and she said: "Shit. Gwen. Where's Gwen?"

Oh, no.

The tall grass obscured what lay within it, so Myra took to the air. From above, with her predator's eyes, it was easy to spot the missing person. There she was. And there. And also there. Stragglers, slower and less mobile than their colleagues on the driveway, had paused like picnickers to consume various chunks of Gwen's body in peace and leisure. Myra struck them from the air, one-two-three, bashing their skulls with the tire iron. Then she landed near the biggest warm spot, Gwen's torso, lying on its back and staring at the sky. They had left the head attached, an arm, and both legs, but had excavated the middle, as if Gwen were a fondue pot. Myra had to turn away, not from revulsion, but before the sight and delicious smell of blood overwhelmed her and caused her do something unfortunate and disturbing.

Myra dropped the tire iron, returned to the driveway, and

collapsed on the cool gravel. Dismembered corpses surrounded her, stinking up the night with their putrescence. She heard footsteps come up. Robin. She stood back a little, out of easy reach. Of course, Myra could still have grabbed her in a flash if she'd wanted to.

Did she want to? Yes, a little. She sat on her hands to help relieve the temptation.

"It wasn't your fault," Robin said. "You did everything you could. There were just too many of them."

Myra shook her head. Of course it was her fault. Had she hadn't prevented it, big strong vampire that she was? No, she had not. What was Chuck going to say? She could hardly wait. And now here he was, rounding a bend in the driveway, breathing hard. He stopped and peered around, partially bent over, hands on his knees, surveying the scene. She could see his expression change as he eyed the corpses, the scattered body parts. His gaze moved to Myra, to Robin, lingered a moment on the armless woman, then returned to Myra.

He said: "Gwen?"

She looked away, shook her head.

After a moment, Chuck said: "Oh." She felt him looking at her. He made a strange noise, and then another one. "Where?"

"You might not want to——"

"Where?"

After a moment, Myra pointed at the spot. "Over there. Just off the driveway."

He went in the direction she had indicated, stopped in the tall grass near Gwen, and stared for what seemed like a long time. Then he turned, stumbled, and collapsed to his knees, making dry, heaving sounds. She wasn't sure if he was crying or puking or both. After a little while the noises stopped; then Chuck came back over and sat down next to Myra, on her left.

"Hey, Chuck," Robin said. "You okay?"

He nodded, wiped his mouth with the back of his hand. "Yeah. Yeah, I'm okay."

But he didn't *look* okay, and he didn't *sound* okay, because, of course, he *wasn't* okay. None of them were. If they held a *not okay* contest, it was anybody's guess who would win.

Well, Gwen would, obviously. But the position of first runner-up was definitely wide open.

~~~~

Toomes fully loaded for the hunt was a creature far removed from Toomes the undertaker and dealer in stolen antiques; if Bob had seen *this* Toomes in a shopping mall parking lot, he would have hidden behind the nearest car and called 911. It wasn't just the backpack full of vampire-hunting gear straight out of an old horror movie, festooned on the outside with garlic heads and stitched leather crosses and filled up with holy water, more garlic, wooden stakes, and a pair of mallets; he also carried a small crossbow——a miniature version of the one he'd used to menace Bob earlier——strapped to his right wrist, an honest-to-god sword in a scabbard on his belt, and an enormous knife with a brass knuckle hilt strapped to his left leg. Bob watched him retrieve a number of arrows for the crossbow from a glass container of water; he wrapped them individually in plastic, like string cheese snacks, and stashed them in an outer pocket of the backpack.

"New thing I'm trying," Toomes said, noting his attention. "Bolts made of ash, blessed by the local shaman and soaked in holy water. Just the thing to ruin a vampire's night."

"Shaman?"

"Shaman. Priest. Whatever."

"What about a blessed machine gun?"

Toomes snorted. "Shoot a vampire full of holes, you'll just piss it off."

"Okay, but what about the human helpers? Guns would work on them, right?"

"Right. That's why you get this." Toomes reached into a cabinet and produced a shotgun, which he proffered to Bob.

Bob just looked at it.

"Well go on," Toomes said. "Take it."

Bob took it, then looked at it some more. "I've never fired a gun before."

"Really." Toomes didn't sound surprised. "That's why you get a shotgun and not something that requires actual skill."

"What do I do with it?"

Toomes said, in the tone of voice one might use when explaining to a small child how to push a toy car around, "You point the end with the holes in it at something you want to destroy, and then you pull the trigger."

"Um. Okay." Bob shifted it from hand to hand and finally held the barrel upright against his shoulder like a marionette.

"Careful you don't blow your own fool head off," Toomes said.

"Isn't the safety on?"

Toomes's expression indicated that this was a ridiculous question. Bob rearranged things so he was carrying the shotgun horizontally in front of him in both hands, aiming it at a wall.

"Better," Toomes said. "And yes, the safety is on. How's that pack feeling? Does it restrict your movement?"

"No." Bob could smell the garlic wafting out of it, as if he had a pizza bag slung over his back. It contained holy water, too, and other arcane accoutrements for dealing with the pointy-toothed undead. He nudged the gold plated cross that hung on a strap around his neck; it lay against his chest, heavy as an X-ray shield in a dentist's chair. It was so blingy that he suspected Toomes had gotten it off a vampiric rapper. "Do I have to wear this thing?"

"Yes, you have to wear it. Most vampires hate them."

"Most?"

Toomes shrugged. "Every once in a while you get an outlier. For them, that crucifix has a little something extra."

"What's that?"

"I'll show you later."

"Why not show me now?"

"Your hands are full. For now, let's just say Jesus saves." Toomes grinned at him. "Come on, let's go."

Bob followed the vampire hunter through the hidden door, stepping out into the cool night air. With their weapons and their backpacks, Bob thought, they must look like a pair of demented runaways as they crossed the front yard to the front gate. Toomes paused there, looked back at Bob, and said: "Last chance to change your mind."

Bob wasn't sure why this was his last chance; if ten minutes from now he decided he'd rather come back and hide in Toomes's basement than go hunting vampires, would Toomes tell him no? But he nodded in affirmation to show he was still game to be a member of the He-Man Vampire Hunter's Club. Toomes held the gate open for him. Nothing happened when they passed the coffins with their night-blooming flowers and left the yard; vampires didn't swoop in to kill them, the house didn't light up the night by exploding into a fireball, steel walls didn't erupt from the ground to bar their return. Bob was a little worried, though, that his mind sifted through all those possibilities and none struck him as particularly outlandish.

They turned right at the road and started walking toward Dr. Zane's office at the other edge of town. Soon they were passing buildings that he recognized from his previous excursions along the main drag. They looked different in the moonlight, shadowed and menacing. More than one front door hung open, as if baleful occupants had awakened and wandered out for a night on the town. He was pretty sure most of these places had been closed up during the day. He mentioned this to Toomes, who brushed it off. "They mostly keep to themselves," he said, gesturing vaguely at the houses with the hand that didn't have an arcane weapon strapped to the wrist. "If you ignore them, they'll ignore you."

"But why——"

"Uh-uh. Asking questions is not ignoring." Then, as if he were making conversation while they walked to the corner store for cigarettes and Top Ramen: "So what brought you folks to Blackberry Hollow, anyway?"

"We just wanted to do a little hiking."

Toomes snorted. "You sure picked the wrong place for that."

"Tell me about it. Anyway we didn't really pick it. It was kind of an impulse thing. We were just driving along and Chuck saw the sign. They were arguing, and——"

"Who was arguing?"

"Chuck and Gwen. About what to do. Chuck was driving, and Gwen—that's Chuck's wife—she wanted to go exploring, but he had a map and a whole big plan for where we were going to go and what we were going to do when we got there. They had a fight and she threw his map in the river."

Toomes chuckled. "Sounds like me and the missus."

Bob, surprised, said: "You're married?"

"I was. Until I had to stake her."

Bob wasn't sure if he was supposed to offer condolences or congratulations. After a moment he decided to just continue the story. "Yeah. So, um, anyway, we saw the sign for Blackberry Hollow, and——"

Suddenly Toomes whirled so fast that Bob, startled, tripped and fell on his ass. He managed to keep the shotgun from hitting the ground and blowing a hole in a passing cloud or his own face. "Toomes, what——" He clammed up because Toomes was pointing the little crossbow at him, or rather, at something behind him, out in the night. Not one of the residents of the yawning houses, obviously, since they were on the *ignore* list. Now that the initial shock had passed Bob realized that someone was speaking, a voice from the darkness, begging over and over again not to be shot. He twisted around to see. A man lay in the grass not far away, on his back, his hands raised defensively. It looked like the guy was missing a leg. Bob scuttled back to Toomes's side and stood, getting a better look at the man's face.

"Holy shit," he said. "Kyle?"

"Yeah! Yeah, it's me, Bob! It's Kyle!"

Toomes looked at Bob, then back to Kyle. "This is one of your missing hikers?" he said.

"Yeah," Bob said. "He's okay. I know him."

"Just because you know him doesn't mean he's okay."

"No, I am! I'm okay!" Kyle said. "But I'm not hiking anywhere anymore, see?" He lifted the stump of his leg and pointed at it. It didn't look like a skillful amputation; the limb had just been twisted off, then crudely cauterized, maybe by sticking it in a fire. A few bits of what looked like surgical tape stuck to the part that was left. How was he even moving around after that?

"What happened to your leg?" Bob said.

"It's gone."

Toomes said, icily, "Gone *where*?"

"Down the hatch!"

Toomes's trigger finger started looking a little twitchy.

Kyle's eyes widened. "There was this hut. And in this hut, I found this arm, half eaten up! And before I could get away, this monster came and knocked me out." He giggled, sounding more than a little unhinged by the experience. He stuck his hand between his teeth and bit down for a few seconds, then took it out again. "When I woke up I was locked in a cage and my leg was gone. I think, I think, he ripped it off and *ate it*."

Bob turned to Toomes, who was regarding Kyle the way somebody might look at a yapping, muck-covered, stinky, possibly rabid little dog. "Does that sound like anything you ever heard of?"

"Yeah. Sure. Sounds like the ogre. Hangs out in the woods. Not my problem." He turned back to Kyle. "So how'd you get away? I mean, locked in a cage with one leg torn off and all. Sounds pretty grim."

"Maybe Paltruck let him out."

Toomes shot Bob an exasperated look, as if he had just said something unbelievably stupid, but Kyle brightened immediately. "Yeah. Yeah, he did! Paltruck saved me!"

"Mind describing this hero of yours, sport?" Toomes said.

"Sure! Short little brown guy. Funny hat. Friendly. *Really* friendly. Like friendly dog friendly."

"Yeah, that's Paltruck all right. He's a sprite."

"That's Paltruck all right, he's a sprite," Kyle said in a sing-song voice. "Hey, that rhymes!" He laughed hysterically, then clamped his hand over his mouth to stop himself.

Toomes scratched his cheek with the crossbow bolt, apparently unconcerned about the possibility of piercing his own nose. "You *sure* you're all right, mister?"

"I'm fine," Kyle said. "Just a little stressed."

"I bet," Toomes said. "Here, catch." He tossed something to Kyle, who fumbled it. The thing landed on his chest. Kyle picked it up and looked at it. Bob saw that it was a small plastic crucifix, powder-puff pink, like it had come from a doll's My First Church playset.

Kyle seemed puzzled. "What's this for?"

"That's for you," Toomes said. "You might need it someday."

Bob turned to the vampire hunter. "So he's coming with us?"

"Hell no," he said. "Are you crazy? At best he'll get in the way. At worst he'll get us both killed."

"We can't just leave him here."

"Sure we can."

"Come on, Toomes. Look at his leg."

Toomes sighed, then pointed up the street. "Okay, Ahab. My house is that way. Look for the house with the caskets full of white flowers out front. You can wait for us on the porch."

While they'd been discussing what to do with him, Kyle had been looking back and forth between them; now he said: "Can't I come along? I won't get you killed. I won't even get in the way. You won't know I'm there. Quiet as a mouse. I promise."

"No," Toomes said, "you cannot come along. You made it this far, you can make it to my porch. That way." He turned and started walking. Bob just stood there gawking at him until Toomes stopped, looked back over his shoulder, and said: "I thought you wanted to kill a vampire? Unless you decided to change your mind. Last chance."

Bob thought his last chance had already passed. "No. I mean, yeah, I do. Want to kill a vampire. I'm coming." He hefted his satchel again, looked at Kyle, who lay there wide-eyed as a castaway watching his rescue ship sail off without him. "Sorry, Kyle. We've got stuff to take care of. Just do like Toomes said and you'll be fine."

"But——"

"I'm sorry, I have to go. Wait for us on the porch. Good luck."

He took off after the vampire hunter, and didn't look back.

~~~~

Chuck would have liked to have gathered up what was left of Gwen and do something appropriate with the remains, but after what had been done to her he would need a bag to carry her in. She would slosh around like a sack full of eels. He didn't even want to think about it. And what was he supposed to do, anyway? Dig a grave with his bare hands? Not going to happen. He couldn't even think of anything decent to say. All he could offer her was a two-sentence eulogy. "Gwen," he said, "I'm sorry I couldn't be there when you needed me. I hope you can forgive me."

He wasn't talking about just this last time; there had been others. Of course there had. Everyone failed everyone else all the time. But Gwen should know what he meant, though, right? Dead folks knew all kinds of things. That was why people were always trying to contact them.

"We're all sorry," Robin said, putting her hand on Chuck's shoulder. He supposed she was apologizing Kyle's behalf. She hadn't seemed all that surprised when Chuck told her what he had done. What was it like to be married to someone and not be shocked to hear he had pushed a friend off a cliff to save his own skin?

So, yeah, it was a regular pity party. Everybody was sorry. Kyle would be the sorriest of all, if Chuck ever caught up to him.

"Come on, Chuck," Robin said. "We should go."

"Okay," he said. "Go where?"

She didn't say, she just took his arm and pulled him away from the spot where most of Gwen lay. He let her lead him across the driveway to Myra and the mutilated lady in the lab coat, Margaret. Myra had been staring at the distant building, but when he and Robin arrived she turned to him and said, "I'm so sorry, Chuck." He wished she would stop saying that. How many times did he have to tell her it was all right, that he didn't blame her? Although he *did* blame her, a little. She had all those new powers—flight, strength, night vision—and she had rescued Robin and some armless stranger, but she hadn't managed to save Gwen from being eaten by zombies. Why was that?

Myra was still looking at him. She was just making it worse, harder. He took her hand—it was cool to the touch, not quite air temperature, but not warm either—pulled her into a hug, and said: "It's okay. You did all you could." Which was true. She was covered in gore, she had been scratched and bitten, though those injuries seemed to have healed already. It was stupid to blame her for the way things had turned out. There had been too many zombies, too much confusion, not enough time.

"Well," Robin said. Then: "I guess we keep going, right? To the Retreat?"

"Why were you guys going there?" Myra said.

"Because Margaret wanted to," Robin said. "She worked here. She was a doctor, I think."

Myra spun around to look at Margaret. "You worked here? What can you tell me about it?"

Margaret shook her head, shrugged.

"She can't tell you anything," Robin said. "She can't talk. She can't write."

Myra stepped closer. "But she can think."

"What's that supposed to mean?"

Chuck, hoping to find a way to be helpful, said: "Maybe you could play hot and cold with her." Crickets. "You know. Hot and cold? Stamp once for warmer, twice for cooler?"

"Oh, no," Myra said. "Hot and cold? That's playground stuff. I have a better idea."

"What?"

She looked at him with those newfangled eyes of hers.

"I'm going to read her mind," Myra said.

~~~~

Myra already knew there was something in the Retreat, something powerful and hidden. If Margaret had some information about that locked in her head, they needed it. She wasn't sure how this mind-reading thing would work, exactly, but she did seem to have been gifted with some of the Count's psychic power; she'd located Chuck on the mountain, after all, and had picked up vague impressions of what he was thinking, what he was feeling. And she hadn't even been trying then. If she *did* try, who knew what she could do?

She held up her hands, palms out. "I'm going to hold your head, okay, Margaret?"

Previously the woman had been watching her warily, but now she squeaked and made a little moue of disgust, maybe because Myra's hands were still gummy with black blood and goo. She wiped them on her bloody clothes, looked at them, wiped them some more on a different patch of clothing. She showed them to Margaret again. "Better?"

Apparently not. Margaret cast a nervous glance at Robin, who said: "Do you have to touch her? I don't think she's comfortable with that."

Myra said, "I'm not going to hurt her. But I don't know how to do this, and I think it'll be easier if——"

"Relax. Nobody said you were going to hurt her. I just think she has issues with being touched at the moment, especially by, um, ah …"

Robin trailed off, evidently unable to think of a diplomatic way to phrase whatever she was thinking, but Myra got the gist of it. Annoyed, she said: "I'm not *um, ah*, a monster. Am I, Chuck?"

Chuck opened his mouth, no doubt planning to sing a paean to the beauty and power and awesomeness that was the new Myra. She gave him the tiniest shake of her head, not wanting him to sound like Renfield waxing sycophantic about Dracula. He picked up on it, and toned it down. "It's okay. You can trust her. She's different now, but she's still Myra. And we really need to find out what the hell is going on."

Robin seemed satisfied. She turned to the armless woman and said, "Margaret?"

Margaret nodded. Myra stepped up to her, put her palms flat against either side of the other woman's head, and tried to find out what was going on in between them. Nothing much happened, except that she found herself eyeing Margaret's neck. She could see it pulsing faintly in time with the rhythm of her heart. All that blood, right there for the taking, just beneath the skin. She pushed the thought aside, and then pushed it aside again when it came back. But this approach obviously wasn't working. The Count hadn't needed to touch her at all; everything he'd done, he'd done with the dusky suns of his eyes. She had fallen right into them. She needed Margaret to fall into hers. She concentrated on her own gaze, trying to change her perception of it from something going out to something drawing in. Suns radiated, yes, but they also attracted.

Gravity: That was what she needed.

Something shifted and lurched inside of her. She felt an impact in the front of her skull as if she had smacked her head against a wall. And then, suddenly, she was walking down a vaguely familiar, harshly lit corridor; or rather, Margaret was walking, with Myra along for the ride as a silent observer. Margaret was on her way somewhere. She was a woman with a purpose. In her hands—her hands, how Margaret missed them!—she held a clipboard; on the clipboard was a patient chart. A sticky note with something scrawled in indecipherable doctor handwriting had been affixed to the top of the chart. The note covered up the patient's name, but Myra was pretty sure she knew who it was.

Carrying Myra along in her head, Margaret entered a small day room. Myra recognized the faux leather couch, and the person who sat on it: Patrick, of course. When she had first seen that piece of furniture it had been on a rotating platform in Patrick's television shrine; now it was sad and stationary, pushed up against the left wall, and instead of being surrounded by screens it faced a single smallish flat-screen television on a table across the room. A black-and-white Dracula type flick was on, a sinister, overdressed fop slinking through darkened castle corridors. Margaret's gaze moved from Patrick to the television to a man in scrubs—not a doctor, but an orderly or something similar; his name tag said *Baxter*—who sat in a chair near Patrick. This man appeared to be trying not to look at Margaret. She called his name, pointed at the sticky note, and told him to turn off the television. The orderly seemed reluctant to comply; he kept shooting nervous glances in Patrick's direction, as if afraid of suffering a rebuke from the patient. Margaret tapped the note with her finger. Who was in charge around here? That was what Margaret wanted to know. She stuck out her hand and asked the orderly for the remote.

The orderly shook his head. He didn't have the remote, Patrick did.

Margaret suggested that maybe he should get it, then.

Patrick started waving the remote around, moving it from hand to hand, engaging in what looked to Myra like a fairly accomplished game of keep-away. She thought the orderly could've been trying a little harder to retrieve it, though. After a minute he gave Margaret a helpless look. You see? Patrick wouldn't give it to him.

Myra could feel Margaret's lips pressing together as if they were her own. She said the employee's name again and speculated aloud if he wanted to get written up, or if he wanted to do his job? Well, which was it? Do his job? Good. Then he needed to get the remote.

The man gave it another try. He still didn't manage to take the remote, but he did knock it out of Patrick's hand while trying. It hit the floor, popped open, and slid over to Margaret in a scatter of plastic and batteries. She knelt down, picked up the pieces, reassembled it, aimed it at the television, and pressed a button.

The screen went black.

Myra was carried along as Margaret went over to Patrick. Now that the television was off, he had lowered his face to his knees and was slowly rocking back and forth. She leaned over and spoke to him. He knew he wasn't supposed to be watching television right now, didn't he? Remember how, after that whole big thing last week, they had all made up a schedule, he and Margaret and the other patients, so that other people could watch what they wanted to watch sometimes?

Patrick nodded slowly.

Okay, good. Margaret was glad Patrick remembered that. So

according to that schedule, it was time for Patrick to let somebody else run the show for a while. And besides, he had a visitor. His father was waiting for him. Margaret had asked him to stop by and have a talk, which they had done, and now he wanted to take Patrick out for a drive or a walk in the forest. Did Patrick think he was up for something like that?

Patrick nodded again.

Good. That was good. They would go down to her office then, where his dad was waiting. Okay? Okay. Margaret made to hand the remote over to the orderly, but Patrick snatched the remote out of her hand and turned the television back on, then stuck the remote into the elastic waistband of his pants.

Margaret sighed. Really, Patrick? Is this how he wanted to behave? Patrick didn't answer, he just craned his neck so he could see around her. She looked at him for a second, then stood up, crossed the room, and unplugged the set from the wall. Turning, she gave Patrick one last chance to return the remote. He didn't answer; he just stared at the blank screen as if puzzled by what had happened, why it had gone dark. Margaret shook her head, turned to the orderly, gave him an instruction. The man's eyes widened as if he couldn't believe what she had said; but she said it again and, after another nervous glance at Patrick, the man came over to Margaret and began disconnecting the set from the box that fed it content.

A flicker passed across Patrick's face, showing other faces, the way sometimes one signal bled into another when watching television over the air. For a second, Margaret could swear there were multiple Patricks sitting on the couch. It was full of Patricks. They were jittery, shaky, out of focus. She barely had time to blink before some kind of shockwave knocked her off her feet.

Margaret hit the wall hard and slid to the floor. As she struggled to stand, the orderly hauled her to her feet. Except he wasn't really the orderly anymore. He had changed, grown thick and twisted, become a huge, hairy monster. He had a firm, rough hold on her and wouldn't let go as her swung his massive head this way and that, scanning the lounge with tiny eyes. He oriented on the window, his bulbous nose working, as if he smelled outside air leaking through the frame. He flung Margaret over his shoulder and began to move.

The television, still unplugged, had switched back on. Now it showed a scene of the day room, except that absolutely nothing was happening. Patrick sat on the sofa, as he had been doing before Margaret came in; Margaret lay on the floor, curled up in a heap, as if she had simply slumped down into a puddle from where she had stood; and the orderly lay on his side near the television stand. The television within the television was on, and Myra was pretty sure the screen within the screen showed a tiny version of the day room in which Margaret was slung over the shoulder of a monster; and in the center of *that* display she could see an even tinier version of the television, showing a yet more tiny scene that she couldn't make out. She suspected it was the lounge again, with Patrick and Margaret and the orderly all motionless, with a microscopic television showing a microscopic monster carrying a microscopic Margaret.

Then the ogre leapt out through the window, smashing the glass and the light grillwork on the outside. The two of them fell to the ground in a shower of stars, landed hard on the pavement of the parking lot. Through Margaret's eyes, Myra watched the institute grow smaller in the distance as they bounded across the grounds. The building was changing; lights were going out across the complex, the walls were beginning to crumble, the grass was growing madly toward the moon. A graveyard appeared, sprouting from the ground like a set of molars, the tombstones darkening to become weathered and ancient. Then the ogre jumped into the air, passed over the fence, and—

And the contact was broken. Margaret stumbled away from Myra, falling down on the driveway, whimpering. Robin went to the armless woman, knelt beside her for a moment, looked at Myra. Her mouth moved, but Myra couldn't hear the words over the roaring of the wind in her ears as she fell on her face.

Breaking and Entering

BOB AND TOOMES stood outside Zane's office, one of them on either side of the door. Toomes was eyeing the entrance like a skeptical buyer reconsidering the curb appeal of a property he'd purchased on the Internet. He favored Bob with a sidelong glance.

Bob said: "What?"

"This is your for real, honest-to-God, *last* last chance to change your mind."

"Why would I do that?"

"Your wife's one of the undead, your friend got his leg eaten by a monster, your other friends are all missing, and we're here paying a house call on a guy you killed earlier today." Toomes shrugged. "Just another day at the office for me, but it might be a little much for some."

"I'm fine," Bob said. "Go."

Toomes eyed him a moment longer, then nodded and gave the door an experimental tug, followed by a harder one. It swung outward, revealing the bloodied, darkened waiting room that Bob had fled not long before. The vampire hunter peeked in and looked around, then led the way forward. Bloody footprints in the carpet showed the way to Zane's body. Toomes eyed them, then followed the sanguine trail to the examination room. The corpse lay where Bob had left it, sprawled on the table, head bashed in, clothes stiff with crusted gore. Toomes stared silently at the doctor for a few seconds. Standing there with his hands in the pockets of his trench coat, he looked like a flasher about to do his thing. Finally he said: "That's some nice work, Bob."

Bob, not sure how to properly accept what was apparently meant as a compliment, merely grunted.

"No, seriously. I'm impressed. You should be proud of yourself, taking him out and getting away alive."

"Dumb luck. And a tire iron. Can you tell if the Count has been here?"

"I don't think so. He would have taken the body with him."

"Taken it? What for?"

"How should I know? Eat it, put it in his fridge, make a lamp out of it, whatever. But he doesn't leave his special friends lying around where just anyone might find them."

"Okay. So do we just, like, hide and wait for him to show up?"

The vampire hunter didn't answer right away. Instead he raised his head and cocked it, as if listening. To what, Bob had no idea.

"Toomes? Are we going to lay an ambush for the Count?"

"Nope."

"Why not?"

From behind them, a dry, papery voice said: "Because what Mr. Toomes has *noticed*, and *you* have not—" The words broke devolved into a raspy chuckle before continuing. "—is that *I* have *already arrived*."

~~~~

After a few seconds of whatever it was Myra was doing, Margaret just collapsed, crumpling in on herself like an emptied juice pack. Chuck took a step forward, but Robin got there first and helped her sit up. The armless woman seemed disoriented, her gaze not quite focusing on anything.

Robin looked at Myra. "What happened?"

Myra didn't answer; she just fell over. Chuck lunged to catch her and failed. Too slow; he was always too slow. She hit the driveway forehead-first, with a solid *thunk* that would've made him very worried, if she had still been a human instead of a vampire goddess. He tripped over her and ended up sprawled on his face in between her and the others.

"Good God," Robin said. "Aren't we a bunch."

Chuck got to his hands and knees and crawled over to Myra,

ignoring the pain from an elbow that felt pretty badly scraped. "I don't think she's breathing."

"Was she breathing before?"

"Um. I don't know?" He reached out to touch her, but then her eyes opened and he scuttled back. She pushed herself up off the ground, rolled over, and sat up. She shook her head as if to clear it, ran her hands through her hair.

"Wow," she said. "That was a trip."

"Did you see anything?"

She slumped forward, cupping her face in her hands. He asked her the question again. She looked up at him and said: "Yeah. I saw stuff." Myra glanced at Margaret, who seemed to have recovered from her own swoon and was now regarding the two of them with an inscrutable gaze. "I saw Patrick."

"Who's Patrick?" Chuck said.

Ignoring the question, or maybe not even hearing it, Myra said: "I guess he watched a lot of television. He wasn't behaving himself, and our Dr. Margaret tried to have the TV removed from the lounge. That's when everything went to hell."

Chuck said, again, "Who's Patrick?"

"The building turned into *that*. This orderly, Baxter, turned into a monster and carried Margaret away. The yard sprouted a graveyard. God knows what else changed that I didn't see." To Margaret: "What happened last week, that you had to make up that schedule you were talking about? Was there a fight? Did Patrick start it? Did he finish it?"

Margaret squeaked and shrugged. "You know she can't answer those questions," Robin said.

"Would somebody *please* tell me who Patrick is?"

Myra turned back to Chuck. "He's a patient here. *Was* a patient. I met him. He had a spinning couch in a room full of televisions. Way better than just the one television he used to watch, right?"

"Seriously?"

"Seriously. They were playing all kinds of stuff. Shows. Movies. News. Bob. Five thousand channels, and everything on." She looked at the sky. "He's probably watching us right now."

"How could he be watching us?" Chuck said. He looked at the distant building. "You think he has a camera pointed out the window?"

"I don't think he needs a camera." She stood up, turned in a circle. "How about it, Patrick?" she yelled. "Are we putting on a good show?

Are you entertained?"

"Okay," Robin said, "Settle down. Let's think this through. You say this Patrick was a patient here? Margaret, is that right?"

She nodded.

"Okay. And there was some kind of, uh, argument, or whatever, about the television? And you tried to take it away?"

She hesitated, then nodded again.

"But that didn't work out, and Myra says that now he has five thousand TV screens and he's watching us for his amusement. Okay. Very nice. Good for him. But if he's the one making all the crazy happen, why would he be watching us? Pretty boring, watching a show you're controlling, isn't it?"

"When I met him, the way he was babbling, he really does think this is all a show," Myra said. "If he's doing it, I'm not sure he knows he's doing it."

Chuck, feeling like the others had left him several steps behind, said: "I don't understand. What do you think he's doing that he doesn't know he's doing?"

"This. All this shit that's been happening. When I was with Margaret, in there, after it happened, before we got carried out of the Retreat, I got a look at the television. It was a show inside a show inside a show, going on forever. I don't know if Margaret noticed it, but I did."

"What does that mean, though?"

"I think it might be, like, something he's projecting us into, or into *us*, if that makes sense. A dream. A mass hallucination. One we're all sharing."

"A dream." Chuck thought about that. "You mean it isn't really happening."

"That's usually how dreams work," Myra said.

"Usually," Robin said, her voice flat.

Myra cocked her head at Robin; to Chuck, it looked a little like the way Gwen's cat might look at a bug just before pouncing on it.

"I mean, *usually*, you're alone in your dream. Usually. But we're all together. I'm assuming here that you're all *you*, of course, and not just figments of my imagination. So ..." She trailed off.

"Go on."

"So where is everyone *else* who was in the Retreat when the shit hit the fan?"

For a moment nobody spoke.

Then Myra said, "Well, let's go knock on the door and find out."

~~~~

They started walking toward the Retreat. Myra led the way, with Chuck slightly behind her and Robin and Margaret bringing up the rear. She could sense them all back there, blobs of heat and blood and plasma, tottering along after their recent traumas. Margaret in particular remained a little unsteady on her feet; Robin helped her stay upright, kept her from falling too far behind. Myra sensed some sort of guilt at work in Robin's attentiveness, but wasn't sure what Robin had done—or thought she had done—that she needed to atone for. It wasn't as if Robin had lopped the woman's arms off with a machete. Had she? Hmm. Maybe she should take a wander through Robin's memories at some point, see what she was hiding in there.

She noticed that Chuck had picked up the pace to get next to her; he was clearly turning something over in his head, trying to figure out how to broach it. "Got a question, Chuck?"

"Uh-huh." He glanced back at Robin, as if afraid she would overhear. "So, this dream we're all in."

"If it is one."

"Right. Yeah. If it is one. But if it is … Do you think Gwen might still be okay? In real life?"

After a moment, she said: "I don't know what the rules are."

"Sure. Of course not. But this Patrick. If you, uh, deal with him, what happens then? Does that make everything go back to normal, do you think?"

"Deal with him?"

"Yeah. You know." He lowered his voice. "Kill him."

"I don't know. It might not do anything. It might fry all our brains. It might strand us all here forever."

"Or we might all wake up in the van and everything would be fine."

"Or we might all wake up in the van." She shrugged. "We just don't know. But I'm not prepared to just march in there and murder someone to find out."

"Murder? Gwen got *ripped apart* and *eaten*. By *zombies*."

"Yes. She did." Myra gave him a hard look, looked *into* him. "Do you want to kill Patrick because you think it'll get us out of here, or because you think it'll be revenge for what happened to Gwen?"

He didn't answer.

"That's what I thought. Look, Chuck, I understand where you're coming from. I do. And I'm not saying it won't come to that. Maybe it will. But we can't make that decision yet. So don't ask me to, all right?"

Chuck didn't look happy—of course he didn't—but he nodded and fell silent. Finally they reached the front entrance, where wide, cracked concrete steps swept up to a large, dark door in the very center of the vast brick face. Dozens of black windows glared unblinkingly down at them, without so much as the flutter of a curtain disturbing the stillness. Myra glanced at the sky. Still not the faintest whiff of dawn. When sunlight started to approach the horizon, she thought, she would smell it on the air.

Robin and Margaret caught up to them. Robin peered up at the building for a moment. "Creepy. I vote Myra checks it out."

Myra snorted and said, "Sure, make the vampire do the dangerous stuff." But she went, of course. If there were a threat to be found—and of course there would be—who better to face it? She took to the air, gliding up towards the top of the steps rather than bothering to climb them.

Behind her, she heard Robin say, "It's nice to have a vampire on the team. As long as it's a good vampire."

A good vampire. Myra wondered if Robin would say that with such confidence had he known how close she'd come to snacking on Chuck like a take-out burger when she'd been carrying him through the air.

She touched down lightly in front of the main entrance and tried the door. Locked. She pulled it open anyway, snapping the bolt. That ought to impress the yokels. The lobby beyond was dark, shadowy, deserted; it looked as if it had been unused for years. Dust and cobwebs lay thick on the chairs, the receptionist's desk, the carpet. The paint on the walls was flaking badly, the plaster crumbling in spots, showing old lath beneath. It reminded Myra of the zombies, with their bones poking out where the covering flesh had rotted or been torn away.

She went inside. Abandoned though it seemed, the place hummed with energy; Patrick was nearby, broadcasting on every frequency. It lent credence to the theory that he was projecting all of this at them. It also made her head hurt. She had hoped, in a vague sort of way, that she would be able to locate him the same way she had located Chuck and the others, but now she knew that wouldn't work. He was the electromagnetic spectrum. He was everywhere.

The others arrived, evidently encouraged by the fact that she hadn't run out screaming. They stood in a little clump near the door, looking around with their eyes, oblivious to the power coursing through the room. Margaret moved a bit away from the others, going to inspect a painting on the wall, a large portrait of a somewhat pinched-looking man in a dark suit standing in front of the table of what appeared to be a corporate boardroom. Some Retreat bigwig, Myra supposed. She realized that he looked familiar. Maybe she had seen him when she'd been riding around in Margaret's head? She stared at the picture, forgetting why she was here. Something about the painted eyes didn't let her turn away.

Without warning, just for a second, the portrait shifted. The man's face changed, his satisfied smile switching to a sharp-toothed leer, his eyes going dark, then lighting up red. Dizziness swept over her and she swooned, almost fell. She stumbled over to the painting as if being pulled, leaned up against it. She could swear she felt a hand come out of it, touch her shoulder, and withdraw.

"Myra?" Chuck's voice was muffled. She barely heard him over the sudden roaring in her ears.

When she raised her head to look at him, all she saw was red, as though peering through a crimson veil.

~~~~

The Count stood in the hallway, holding a limp Kyle over his shoulder like a rucksack. Bob couldn't tell if Kyle was dead or had been bitten or what, but he wasn't struggling.

"Nothing to *say*, Mr. Toomes?" The Count cocked his head. "You *disappoint* me. After all the *stories* I've heard about you from the gibbering *fiends* you've terrorized, I expected something more *interesting* from our meeting. Repartee. Banter. An *insult*, at the very *least*. Yet you do not *move*. You do not *speak*. Do I *terrify* you so?"

"Oh, yeah," Toomes said. "I'm petrified."

Chuckling, the Count turned his gaze on Bob. "And *you*. I caught *this* fool crawling in the *dirt* like an *insect*, trying to *follow* your little duo. He *told* me he *knows* you, *Bob*."

"Never seen him before in my life," Bob said.

The Count sneered, unimpressed with the obvious lie. He looked at Bob, then at Kyle, then grinned toothily and flung Kyle at them. Toomes ducked, evading the human projectile, but Bob was not so agile and ended up on the floor with Kyle on top of him. His shotgun went off, blowing a hole in the wall to his Bob's left. He could see a little bit of the waiting room through the new opening. As he struggled to extricate himself from the deadweight that was Kyle, Toomes went on the attack, firing an ash-and-holy-water crossbow bolt into the Count's shoulder. It smoked faintly where it sunk into in his flesh. Toomes advanced, crucifix extended, driving the hissing vampire ahead of him.

"If I'd known you would go down this easy," Toomes said, "I would have come after you years ago."

The hiss changed to a sound like a brittle, rusted hinge swinging in a cold, dry wind. It took Bob a moment to realize this was laughter. "Do I, Mr. Toomes?" he said. "Do I go down *easy*, like that *expensive Scotch* you love so well?"

Bob finally freed himself through a combination of worming and shoving, but before he could stand up and join the fray, he noticed that Kyle's eyes had opened. He opened his mouth to tell Kyle to scurry off and take cover, but before he could say anything, Kyle head-butted him in the face. Stars exploded in Bob's head. He fumbled for the shotgun, but Kyle kicked it through the opening and into the waiting room, out of easy reach. The Count cackled.

Toomes, not turning, said: "What's going on back there, Bob?"

"Little problem," Bob said, still on his back, trying to fend off a flurry of blows.

"Perhaps it is your new friend *Bob* who goes down like *whiskey*," the Count said, "and not *I*."

"Maybe you both do."   Toomes produced a crucifix-handled dagger from somewhere on his person and stabbed it into the Count's abdomen. The vampire howled. Kyle, using his hands like a gymnast on the pommel horse, flipped himself over Bob, slid between Toomes's legs, and yanked the blade out of his master's stomach. A ribbon of thick black fluid came with it. Kyle tried to reverse the weapon and use it against its owner, but Toomes smacked his wrist with a wooden mallet to knock the blade aside, then used Kyle's shoulders as a platform to launch himself at the Count's face. Now he had a handful of dripping garlic—how did he always manage to get hold of exactly what he needed, exactly when he needed it?—which he shoved into his foe's shadowed eye sockets. The Count snarled and fell back, catching Toomes's rush with his clawed hands. The two of them tumbled through the office door in a tangle of fists and noise and acrid smoke.

Bob, the slow and stupid sidekick, had just barely regained his footing while all that was going on. He moved forward to help Toomes, but Kyle blocked his way like a speed bump. A speed bump with a dagger.

"Come on, Kyle," Bob said. "You don't really want to do this."

"Don't tell me what I want to do," Kyle said as he thrust the blackened steel towards Bob's groin. "You don't even know me!" Bob jumped back and Kyle came at him, brandishing the weapon in one hand while scuttling on one leg and one arm like an angry, demented, mutilated crab. Unnerved by his crazed speed and contortionist pose, Bob retreated into the examination room, slammed the door, and thumbed the lock. A moment later, Kyle began pounding on the other side. "Bob!" he shouted. "Hey Bob! It's me, Kyle! Help! Let me in! There's a *vampire* out here!"

"Kyle! Come on, man! Think about what you're doing!"

Bang! "I don't need to think anymore, Bob!" *Bang!* "I've got the Count now!" *Bang!* "He thinks for me!" *Bang bang!*

Bob kicked away the stool where the doctor sat, tossed his satchel onto the counter, and rifled through it, looking for something useful. Garlic and crosses and holy water and seriously, what the fuck, Toomes? Where were the weapons? None of this anti-vampire crap would do shit against Kyle, still out there pounding on the door like a demented knife salesman who wouldn't take no for an answer. Bob fingered the crucifix around his neck, took it off, hefted it. Heavy. Maybe he could club Kyle over the head with it and knock him out until he came to his senses.

Bob went to the shuddering door and flattened himself against the wall next to it. After one or two more hits, the door flew inward. Splinters of the broken jamb spun across the room. Bob leaped into the doorway, the sturdy cross raised over his head. But Kyle wasn't there. Where had he gone? It was a *hallway*. There was nowhere to—

"Hi Bob!" Kyle dropped down from above the door, where he had somehow wedged himself between the walls, and planted a foot in Bob's stomach. He staggered backwards as Kyle scurried into the room, brandishing the dagger. Recovering his balance, Bob swung the crucifix in a wild arc, hitting nothing. Kyle slashed with the blade and Bob jumped back, just barely escaping disembowelment. He lost his footing and stumbled, giving Kyle the opportunity to deliver a vicious kick to the side of his head. He stumbled to the side, hit the wall, and slid to the floor. When the stars cleared from his vision he saw that Kyle had shoved Zane mostly off the examination bed and taken his place, where he perched, glaring down at Bob like a scruffy one-legged gargoyle. He was playing pinfinger with the dagger and one of Zane's hands, which he held in place with his remaining foot.

Bob stared up at him, feeling slack-jawed and stupid.

"Look at you," Kyle said. "What a pathetic performance, getting your ass kicked by a dude whose leg just got ripped off."

He had somehow managed to hang onto was the big crucifix. Toomes had said it had a secret. Something extra. What was it? Something he could use now? It sure would have been nice if Toomes had fucking deigned to fucking clue him in as to what the fuck the fucking secret was.

"Come on, Bob. Say something."

Bob ran his fingers over the crucifix, hoping it would yield a clue to its alleged enigma. He thought he felt the Jesus figure slide a little bit. Maybe it was just loose. Maybe it did something. What was it Toomes had told him? *Jesus saves*, right?

"What's the matter, Bob? Did you forget how to talk? Did I kick you too hard?" Kyle's voice was full of mock concern. "Come on, think. What day is it? Who's the president? What's your wife's name?"

Bob looked up sharply.

"Oh, that got your attention, didn't it? I'll give you a hint. Her name's Myra. Hey, you know the Count fucked her, right? Maybe after you're dead he'll let me fuck her too."

Bob put the crucifix down on the floor and pretended to use that hand to push himself up, while surreptitiously transferring most of his weight to his other hand. "You little toad-faced bastard—"

Kyle grinned and pounced, stabbing downward with the dagger.

Bob pivoted, raised the crucifix, pointed the long piece at Kyle, and—praying something would happen—pushed the little Christ figure forward.

A highly polished wooden spike popped out of the bottom of the cross, impaling Kyle at an upward angle through the diaphragm. Kyle's dagger thrust went wide, opening a thin cut along Bob's shoulder instead of sliding between his ribs. Kyle made a strange grunting noise and scrabbled at the cross. Bob threw him off and retreated to the other side of the room, putting some distance between the two of them. He had somehow held onto the crucifix; he didn't remember yanking it out, but there it was in his hands. Kyle was still alive, but didn't seem to be in any condition to continue fighting. He had righted himself, pressing both hands to the hole in his chest. Bright red blood oozed from between his fingers. Not taking his gaze off of Kyle, Bob slid the Christ figure forward again. The spike retracted into the cross. Where had Toomes had picked up this pneumatic trinket? Not from a vampire's lair, he was sure. Maybe he had machined it in a shop in his basement.

"Hey, Bob." Kyle's voice was thin, weak.

"Yeah?" Bob said.

"The Count … is really gonna be … pissed at you … when he …" Kyle trailed off into a gurgle; his eyes became glazed, unfocused.

Bob detected movement in the doorway, and glanced that way, hoping to see Toomes. He didn't. It was the Count. He didn't look nearly as composed as he once had. The skin of his face was burned in a pattern that suggested an acid splash, probably inflicted by holy water. The creature's black cloak was rent and torn, and further darkened by inky fluid. The crossbow bolt still stuck out of his shoulder. One of his eyes was missing, the socket a smoking, blackened hole; Bob thought a clove of garlic might still be in there, fused and bubbling. The Count's remaining eye, red and baleful, swiveled as it took in the scene.

"I think he's pretty pissed at me already," Bob told the dead man.

~~~~

Chuck knew they were in trouble when Myra turned and showed him that other face of hers.

He grabbed Robin and moved her around behind him, began backing toward the door. Margaret had moved a little farther into the lobby. She seemed to understand that something was wrong; she took half a step forward and Myra was instantly in her way, hissing, fingers splayed like talons reaching for prey.

"Myra!" She spun on him, hands curled into claws, mouth full of sharp little teeth surrounding the four twisted daggers of her canines.

Okay, he had her attention. Now what?

Babble.

"Myra, think," Chuck said. "You don't want to do—*shit!*"

Margaret had tried to scurry around Myra's back to reach Chuck and Robin, but the attempt was an abject failure; Myra caught her without turning or even looking in her direction. She hauled the doctor in close, spun her around, grabbed her with both hands, and moved her into the classic vampire-victim pose, but she didn't clamp down with those jaws; not yet. She was still looking at Chuck. Why didn't she bite? What was she waiting for? Did she want him to talk her out of it?

Chuck raised his hands, palms up. "Come on, Myra," he said. "Let her go."

Myra cocked her head at him like an animal. Margaret hung limp in her grasp. Chuck didn't think she was hurt, but she probably feared that any movement would prompt Myra to finish the kill. So did he.

"I don't think Myra's in there anymore," Robin whispered.

Myra seemed to hear that. Her dusky eyes narrowed.

"Yes she is," Chuck said. "You're in there, aren't you, Myra?"

She tossed Margaret aside and lunged at Chuck, but before she reached him Robin gave him a powerful shove out of the way. She was a lot stronger than she looked, but nowhere near strong enough to resist when Myra plowed into her and carried her out the front door. Chuck righted himself and scrambled after them. They were struggling on the top step, at the edge of the big staircase that led down to the driveway. Myra was on top—no surprise—and it looked like she was getting ready to take a chunk out of Robin's throat. Chuck grabbed her and tried to yank her off, but it was like trying to rip a tree out of the ground. She easily reversed his grip and flung him across the landing. He tumbled head over heels along the crumbling brick before coming to rest up against the Retreat. He was on his back, legs vertical, looking up the wall toward the roof. The building seemed to be leaning over him, having itself a good laugh. A moment later Myra was on him, all glowing eyes and slavering fangs, dripping icy saliva onto his face as she pinned him to the ground. He could see Robin out of the corner of his eye. She was still alive; Myra had abandoned her to come after him.

Robin got shakily to her feet. Myra whirled to Robin and hissed. Then Margaret appeared, peeking out of the entrance, and Myra oriented on her. Her body tensed. A newborn predator, she seemed to have difficulty focusing on her prey, was easily distracted from one target by the actions of another. That was the only thing keeping them alive at the moment. But Chuck didn't want her going after the others. This was his responsibility. He had told them she could be trusted. Besides, she was *his* vampire goddess. If anybody was going to feed her, it would be *him*.

He stretched and tilted his head to the side, exposing as much of his neck as he could. Myra's attention returned to him. She made a funny noise deep in her throat, something between a choke and a growl. She still didn't move to bite him. What was she waiting for?

He reached up, grabbed the side of her head, and pulled her down towards his throat. He almost had an orgasm when her cold lips touched his skin.

And when they parted and he felt her teeth, he did.

~~~~

The Count lurched forward, limping slightly. Toomes had clearly inflicted a lot of damage; but Toomes was not here.

"*You.*" The vampire pointed a bony finger at Bob. "You *killed* my *good servant* Zane. You *persuaded* Toomes to *move* against me. And *now* you have *killed* this *fool* as well. Yet *you* will *serve* me. You will serve me *well*."

Bob raised the crucifix, holding it in front of him like a shield. "Stop," he said.

The Count stopped.

"Sit. Stay. Good dog."

"You call *me* a dog? You will *whine* and *grovel* before me. You will *lick* my *heel*. I will *kick* you, and you will *thank me* and ask me to *do it again*. I will *take* your *wife* in front of you again and again, and you will *stand* and *watch* and *masturbate* like the *pathetic creature* you are."

"I hear a lot of talking." Bob took a step forward, stretching out his arm, moving the cross closer to the vampire. "I don't see any doing."

"You think that *trinket* will *protect* you? I do not *fear* it."

"No? You still have that arrow in your shoulder. Doesn't it hurt? Why haven't you pulled it out? Is it because the holy water burns your lily white skin when you touch it?"

The Count's lips twisted into a snarl.

"Too bad I killed Kyle, huh? Otherwise he could have pulled it out for you, since you can't do it yourself. So who's pathetic now, one-eye?"

Dark, dusky color—other peoples' blood, Bob supposed—flooded the Count's face. "*I* will *show you* what *I* can *do*." He reached up, closing skeletal fingers around the protruding shaft. Smoke rose from his hand, just like it had before. Bob took the opportunity to lunge forward, jabbing the end of the heavy crucifix at the vampire's chest while sliding the Christ figure forward. The mechanism inside fired without a sound, ejecting the stake with enough force to separate the Count's ribs and pierce his heart. The Count screeched and his pale hands clutched at the gilded metal. Wisps of sulfurous vapor rose from his fingers as they burned. Bob let go of the device and scrambled away as the Count staggered back, trying to pull the crucifix out but seemingly unable to get a grip on it. He was starting to fall apart; bits of his skin flaked off, and his flesh sagged as if melting.

"*You* will *die* for *this*," the Count said, his voice a hissing gurgle. "Your *blood* will *flow* like a *river!*"

The bag Toomes had given him lay on the counter near Kyle, half open, the material darkened by the fluid from broken vials of holy water. Bob darted for it. The Count flew at him like a flapping shadow, long arms raised, black fingernails sharp as razors. Bob's outstretched hand found the strap. He grabbed it and flung the satchel at the Count. It caught the vampire's head like a hood, and immediately tightened over the skull as the blessed water did its work. Sulfurous steam bloomed from the fabric; noisome stuff oozed out beneath it, waxy molten flesh forming a pallid cascade on the creature's dark clothes. He wailed and gnashed his teeth, fangs like daggers scissoring through the wet fabric. His urbane facade shed, the Count became a blind, raging, flailing monster, swinging his arms wildly. Even now, Bob thought, one of those blows would be enough to kill him. He dove behind the examination table, scuttled along the floor, and grabbed an overturned stool he found near the wall. Rising up, he smashed it over the Count's, striking head again and again until the shape inside the bag had been pounded from a sphere to a flattened mushroom.

The Count finally fell, melting away to nothing, leaving behind his sodden black cloak and the golden crucifix and the cross-fletched arrow. Bob collapsed against the wall and slid to the floor and lay there panting for a little while.

When he finally thought he'd be able to move without puking his guts out, he stood and went to give the Count's cloak a kick. It flew across the room and smacked into the wall with a wet *splat*, stuck there a moment, then slurped to the floor. But it left a stain on the wall, a blood-black stain in the pattern of a face: Narrow eyes, flattened nose, wide thin lips.

As Bob stared, horrified, the lips on the wall curled into a sneer, then moved. A whisper of a voice tickled his ears.

It said, *You think I am done, Bob? You think I am finished? With you? With your wife? With this world? Think again, Bob. Think again.*

Unnerved, Bob picked up the stool and bashed the wall-face with it over and over again, until the paint and plaster was gone.

~~~~

Meat. They were all meat, all blood. Meat and blood. Blood and meat. And Myra was so, so hungry. She should feed. She wanted to feed. She *needed* to feed.

She had been a little disoriented at first, couldn't decide who to start with, and they kept *talking* at her, bleating like sheep. But now she had Chuck pinned, and he was practically begging for him to bite her. He wanted it. Of course he did. Sheep wanted to be eaten. They knew it was what they deserved. Robin would be next. Then Margaret. Then she would go back and find Bob and give him what she knew he wanted.

Chuck tried to pull her head down. She let him. Lips on skin. Teeth on skin. She felt him shudder. He was going to die happy. But before she could sink the bite, someone jammed a spear through Myra's heart. At least that was what it felt like. Her limbs went weak, weak as a baby's; and everything went dark around her, the brilliance of the night gone, replaced by inky blackness. Hands grabbed her from behind and somehow pulled her off of Chuck, threw her to the side. She rolled to a floppy stop at the edge of the stairs, lying on her back, looking up into a sky that had been stripped of the black light she'd gotten used to seeing. The Count's voice faded from her head, swirled and vanished like crud down the toilet. The moonlight had been silenced. All she heard now was the faint, lifeless whisper of the wind whisking the trees and grass and whistling through the high-up eaves of the Retreat.

As her senses returned she saw that the others had gathered near her, but not *too* near; Robin and Chuck stood together, with Margaret behind, peering between their shoulders. Robin and Chuck were whispering to each other, but she couldn't hear the words. What had happened? Why wasn't the moonlight talking to her? Why couldn't she hear the words? She could *always* hear the words. She pushed herself up onto one elbow. The others took a wary step back with a unison that would have been comical if Myra were in the mood to appreciate it. As it was, though, just sitting up made her feel dizzy, like she needed to puke. She put a hand to her chest. The pain was beginning to fade. But she felt so weak, so drained, so … *human.*

She rubbed her temples and said: "Ouch."

"*Ouch?*" Robin's voice was hard. "*You* don't get to say ouch. Not after what you just did."

"What … What did I do?"

"Don't you remember?" Chuck's voice sounded hoarse. Why? He was covered with small cuts and scrapes and his pants were stained like he'd wet himself. Robin had a bloody ear and elbow and one hand pressed to her stomach. Whatever had happened, they obviously blamed her for it.

"No."

"You went nuts and tried to kill us," Robin said. "Remember now?"

"I'm sorry," she said. "I don't. Not really. But I think … The Count … In the painting … He got back inside my head, and I—"

"Is he still there?"

"No. He's gone." She stood up, swooned, nearly fell. Nobody

tried to catch her this time. They all backed off again, moving as if they were a single unit. She recovered her balance on her own. "Look, I know you guys must be freaked out, but I'm back to normal now. I think … I think the Count is dead. I think someone killed him."

"Great," Robin said. "He sounds like a dick. How do we know you won't come after us again on your own authority?"

"Because I can't. I'm just Myra now. No more vampire powers. Look. See? No more flying." She hopped into the air, hoping against all her senses that she would still be able to soar; but of course she couldn't, and instead landed hard on her unsteady feet. Bad move. This time she really did fall down. The others looked on suspiciously while she picked herself up, as if this were some elaborate ruse to fool them. They were paranoid, but only because everything was out to get them. "All right," she said, rubbing a bruised knee. "What do you want me to do?"

Chuck and Robin looked at each other and had a hastily whispered conversation; Robin kept looking towards the small cemetery, and when their huddle broke up, she pointed at it.

"You want me to go in there?" Myra said.

They nodded.

"And then what?"

"Climb the tombstone with the cross on it," Robin said.

Myra peered at the grave marker in question. It reminded her of a chess piece, with a slender fluted column and a flared cap with a cross on top. Dead ivy clung to the bottom like skeletal fingers. "Climb it? Really?"

"You don't have to sit on top of it. Just get high enough to touch the cross." Robin folded her arms. "If you can do that, then I'll believe you."

Myra said: "Chuck? Margaret?"

Chuck nodded. The armless doctor just looked at her. A united front. And so Myra turned and staggered down the steps and tottered off down the driveway toward the graveyard. She supposed their demand made sense, like in the movies when people would make suspected vampires grab a cross or look in a mirror to prove they were human. But nobody had a cross, nobody had a mirror, and sure as shit no one wanted to go exploring the Retreat looking for either.

She reached the spot where she had battled the zombies. No way would she be able to do that now. She hoped she hadn't left any with the capacity to move. She wished now she hadn't dropped the tire iron, but she would never find it again in the tall grass. She passed by Gwen, or what remained of her, lying in the various spots the undead had dropped her. Myra tried not to look at the pieces. She cut over to the graveyard. Once there, she circled the fence until she found a partially fallen gate, then clambered over it to get inside, then walked up to the designated tombstone. It was slightly taller than she was, the cross on top bigger than she'd thought. She really *could* have sat on it, if she wanted to, and could muster the strength to drag her sorry ass up there. Which she couldn't.

A glance up the driveway showed her that the others stood near the top of the steps, watching her from the high ground, shadowy figures in the moonlight. Fifteen minutes ago, she could have picked out every freckle on their skin from here. Of course, after doing that, she might have tried to kill them. Tradeoffs, you know? She sighed, took hold of the ridge around the crown of the tombstone, and hauled herself up onto the base, then stretched up far enough to drape her arms over the cross. She pushed herself a little higher onto the marker to make sure they could see her properly, then hung there, exhausted, clinging to the crosspiece. She was still wiped out from her sudden return to humanity; or maybe being human always felt this way, and she only realized it now because she had briefly been so much more.

Suddenly she felt the marker shift beneath her like a loose tooth; her unaccustomed weight up towards the top must have unbalanced it. Where once she could have simply sprung off it and soared away, now she had no choice but to ride it down as it tipped over. The ground gave way beneath it. She fell in a shower of earth and rocks, tumbling head over heels before landing flat on her back in some sort of pit, looking up at the sky through a frame of dirt and overhanging grass. The tombstone slid down on top of her, pinning her up to the shoulder, while loose soil and debris and more than a few old bones covered her up to her waist.

Well, look at this. Saved from being a vampire, returned to being a human, and now her life was going to be snuffed out by a cross.

Oh, the irony.

Inside Underground

WEAPONS. HE NEEDED more weapons. Real ones this time.

Bob started with the dagger, tucking it between his belt and his pants, as if it were a screwdriver or a hammer. He couldn't bring himself fish the trick cross out of the oozing pile of goo and muck that had once been the Count, though. Leaving it there, he went out into the hallway, reached through the hole in the wall, and retrieved the shotgun. Then he went looking for Toomes. He found the man lying in disarticulated pieces in the doctor's office; the Count had been pretty busy exacting revenge for his injuries while Bob had been mixing it up with Kyle. He wondered if Kyle had already been the vampire's slave when they'd met him on the road. Probably. He should have just let Toomes off Kyle like he'd wanted to. Then things would have turned out very differently here. Probably.

Lesson learned.

Toomes's wrist crossbow lay near the door. Bob carefully picked up the weapon and strapped it to his own forearm. It hardly got in the way at all. He had watched Toomes load the thing—it snapped back with a lever, had a nice slot for loading the arrows, and fired with the pull of a trigger—so if he could locate some ammunition, it might come in handy, even though he would probably miss anything that he couldn't shoot point-blank in the face.

A quick search turned up the vampire hunter's satchel under the desk. He opened it and started rummaging around inside, and immediately sliced his hand on something sharp. Cursing, he turned the bag over and dumped its contents out onto the bloody floor. "Cut me *now*, motherfucker," he muttered, shifting the stuff around with a booted foot. He found bolts for the small crossbow, a bunch of stakes and garlic, a wooden mallet, another cross, lots of broken holy water vials, some throwing stars, a case of shotgun shells. He didn't have much use for most of that stuff, but the shells? Those would be his. He shoved the box into his own pack, as well as the mallet and a few of the stakes and the cross and all the garlic, just in case there were more vampires running around that he didn't know about. He hefted a throwing star, and cut himself again on one of its many points. Yeah, he had no idea what the fuck to do with those. He shouldn't have slept through ninja class.

The bag fully exploited, Bob moved on to pillage the remainder of Toomes's body. The man still wore his sword belt, but the sword wasn't in it. Bob found it hilt-first behind a bookshelf. He gingerly took hold of the wickedly sharp blade and slid the weapon out, somehow managing not to slice his own fingers off. He took a couple of experimental swings and found it manageable. He couldn't wield it with any degree of skill, of course, but he figured not too many things would approach a guy who was wildly waving a blade around. He unbuckled the belt and tugged it free of Toomes's torso. It was a bit big for his own waist. He tried to use the dagger to poke a few extra holes in the thick leather, but that didn't work so he just secured it as best he could. It sagged over his hips and the tip of the scabbard tended to drag, like he was a kid who had gotten into his warrior-king father's things. Well, he'd just have to deal with it.

Having looted everything serviceable, Bob stood, slung his bag over his shoulder, and headed for the front door. He paused before opening it, taking in his dim reflection in the glass: Crossbow on one wrist, shotgun in his left hand, sword at his hip, dagger in his belt, bag full of stinky garlic and pointy objects. He looked like an honest-to-God vampire hunter now, didn't he? Toomes two-point-oh. He spared a backward glance towards where the bodies lay, touched his forehead in a final salute, and moved out onto Dr. Zane's porch. The sky was black, still in the grip of the deepest part of the night. How much longer until morning? There would be a morning, right? There had been a sunset, so there had to be a sunrise, didn't there?

He was having a little trouble convincing himself of that.

Bob hadn't counted on Toomes's death; he'd expected to follow the vampire hunter's lead, to be told where to go and what to do and how to do it. To be the sidekick, not the hero. On his own, he had no clue what his next move should be. Myra was still out there somewhere, but how could he track her down? Maybe he could find Paltruck again, collect some more cryptic advice. So far the little guy's suggestions hadn't worked out all that well, but at least he *had* suggestions. It beat drifting in the current like a log. He headed for the woods, hoping the sprite would put in an appearance; sure enough, when he reached the path, he found Paltruck sitting on a moldering stump just inside the woods, his posture suggestive of a visit to the toilet. The only thing he needed was a magazine. *Pinecones Today*, maybe.

Paltruck looked up at Bob's approach. "Look at you," he said. "Loaded for bear. Ready to take on an army."

"If I have to," Bob said.

"Bravado! I love it. This isn't the Bob I first met." The small creature looked around. "Where's Toomes?"

After a moment, Bob said: "The Count got him."

"He did?"

Bob nodded.

"Oh. That's too bad." Paltruck kicked his heels against the stump. "He used to bring me things. When he would visit."

"He did? Like what."

"Doesn't matter." Then: "He didn't suffer much, did he?"

"Um, I don't think so," Bob lied. "I evened it up. I finished the job."

"Finished it how?"

"By killing the Count."

"Ah," Paltruck said. "I thought I felt something foul in the air. Must've been the Count's spirit passing by."

Bob wondered where Paltruck thought the spirit had been going. Maybe back to Route 28, to hitch a ride to warmer climes. "Good riddance," he said.

"Riddance? You wish. I said passing *by*, not passing *on*. Spirits like his have a way of hanging around to cause trouble."

Bob didn't like the sound of that at all. He decided not to mention the part where the Count had turned into a talking wall tattoo; the look on Paltruck's face was grave enough already. "Do you have any idea where Myra is?" he said. "Is she back to normal now that I killed the Count?"

"*Normal.* Such a relative concept." Paltruck rubbed his little hands together. "The wind tells me there was a big commotion up on the mountain, near the Retreat. She was part of it."

"The wind told you that?"

"Yep! You can learn a lot from the wind, if you listen to it."

"Uh, okay, sure," Bob said. He didn't think listening to the wind was on his list of skills. "Did the wind tell you what the commotion was, exactly?"

Paltruck shook his head. "The wind outside doesn't talk to the wind inside. There's a barrier, see. Not much crosses it."

A failure to communicate. Why was Bob not surprised? "All right. So how do I get there from here?"

The sprite pointed with a stubby finger. "Straight up the road there. You can't miss it. Just watch out for the zombies and stuff."

"Zombies? Stuff? What kind of stuff?"

"Better get going or you'll miss all the fun."

"Paltruck, what—"

"That's all I can tell you. Anything else would be spoilers."

"Are you kidding me? *Spoilers?*"

"Can't give them out. It's not allowed."

"What if I point my crossbow at you?" Bob did so.

"That would only work if I thought you might use it."

Bob sighed and lowered the weapon.

"Hey, it was worth a try." Paltruck stood up and patted him on the shoulder. The only reason he could reach that high was because of the extra boost provided by the stump. "You looked super dangerous. If I didn't know you were bluffing, I'm sure I would have been very intimidated."

"You're just saying that."

"Suit yourself. Anyway you really don't have time to stand around trying to pry information out of me. You need to get going. Follow the road. It'll take you up the mountain."

"To the Retreat."

"Right. To the Retreat."

"And Myra will be there?"

"Oh, absolutely," Paltruck said. "There's a new show starting up, and believe me, that woman is going to be a star."

~~~~

For the first second or two after the graveyard swallowed Myra, Chuck and Robin just stood there gawking at the place where she had been. Then Chuck realized that the ground was collapsing in a line, a ragged dark crevice, a tunnel with the roof caving in, running straight toward their position. The two of them exchanged a glance, and then they bolted; or rather, Robin bolted. Chuck lumbered, and was caught when the stairway cracked up the middle, crumbled, and caved in on itself. He fell in a shower of mortar and broken bricks. He landed hard on his backside, scraped and battered but not really injured otherwise.

Chuck got to his feet, shaking ruddy dust out of his hair and clothes, and looked around. He was at the bottom of a rectangular pit, with walls of loose dirt and rubble and a floor of packed earth strewn with broken fragments of the steps he had until recently been standing on. A narrow, roughly carved trench, maybe five feet wide and twice that deep, exited from the side of the pit that faced the cemetery. Apparently something had dug through the earth from the building to the graveyard, and when the large tombstone had tipped over it triggered a collapse of the entire burrow.

What sort of creature or creatures would dig a secret tunnel connecting the graveyard and the Retreat? Nothing he wanted to meet.

He got bumped from behind and whirled, flattening himself against the wall, but it was only Margaret. She looked even filthier than before, thanks to the new layer of white and red particulates that had settled on her. She must've gotten caught in the collapse, too, and had managed to ride it to the bottom without getting hurt. Both of them were having lucky nights. Yeah, so fucking lucky.

From the foot or two of stairway on the left, which had escaped the collapse, Robin's head appeared, peering over the edge at them. "Everybody okay down there?" she said.

Margaret nodded. Chuck said: "We're peachy. How are you?"

"Well, I'm not in a hole, so there's that." She looked the pit over. "Do you think you can climb out?"

Chuck tested the steep earthen wall. Crumbly and unstable, and made even more treacherous by all the broken bricks and chunks of mortar. He shook his head. "Not a chance."

"Okay." She looked at the Retreat, then in the direction of the graveyard. "Stay put for a minute. I'm going to run the length, see what it looks like, check on the ex-vampire."

"Yeah, sure," Chuck said. "We'll be right here."

Robin nodded. Her head disappeared. He heard her light footsteps on the stairs, then on the gravel, and then there was silence, except for his own breathing and the faint skittering of stones where the walls were still collapsing a little. He looked at Margaret. "I don't know where she thinks we might go," he told her. Margaret shrugged.

A section of the Retreat's foundation chose that exact moment to give way, cinderblocks clattering inward to reveal a dark opening into the basement, or whatever sort of subterranean hell lay beneath the building. A wash of fetid, smoky air emerged and rolled over them, along with a fresh cloud of cement dust. Chuck waved it away from his face like a cloud of flies, then crept over to inspect the opening. The mortar in that area looked to have been deliberately scraped away, the blocks stacked up into an unsecured barrier. Whatever had dug the tunnel had, apparently, rebuilt the wall, but left it easily disassembled. He was surprised it hadn't fallen apart immediately after the collapse. Chuck looked at Margaret, who shrugged. She had no clue who or what had done this, either. But now he had an answer as to where they might go, anyway.

Robin returned, breathless and flushed, her head poking over the side of the pit. Her gaze flicked to the hole in the basement, then back to him. "I have bad news, and I have worse news," she said. "The bad news is that there's no easy way out of there. Uh, except for that hole in the wall. Did you do that?"

"No, it just happened on its own. What's the worse news?"

"The worse news is that Myra is half-buried in crap and having trouble breathing. You need to get to her as soon as you can."

"Oh." Chuck looked at the trench that exited from the side of the pit opposite the Retreat. "That way?"

"Yeah. While you're doing that, I'll go inside, look for a rope or something that I can lower down to pull you guys out with."

"Margaret can't hold onto a rope."

"We'll tie it around her waist. Once you and Myra are up, we can haul her out."

Chuck rubbed the back of his head. "I don't like it. You shouldn't go in there alone."

"There's not much choice. You can't climb out, I'd rather not climb in, and Fang-Face Airways has been grounded." She stood, looking at the Retreat.

"Robin, don't—"

"You can't stop me. There's no time to argue." She stood. "Go help Myra. She's in trouble."

"Aren't we all," Chuck muttered, watching Robin head up the steps towards the Retreat.

~~~~

While Chuck and Margaret started picking their way along the collapsed tunnel in search of Myra, Robin stood up and looked at the Retreat or——as she had started to think of it——the Asylum. It seemed to have gotten bigger since their abortive first attempt to explore it. Was it her imagination, or had the wings sprouted a few extra vertical floors, stretched a few hundred extra horizontal yards? In this nuthouse of a world, she supposed, anything could happen. Going in was reckless, but she didn't have a better plan at the moment for getting the others out of the hole they were in.

At the top of the stairs she peeked into the lobby; she hadn't gotten that good a look at it before Myra had gone nuts and attacked them. Two large doors exited from it, one on either side, each with a small, square, metal-screened window, through which she could see long, dim corridors. Residential wings, she thought. A wide, solid, wooden door was near the back left corner; enough was left of a broken wall sign to indicate it had been a unisex bathroom. A final door, smaller than the others, stood opposite the entrance, behind a reception desk. She supposed that must lead to an administrative office of some sort. Everything was dead silent and deserted; this didn't make her any less suspicious of the place or its intentions. And it *did* have intentions. She was sure of it.

Robin stepped inside and waited a moment. Nothing happened. Slightly emboldened, she moved forward. She went and stood in front of the portrait for a minute, the one Myra had been staring at just before she went crazy and attacked them. A plaque underneath it said *Edward B. Collins, Director*. He had a pinched and hungry expression that she didn't like, not the sort of self-satisfied aura you were used to seeing on congratulatory paintings of bigwigs. The eyes were a little creepy, like he was aware of her scrutiny. She felt an urge to cover the frame with a cloth. She turned her back on it and headed over to take a peek into the bathroom. It was dark in there, dusty, the fixtures dirty and disused. A side door labeled *Maintenance* stood in the wall to her right. It had no knob or handle on this side, just a metal push-plate and a keyed deadbolt. She gave it a shove. Locked. She withdrew and went to the reception desk. On top of it she saw a telephone, a calendar pad, and a visitor sign-in book, open, with a pen lying in the middle. She picked up the telephone. No dial tone, of course. She hung it up and eyed the book. It had columns for the date, the time in and time out, your name, and the name of the patient you were visiting. The last entry was from earlier today; the last visitor was an Robert Toomes, who had come to see a patient named Patrick Toomes.

Patrick. Hmm. Interesting.

She checked all the items on the desk; none had a key hidden underneath. The pad was scrawled with disturbing doodles that seemed different every time she glanced at it. She turned it face-down. Rifling the few desk drawers turned up nothing except thumbtacks, sticky note pads, a few more pens, and a spent emery board. She found a small first-aid cabinet, locked. Well, there wouldn't be any rope in there anyway. She tried the door behind the desk. That was locked too. Fuck. Everything was locked around here.

She was still rattling the knob when she became aware of a scratching noise from behind her.

Robin slowly turned, and saw the pen moving across the visitor log, writing in red ink, completing a new entry. As she watched, it scrawled the current date, followed by what she supposed must be the current time. It left the time out blank, of course, skipping over to the column for the visitor name, where it drew a perfect imitation of her signature. Then, finally, it filled in the name of the person she was visiting.

D-E-A-T-H.

Robin stared at the page for a moment. So she was here to see Death, was she? Sorry, but that august personage would have to wait. She had things to do.

Picking the nearer of the two large doors, she gave it a push. At last, something that wasn't locked! She went through, entering a wing corridor dimly lit by emergency lights. They seemed close to exhausted. The emergency was outlasting the lights. The hallway went on forever, running off into darkness. Plenty of patient rooms to raid for sheets. Four of them knotted together would do, or maybe six, just to be sure. She tried the door nearest her. Locked. She moved to another. Also locked. So was the third one. Access denied.

Robin gave it up as a bad job and returned to the door to the lobby. She gave it a tug, and would it open now? Of course not. She couldn't push it, she couldn't pull it. It might as well have been painted on. She peered through the window. The lobby, formerly derelict and deserted, was now occupied by a receptionist behind the desk, furiously scribbling on the calendar pad. Was she making the doodles Robin had seen? The sun shone outside the front doors. Robin felt a sudden, desperate need to get out into that daylight. She drew back her hands and pounded on the door with both fists, hard. The thump echoed in the corridor. The scene through the window flickered like a television with a wonky tube. She hit the doors again and the picture faded completely, returning the lobby to its state of abandoned vacancy. But the door still wouldn't open.

Then she heard a *click*, which was instantly echoed by a hundred more behind her. She turned. All the doors she could see, on both sides of the hallway, had opened just a crack, showing darkness beyond.

Oh, she didn't like that. Not one bit.

Robin took off running, paying no attention to the doors or to anything else. She came to a corner, rounded it and kept going. The sound of her feet hitting the floor bounced off the tiled walls. When she finally stumbled to a stop, in a stretch where the doors were still closed, the sound of footfalls continued to reverberate from the walls. She quickly realized that they were going on too long to be echoes. These were new sounds. A horde of *something* was in here with her, and it was running, too. Behind her? Ahead of her? Coming? Going? She couldn't tell. The corridor stretched out in both directions, identical, empty, going on and on and on, lined with closed, unnumbered doors. The corner she had turned had faded from view. It was as if she had wandered into one of those trick funhouse rooms where they positioned mirrors face to face, reflecting each other to infinity, except she was willing to bet that she could run and run in either direction and she would never crash into a wall of shiny glass.

She tried several of the knobs in the immediate vicinity. All of them were locked. With a frustrated shriek she spun and slammed her back against the last one, giving it a hard little kick with the heel of her boot. She looked left, looked right. The footsteps continued to echo. She thought they were getting louder, but she couldn't see what was making them in the dimly lit distance.

Then she heard another *click*. The door opposite her swung inward, exposing blackness beyond.

Robin looked at the ceiling. "Oh, *come on*," she said.

The ceiling didn't answer her.

"Well, fine," Robin said, moving towards the opening, "but you'd better show me something interesting."

~~~~

Unable to wriggle out from under the dirt and debris, the bones and pieces of coffin, and the tombstone with the cross on top, Myra remained where she'd fallen, stuck and stuck good. Her earlier struggles to escape had shifted the rubble just enough to let it compress on her and further restrict her breathing and her movement. Now, instead of trying to escape, she was just trying to stay conscious and distinguish between reality and hypoxic delusions. For instance, she thought she had seen Robin at one point, peering at her from above, but the real Robin would have come down to help her, right? This one just gave her a Robin-style frown and disappeared. Myra had lacked the wind even to scream for her to come back. Things had only gotten worse since then. Black spots gathered around the periphery of her vision, like ants trying to work up the nerve to raid a sugar bowl. They joined and spread, deepening into a dusky silent movie-style frame, then spreading inward, blotting out the pale and silent light of the moon.

Then Chuck appeared, followed by Margaret. More hallucinations, maybe. She tried to greet these figments of her imagination, but couldn't muster the breath. Chuck rushed over and crouched beside her, getting his hands underneath the tombstone and lifting with his legs like a good boy who listened to his chiropractor. The heavy weight shifted a little and she drew a huge, deep, eager lungful of air, then a few more. Chuck's face was turning red with the strain of giving her breathing room. She worked her own hands underneath the gravestone and pushed. Together, they managed to heave it up and to the side. Loose dirt showered all around With that obstacle removed, she was able to start digging herself out. Chuck joined in, the two of them laboring in silence as Margaret looked on, until at last Myra squirmed free. She sat on the edge of the fallen tombstone for a few moments, gulping air, then working through an attack of hiccups. Once she had gotten over that, she lifted her gaze and said: "Thanks."

"You're welcome," he said, a little bit warily, keeping his distance. It bothered her a little. Weren't they all supposed to be friends again?

Speaking of friends, one of them was missing. She looked around. "Where's Robin?"

"Inside."

"Inside what?"

"The Retreat. She went looking for a rope or something to haul us up, on account of we can't climb out."

"Oh, Chuck." She looked at the building, looming over them even at this distance. Had it gotten bigger, or was it just the angle, being down in the trench, that made it seem that way? "She shouldn't have gone in there."

"That's what I told her, but I couldn't exactly stop her. She's the only one who didn't fall in when the tunnel collapsed."

"Tunnel?"

"Uh-huh. That's what we're in. It goes all the way to the building.

The whole thing collapsed after you fell, and we—" He indicated Margaret with a tilt of his head. "—both got caught. Robin didn't." He shrugged. "She's nimble, I guess."

Myra eyed the sides of the burrow.   Taller than a person, crumbling, nearly vertical, and curving back inward near the top, they didn't look the least bit climbable. Certainly Margaret couldn't do it. That was probably why Robin had gone into the Retreat; she wouldn't abandon the armless woman. Myra remembered the guilt she had felt coming off Robin with respect to Margaret, and wondered again what lay behind it. She'd probably never find out; there was an excellent chance she wouldn't be seeing Robin again.

"Are you ready to go? We should get back to the stairs. In case she's waiting for us."

Myra could tell he didn't really believe that Robin would be waiting there. Neither did she. Still, it wasn't like they had anything better to do. "Sure," she said. "Lead the way."

"It's just the one tunnel," Chuck said.   "We won't even need to scratch arrows into the wall to find out way back."

~~~~

Bob hurried up the road to the Retreat, making an enormous racket as he walked, his weapons and accoutrements and shit all clinking and clanking and banging around. Toomes hadn't made this much noise when he walked. It must have taken a lot of practice for him to move stealthily while loaded down with all this crap. Maybe someday he, too, would become an expert at it, and then Paltruck would tell people they needed to go see Bob, the vampire hunter, because he could help them with their problem.

Fuck. He hoped that never happened. He didn't want to be here long enough to get that good at this.

The road followed the contours of the mountain in a series of switchbacks. The woods had grown steadily quieter as he climbed, and now were dead silent. That was never a good sign. He thought of those houses down below, their open doors, their air of emptiness. Where had their wandering occupants gone?   Were they out there lurking among the trees, unheard, unseen, shadowing his ascent toward the Retreat, scaring away the birds and silencing the frogs? Toomes had said he should ignore them, but what if *they* decided not to ignore *him*? What then?

The sensation of being observed stayed strong, but no attack came. Maybe schlepping around Toomes's arsenal gave pause to whatever was watching him from the woods.   Maybe they thought he *was*

Toomes. The idea offered some comfort; protected by Toomes's apparently fearsome reputation, he just might make it to the top unmolested. He hoped so, because he didn't actually know how to *use* most of this stuff. Sure, any bozo could swing a sword, but actually demonstrating some skill—fending off a determined enemy—that was a different story. If forced into a fight it would quickly become apparent that Toomes, he was not.

He rounded a final curve in the road, which brought him to the end of the trees. Straight ahead through the pine forest, he saw a gate; beyond that, the trees gave way to overgrown grass, high and scraggly and swaying in a light breeze, with a shadowed structure looming over everything. This could only be the Retreat. The name made it sound like somewhere you would go to relax and get away from it all, but he didn't think he'd find the others around a bonfire, sitting on Adirondack chairs and drinking root beer floats. The building was squat and drab, reminding him of a haunted orphanage from some supernatural gothic drama. Two enormous wings flanked the central structure, running off at angles into the darkness. He could imagine the place scissoring itself out of the mountaintop and shambling across the summit, the wings transforming into legs, shedding earth and bricks and shingles and broken glass as it lumbered about, hunting for smaller structures to gobble up, for animals and people to stomp on.

Well. This was his destination. If Paltruck was right, he would find Myra here.

He just hoped he wouldn't have to kill her.

~~~~

They walked back up the collapsed tunnel, picking their way over the debris, heading back toward the Retreat. Myra led the way, followed by Margaret and Chuck. He helped the armless woman through the rough spots, and kept a careful eye on Myra. Sure, she seemed normal now, but if she suddenly suffered a vampiric relapse he'd rather have it happen in front of him than behind.

At length they returned to pit formed by the collapsed stairway. There was no rope dangling down for them to grab, no sign that Robin had returned. He called her name, trying to be loud and quiet at the same time. No answer. He called again. Still no answer. He opened his mouth to call a third time, but Myra's hand on his arm stopped him. "She's not there."

"She should be back by now." The Retreat loomed overhead, an ominous, dirty glacier scraping its way along the mountaintop. A bitter, faintly rancid odor wafted from the nearby hole in the foundation. It reminded Chuck of a pen at the zoo that was long overdue for a cleaning. He didn't remember that smell from before, but the collapse had been fresher then, the air full of freshly churned dust. Chuck craned his neck, as if that might let him see into the building. "She promised she wouldn't go far."

"I think all promises are null and void in there."

"I guess." Chuck ran his hand along the side of the pit. "I can't climb this. Do you think you can?"

"No. Even if I could, it wouldn't help you or Margaret. I won't be able to pull you out." She looked at the sky. "If I could still fly, I could carry you both out of here."

"Yeah, well, a side effect of flying was you nearly killed all of us, so I'm kind of glad you can't anymore. To be honest."

"That wasn't me. That was … Whatever the Count put inside me. And it's gone. Really, Chuck. It's gone. I'm just me again. I wouldn't be down here otherwise."

"I know." He sighed. "I hope she comes back soon."

Myra said nothing.

"You don't think she will, do you?"

"Not really, no. Do you?"

"She might."

Myra shrugged.

"What else can we do?"

She tipped her head toward the hole in the foundation.

"Are you kidding? You said yourself we shouldn't go in there. You said in there, all promises are null—"

"And void. Yeah. But if Robin doesn't come to rescue us, what are we going to do? Stay down here forever? At least that's a way forward."

"Forward into *what?*"

"I don't know," she said. "But this place seems to have ways of making offers you can't refuse."

~~~~

Robin stood at the edge of the darkened room. The harsh light of the hallway crossed the threshold and thudded to the floor like a shotgunned bird, illuminating nothing of the room beyond. She felt around the wall for a light switch, found one, flicked it a few times. Nothing happened. This scene was supposed to play out in the dark. Of course.

As she hesitated, someone said: "I know that perfume."

The voice sounded wrong somehow, off, bubbly and sticky and

hollow, but she recognized it. "Kyle?"

"Yeah." He was somewhere in the room, off to her left, but she couldn't see him. "Is that you, babe?"

"It's pretty sad that I have to ask this," she said, "but are you talking to me? Your wife? Robin?"

"Who else would I be calling *babe*, babe?"

"You want a list? I can recite one. From memory." Then: "And I'm not wearing any perfume."

"Not today," he said, "but you were yesterday. It's left over on your skin. I can smell it. Perfume is like blood, you know. You can't get rid of it no matter how hard you scrub."

Robin, not caring much for that analogy, said: "How did you get here?"

She heard him shifting around. Something creaked underneath him. "Not sure. One minute I was in the doc's office, the next I was here."

"Really? Last I knew, you were pushing people off cliffs."

"You heard about that, huh? I guess that means you bumped into Chuck."

"I did," she said. "But I heard it from Gwen, actually."

After a moment he said, "Gwen's alive?"

"Not anymore."

There was a pause. Kyle made a sickly, phlegmy, coughing sound, then spat. Something splattered to the floor. She was glad she couldn't see what it was.

"You don't sound so good, Kyle."

He laughed weakly. "I don't feel so good, either." Then: "How about you come in here and make me feel better?"

"Tempting, but no thanks."

"You got something better to do?"

"Yeah, I do. Again, you want a list?"

"It's not my fault," Kyle said. It sounded like he was on the move, coming closer to the door.

"What's not your fault?"

"I'm not a fat gasbag like Chuck or a dopey schmuck like Bob. Women come on to me. What am I supposed to do, turn them down?"

"Are you fucking kidding me? Of course you are."

"But that would be rude."

"Oh, please. God's gift to women, performing a public service? You're so full of shit."

"Am I?" His voice was nearby now, off to the left, and elevated, like he had climbed on top of a dresser or something. What was he going to do, pounce on her like a cat?

"Yeah, you are. You always were." She backed into the hallway. "And we're done here."

"Oh, no," Kyle said. There was a *thud* and he landed in front of her, a smudgy blot against the darkness of the room. He grabbed her ankle in a cold grip and pulled, hard. "We're not even close to done, babe." She went down on her backside, fingers scrabbling for purchase on the unblemished tile as he dragged her forward. For a few seconds—just an instant—she could see him in the glare of the hallway lights. His skin was blue and mottled, darkened by bruises, stained with blood; his face was swollen and distorted, his eyes crazed and yellowed, his flesh rubbery. That was all she saw, his face and his arm, but it was enough to finally wring a shriek from her lips.

"Now that's what I like to hear," Kyle said, as he pulled her into the darkness and kicked the door closed behind her. "Beautiful women, screaming my name."

Goblins

WITH HIS GOAL finally in sight, Bob broke into a run, clanking and rattling as he hurried towards the gate. Maybe that lack of Toomes-like discipline was what finally brought the creatures boiling out of the forest.

They started swarming before Bob reached the gate, a horde of short, twisted creatures, mostly naked, although some wore the tattered remains of unidentifiable garments, and mostly hairless, except for tufts that sprouted here and there, but never where such tufts belonged. Their faces were broad and round, their mouths full of sharp little teeth; their long arms nearly touched the ground, and their thick, muscular legs, unnaturally long and oddly bent, with knees near their shoulders, made them seem like giant mutant crickets. And there were so many of them; a handful, then a dozen, then more, jabbering and gibbering and capering every which-way, big flat feet leaving odd tracks stamped into the dust. They didn't look the least bit friendly, whatever the fuck they were. Not vampires, not ghosts, not zombies. Not any sort of undead at all. These goblins were some manner of living thing. He could see them breathing, their skinny chests expanding and contracting.

If they were alive, he could kill them.

Bob whipped out the shotgun. The creatures raised their red

hands, their yellow eyes going wide. He fired. The muzzle flash of the shotgun lit up their faces. Four of the little monsters—the ones right in front of him—went tumbling backwards in a spray of black blood and umber fragments. The pieces were still in the air when he spun and fired again. Three more of them did involuntary backflips. He spun and fired again.

Click.

They surged in the instant they realized he was out of ammo, waving their long arms, slashing with their sharp claws. He used the gun as a cudgel to buy himself enough space to draw his sword, then spun and spun and spun again, slashing and stabbing wildly. He felt the hits shuddering up the blade, through the hilt, into his hands, until he wasn't hitting anything anymore; they had withdrawn, snarling and grumbling in some guttural language. Panting, Bob turned in a slow circle, keeping the blade leveled. His body stung in any number of places. He hadn't been the only one to draw blood.

The goblins regrouped, muttering to each other, maybe trying to think up a plan to take him down without sacrificing more of their colleagues.

Planning? Fuck that. He raised his sword and charged right into them.

They screeched and fell back, they sprang into the air, they gibbered and drooled and gnashed their teeth. He hacked and thrust blindly, but the sword seemed to know what it was doing, spitting and slicing. The air began to stink of black blood. He pressed his advantage, driving the goblins back, until hit him in the base of the skull, something hard as a rock. He staggered forward. The creatures pounced. They bit and scratched and pulled like a throng of teen-age pop fans who, disappointed by their idol, had graduated from hysterical adulation to homicidal mania. But Bob had managed to hold onto his sword and, recovering his senses, he swung it like a baseball bat, no finesse at all, just a fast arc. One ducked beneath the blade, came up right in front of him. He punched it in the face and nearly broke his knuckles. It felt like hitting a bowling ball. The goblin snarled at him. He reversed his swing and cut its head off with a single sweep of blue steel. The head hit the ground, rolled a little ways, and came to stop, looking back at Bob with a surprised expression on its face.

And then he was alone. It took him a moment to realize that the remaining creatures had fled. He could hear them scuffing and shuffling through the brush, the sounds growing fainter as they retreated.

He turned in a slow circle, bloody blade held out in front of him. "That's right!" he shouted. "Fuck with me, you see what you get!"

The woods had fallen silent. The goblins, if they were still watching, didn't answer.

"That's right," he said again, more softly this time, as he sheathed the sword. The scabbard squeegeed some of the blood off the blade; it oozed down the ornate leather, dripped from the tip to the ground. Toomes would never approve. But Toomes wasn't here.

Victorious, if a bit bloodied, Bob the Goblin Hunter continued onward, toward the chained-up gates of the Retreat.

~~~~

Myra was crouched down in front of the opening in the foundation of the Retreat when a not-so-distant *boom* attracted her attention. She looked over her shoulder at Chuck. He was looking over his shoulder in the direction of the gate. "Tell me that was thunder," she said.

Another blast split the air. It was followed by a horrific din, like an army of angry, drunken, chattering chimpanzees gearing up for battle. She wasn't sure how far all this action was. Not far enough.

"Yeah," Chuck said. "Not thunder. That's somebody shooting at something."

"Who? At what?"

"Fuck if I know." He peered up at the Retreat. "All I know is we need to get our asses out of this hole."

"That's not happening. Robin isn't coming back."

He glanced at her, then tried a half-hearted hop, as if that would let him see over the top of the pit. He landed, slipped on the loose soil, and fell on his ass. As he stood up and dusted off his backside, Myra said: "Chuck."

He looked at her.

"Robin is not coming back. Okay? Something happened to her and she's not coming back."

"But she said she wouldn't go in too far. She said——"

"It doesn't matter what she said. She would only have to take one step in the wrong direction. That's what it comes down to, Chuck. One step in the wrong direction. Tell me I'm wrong."

He sighed and folded his arms, but he didn't tell her she was wrong. "So what do we do?" he said. "We can't climb out."

"No, we can't. That leaves ..." She trailed off, gestured at the opening.

"In *there*?" He laughed, or choked. Maybe both. "What was that you just said about one step in the wrong direction?"

"Nobody is coming to save us, Chuck. Not Robin, not Bob, not Kyle. I don't want to take my chances with whoever is out there shooting off guns, do you?"

He opened his mouth, closed it. He looked at Margaret. "What do you think?"

The armless woman squeaked and shrugged as best she could.

"It's the only thing we can do, Chuck," Myra said. "You know it is."

He kicked some dirt around.

"Chuck?"

"All right. Let's go. We'll have to hold onto each other until we find some light. Me first, Margaret in the middle, you at the end."

"Okay."

They lined up in front of the hole, each of them with a grip on one of Margaret's shoulders, because she had no hands to hold. Chuck moved cautiously forward. He had to turn sideways to fit through the crack, and disappeared into the black until all Myra could see of him was the hand that was hanging onto Margaret. The armless doctor went next, and then it was Myra's turn. She sidled through the gap and into an open space. "Chuck?" she whispered. "You there?"

"Yeah, I'm here."

"What've we got? Can you tell?"

"Seems to be a hallway. Narrow. Goes left and right."

"Which way do you want to go?"

"Uh, I don't know. Left?"

"Okay."

He started moving, and then Margaret moved too, and she followed, slow and cautious in the utter dark. The split in the wall receded, becoming nothing but a finger of moonlight across a rough floor. The air grew stale. Suddenly Chuck made some sort of startled exclamation, and then Margaret's shoulder pulled away from her. Unbalanced, Myra stumbled and fell on the hard, cold floor. She heard a sound like something sliding along stone. Her fingers felt something, the edge of a pit or slide. Shit. Chuck and Margaret must have fallen into it.

She leaned over the edge and whisper-shouted, "Chuck?"

No answer.

"Margaret?"

No squeak.

She reached down with her arms, probing the opening. She

couldn't reach the other side. The downward slope was relatively smooth, though it had what felt like small handholds, for if she felt like climbing down in the dark. She didn't. She found a narrow ledge on one side, wide enough to sidle along. She used it to get across. The pit wasn't very wide, less than five feet, she thought, but that was more than enough to have swallowed up her companions.

All because somebody took one step in the wrong direction.

She backed off from the edge of the hole that had claimed Chuck and Margaret, trying to decide what to do next, and almost immediately slipped on some rubble, staggered into a door that swung open, and fell down a short flight of stairs. The door closed behind her and wouldn't open from this side; she found a handle, but it wouldn't turn, no matter how hard she pulled on it. That vampire strength would have come in handy now, along with that vampire vision. Pounding on the door would be futile, and only attract attention. Instead, she turned and started picking her way along the twists and turns of the corridor she had landed in. Lined with cold pipes and moldering wire, it seemed to be some kind of utility tunnel, and smelled exactly the way you would expect a cellar that had been sealed up for twenty years to smell.

She didn't realize the corridor had ended at another set of stairs until she stumbled into a railing and flipped over it like a drunken gymnast. Fortunately the drop was short, and ended in a pile of rags and assorted other soft crap, so she didn't crack her skull open on the concrete floor below. But she didn't have time to be relieved about her unbroken neck; the pile immediately began to writhe beneath her, sprouting arms and hands and sharp, sharp fingers that clutched and grabbed. She flailed at the unseen attackers but they quickly seized both of her arms and one of her legs. Her last free foot connected with a head that felt as hard as a rock. Instead of flinching, the thing grabbed her ankle, and then it was all over; they lifted her up and carried her off into the inky blackness.

If she had still been a vampire, this would *so* not be happening to her.

~~~~

Kyle flung Robin onto a hard, narrow bed. She bounced across the thin pad and quickly sat up, pulled her knees into a crouch. She could hear his ragged breathing nearby. She got ready to spring, but didn't, waiting for his next move.

"You can't see me," he said in a sing-song voice, "but I can see you."

"Yeah? Can you see this?" She flipped him the bird.

"Naughty," he said.

She switched to her pinky, held it in front of her face and wiggled it. "Hmm, what does this remind me of?"

"Bitch. And you wonder why I cat around?"

"Yeah, yeah, yeah. Everything is my fault." She moved to the edge of the mattress, which was more like a chip of foam rubber encased in vinyl. Maybe it was an immobilized stretcher or a cheap cot. When Kyle came crashing down next to her, she punched in his direction, her knuckles connecting with his chest. He grunted and exhaled foul air into her face. His shirt felt cold and soggy. She hit him again, in the same spot, with her other fist, and would have kept pummeling him except he caught her wrists and held them. His grip wasn't what it used to be. She thought she could break it, but she didn't try. She opened her fists instead. After a moment Kyle let go of one of her hands. She brushed her fingertips across his chest, along what felt like an open sore.

"Kyle?" she said.

"Yeah?"

"What is that?"

"Stab wound," he said.

"Who did it?"

"Bobby-boy. With a spring-loaded stake in a trick cross. But don't be too mad at him. I was trying to kill him at the time."

"Why were you doing that?"

A flat chuckle. "Somebody made me an offer I couldn't refuse."

"Who?"

"Nobody you'd care to meet." Then: "Want to see it? Interested in taking a look? Hmm?"

After a moment, she said: "Okay."

"You won't like it."

"I already don't like it. Show me anyway."

"Say please."

"Oh, for fuck's sake, Kyle."

He chuckled. "Okay, babe. Just remember, I warned you." He got up and started moving around again. A dim light came on, close to the ground. Not a flashlight or a lantern; it was one of those gadgets doctors used to look in your ears. Kyle was holding it like a blowtorch. He passed the light along himself, giving her a look at what was left of him. His right leg ended at the knee joint in an ugly patch of twisted, blackened flesh. The skin that wasn't burned was blotchy and bluish. There was the hole she'd felt in his chest, a dark pucker crusted with drying blood, peeking through a rent in his shirt. His eyes were yellow where they should have been white, glazed instead of glossy.

He scuttled back to the hospital bed. "So. Notice anything different about me?"

"A few things," Robin said. "What happened to your leg?"

"I gave it to a friend." Kyle laughed crazily. "He was hungry, see."

"A friend?"

"That thing I threw Gwen to? I broke into its shack—I thought I could hide there—and it came back and caught me. Isn't that funny? I know how you enjoy irony."

He meant the ogre. It must have learned from experience with her and Margaret, and started with Kyle's leg so its meat couldn't run away. "Is he the one who made you try to kill Bob?"

"Oh, no," Kyle said. "That was somebody else. Hey. Want to see another thing?"

Show-and-tell wasn't over yet. "Sure. Thrill me again."

He stood the ear-light on a nearby dresser, then reached underneath the cot and pulled out a big gold crucifix. "Nice, huh?" He held it up for her to see, turning it this way and that so she could inspect it. This must be the trick cross he had mentioned. The little carven Christ seemed to float just above the long piece, so she figured it might move. Maybe it was a switch.

"Did you go and get religion on me, Kyle?"

"No. Religion got me. Here, watch this." He turned the crucifix so that the shaft was over the hole in his chest, then slid Jesus down a little. There was a faint *click*. He made a little noise as his body jerked a little. "You never do get used to that," he said, turning sideways so she could see the tip of a wooden stake sticking out of his back. "See how the spike goes all the way through? Isn't that neat? That's how Bobby-boy did me. Thinks he's a hero or something. What an asshole, right?" Kyle pulled the device out, then pushed the switch again. The spike retracted and a little lid closed over it. "Pretty cool, huh?"

"Yeah," Robin said, "that's quite the gadget. How did you get hold of it?"

"I guess Bob didn't think he needed it anymore. It was on the floor next to me when I woke up dead."

Kyle slithered onto the bed, cozied up next to her. He pressed the business end of the crucifix against her chest, right between her breasts.

"Want to see it again?" he said.

~~~~

Chuck woke up face-down on the floor like he'd been on the world's worst bender. Everything hurt. He remembered stepping off into space, toppling forward, his fingers involuntarily clutching at Margaret's shoulder as he fell. He might have pulled her in after him. He rolled over, sat up, and whispered her name. He heard an answering squeak from his left. He crawled in that direction. His questing hand soon found the rough, dirty fabric of her lab coat. "Are you hurt? Squeak once for no, twice for yes."

One squeak. That was good.

"Any idea where we are?"

One squeak. No surprise; even if she had ever come into the basement, it must have changed along with everything else in this hellhole. He was pretty sure an open pit in an unlit hallway wouldn't have passed inspection.

"Any sign of Myra?"

One squeak. So, nope. But that didn't mean Myra wasn't here and unconscious.

"Should we look for her?"

Two squeaks.

He stood and helped Margaret up, then took hold of her shoulder. "Okay. I've got you. Here we go. I should be more careful this time, right?"

This elicited a light snort that was almost a laugh, and two squeaks. He moved forward with extreme slowness, bringing the doctor with him, tapping ahead with one toe to test for holes before committing to each step. He periodically called for Myra, who never answered, and at some point he realized that he had given up. She wasn't here.

Eventually, a glow began to seep in from somewhere ahead of them. It showed him he was about to walk into the wall of a T-intersection. As his eyes adjusted he discovered that they were in what looked like a stereotypical mine tunnel: Rough-hewn but more or less squared off, with wooden braces at intervals to shore up the roof. All that was missing was the metal railway along the middle of the floor where the carts would run. He glanced over his shoulder at Margaret; she was peering at their surroundings with wide eyes. Obviously she'd had no idea that her hospital had been built on top of a network of abandoned tunnels. He was sure it hadn't been, that this was yet another feature of their new and improved fucked-up environment. He tugged on her coat and tipped his head in the direction of the light.

She nodded and they moved off that way, following the tunnel as it made a long arc down and to the left. Other tunnels of various slopes and diameters opened off of this one, not only in the walls but also in the ceiling and floor. The mountain was Swiss-cheesed with holes. The extensive ventilation did little to alleviate a pervasive odor of smoke and oil; something greasy and noxious burned nearby. It was like being locked inside the world's worst rotisserie.

Eventually, the tunnel leveled out and straightened. It opened onto a large room up ahead. Whatever was providing the illumination came from in there. He turned to the doctor, indicated for her to stay put, and put a finger to his lips. She raised an eyebrow at him. Oh, yeah, right: Shushing Margaret, of all people, was hardly necessary.

Leaving her in the shadows, he crept forward to peer into the big chamber. Unlike the tunnel, it appeared to be a legitimate part of the Retreat: A subterranean gymnasium, somewhere for the patients or staff to exercise during what must be interminable winters. But it wasn't in very good condition; the walls were peeling and stained with moisture and mildew, the varnish almost totally worn off the warped wooden floor. It seemed as if a large number of people had moved in; crude bedding lay scattered everywhere, along with several large piles of what looked like discarded clothes. He might have taken it for an emergency shelter, if it weren't for the statue.

A representation of a young man, this enormous icon stood on a pedestal at one end of the room, regarding its shabby domain with a baleful gaze, as if it had expected to wake up in some classy museum or temple rather than this shithole. Its arms were stretched out in front and slightly to the side; each hand held a bowl-shaped brazier. The fiery contents were the source of the red light and burnt-meat odor. Black smoke dribbled over the lips of the pans, drifted reluctantly upward, and collected in a puddle beneath the ceiling before being drawn through an ancient ventilator grate.

The gym was pocked with dark openings in the walls like the one he stood in, but he was more interested in the doors. The real ones. One set was directly across from him and another was off to the left, near the statue. Real doors might go to real hallways, which might go to real stairs, which might go to the Retreat proper, if such a thing still existed, which might let them go back outside. Not that outside wasn't awful, too, but still. He turned to Margaret, hanging back in the dimness. He wondered if she had ever been in this room before. Maybe she would know which doors to choose. He went back to where she waited, described what he had seen, asked if she knew the place. Two squeaks. She'd been there. Good. Very good.

"Do you think you can you find your way upstairs?"

Two squeaks again.

"Okay. I think it's deserted for now. Let's go before anyone comes back. You lead the way this time, okay?"

She nodded and brushed past him. He followed, and almost ran into her when she came to a dead stop just inside the gym, staring wide-eyed at the statue.

"What's the matter?"

She looked at him, tipped her head at the figure.

"Yeah, I know. Crazy, right?"

Margaret shook her head, stamped her foot, emitted a frustrated grunt.

"Not crazy?"

She shrugged.

"Do you know who that is?"

She squeaked and nodded.

"Who is it?" She sighed, because she couldn't tell him that, of course. But then something clicked and he said: "Is that Patrick?"

She nodded again. So that was it. They had stumbled into the Church of Patrick, Maker of the Crazy. Terrific. Fortunately, services weren't being held right now.

"Well, I don't know who built that statue or who lives here, and I don't want to meet them," Chuck said. "Which doors do we take to get out of here?"

Margaret grunted and scurried forward, weaving through the dozens of grimy ad hoc bedrolls. He followed close behind. They were heading for the doors near the statue. Bits of trash that might have been offerings littered the base: Small piles of bones, crudely carved sticks covered with scratched symbols, a few rotting animal carcasses, even some candy bars in bright wrapping, incongruous reminders of the normal world of junk food and sugar that they had left behind. He was tempted to collect them for later, but the thought of touching—let alone eating—anything that had been lying on this floor nauseated him.

They reached the doors. Chuck barreled into them with his shoulder. They shuddered and wobbled but refused to open, as if locked or jammed or chained on the other side. Through the grimy glass he could just make out a short flight of steps leading upward. He bashed the door a few more times, with the same results. He turned Margaret. "What about the other doors? Where do those go?"

She shook her head, then retreated into the narrow space behind the statue. He hurried after her, because if Margaret was running, he assumed she had a reason. As they crouched in the shadow of Patrick's knees, he realized why she'd gone to ground: Something was coming. He could hear it now, running footsteps echoing into the room from one of the tunnels, God knew which. Patrick's worshipers, returning for nightly prayers. Sounded like he had a lot of them.

It wasn't long before a small army of stunted, misshapen creatures began streaming into the room, first from one opening, then from more. They muttered amongst themselves, making little noises that sounded like some sort of guttural language. He wondered what they were talking about. Sports scores? Politics? Dinner plans? The people hiding behind the statue? Not that last one, he hoped.

Then a phalanx arrived carrying Myra on their shoulders, and the room fell silent.

So they must have been talking about her.

~~~~

When Bob sidled between through the gap between the gates and entered the grounds of the Retreat, it felt as if he had stumbled out of summer and into the hollow, winter-facing side of autumn. The warm night breeze died away, then started up again, blowing from a different direction, ten degrees cooler, liquid with the threat of rain. He felt the misty chill through his layers of gear, along his bare arms, through his hiking boots. He slowed to a deliberate walk as he crunched up the driveway, pondering the very existence of this place. Why here? Why so remote? He recalled, in a vague sort of way, that there used to be tuberculosis sanatoriums in the Adirondacks, back in those ancient-history days before antibiotics, when you either died or you didn't. Maybe the Retreat had once been such a place, now repurposed as something else. But what? Why wouldn't Paltruck just *tell* him these things?

He slowed as he noticed, off to his right, a fenced graveyard and what looked like a large hole in the ground. Curious, he headed that way, cutting at an angle through the tall grass. A nasty odor pervaded the air, like a particularly putrid swamp or a large, decaying animal. He soon reached the black iron fence and paused there, eyeing the cemetery. The markers were mostly nondescript, with scrawled, unreadable epitaphs. A number of tombstones had toppled into a pit or sinkhole, which was connected to a crumbling ditch that ran off across the yard. It looked fresh, unstable; loose stones and rubble continued to trickle to the bottom. He sighted along the ditch. It ran more or less straight across the yard, up to the big building at the top. He wondered what the deal was with that.

Leaving the cemetery, he headed back towards the driveway, then steered himself at an old tractor that poked out of the tall grass like a mechanical island. It looked like it had been sitting out in the elements for a good long time; the rubber of the tires was cracked and powdery, and rust bloomed through the paint in various spots. The key was still in the ignition, but it wouldn't turn. He climbed up onto the tractor for a quick look around, and spotted a body lying nearby, in a bed of flattened, splotchy grass.

Fuck. Was that Gwen?

Bob hopped off the tractor and hurried over. It *was* Gwen. Most of her, anyway. She was missing an arm and part of a leg, and he didn't even want to look at her abdomen, which had been torn open, shredded, and partially excavated, like a fondue pot or a dish of pâté. God. He moved around and crouched down beside her. Her eyes, wide open, stared up at the sky. He reached out to close them.

They rolled in their sockets to look at him.

Before Bob could react, Gwen's remaining arm shot out. She grabbed his wrist and yanked his hand into her mouth. Her perfect white teeth bit down hard.

Howling, Bob pulled back, leaving a couple of minor fingers behind in Gwen's jaws. She chewed contentedly, splintering the small bones, a look of vacant satisfaction on her pretty, bloodied face. He scuttled back. Her head lolled in his direction and she reached out with an open palm, imploring him to come back, maybe offer her a nose, an ear, a few toes. He had ten toes. Surely he could spare a few.

Shit. Shit, shit, shit! What the fuck? What was going on here? What was this?

But, yeah, he knew what was going on here. He knew what this was. An empty graveyard, a horrible smell, a dead Gwen hungry for human flesh? That meant zombies. And the thing with zombies was that when you got bitten by one, you turned into one, right?

After Dr. Zane's scalpel, Kyle's treachery, the Count's fangs, the claws and teeth of an entire horde of ravening goblins, after all that, *Gwen* had gotten him. Of all the fucking sick jokes.

He discovered that he had somehow stumbled back to the driveway. His injured hand had already started to go numb where his pinky and ring finger had once been. Was that shock setting in? Or did it mean he would soon be shuffling around looking for yummy brains to devour? Maybe he would be saved if he cut his hand off. He knelt and held his sword over his wrist. The blade trembled. He didn't take the swing. He was being idiotic. He would just bleed out, and die that much faster. He needed to bandage it up, not make it worse. The only place he could think of where there might be bandages was the Retreat. He sheathed his sword and, keeping his injured hand squeezed inside the opposite armpit, half-ran, half-stumbled up the driveway. He quickly found himself slogging through a carpet of wriggling, crawling, writhing squick, a minefield of animated body parts squirming in the dirt. There'd been some kind of zombie massacre here. He slowed up, picking his way through legs with feet, legs without feet, arms with hands, arms without hands, twitching fingers, even a few heads with snapping mouths and milky eyes. Something really bad had happened here, and not long ago. Obviously Gwen had been involved. Maybe Myra had been, too. He checked as many heads as he could, but didn't spot Myra, or anybody else he knew. So that was one good thing, anyway.

Bob was so focused on both examining and avoiding the body parts that he almost fell into the trench from the cemetery. It knifed across the mountaintop, heading straight for the front of the Retreat, sectioning the driveway into a number of disconnected arcs. He couldn't cross the gap, so he cut through the tall grass instead, treading carefully and keeping well away from the edge of the ditch. Before long he reached the steps that led up to the entrance. These had mostly collapsed into a rubble-filled pit. The trench led into it, and then on into the building, through a black opening in the foundation. A narrow section of steps still clung to the wall on the left, giving him a way up to the landing and the big front door. He didn't have to try to climb the rubble.

Must be his lucky night.

~~~~

When the tunnel began to grow lighter, illumination seeping in from somewhere up ahead, Myra finally got a look at the things that were carrying her. They were small, maybe four feet tall. They had thick, gnarled, sturdy shoulders and no visible necks, as if their cannonball heads were screwed directly into their bodies. Their ears were pointy, not like an elf but like a bat, and their patchy hair was an odd shade of greenish-white, standing out sharply against rubbery skin of such a deep red that it looked burnt. They looked at her with vast yellow eyes, sniffed her with flattened noses, sneered at her with toothy thin-lipped mouths. They seemed to be taking care not to hurt her, not to scratch her with their sharp black claws. They were saving her for something. But what?

Soon they entered a large room. It appeared to be an old gymnasium; she saw padded walls and exposed beams below a ceiling obscured by thick, oily smoke. Big round lights hung down, emerging from the vapor like rocket thrusters. The room stank in half a dozen ways, each worse than the one before. Urine? Check. Shit? Check. Vomit? Check. Burning fat? Check. She spotted a large statue across the room and craned her neck, trying to get a look at it as she was carried nearer. It seemed to be a crude likeness of Patrick, carved or assembled out of rocks and bricks and knotted sheets and all kinds of other crap, the end result being this hulking brutalist figure that glowered down at her as she passed by. Its hands held bowls that leaked heat and black smoke. She almost expected it to pour fire on her as she went by.

A number of her little friends broke away from the pack and went over to line up in front of the statue, falling down on their bony knees, raising their clawed hands in the air, turning their bulbous eyes to the smoky heights. It was like some sort of bizarre revival. Next up: Speaking in tongues. Then snake-handling.

They carried her to a pile of torn clothes directly in front of the statue, out in the middle of the room, and tossed her into it. Several of the creatures took up guard positions, but they didn't interfere as she rifled through the heap, presumably because they knew she wouldn't find anything useful. She turned up a lot of torn uniforms in blue and black, as might be worn by maintenance or security people, as well as smocks and scrubs and coats with name tags attached or embroidered, like Margaret's, a smattering of hospital gowns, and street clothes. A sleeve here, a pant leg there, a shredded shirt, a dirty shoe. She would have been hard-pressed to assemble even a single outfit from the pieces; pretty much everything in the midden had been shredded into rags.

What was this? Why clothes? Had these garments belonged to the people who were in the Retreat when everything had gone crazy? What had happened to their former wearers? Had something dragged them all off and killed them? Or … She peered at her captors. Had they been humans once? Staff, patients, visitors? Were these *their* clothes? Maybe the ones who weren't of any particular importance to Patrick had morphed into the background, becoming generic threats like the zombies and these small things, while a few became more important characters. The Count, the ogre Robin had described. Even Margaret was a character, in a way.

So what about her, Myra? Was she going to be expected to become one of the Patrick-worshipers, to get all red and shriveled and bug-eyed, to join in their rituals?

Ugh.

No fucking way was she handling snakes.

Gods

"JESUS IS COMING to *save* you, Robin!" Kyle said. "Are you *ready* to be *saved?*"

He kept his finger close to the Christ figure as he pressed the bottom of the cross up against Robin's chest. All he had to do was slide the figure forward. He wouldn't even have to do it intentionally; a little muscle spasm would be enough to make her day even worse than it already was.

"Kyle—" Robin said.

"Look, Robin! Jesus is on his way!" He gave the figure a tiny nudge. "How *close* can he get before it's *too late* to *repent?*"

"Kyle—"

"Oh, wait, he changed his mind. Look, he's going away! I guess he's not ready to *save* you yet. There's still time. Are you *ready* to *repent?*"

God, he had totally lost it: Speaking like a malevolent movie preacher, acting like a sadistic child. Maybe Kyle wasn't even in there anymore. Maybe something strange had moved into his body, some creature of this lunatic world that knew what Kyle had known, talked like Kyle had talked, justified itself the way Kyle had justified himself. Or maybe this was just Kyle with the filters removed.

"Answer Jesus," Kyle said. "Are you ready to repent, or not?"

She just stared at him, not bothering to conceal her disgust or her pity. He didn't seem to like it. "Don't look at me that way, bitch," he said, jabbing two fingers at her forehead.

Which meant he had taken one of his hands off of the crucifix.

Robin smacked the cross hard from below, knocking it up and out of his grip. Both of them grabbed for it as it spun in midair. He blocked her arm and caught the gadget at about head level. His fingers were on the Jesus figure. He didn't seem to notice or care that the business end was pointing at his own head.

She grabbed the crosspiece and pulled it towards herself.

Because Kyle's finger was on the trigger and he wasn't quick enough to let go, Jesus slid down to the firing position. The stake popped out, stabbing Kyle in the face, just above the bridge of his nose. She heard a *crunch* as it punched through cartilage and bone. Kyle's body jerked; his eyes widened and crossed inward, as if he had been surprised by a bee landed there and stung him. His fingers went slack and started to quiver. She yanked the cross straight back. Twitching crazily, Kyle collapsed sideways onto the bed. Dark blood oozed out of the hole in his face.

Surely he was dead for real now, right? Surely he wouldn't be getting up again? Oh, surely. But Robin bet Bob had thought that, too.

So she pounded on his head with the crucifix until the back of his skull caved in and all sorts of interesting things started to ooze out of it.

Because if she knew one thing, it was that they *always* got up again.

~~~~

The lobby of the Retreat was utterly silent, dark and deserted. There was a big painting on one wall, of a board room, a big broad table surrounded by chairs, but no people. Everything human had deserted this place. Bob went to the front desk and eyed the visitor log. The last entry, written in red, had Robin's name in it, and said she was here to visit Death. Had Robin really been here? Had she written this? What did it mean? He stared at it for a minute, then closed the book and dropped it into the trash bin behind the desk. Visiting hours were over.

He noticed some small cabinets underneath the desk, including one with a red cross stenciled on it. It was locked, but the chipboard panel was no match for his sword. True to the labeling, it contained a first aid kit. He sat behind the desk for a few minutes bandaging up his injured hand, probably using way more gauze and tape than was actually necessary; the stumps of his fingers had already stopped bleeding, getting all congealed and scabby, and edging towards what seemed to be a dangerous shade of purplish-black. He popped a few painkillers, swallowing them without water. Then, just because it seemed like the prudent thing to do, he stuffed the whole kit into his bag. The mighty Toomes may have eschewed adhesive strips and disinfectant, so confident was he in his ability to avoid the slightest nick or blister, but any delusions of indestructibility that Bob might have harbored had been destroyed by his encounter with Gwen's hungry jaws.

Hand attended to as best it could be, he stood and headed for the exit, then stopped. He thought he heard something coming from one of the interior doors. Running footsteps? He hesitated. Paltruck had said he would find Myra here. Could that be her? He went to the door, eyeing it with suspicion. The footsteps were getting louder. They had the echoey character of someone racing up from the other end of a long, empty corridor. He sidestepped as the door burst inward and something came tumbling out into the lobby. His dagger was suddenly in his good hand, which was driving it down toward his attacker. The blade struck something hard and turned aside, stabbing into the floor.

"What the *fuck*, Bob?" Robin said. "Jesus Christ."

She clutched a massive gilded cross to her chest, now with a dent and a scratch along one of the horizontal bars; that was what had diverted his strike. "Where did you get that?" Bob said, staring at the crucifix.

"Yeah, nice to see you, too. I got it from Kyle."

"Kyle's here? That's impossible. I—" He broke off suddenly, realizing who he was talking to and what he was about to say.

"Killed him? Yeah, I know. He told me." She got to her feet and inspected her side. Bob had cut her after all; the wound looked shallow, just a graze really, but it was bleeding profusely all over her grimy shirt. "What happened to your hand?"

"I got bitten."

Now she looked at him sharply. "By what?"

He almost told her it was a zombie, then decided she might freak out and decide he was going to try to eat her brains or something. "I don't know. Goblins, I guess. I came in here looking for bandages."

"And you actually *found* some? Amazing. Give me one."

He handed over the first aid kit, then looked away as she took off her top and patched herself up with gauze and tape. "What are *you* doing here, anyway?" he said.

"Most recently, I've been running down an endless corridor for I don't know how long. It conveniently ended just in time for you to try and stab me. I came in looking for a rope or something to help the others get out of that hole they fell in, but it didn't work out. You can look again, I'm finished."

He turned around. She was just tucking the remains of her shirt back in. "You said the others? What others?"

Hanging the crucifix around her neck, she said: "You know. The others. Chuck, Myra—"

"Myra? You were with Myra?"

"Yeah. Like I said, they fell in a hole. Right out front." She pointed at the entrance. "Are they not there anymore?"

But he was already heading for the front door, ignoring Robin's startled noise and exhortation to wait. He banged through it, went partway down the scrap of ruined staircase, and shouted: "Myra!"

His voice echoed around the mountaintop. Myra didn't answer, of course. She wasn't there. He heard the door of the Retreat open behind him. Robin came out, stopping at the edge of the landing. He looked up at her. "They're gone," he said.

"Yeah, well, they were supposed to wait for me," she said. "But I was detained."

Bob pointed at a black opening in the foundation of the Retreat. "Maybe they went in there."

She eyed the opening. "Why would they do that?"

"I don't know, but unless they climbed out ..." He trailed off, staring at the crack.

"They couldn't have climbed out," Robin said. "The sides are too crumbly. And anyway, Margaret doesn't have any arms."

He started to ask who Margaret was and why she didn't have any arms, but decided it was probably a long story that didn't really matter to him. He studied the opening in the foundation. If Chuck could fit through it, then so could he. How could he get to the bottom? Slide down the edge? He didn't want to trigger a further collapse and end up buried under bricks and rubble.

Robin said, "You're not thinking about going down there, are you?"

"Actually I am."

"I don't suppose I can persuade you not to do that?"

"Not if Myra's in there."

"Maybe she is, maybe she isn't," Robin said. "You can never tell with this place. It has its own set of rules."

"Rules. You sound like Paltruck."

"You met Paltruck?"

"Yeah. You did too?"

"Uh-huh. He let me out of a cage where I was being held prisoner. Did he help you too?"

"Yeah. Sort of. He told me where to find Myra, but I got there too late to save her from the Count. Then he sent me to see a vampire-hunting undertaker named Toomes. Funny, right? Ha ha ha."

"Toomes?" she said. "*Robert* Toomes?"

He finally looked up at her. "How did you know that?"

"Come back inside," she said. "I want to show you something."

~~~~

After they brought Myra in, the small red hobgoblins continued to stream into the gymnasium, as if it were Halloween and that was the only costume anyone had in stock this year. Most of the little umber monkeys gathered in front of the statue. They danced and bowed and waved their hands in the air, they grunted and chanted, they hummed, they sang crazy gibberish songs, they stared at Patrick's statue in rapt admiration. He hoped they didn't decide to come around the back to worship its glorious posterior. This went on until they reached some sort of critical mass of monsters, at which point they all abruptly shut up and formed themselves into two parallel lines a couple of arm's-widths apart, creating a straight path between the statue and a pile of rags. They had their claws raised and their teeth bared, but remained perfectly still as the two on the end nearest the statue broke formation and started marching down the aisle toward the heap of fabric.

Sitting in the heap, with an *oh shit* expression on her face? Myra. The fashion show was about to start, and the critics were going to rip her to pieces. But what was he going to do about it? What *could* he do? Charge out and save her? That would be a brief scuffle with a sad ending.

The two creatures reached Myra. They poked and prodded her to her feet and out of the clothes pile and forced her into the gauntlet.

Before he had time to think better of it, Chuck cupped his hands around his mouth and shouted, "Stop!"

Myra stopped.

The creatures behind her stopped.

A mutter swept through the gymnasium as they all turned to gawk at the statue.

Chuck stood there, feeling paralyzed by the attention, even though they couldn't really see him. Margaret gave him an encouraging shoulder bump, or maybe it was her version of a dope slap. Either way, she was telling him he needed to do something. Chuck drew a deep breath, steadied himself. His voice couldn't betray any nervousness. Patrick was their god, and gods weren't supposed to get nervous around their worshipers. "Let the woman go!" he boomed. At least, he hoped he boomed it. That was what he was going for.

Plaintive-sounding grunts traveled around the room, as if the creatures were trying to figure out what to do. Probably their statue had never talked to them before. Did they even comprehend English? How did you say *Get the fuck out!* in monsterese?

Like this.

Reaching as far into his belly as he could, making his voice as big and as deep as possible, Chuck roared: "Get the fuck out!"

They understood the tone if not the words, and fled, retreating into the numerous holes and tunnels, their big flat feet flapping against the once-polished floor of the gymnasium. They sounded like a small army as they swarmed away in all different directions. Once the echoes had faded, Chuck ventured out from his hiding place. Myra stood nearby, looking very puzzled, but she broke into a big grin when she saw him step out of the shadows. "Well, if it isn't the Great and Powerful Oz," she said.

"Pay no attention to the man behind the statue." Chuck jerked a thumb at the nearby doors. "We have to get out of here before they come back. Those are locked. Let's try these."

She nodded and headed for the far exit. Chuck hurried to join her, Margaret tottering along behind. He and Myra reached the doors at the same time. He took one and she took the other, but before they pushed or pulled, an amber-red light bloomed behind the scratched and filthy windows. The doors groaned and trembled and bulged inward. Chuck and Myra exchanged a glance and bolted in opposite directions, just as the doors blew off their hinges. Margaret shrieked and cringed. The sideways force of the blast caught Chuck as if it had reached around to grab him. It sent him skidding like a hockey puck. He slammed up against the padded wall on the opposite side, looking back towards the opening. Myra landed some distance away, covering her head with her hands. The doors clattered to the floor like leaden butterfly wings.

The glow in the doorway faded, revealing a shadow in its center, which resolved into a smaller, flesh-and-bone version of the statue: The human Patrick, glaring at Chuck, his face dusky and dangerous.

"There's only *one* god around here," he said, "and it's not you."

~~~~

Robin brought Bob to the reception desk, then looked around. "There was a book——"

He didn't seem overly impressed. "Yeah. I saw that already. It said you were here to visit Death. I threw it in the trash."

"Okay, but did you see who else was here?" She retrieved the book, laid it on the desk, and turned to the last page of signatures. "Robert Toomes came to visit Patrick. That's the same name as your vampire hunter, right?"

"Yeah. Yeah, it is." He tapped the entry with his finger. "Who's Patrick?"

"Myra thinks he's the one who's making all the crazy. Controlling it. She used her vampire powers to read Margaret's mind and found out that——"

Bob said: "She's still a vampire?"

"What? No. Put that thing away." He had drawn his sword so fast she hadn't even seen him do it, as if he thought saying Myra's name might cause her to come shrieking out the hallway to attack them. Paranoid much? "She went back to normal after she … Well, not long after the zombie incident." If he heard that Myra had gone crazy and attacked them, he would probably wander off on that tangent for a while, and she needed him to focus. If he could. Which she was starting to doubt.

"Zombie incident." Bob sheathed his sword. "Is that where all those pieces out there came from?"

"Yeah. Myra did that. She took them apart and saved us from getting eaten."

"She didn't save Gwen."

"No. She didn't." After a moment she said: "You, uh, you saw her?"

"What's left of her." Bob held up the hand that was swaddled in bandages. "She bit my fingers off."

Robin cocked her head at him. "You said a goblin did that."

"I lied. I didn't want you to think I was going to turn into a zombie."

"Okay." She eyed him carefully. "Are you?"

"I don't know. I haven't so far."

"Good to know. Well, there were a lot of zombies. Myra did the best she could, but, yeah. They got Gwen." Then: "They didn't just get her, they tore her apart. How did she manage to bite your fingers off?"

"I was careless. It won't happen again. Tell me more about

Toomes."

"Well, you saw it. You know as much as I do now. He came to visit Patrick. They had the same last name."

"So you think they were related."

"Of course. It makes sense. Dad? Brother? Uncle? I don't know. But he was important to Patrick, so Patrick made him into a vampire hunter, some kind of hero."

Bob grunted. "Yeah. The dead kind."

"All right, he's dead, but maybe that's because we're here meddling with the plot. We blundered in and Patrick hasn't figured out how we fit yet. We're making his characters do things they wouldn't do otherwise."

"You're saying it's *my* fault Toomes got killed?"

"No, that's not what I—"

"This book is useless. It doesn't say anything that helps us." He swept it back into the trash.

"Look, Bob, I'm not accusing you of anything. I'm just saying, I think we can do something about this situation. We can change things. Are you even listening to me?"

"What? No. Sorry. Where'd the guy in that big painting come from?"

He was looking at the portrait. She had grown to hate that picture, the way its occupant smugly surveyed the room like he owned the place. "I don't know. Somebody painted him I guess. Why are you asking me that?"

"He wasn't in it when I first got here. It was just the table and chairs."

"No shit? Are you sure you weren't just distracted and didn't notice him?"

"I'm sure. Who is he?"

"Edward Collins. He's the Director of the Retreat."

"I think he's the Count."

"Seriously?"

"Yeah."

Robin took a fresh look at the portrait. Sure, she could see him as a vampire. You wouldn't even need to change his features much, or his expression. Just add some fangs and a little dribble of crimson from one corner of his mouth, brush on a little extra white to pale him up, and bang. Instant undead.

"You know what?" Bob said. "I feel like he knows we're here. Like he's watching us. Is that crazy?"

"No," she said. As if it were listening to them, the figure in the portrait seemed to shift a little. Its lips curled into a tight smile, or maybe a sneer, as if enjoying and disdaining their unease. She heard a whisking sound and glanced at Bob. He had drawn his sword again. She said: "What are you doing?"

"I'm going to make him stop looking at us."

"You're not serious."

"Yes I am."

"Forget about the painting, Bob. Let's just go."

"You don't understand. When I killed the Count, he sort of went into the wall. Like graffiti. And now here he is again, in there, gloating. I have to kill him again."

"So you're going to just hack it up while it's hanging there?"

Bob stopped. He looked thoughtful. "You're right. I can't do a proper job while it's on the wall. Take it down for me."

"What? No. Fuck that. I am not touching the magic evil painting. You want it off the wall, *you* take it off the wall."

"It's too big. I only have one working hand."

"Then I guess you're shit out of luck."

He raised the small crossbow and pointed it at her.

She stared at him. "You have *got* to be fucking kidding me."

He didn't say anything, just gestured her forward with the crossbow. Robin studied him for a moment, trying to decide if he would actually shoot at her with that thing, and if he did, if he was likely to hit her. He could hardly miss at this range. The sheen of sweat glistening across his slightly deranged expression suggested that the Bob Express might well be on the verge of jumping the rails, if it hadn't already. Maybe the bite from Gwen really *was* rotting his brain. She sighed and went to examine the portrait. It was very large. She grasped the frame; it felt slick and surprisingly cold. She gave it a tug, but it was firmly affixed to the wall. Now that she was close to it, she could see any number of brass screw heads in the frame, holding it securely in place. She glanced up at the painting. Collins was looking back at her now, head tipped forward, giving her a little smile.

Robin really wanted to be somewhere else right now.

She looked at Bob over her shoulder. "I can't take it down," she said. "It's screwed in like motel art. *Now* can we go?"

Before Bob could answer, strong hands latched onto her shoulders and pulled. She felt a wrenching sensation as she was yanked off her feet, then a sickening lurch in her stomach. She landed on the floor in a place that smelled of dust and old paint and stagnant air. As she got to her feet she saw that she was in a boardroom, complete with a big table and leather chairs and corporate gewgaws on display. Everything had a painted look, as if it had all been done with oils. Standing over her was the man in the picture, Edward Collins, the Count, the Director of the Retreat, a portrait come to life, a thing made out of brush strokes and pigments. Except for the cinnabar vermilion slash of his still-smiling lips

That looked like it had been done with a knife.

~~~~

Bob stared at the spot where, until a moment before, Robin had been. He wasn't sure if the guy in the portrait had reached out and grabbed her or if she had somehow fallen into the painting; all he knew was that she was gone. He raised his gaze to the painting. Its smug asshole subject smirked back at him, and no wonder. Maybe Bob had managed to kill Kyle and the Count, maybe Bob had managed to bull his way through a horde of goblins, but who was winning now? Collins had snatched Robin away just like he had snatched Myra, and Bob didn't have all his fingers because Gwen had bitten them off, and she had infected him with zombie juice so that soon he would be just like her, shuffling around and looking for delicious brains to eat. He'd gone from weekend hiker to vampire hunter to goblin slayer to mindless undead in the space of a few hours. What a fucking loser.

Wanting to get away from the Director's insolent stare, Bob moved towards the front door, with no real plan other than to maybe sit on the front step until his brain turned to mush and he could quit worrying and stagger away; but then he realized that numerous small, red things—goblins, as many or more than he had fought the first time—were swarming up out of the hole in the stairs outside, like venomous ants preparing to invade a picnic. They were coming for him, and he was in no condition to face them again. He switched directions, lurching over to the door Robin had entered from, and stumbled through it. He experienced a momentary wrenching sensation, as if someone had jabbed a fork into his skull and given his brain a spaghetti twirl. Was this his final descent into zombie-hood?

No. The episode of vertigo passed and his head cleared, more or less. He found himself standing in a brightly lit, antiseptic-looking hallway. He felt oddly underdressed. His weapons and clothes were gone. Instead of a satchel full of vampire-hunting gear, he carried a teddy bear knapsack full of actual teddy bears, and instead of bloodied jeans and a shirt and hiking boots, he wore old sweat pants, a T-shirt, a tattered flannel bathrobe, and threadbare slippers. They didn't do much to keep the warmth from draining out of his body and into the icy floor.

"Sinclair?"

Bob turned as a man in scrubs approached. He held a tiny plastic tub in one hand and a paper cup full of water in the other. He looked annoyed. "What were you doing wandering around in the lobby again? You know better than that."

Bob considered this. What *had* he been doing in the lobby, anyway? Oh, right. Looking for bandages. For his hand. How had he hurt it again? And how bad was it? He didn't remember, so he lifted his hand to check. It was already bandaged. Had he done that? When?

The scrub apparently thought Bob was waving to him. "Yeah, I'm happy to see you too," he said, "because it's time for your meds. Here." He thrust the tub forward.

Bob could see colorful pills inside the container. "What's that?"

"That's dinner and a movie, partner. Eat up."

"Where am I? Who are you?"

The man gave him a look that suggested he heard this question all the time. "You're at your vacation home in Aspen, and I'm your chauffeur, your butler, your chef, your brother."

"This … This isn't right. I'm not supposed to be here. I'm a vampire hunter."

"A vampire hunter? Really? Last week you were Buck Rogers. Maybe next week you'll be President. Take the pills, would you? I have other clients to visit."

Bob shifted the teddy bear knapsack to the crook of his arm and took the tub with his good hand. The pills were bright as candy-coated chocolates. What were they? Did it matter? He looked at his chauffeur, his butler, his chef, his brother. "I need to find Patrick. Do you know where he is?"

"Patrick is where Patrick always is. Did you forget? If you're a good boy and you take your meds, maybe you'll remember."

"I don't need medicine," Bob said.

"Uh, it seems you do, if you want to find Patrick."

Bob examined the capsules again, gave the cup a little shake. One, two, three of them, red and green and blue. He did want to find Patrick. Maybe this was the way to get to him, the price of admission. He knocked the meds back, traded the tub for the cup, drank the water, and swallowed everything down.

"Good job, bro," the man said. "Patrick's in the AV lounge. South side. You remember the way now, yeah?"

And you know what? He did.

~~~~

The concussive wave that blew the doors off their hinges stunned Myra for a moment; when she recovered and raised her head from beneath her hands, she saw Patrick advancing into the room, so intently focused on Chuck that Myra was surprised he didn't catch fire or explode. Patrick's purposeful movement conveyed the impression of striding, but wasn't even a walk; he was floating just above the ground, toes not even scraping the old lacquered wood, because gods didn't need to tread the earth like everyone else did. Hadn't she learned that, when she had briefly been a small god herself?

Chuck, clearly aware that he was in trouble, scrambled to put some distance between himself and the new arrival. This attempt was unsuccessful. Patrick just glided along with severe serenity, erasing exit tunnels with waves of one hand or another, until his quarry was trapped and cowering in a corner. "Didn't your parents teach you not to pretend to be something you aren't?" he said, drifting closer. "I guess I'll have to do it for them."

Myra stood up and shouted, "Patrick! Leave him alone!"

He glanced at her, but his eyes betrayed no recognition; but then his gaze flicked to Margaret, who lurked nearby, and his face lit up with a poisonous gleam. He immediately abandoned Chuck, piloting himself towards the armless doctor. Margaret was evidently much bigger potatoes than a god-impersonating nobody. "Doc!" Patrick said. "I never thought I would see *you* here again. Didn't you leave with Baxter?"

Margaret squeaked miserably.

"Oh, that's right," Patrick said, drifting closer. "*He* left with *you*. It's important to be accurate, isn't it?"

"Patrick," Myra said, "what are you doing?"

He didn't even look at her. "I'm going to see the doctor."

Myra intercepted him. "The hell you are," she said.

He stopped, looking annoyed, and maybe a little surprised. "I don't think we've been introduced."

"Yes we have."

"I forget things sometimes. You'll have to remind me. Who are you?"

"I'm Myra."

"Pleased to meet you, Myra. Get out of my way."

"Go around me."

"Gods don't go around. We go through."

"Go through me, then." She cocked her head at him. "Unless you're not a god."

"Maybe I'm a god. Maybe I'm not. Like I said, I forget things sometimes." Invisible hands picked Myra up. "But when I say get out of my way, I mean *get out of my way*."

The hands flung Myra across the room. She landed hard and slid along the floor, picking up a corona of noisome rags, some that came with her and some that she left behind like a comet's tail. She finally came to rest in a tangle of fabric up against the padding of the far wall. Patrick had reached Margaret, hovering over her, a hawk who had found a squirrel. "Doc, Doc, Doc," he said, shaking his head. "What were you thinking, coming back here?"

Margaret squeaked.

"What's the matter, Doc? Cat got your tongue?" Then he laughed and said, "Oh, no, wait. Baxter's got it." He closed his eyes, made a fist, then opened it and looked in his palm. It held something short and bloody that Myra didn't want to look at too closely. "Now *I've* got it. Does that make me the cat? What do you think, Doc?"

A hand closed on Myra's wrist. She gasped, but it was only Chuck. He had stolen across the gymnasium while Patrick was occupied. "We have got a *big* problem," he said.

"Yeah, no shit." Myra watched Patrick circle Margaret like a buyer appraising cattle at a slaughterhouse, and maybe with the same intent. He raised his hands. Margaret's feet left the floor as if he had her on a string. Turning, Patrick glided out the way he had come in, with Margaret bobbing along after him. Myra chanced another shout. "Patrick! Where are you going?"

"Upstairs. And I'm taking the Doc with me. We need to run some tests." He glanced back at them, and grinned. "But don't be sad! I haven't forgotten about you two kids. Your other playmates are on their way back."

"Other playmates?" Chuck looked at the walls as the dark openings Patrick had sealed reopened one by one, *pop pop pop*. "Fuck. He means those little freaks."

"Is that any way to talk about your friends?" Patrick said. He waggled his finger at Chuck. "You're more like them than you know."

Chuckling, Patrick exited. Margaret went with him. She gave them one last wide-eyed look over her ruined shoulder before vanishing into the darkness.

Myra heard a metallic rattling noise. The doors that Patrick had blown off their hinges had begun to vibrate, then to slide. Her eyes met Chuck's; neither of them said a word, but they both ran for the hallway, racing the doors to see who could get there first. One of them left the floor and flew past, and might have taken Myra's head off if she hadn't felt it coming and ducked just in time. It slammed into place in front of her. She leaped for the opening that remained. The other door struck her and knocked her sprawling forward onto cold tile. A loud *bang* echoed and faded behind her.

She lay there stunned for a few seconds before rolling over. She had made it out of the gym and into the hallway; the door had shoved her through like a piston. Dim light filtered in through the small, smeared windows in the doors, but it was enough for her to see that she was alone. She peered through the window. Chuck was on the wrong side. He stood with his back to her as the room filled up with monsters. Myra grabbed the door handles and pulled, but they might as well have been part of the wall; they didn't budge, didn't even rattle, as if they'd been fused. She was suddenly sure Patrick had arranged it this way, allowing her to escape, trapping Chuck in the gym as punishment for his impersonation.

The little creatures came swarming towards Chuck. She could hear them screeching and gibbering, the sound muffled by the door. She turned away. Whatever was coming next, it wouldn't be pretty, and there was nothing she could do about it. Nothing at all.

Trying not to listen to the sounds from behind her, she crept off into the darkness, in pursuit of Patrick the self-styled god.

~~~~

Robin scrambled to her feet and quickly assessed her new situation. The boardroom only had one door, a big black one. Artwork-Collins stood in front of it, blocking it like a bouncer outside the VIP room. A photograph hanging on the wall to her right depicted the lobby of the Retreat. She figured that must be the way she had come in; it was the only thing here, herself not excepted, that didn't look like it had been rendered with oil and brush. The photo was surrounded by a thick wooden frame, ornate with swoops and curves. The bottom piece of it connected to a large, shield-shaped brass plate with a cartoon-style keyhole in the middle of it. Finally she moved her gaze on to the other occupant of the painting, who was studying her with interest, and a certain amount of impatience.

"Oh," Robin said. "Hi."

"Hello," he said. "I don't know you. Are you a new employee?"

"No."

"Are you a patient?"

"No."

"If you're not a patient, and you're not an employee, then you must be a visitor." His knife-slash mouth quirked on one side. "I hope you signed in."

"Someone signed in on my behalf."

Collins began approaching her. She circled the table to avoid him. When she passed by the doors, she grabbed the knobs and tried to open them, but they didn't budge. She probably shouldn't have been surprised. After all, they were painted shut. Ha ha ha. Collins kept coming, so she kept going. He stopped when he had the doors at his back and she was on the opposite side, with the long table between them, like they were about to face off in an epic air hockey match.

Collins said, "Are you running away from me?"

"I'd call it *edging* away," she said. "If you start to really chase me, then I'll run."

"What makes you think I might chase you?"

"My friend Bob says you're a vampire," Robin said. "Or used to be. He says he killed you, but here you are, pulling people into paintings."

"Your friend Bob sounds a little off. Is *he* a patient?"

"No," she said, "but maybe he should be."

"That can be arranged. Why are you here?"

"I'm here because you dragged me into your portrait."

"Not here in the painting. Here at the Retreat. You're a visitor? Who were you visiting? Why now? Where did you come from?"

"What is this, an interrogation? Are you going to shine a light in my face and ask me where I was on Tuesday night?"

"Good idea." Collins snapped his fingers and the light on the table flared, glaring cadmium yellow right into her face. It wasn't real light, so the effect wasn't blinding; it was more like looking at an extremely garish painting of a flower that blocked her view of half the room. "Where were you on Tuesday night?"

She stared at him, or, more accurately, at the fake klieg light that obscured most of him. "Are you fucking kidding me?" she said.

"We discourage the use of profanity around here."

"Oh for fuck's sake. Look. We had no idea this place existed. We were just out for a drive and we decided to try the Blackberry Mountain trail. That's all."

"Is it? Who picked the trail? Did one of you suggest it? Did anyone seem to be ... affected in some way, beforehand? Impaired? Afflicted?"

Robin immediately thought of Myra, and the sudden onset of her mysterious, crushing migraine in the parking lot.

"No," she said.

He snorted.

"Okay, fine. Yes. But what is it to you if somebody had a headache in the car? Does that mean something?"

"It means that—" He broke off, then grinned. "Aren't you clever."

"I like to think so, yeah."

"But not clever enough to understand why you're here. You're hoping I'll enlighten you, but I won't."

"Aw, come on. Play along."

"I don't think so." He snapped his fingers and the light went out, the painted bloom folding back into itself and disappearing. As she watched, he went to the photo, produced a large, cartoonish key, inserted it into the keyhole beneath the frame, and started twisting it. Each time the key turned, the scene in the photo changed, showing some other room: A cafeteria, a break room, a decrepit gymnasium. He stopped on an institutional-looking hallway not unlike the one she had been in earlier, when she had encountered Kyle. This must be how he had temporarily disappeared from the portrait in the lobby; she imagined him here in his little boardroom, keeping an eye on various parts of the Retreat, using the key to move through the system like cancer traveling through the lymphatic system.

Collins removed the key and glanced over at her. "This is where I leave you."

"So sorry to see you go."

"I'm not going. You are." He left the picture and headed for the doors, key held out in front of him. So that was it; the key moved the picture, and it also opened the doors. How useful.

She wanted it.

Robin took the crucifix off from around her neck and held it by the long piece, letting the looped cord dangle. He touched the key to the doors. They rolled open, sort of disintegrating, like paint being brushed with thinner. As they did, she felt a force pulling her towards them, not like the rush of atmosphere through an airlock, but more like she was covered in magnets and the door was a big iron plate. She hopped up onto the tabletop and pushed off the wall with her legs, giving herself a burst of speed. Collins, a look of astonishment on his painted face, just stood there as she went by and lassoed the key with the leather thong of the crucifix. Her momentum tore it out of his grip. He cried out and lunged for her, catching hold of the cross's strap. She snatched the key and swiveled it loose, giving up the crucifix in exchange for her prize.

Key in hand, she passed through the doors and out of the painting.

TELEVISION MAN

In The Cards

BOB SHUFFLED INTO the lounge at the end of the hallway. The room was empty except for a guy on a couch who was staring at the television. There were a couple of other chairs in the room but Bob thought they looked comically small; if he tried to sit in one he might fall off, or it might collapsed under his weight. Instead, he plopped down on the sofa, shifting his teddy bear knapsack around to his lap so he wouldn't squash all the little bears inside it.

The other guy on the couch looked at him. "Hi," he said.

"Hrm," Bob said.

"You're new, aren't you? What's your name?"

"Bbb."

"I'm Patrick."

Patrick? Wasn't he looking for somebody named Patrick? Bob wasn't sure. His head felt all fuzzy. The back of his hand was wet and he couldn't really remember why until he wiped his mouth with it and it came away coated with saliva, dragging along a thin line of spittle that broke and fell, drawing a line across his leg.

Patrick said, "Eww."

Bob mumbled something that was supposed to be an apology.

"It's okay. You look like a zombie. Did they just up your meds or something?"

Bob shrugged. He didn't know whether they had just upped his meds or not. He wasn't even sure what meds were.

"Never mind. You can just watch TV with me."

Bob raised his gaze to the television. It required a lot of effort. His neck muscles felt all rubbery, and his head weighed at least a hundred pounds. The screen was blurry, like it needed to be wiped off. In fact, everything was blurry. Maybe the whole room could use a cleaning. Bob couldn't really tell what was happening in the movie. He made a noise that ended with a question sound.

"I don't know. It's a movie I haven't seen before. But everybody is in big trouble." Patrick gestured with the remote towards the screen, which showed a dark, smoky place full of fuzzy red objects and a vaguely Chuck-shaped blob. "See that guy? He's trapped in a room full of goblins. I think they're going to eat him. This girl got pulled into an ugly painting—she just escaped but I don't know where she ended up—and this other girl is walking up a dark hallway all alone. You know how *that* always turns out."

Did he know how that always turns out? Bob wasn't sure. The scene switched to a dimly lit corridor. A person who may have been Myra stood in it, moving toward the camera, silhouetted against the ruddy light of a dirty window some distance behind her. Bob raised a hand to point, but it was too much effort and he let it drop again. "Mrmm," he said.

"No, not yours. Mine." Patrick transferred the remote to the hand farther away from Bob. "So that's who's left. There used to be another guy, but he disappeared. I'm not sure what happened to him. He kind of looked like you. And there were a couple more characters earlier, but they got killed." He sighed. "I don't know how they're going to get out of this mess. We'll see. It's fun not to know what's going to happen, isn't it?"

"Unnhnn," Bob said.

"You don't think so? You'd rather have spoilers?" Patrick shook his head. "If you always knew everything everyone was up to, what everyone was thinking, you wouldn't like it. Trust me."

Bob tried to say that he wanted whatever spoilers Patrick could give him, but it all came out as a string of mumbled consonants. Patrick seemed to take it as an inquiry on what had happened before Bob got there, and launched into a recap of everything that had led up to the each character's current predicament. Sometimes he seemed to be describing events that Bob vaguely remembered participating in, which didn't really make sense if it was just a movie. Maybe he had already seen it, and was projecting himself into it as one of the characters.

Well, if he had seen it before, he didn't really need to see it again. Especially when it was so much effort to stay awake.

He let himself slump sideways to have a little nap.

~~~~

Myra kept one hand on the wall as she walked along the darkened hallway, away from the gymnasium where Chuck had been trapped. The tiles were cool and slick with condensation. She passed a number of side corridors; every time the surface fell away from her fingers she was afraid that it wouldn't come back, leaving her to creep through a wide-open space with nothing to guide her until she stumbled into a swimming pool full of piranhas or something. But the wall always came back, and eventually the corridor ended in a cold metal door that felt like it belonged to an elevator. She located a panel off to the left. There was only one button. She pressed it, expecting nothing to happen, but a plastic ring around the button lit up just like it was supposed to, illuminating the hallway with a feeble, pallid glow. The button was revealed to be unmarked, black and glossy like a shark's eye, showing neither up nor down. From the shaft beyond the door, she heard a great deal of groaning and creaking as the elevator trundled to life. She hoped it wasn't loud enough for the monsters back in the gym to notice. She turned and surveyed the hallway in the dim light from the button, half-expecting to see an array of globular eyes gleaming back at her, but no, nothing but tile. Tile floor, tile walls, tile ceiling. It may as well have been a big shower stall. Only the nearest side corridor was visible, a few yards away, black as the entrance to an unlit morgue at midnight, going off to who knew where. She kept an eye on it, but nothing slurped out to get her.

There was a *ding* and the doors moaned open behind her. She backed into the elevator. A flickering fluorescent halo in the ceiling illuminated the trashed interior; the walls were crisscrossed by jagged slashes, the railings had been pulled off the walls and lay on the floor like discarded skis, the floor was splashed with something brown and crusty. A hole yawned in the back left corner, the floor twisted up around it in jags and curlicues, as if something had burst up through the bottom and had proceeded to wreck the place.

There were only two buttons available inside the box. They didn't look like any other elevator buttons she had ever seen. Both were nearly the size of her fist, comically protruding from the wall, making her feel like she had wandered into some sort of "My First Elevator" play set. One button said *UP* and the other said *DOWN*.

Myra was pretty sure she didn't want to go any farther down.

She mashed the *UP* button with her fist. The elevator didn't do anything for a very long few seconds; then the doors rattled shut and, with a lurch, the box began to drag itself upward. She stayed as close to the door as she could, keeping an eye on the hole in the floor, wondering if whatever had come through it might still be around. Just in case, she picked up one of the shorter sections of handrail. A snapped-off support still protruded from one end, forming a sort of handle that let her wield the thing like the bastard child of a sword and a truncheon. Despite the elevator's horribly loud metallic screeching and grinding, though, nothing erupted from the opening to claw and drool and gibber at her. When, after several minutes, the conveyance finally shuddered to a halt—seemingly from exhaustion more than anything else—and the doors sighed open, she dropped her makeshift weapon and stepped out into the smallish chamber outside. It was unremarkable, except for the wall opposite the elevator, which sported an enormous tinted window. Myra stepped out of the elevator, then stole to the window and peeked through. On the other side, Margaret sat in a wooden chair, secured to it by what looked like a straitjacket. There was a table in front of her, with a tall screen across the middle, separating her from the man on the other side. She recognized him from the painting in the lobby, and also from when she had met him at the castle. His suit, funereal black, looked like something the Count might have had hanging in his wardrobe for those times when formalwear was required.

She didn't see a way into that other room from here; the only door was to her right, and it was boarded up. The boards didn't look all that sturdy. Maybe she could pry them off with the broken handrail. Or maybe she could just use the handrail to smash the window, assuming it wasn't smash-proof.

A voice from behind her said: "I wouldn't do that if I were you."

She whirled and spotted Patrick, lying on the wall next to the elevator door as if on a grassy riverbank, watching the scene through the window. He was still surrounded by the amber-red glow, dialed down from earlier. He didn't seem inclined to pick her up and smash her against the ceiling. At least, not at the moment.

"You wouldn't do what?"

His head rolled to look at her. "Interfere." Then it rolled back to its previous position.

That curdled the stale air for a little while. "Okay," she said. "I won't." Then: "What am I not interfering with, exactly?"

"I told you before. We're running some tests."

"Why?"

"We test everybody we can. Dr. Collins thinks patients are better at it than regular people."

"Better at what?"

"Why don't you go and see?"

Taking that as an order, Myra turned back to the window, just as Collins flipped over a card. She craned her neck to see what it was. Instead of a king or a queen or a jack, it had a bunch of wavy lines on it. After a moment, Margaret tapped her foot a couple of times. Collins, unseen by Margaret behind the divider, shook his head and made a red mark on the paper in front of him. It had a lot of other red marks on it, and a smattering of green ones. He turned over another card. This one showed a circle.

Myra looked back to Patrick, hovering on the wall. "Is she supposed to guess what card he's looking at?"

"She's not supposed to guess. She's supposed to know."

"How would she know if she can't see it?"

"She just would. Or else she wouldn't."

"Okay." For a little while Myra didn't say anything. "You brought her up here and handed her off to be tested."

"Yes."

"But you don't do the testing yourself."

The look Patrick gave her told her that she didn't seem to be very bright. "Obviously not. Dr. Collins does it."

"Why not you? You seem to know all about it."

"Oh, I do. But Dr. Collins says that my abilities would make the results suspect."

"Your abilities?"

"Yes." He cocked his head at her and smiled a little, not nicely. "You must have noticed that I have some."

She sure had. Myra thought about this for a minute. "So he tests everybody?"

"Everybody he can."

"He tested you?"

"Of course."

"How did you do?"

He didn't answer; he was looking through the one-way glass again.

"Patrick?"

"Square."

"What?"

"Go check."

She shuffled over to the window again. The current card was a plus symbol. She opened her mouth to tell Patrick he had been wrong, but then Collins moved on to the next one.

Square.

"Patrick," she said, "how many cards did you get right?"

He grinned widely. "All of them."

~~~~

The goblins had Chuck surrounded, backing him away from the exit, up against the wall, then herding him into the corner nearest the statue, where the clothes were piled particularly high. He looked them over, their hungry, sharp little faces, their fangs, their razor claws. They seemed to be waiting for something, but what? He soon found out as some of them sprang into the air and landed on the statue's right arm. Under the additional weight, the arm pivoted at the shoulder, bringing the smoldering bowl close to the floor. As it neared the bottom of its arc, the hand that held the bowl tipped it forward, turning it into a sort of scoop. When that happened, a cohort of the little monsters surged forward and grabbed him with their hard, sharp hands, cut away his clothes with their razor-edged talons. In short order they had stripped him bare, somehow managing not to injure him beyond a few light scratches. They carried off the scraps of his clothing, capering and gibbering as if they'd won some great prize. The others dragged him across the floor, bringing him over to the statue of Patrick. They lifted him up onto their shoulders. Hail the conquering hero. Heat washed over him, like standing too close to a bonfire. Maybe they were planning to cook him so they could eat him later. Chuck roast. Mmm, tasty. A little fatty though.

He hit the edge of the bowl and slid into the flames. The goblins jumped off its arm and the statue pivoted again, scooping him up, letting him settle into the bottom of the fiery platter. Whatever was in there was sticky and viscous and burned like napalm. He squirmed and writhed inside the inferno as his skin crisped away, his fat sizzled, his hair burned. He screamed and the fire invaded his mouth, flash-frying his tongue, scorching down his throat to collect in his belly and cook him from the inside out. At last, he blacked out.

When he came to, he was no longer burning. Now he drifted with the smoke beneath the ceiling of the gym. A weak current pulled him into the grille of an air shaft. He slid through the darkness for a while, now sideways, now up, now diagonally, now up again. He swirled through a spinning ventilator and emerged into the moonlight above the Retreat. The grounds stretched out beneath him, curving at the edges like he was looking through a fisheye lens. He drifted along the roof, floating above a tarry pebbled surface, then a cracked solid one, then over a strange dome that bulged like a pimple and seemed to be expanding and contracting as if taking measured breaths.

Chuck became aware of a small shape picking its way along the roof, heading in his direction. At first thought it might be a goblin, but it didn't move the right way. The thing neared, then scrambled up the dome to the top. It got there just before Chuck did, and when he drifted past, the figure reached out and grabbed him and somehow held him in place, despite the fact that Chuck was nothing but vapor. A pretty neat trick, Chuck thought, catching a cloud.

"What's this?" the figure said in a reedy voice. "A new goblin? Don't we have enough goblins?"

An answer came, faint, hollow as the wind, seeming to rise from the dome beneath them: "Goblins are so disposable. We can never have too many. And he provoked us."

"But he came from outside. We weren't going to make goblins out of the ones from outside."

"Outside. Inside. Is there really a difference?"

"There used to be," the figure said, pouting. "There's *supposed* to be."

"Don't be naïve." Then: "You shouldn't be here. You haven't got any authority here."

"I have some."

"Not enough. Go back to the forest."

"But—"

"Go back to the forest, Paltruck. That's where you belong."

Chuck felt the other presence withdraw. It didn't speak again. The small creature—Paltruck, apparently—sat there silently, holding onto Chuck, like a comic book character who had grabbed someone else's thought balloon and refused to let go of it. After a little while, Paltruck muttered: "It's not fair."

Chuck was inclined to agree.

More time passed. Chuck had no idea how much. Then Paltruck said: "I don't care what he says. This has to stop. He's right, I don't have much authority here, but I can send you back down. Don't tell, okay? It'll be our secret."

Chuck wondered what Paltruck thought he might tell and who he might tell it to. A moment later he was racing away, leaving the small creature behind, scudding back across the roof and through the ventilator, which was now spinning the opposite direction from before. He flowed swiftly through the darkness of the air shaft network, poured out into the dim and smoky gymnasium, plunged straight down into the fire. His shriveled, screaming body was still in there, writhing, shrunken. He reentered it like an intaken breath, dislodging something else that was trying to take up residence there. The platter tipped downward and spilled him out onto the floor. He rolled a little way and ended up facedown on the beaten wood.

He heard footsteps gather around him and raised his head, blinking away the tears that blurred his vision. The goblins had surrounded him again, but kept their distance, looking down at him with yellow eyes. He stood up, ready to face the little monsters, and realized that he wasn't taller than they were anymore. He looked at his hands, or what used to be his hands; now they belonged to something else, something with spindly fingers and sharp claws, with wiry arms and orange-red skin. He took a look around the room. The shadowy recesses weren't so shadowy anymore; he could see into them in shades of green and grey. He could see a heat-bloom radiating from the fire, bright as a star.

He'd gone into those flames a man and had come out a goblin, but he was still himself on the inside. That was what Paltruck had done. That was their little secret. He could move unnoticed, a double agent among the horde. Except that the other goblins stayed back, watching him expectantly. Could they tell he was different from them? Were they waiting for him to say something? Was there a password?

Just as he began to think the stillness was dragging on too long, he heard a creaking noise. The doors through which Patrick had taken Margaret and then Myra had escaped, the doors that had closed and trapped him in here, were swinging open.

As a single unit, the other goblins turned in that direction. A great shout went up, a shriek or a war cry or whatever, and then they streamed toward the doors, the sound of the their feet echoing through the gymnasium. It seemed as if they'd been waiting all their miserable lives for those doors to open, and now they didn't have a second to waste.

In a moment they were gone, leaving Chuck standing there, all alone, a confused man in a little goblin body.

~~~~

Somebody was gently shaking her.

Robin opened her eyes to find a man in navy scrubs bent over her. He carried a clipboard in one hand, folded against his chest, and had his other hand on her shoulder. As she blinked up at him, he said: "You're not supposed to sleep in the hallway."

"Oh," she said. "Sorry."

The man—an orderly?—reached out to help her up. She started to move to take his hand with her right, only to realize that she was already holding onto something: The key she had taken from Collins. She quickly hid it behind her back and let him pull her up by her left hand instead. She felt tired, sore, oddly slack. Her toes were cold. Her hiking shorts and boots had been replaced by loose sweat pants, a flannel hoodie, and flip-flops. She hated flip-flops. She said: "Where am I and why am I dressed like this? Where are my regular clothes?"

He didn't seem surprised at the questions. "I don't know why you're dressed like that or where your regular clothes are, but you're in the Retreat, just like always."

"Always? But before, I was in …"

She trailed off. If she had landed in some version of the Retreat that was actually functioning as an institution, then telling a staff member she had just been inside a painting most likely wasn't the best idea.

"You were in what?" The man actually sounded interested in hearing the answer, which was probably a bad sign.

"I was, uh, in the Retreat. Just like always. Hey, is Patrick around?"

"Patrick? He should be. When is he not?"

"Do you know where?"

"No, but check the TV lounge. He's usually there."

"Right. Of course." Then: "Um, where is that, again?"

He raised an eyebrow. "Are you sure you're okay? You seem disoriented. Did you hit your head?" He inspected his clipboard. "Oh, I see. It's time for your meds. I'll go get them from—"

"I had them already," Robin said.

The orderly gave her a narrow look. "Really? You're not checked off on the list."

"Yeah. He was going to mark it down but his pen was out of ink. He said he would do it when he got back to the station. I guess he forgot."

"Who was this?"

"Uh, Baxter?" Robin half-asked.

"Oh. Baxter." From the orderly's tone of voice, Baxter's involvement explained everything. "All right. You can go to the lounge and find Patrick." He pointed up the hallway. "I'll track down Baxter and make sure you got the right meds at the right time. If he tells me something different, you'll be seeing me again soon. Yeah?"

"Okay. Thanks." She went in the direction the man had indicated, shifting the key around in front of her in what she hoped was a surreptitious manner. She inspected it as she walked. It wasn't made of paint anymore; now it was actual metal. Brass, she thought, badly tarnished. So she wasn't crazy; that whole incident inside the portrait had actually happened. Or had it? Was she really so crafty with her sleight of hand that the orderly hadn't noticed she was carrying something? Maybe it was an imaginary key and only she could see it.

Maybe. But that didn't mean it was useless.

She hadn't gone far when she heard what sounded like a television coming from a door to her left. She went inside. Two people sat on a couch. One of them might have been Patrick; the other was definitely Bob. He wasn't dressed like she remembered, and he wasn't carrying his weapons anymore. He still had his satchel, sort of, except now it looked like a big teddy bear and was full of other teddy bears. He couldn't threaten to shoot her with those. She wasn't sure he was even awake. Robin bent over, trying to get a look at his face, which was aimed at the floor. Was he drooling?

"You're blocking the TV," Patrick said.

She looked at him for a moment, then sidled out of the way and moved closer to Bob. He wasn't faking it; he really was in some kind of stupor. She considered slapping him a few times to snap him out of it, which would have been satisfying even if it didn't work, but settled for nudging his shin with her foot instead. No response. "Hey, Bob," she said. "Wake up."

Patrick said, "Don't bother. He's totally out of it. He won't even watch television."

She grabbed Bob's shoulders and gave him a good shake; his head lolled from one shoulder to the other like a fading balloon that could barely lift its string. "Bob! Is this any way for a vampire hunter to behave? Come on!"

"Vampire hunter? Better not to let them hear you validating his fantasy world."

Robin let go of Bob. He slumped sideways on the couch. Then, to Patrick: "What's wrong with him?"

"Nothing," Patrick said. "He just had his meds, is all."

"What did they give him?"

Patrick shrugged. "Meds."

Meds. That was helpful. Well, whatever he had taken, Bob was definitely checked out of the hotel. She backed off a step and looked around, trying to figure out her next move.

Patrick said, hopefully: "Leaving?"

"Not yet."

"Well, can you just sit down then? I'm trying to watch TV."

"Yeah? What are you watching?"

"Stuff."

"Sounds riveting," she said.

"It's better than wandering around out there." He gave her a significant look. "You never know when you might get kidnapped by an ogre or pulled inside a painting."

After a moment, she said: "You saw all that, did you?"

"Uh-huh." He pointed at the set. "In the movie."

She turned to the television. It showed a small, dim room, where somebody who looked a lot like Myra was talking to somebody who looked a lot like Patrick.

"That's you," Robin said.

"Nah. He only looks like me."

"He looks *exactly* like you."

Patrick shrugged, as if to say that lots of people looked exactly like him.

"So that's not you."

"Nope."

"And you've never been in that room."

"Oh, I've been there lots of times. But I'm not there now." His tone of voice suggested that she must be incredibly dense. "I'm here. In *this* room. With you."

"Where is that room? Can you take me to it?"

He shook his head. "It's here, in the Retreat, but we can't go there now. We'll miss the movie."

"I'll go by myself. I don't care about the movie."

"You can't go by yourself. You have to go through the walls."

"Through the walls? You mean like secret passages?"

"The passages aren't a secret. Everybody knows they're there. Getting into them is the hard part. Getting out again is even harder."

"Is there a way into them from this room?"

"Sure. Like I said, I don't go wandering around out there."

Robin glanced around the room, looking for a hidden door into the passages that weren't a secret because everyone knew about them. Where might such a door be? Her gaze settled on a battered radiator that stood against the wall to her right. "Is that it?"

"Yep."

"How do I open it?"

"You just pull on it. But you need a special key to unlock it."

"Who has these special keys?"

"Baxter does. And Dr. Collins."

"Collins has a key?"

"Uh-huh."

She showed him her prize from the portrait. "Does it look like this?"

His eyes widened.

She stuck her finger through the loop on the end and gave the key a gunfighter-style twirl. "Didn't see *that* in the movie, did you?" she said.

~~~~

Myra stood near the one-way glass, watching Margaret get nearly all of the cards wrong. Every once in a while the doctor guessed correctly and got herself a green mark on the paper, which eventually gave Myra enough information to identify the code; she stomped her foot once for a square, twice for a circle, three times for wavy lines, and so on. But mostly the marks were red. Periodically, Myra shifted her gaze to a section of the window that showed Patrick's reflection. He stayed where he was, stuck to the wall as if he had been cocooned there in a wad of glowing amber goo. She knew he was studying her, but didn't know why.

Collins turned over the last card. Margaret earned another red mark. Collins shook his head and his mouth moved, though Myra couldn't hear what he was saying. The door in the other room opened and an orderly entered. Myra recognized him as Baxter, the one from Margaret's memories who had morphed into an ogre and taken her away. Now he did it again, picking her up, chair and all. Margaret squeaked and squirmed and kicked her feet as he carried her out of the room.

Myra smacked the window with her open palm, once, hard, and shouted, "No!" The surface instantly shattered into thousands of tiny pieces. They hung together for a moment, a vertical jigsaw puzzle of fragments, before cascading to the floor—all on her side—in a shower of jagged blue-green jewels.

Collins turned his head to look at her. There was no surprise on his face; he had known all along that she was there. He smiled at her. So cold, so wide, so toothy. The Count had smiled at her that way, but

Collins wasn't a vampire now, he was a man; and somehow, on a man, the smile looked even worse.

The orderly reentered the other room, carrying a new chair, a regular office one with arms and rollers and burgundy fabric cushions. He set it down in front of the table, then departed. Collins showed Myra the reformed deck of cards and gestured her towards the spot Margaret had vacated. Instead, she backed away until she got to the elevator. Patrick, still glued to the wall, regarded her with disdain as she pawed around behind her back looking for the call button. There it was. She pressed it with her palm. Grinding noises ensued. Patrick yawned. Collins just waited, idly shuffling his deck.

The elevator emitted a sickly *ding*. She turned around to face it as the doors groaned open, revealing a horde of small grinning creatures, a fresh contingent of the little monsters from the subterranean gymnasium. They smelled like a pack of sweaty office workers returning to work after a long run and a smoke break and no shower. They flapped into the room, parting around her, leaving a small contingent to stop her from entering the elevator. Patrick, looking utterly bored, slurped off the wall, flowed over their heads into the battered box, and vanished through the hole in the floor.

Behind her, Collins clapped his hands sharply, jerking her attention around to him. She was startled to see that the creatures had positioned themselves into a little stepped pyramid in front of the broken window, forming stairs for her to climb.

"Enough dawdling," Collins said. "Come and sit down. I've got some things for you to look at."

She stood there gawking at him.

"Please. I'm asking nicely." He gestured at the window. "You can see I've rolled out the red carpet."

What a comedian. She eyed the elevator. She wouldn't be able to get past the three little guards, and if she did, she wouldn't be able to get it going before they dragged her out of it. Her gaze moved to the barricaded door. Collins laughed. "Don't be ridiculous. You wouldn't get two steps before the goblins stopped you. Come and sit down." His voice congealed into something waxy and toxic. "You really have no other option."

Well, fuck and damn. Myra sighed and went to the window. She studied the goblin steps for a moment, then hoisted herself up onto the frame, pivoted over the barrier, and dropped to the other side. Maybe Collins could make her dance, but he couldn't dictate the steps. So there. He didn't react to this gesture of useless defiance; he just tilted his head at the empty chair. Myra went to it and sat down. From here, Collins was hidden behind the big screen that cut across the middle of the table. "So what are we playing? Go Fish?"

"No. We're conducting a little test. Patrick told you what these cards are for?"

"Yeah. You want to see if I can read your mind."

"Not my whole mind. Just the part that's concentrating on these cards. I draw a card, and you tell me what you think I see."

"What's the point?"

"I'm studying your potential."

"Maybe I don't want my potential studied."

"Why not? Wouldn't you like to know what you're capable of?"

"Is that something any of us should really know?"

"Oh I think it is. So let's get started, shall we? We have circles, squares, a Greek cross—you might call it a plus sign—stars, and wavy lines. Tell me which one I see."

She heard him turn over a card. She looked at the screen, slate grey and featureless, then glanced through the window. The goblins were gone, though she hadn't noticed them disperse. She was sure they lurked nearby, ready to reappear if they were needed.

"I'm waiting," Collins said.

For some reason, she thought he was looking at a bunch of wavy lines.

"Circle," she told him.

~~~~

Chuck wandered through the doors into the hallway beyond, up a short flight of stairs, then along a dingy, echoing corridor. There were several side passages, which he ignored; he could tell they hadn't been used in a long time. He stopped when he came to a rickety elevator. This showed signs of recent activity; the others must have gone up in it, as, he imagined, Myra had done. Now it was his turn. Feeling vaguely ridiculous, he pressed the button. It lit up with an unsteady flicker, but there was no sign that anything was happening, no whirr of machinery to indicate that the box was on its way.

He waited a little while, then decided the elevator wasn't coming. Maybe the goblins had wedged the door open when they got to their floor. Maybe the elevator just didn't work. He inspected his fingers, their powerful joints, their curved claws, then jammed them into the space where the door met the wall and started pulling. The door creaked and protested, but it moved, revealing an empty shaft beyond. Ropy cables snaked down from above, swaying slightly. With this new body, he could climb the shit out of those. Before he got started, though, he noticed dark shapes swarming into the shaft high above. The cables began to twang and vibrate like harp strings. He retreated and ducked back into one of the branching corridors, and waited there as the other goblins tromped by on their way back to the gym. If they noticed him skulking around in the shadows, they didn't pay him any attention.

Once his colleagues had passed through, Chuck scampered out, leaped into the shaft, and grabbed one of the cables. The braided steel retained only the barest sheen of lubrication. He felt the frayed ends of individual strands poking at his hardened skin. This would have drawn blood once, but now it wasn't even an annoyance. In fact it made for a better grip. He started shimmying up the metal rope. The only sound was the faint scraping of his hands and feet as he climbed. It grew dark, then lighter again as he approached the bottom of the elevator car. It had a hole ripped in it, letting feeble illumination drip through. In addition to the light of a sickly fluorescent bulb, there was also a weak, liquid, lambent yellow gloss around the bottom of the car and the shaft immediately below, as if someone had splattered it with the ooze from a broken glow-stick. He wondered what that stuff was. It had all faded by the time he got there. Chuck hopped over to one of the walls where it had been, clinging with his fingers and toes, and sniffed around a little. Nothing. When it disappeared, it disappeared completely.

He tilted his head to look at the hole in the bottom of the car. His long arms couldn't quite reach it to pull himself through; he would have to jump for it. A real goblin would make it with no trouble, but could he?

Only one way to find out.

Chuck planted his big feet on the wall, tilted his head so he could see the target, and sprang forward. He shot through the opening and bounced off the wall of the elevator, then off the ceiling, then off the opposite wall. He ended up on his back next to the hole, momentarily stunned, staring up at the dent he had made in the roof. His new goblin legs had a lot of kick in them.

As he'd suspected, the elevator door was jammed open; stuff that looked like fragments of tempered glass had gotten wedged into the track. He exited, turned, and started to pick the glass out of the way, then thought better of it, lest the elevator should be called into service by something he didn't want to meet. He turned to inspect the room he had entered. A sheet of more sharp, tiny crystals covered the floor, apparently from a big broken window in the wall ahead of him. He heard a voice—Myra's—from beyond the opening, periodically saying different shapes. Square. Circle. Star. Was she playing some kind of game? He crept over to the window. She wasn't alone. His goblin nose smelled her perfume or soap or shampoo, but also a masculine scent. Aftershave? Deodorant? Cologne? He wasn't sure. He stayed where he was, out of sight, listening. He could hear other sounds, faint sliding noises, like plastic or laminated paper. Those sounds seemed to precede Myra's words by a moment or two, so they must be related, but he didn't understand what it was all about.

Well, whatever was going on, it didn't seem as if Myra was in any immediate danger. Chuck sat down with his back against the dividing wall, out of sight, and for once tried to plan his next move. What to do? He couldn't just leap through the window, waving his arms and gibbering in goblin-talk, and carry her off slung over his shoulder like a prize. For one thing, he didn't know who she was with; and for another, she would think he was yet another monster coming to harass her. He would have to demonstrate who he really was before she would be willing to go anywhere with him. And where would he take her? Back down the shaft to where his little red comrades waited? No. Obviously. But maybe that barricaded door went somewhere better. He bet he could rip it right of its frame if he tried.

Funny thing about being a goblin.

He felt better than he had in years.

Let's Make A Deal

MYRA STARED AT the divider separating her from Collins. She couldn't see him, but she heard a faint whisking sound every time he turned a card over, and offered her guess without prompting. There went another one. She thought it was a square, but she said it was a circle. He turned over another; square again. She called it a star.

"That was the last one." It was the first thing he had said in a while. She heard him shuffling some papers. "That was quite a remarkable performance."

"Was it?"

"Oh, yes. You got every single one wrong. You should have gotten about a fifth of them right, just by chance." He suddenly folded the barrier so that she could see him. "One can only conclude that you knew which card I had and deliberately chose wrong every time."

Fuck. Look at him, so pleased with himself. "Maybe I'm just a lousy guesser," she said.

"The law of averages doesn't care how lousy a guesser you are." He banged the cards on the table a couple of times, squaring the deck. "I think it's time we moved on to another test."

"What, more cards?"

"No. You're done with cards. I need to put you into a scenario where you're less likely to cheat."

"How are you going to stop me from cheating?"

He set the cards down on top of the paper that showed her perfectly imperfect score. "You'll see," he said.

She felt a presence move in behind her, and wasn't surprised to see Baxter lurking there when she glanced over her shoulder. She turned back to Collins. "Are we going somewhere?"

"Yes. I have to retrieve something before we perform the next trial, so my colleague here will be taking you to the auditorium to wait for me."

"The auditorium? Is that where you took Margaret?"

"It is."

"Is she safe?"

"She is out of harm's way, for now, which is more than I can say for your other friends, or for your husband. Bob, isn't it?"

"Bob is here?"

"He's in the building, but he won't be joining us. Not yet. You might say that he's being held in reserve against the possibility that you continue to be uncooperative. Should that happen, you can expect me to raise the stakes again by involving him in your testing." Collins smiled, showing her his teeth. "I hope you take advantage of the opportunity to avoid that." He looked past her, at the orderly, and nodded; hands gripped her shoulders and pulled her out of her seat. The chair tipped over and clattered to the floor.

Collins made a *tsking* sound, got up, came around the table, righted the chair, and rolled it back into place.

"Clumsy Baxter," he said. "Always such an ogre."

~~~~

After the game of cards, or whatever it was, had broken up in the other room, Chuck waited for a minute or two, then peeked over the wall. The cards remained neatly stacked on the table, along with a few sheets of paper and a folded cardboard screen, but everyone was gone. A narrow door in the wall to his right stood partly open; he didn't see any other way in or out of that room, so they all must have exited that way. He flipped himself over the divider, ninja-style. With his weirdly enormous feet, he stuck the landing like a boss. He slunk to the door and peered into the corridor beyond. The walls consisted of exposed lath and beams, crumbling plaster protruding between ribs of flat, water-stained wood; the ceiling looked like the underside of a derelict ship, with a floor of unfinished boards, patched here and there with mismatched bits of plywood, linoleum, even roofing shingles. A single naked bulb burned near the door; its light extended to a T-intersection maybe five yards away. The corridor was exceedingly narrow; had he still been a Chuck-sized Chuck instead of a goblin-sized one, he would have found it difficult going, but as it was he had plenty of room to move. He scurried to the intersection. It ran off into darkness in both directions. No one was in sight, and he had no idea which way they had gone. Maybe his new and improved goblin ears could help him out. He cocked his head and listened, and heard something, but not what he had expected; it sounded like a dozen sets of footsteps were tramping along somewhere in the maze of twisty corridors, drowning out whatever other sounds might be echoing around in here. More goblins? Where had they come from? And where were they going?

His ears, clever things that they were, swiveled of their own accord, isolating the source of the footsteps. They were coming from his left. He used the sharp nail of his forefinger to scratch an arrow into the wall to show which way he was going, just in case he needed to find his way back; then he headed toward the sounds. Once he got away from the incandescent bulb, he found that the place sort of lit up in his vision, everything cast in shades of grey and black and purple, so he wasn't moving blind. Plus he had his ears to guide him; the sounds of the other goblins faded and strengthened as he took wrong turns and corrected his mistakes. The place was a maze; it reminded him of those crazy funhouse hallways, but on an epic scale, the way it crooked and bent, went up a few steps, then down a few, following the contours of the surrounding rooms. Numerous side corridors branched off from this one, dark openings that beckoned like comforting caves; black chimneys rose overhead, some with crude ladders and some without; pits opened beneath him, spanned by rickety boards or perilous lips of crumbling plaster. He kept scratching arrows into the wall, used the rough heel of his palm to scratch them out or correct them if he passed them again after going in a circle, which happened more than once. The last thing he wanted to do was get stuck in here forever, which he could totally see happening if he wasn't careful. Maybe he could become the Retreat's resident ghost, creeping through the corridors, scratching on the inside of the walls to freak out the staff, stealing out at night to grab food and frighten the residents.

Chuck shook his head to clear it of such crazily appealing ideas, such goblin-think. That way lay madness.

And there was already more than enough madness to go around.

~~~~

Robin inspected the radiator, but she didn't find anywhere to insert the key. She turned to Patrick and said, "Are you sure this is a secret door?"

"Uh-huh."

"You're not just telling me that to get me out of your hair?"

He looked at her. "*Are* you out of my hair?"

Robin could take a hint. Leaving him to stare at his screen, which was showing God knew what—the inside of an elevator shaft or something—she knelt down and felt along the warm metal sides, the paint rough under her fingers. She stopped at the bleed valve. Someone had left the radiator key in it. Green with corrosion, it looked like it was probably stuck, but that didn't mean it was. She pinched it between her fingers and gave it a twist. It wouldn't move. Then she pulled it and it slid right out, valve and all, smooth as butter, revealing a deep socket underneath, ending in a keyhole.

Bingo.

She inserted the key, but before she turned it, she realized that it was transmitting vibrations into her fingertips, and not from water moving through pipes. This was something else. She cocked her head, lowering her ear closer to the fixture. The vibrations resolved themselves into sounds.

Tramping feet. Lots of them. Getting closer.

Shit.

Suddenly concerned that the secret door would be opening soon, from the other side, to admit visitors she probably didn't want to meet, Robin removed the key and replaced the valve. She retreated to the couch, ignoring Patrick's exasperated grunt as she passed between his face and the glowing boob tube. She grabbed Bob's hand. "We have to go." She pulled him to his feet, or tried to; Bob was having trouble sitting, let alone standing. He slumped forward, hanging off her shoulders like a drunk. Robin tried to adjust him around to her side, but it was like manipulating a giant sack of cooked spaghetti.

"Still refusing to leave people behind who would best be abandoned? No wonder you keep getting caught."

She remembered that voice. Collins, now made of flesh and bone instead of oil and pigment, stood in the doorway, wearing a charcoal suit and matching bowtie. She looked him over and said: "Did you just come from a funeral?"

"No," Collins said, "though I may be going to one. But first. You have something that belongs to me. I want it back."

She let go of Bob, giving him a little push so he fell back onto the couch, and turned to face the Director. "Are you sure it's yours? Because the guy I stole it from was more colorful than you."

"Very funny." He smiled thinly, just to show her how funny she was. "Return it."

"I threw it away."

"I don't believe you. Show me your hands."

Because Robin no longer had the key, having stuffed it into Bob's teddy bear knapsack when she dropped him on the sofa, she readily complied.

Collins's eyes narrowed. "What did you do with it? Is it in your pockets?"

"I don't have pockets. I told you, I threw it away. I only took it because you were using it. I didn't think it would do me any good out here."

"Please. You're not that stupid."

"Maybe I'm *exactly* that stupid."

"I guess we'll find out. Because you have—" He checked his wristwatch. "—Five seconds to tell me where it is."

Robin cocked her head at him. "What happens in five seconds?"

As she spoke, she heard a metallic *click* from behind the radiator, as of a latch being released.

"Something you won't like," Collins said.

~~~~

Bob felt like he'd guzzled a bucket or two of vodka with a chaser of cough syrup. His head spun every time he moved his eyes, and when Robin forced him to his feet, well, forget it. He had to hang off her, and it was all he could do to keep from puking over her shoulder and down her back like a colicky baby. Then Collins showed up, and Robin stuffed something into his knapsack and pushed onto the sofa, where he collapsed in a barely-there stupor as she and Collins exchanged unpleasantries.

Then he noticed fingers sliding along the gap between the radiator and the wall. Spindly reddish fingers with sharp black nails. Goblin fingers. He fumbled for his weapons, remembered he didn't have them anymore, and tried to stand, as if he could block them with his body, but all he managed to do was land sprawling on the floor right in front of the radiator. He had barely gotten even one step. The teddy bears cushioned his fall so he didn't smash his face. The metal thing Robin had slipped into his sack jabbed him in the belly. He could only watch as the radiator swung outward on unseen hinges, pivoting on the pipe that fed it hot water, revealing a hole in the wall behind it. Light spilled into the opening, which was occupied by a number of goblins, all of them eager for another chance to slice him with their claws and bite him with their teeth. They boiled into the room, or tried to, but something seemed to stop them, bouncing them back, as if they had run into an invisible barrier. They clawed and scratched at the air, but couldn't get through.

Collins looked at Patrick.

Patrick said: "You're not doing this here. I'm trying to watch my show. Sit down and be quiet, or go away."

Collins opened his mouth to speak, but the volume on the television suddenly increased, drowning him out. The sounds of battle filled the room. Bob managed to roll his head around to look at the screen. It showed his first encounter with the goblins, hours earlier, when he had still been a vampire hunter, still had a shot at being the hero. Look at him go, laying waste to the goblin horde with Toomes's shotgun and sword. That was who he wanted to be again: A vampire hunter, not a drugged-up zombie nothing who could only mumble and couldn't stand up on his own. He wanted his equipment, his clothes, all the things that had been taken away. Sure, he'd been using someone else's weapons, playing someone else's role, but, really, wasn't that what everyone was doing most of the time? Why couldn't he be the big hero?

Bob squeezed his eyes shut, clenched his fists as tight as he could, as if that would push the meds out of his body and bring back his gear. The floor seemed to tilt a little beneath him, like a big ship riding a wave. At first he thought it was just a wave of nausea, but when it passed, his head felt clear for the first time in what seemed like days.

Bob opened his eyes.

He was back in his own clothes. His sword lay just inches away from his outstretched fingers. The light from the television reflected along its shiny blade, giving it an enchanted blue-green blow. His teddy bear knapsack had turned back into the bag of tricks he'd assembled after Toomes's demise. Even his wrist crossbow had returned, strapped to his arm, cocked and ready. He didn't have his missing fingers back, he wasn't going to be greedy.

Bob grabbed the sword, jumped to his feet, and—ignoring her startled expletive—pushed Robin aside to confront Collins. "Where's my wife, you son of a bitch?"

Collins raised an eyebrow. Behind him, Bob heard Patrick sigh. The television went mute; the picture froze. The barrier holding back the goblins evaporated.

Bob pivoted and met the goblin pack head-on, hacking with his newly-recovered blade as Robin scrambled out of the way. Burnt sienna body parts spun through the air, spraying black blood across the white walls and floor. The creatures broke immediately, turned and fled, climbing over each other in a panic to get away. He slashed at their retreating backsides as they vanished into the hidden passage, and would have gone after them if Robin hadn't grabbed him by the belt and spun him around. She was quick enough to dodge his reflexive sword thrust. Maybe she'd been expecting it.

"Jesus Christ, Bob, are you *trying* to kill me?" she said. "They're gone. Calm the fuck down."

"Sorry." He was breathing hard, all wound up. "Sorry. Got carried away."

"No shit. What just happened? How did the drugs wear off? Where did that sword come from? And the bag of crap? And the clothes?" She looked down at herself. "And why don't I have *my* clothes?"

"Patrick must have done it." He looked around. "Where'd Collins go?"

"He took off when you went after those things."

"Goblins," Bob said.

"What?"

"That's what I call them. Goblins." He went to the door, looked up and down the corridor. The long corridor was empty in both directions, just an endless series of doors. Chasing after Collins would be a waste of time right now. He returned to the lounge. Robin was peering into the passage behind the radiator. He went over to Patrick. "Thanks," he said.

"For what?"

"For giving me back my weapons and clearing up my head."

"I didn't do that."

"You didn't?"

"No. I was just trying to watch my show."

"Then who did?"

"If you don't know," Patrick said, "then I'm not going to tell you."

Before Bob could pursue line of inquiry any further, Robin yelped and scrambled away from the opening. Bob turned and saw that another goblin had come through. The thing gibbered at them, emitting an urgent a series of grunts and squeals, waving its arms and gesturing at the secret door.

Bob stepped up and shot it point-black in the face with his crossbow.

~~~~

Baxter took Myra on a winding path through the narrow corridors. At times the walls became so close that they had to turn sideways to slide between; at other times they had to stoop, backs scraping against the rough ceiling. The passage finally widened into an almost human-sized hallway before ending at an old wooden door. The orderly drew back a bolt and pushed the door inward, revealing a darkened area beyond. He gave Myra a shove through the opening. She stumbled into the room, tripped over something, and fell. Baxter exited and pulled the door shut. She heard a bolt slide into place on the other side.

Myra rolled over and sat up and looked to see what she had tripped over. It turned out to be Margaret, still tied to that chair, lying on her side, not moving. Myra hauled the chair upright and felt the doctor's throat. She was warm and had a pulse, but she was definitely out of it. Maybe they had bopped her one, or drugged her. Myra fussed with the straps for a minute, but the cunning knots were smarter than she was. Just as well. If she weren't strapped in, Margaret would probably fall out into a heap on the floor. After a moment Myra dragged the chair off to the side and left it against the wall.

That done, Myra crept away and looked around the room, or tried to. It was a rather large space, but very dim, the only illumination coming from the feeble glow of distant *EXIT* signs. The signs were quite a bit above her, suggesting she was at the bottom of a downward-sloping floor. She realized that there were noises coming from the far places of the room, as of attendees moving around, shuffling their feet, breathing, muttering, clearing their throats. It reminded her of a movie theatre filling up before a show. Well, Collins had mentioned an auditorium; that implied an audience. Perhaps her next trick was going to be performing feats of mind-reading for the amazement of the spectators.

The sounds of movement died down. A few seconds later, she heard something like flashbulbs popping and all the lights suddenly came on at once, blindingly bright. She cringed as a roar went up from all around, but it was applause, not a war cry. As her eyes adjusted, she saw that she and Margaret were on a stage, surrounded by rows and rows of tiered seating. The audience consisted of a few dozen goblins, draped in the tattered rags she had seen in the gymnasium. They had dressed up in finery for a night out on the town. The back wall of the stage was obscured by thick red curtains. She wondered what was behind them.

Collins emerged from the wings and strode onto the stage, looking like he had just wandered in from the swinging Seventies. That hair! That grin! They both seemed to be made out of plastic. Myra could almost see light sparkling off his teeth. He waved to the audience as he sauntered over to where Myra stood, then hung around waiting for the applause to die down. It didn't. Finally he raised his hands—one of which held a microphone so gigantic he could have clubbed baby seals with it—then lowered them again. The roar of the crowd faded.

Collins turned to Myra. He offered her his free hand; too dumbfounded to do anything else, she took it and let him lead her to the front edge of the stage.

"Welcome!" he said. "You're our next contestant! Are you ready?"

Myra said, "Ready for what?"

The curtains along the back wall retracted, revealing three huge padlocked doors, arrayed in a row facing the spectators, advertised themselves in garish lettering as *ONE*, *TWO*, and *THREE*, just like in that old game show with the silly costumes, where you had to decide whether to keep what you had already one or forfeit it in favor of something else—maybe better, maybe worse—hidden away from sight.

"To make a deal, of course," Collins said.

~~~~

Robin dragged the dead goblin away from the secret door, putting it in a corner with the others. She tried not to look at the crossbow bolt sticking out of its eye, waggling as the thing's head bobbed up and down. She remembered how Bob had threatened her with that same crossbow, trying to get her to remove the painting from the wall so he could hack it up with his sword. Would he really have shot her? She wasn't sure. But she'd felt safer around him when he'd been disarmed.

She glanced sidelong at Patrick and Bob. Patrick had returned to watching television, while Bob had taken Robin's place at the secret door, peering down the narrow dark corridor beyond. What was he doing, waiting for something else to emerge and suffer his mighty wrath? Patrick noticed her looking at him. His oblique gaze flicked to her, then to the television, then back to her, then back to the television, then back to her. He tipped his head slightly, telling her she should look at the screen, so she did. It showed Chuck being carried along by a bunch of the little red guys who had so recently invaded the lounge. They pitched him into a fiery brazier held in what looked like the hand of a large statue. The ensuing screams, aided by a sudden increase in the audio volume, attracted Bob's attention. The camera, if that was what you wanted to call it, zoomed in as Chuck squirmed and crackled and blackened in the flames. Robin wanted to look away, but couldn't; in some weird way, she felt like she owed him this, after she had basically shoved Margaret at the ogre, then failed to save Gwen, then failed to fulfill her promise to return with a rope to haul Chuck and the others out of the hole. She seemed to be pretty bad at helping people. She should probably stop trying.

At last, the screaming stopped. Robin realized she was holding her breath, and let it out. God. Was that worse than what happened to Gwen? She wasn't sure.

Bob said: "They burned Chuck alive, those little——"

He broke off as the statue's arm suddenly tipped forward and the brazier vomited a smoldering goblin out onto the floor. It rolled and tumbled and stood up, looking at its hands and arms as wisps of vapor rose and dissipated. It stood there with a puzzled expression on its little pug face. The camera pulled back, showing all the other goblins leaving in a hurry. Eventually the remaining one scurried off as well. The camera followed this lone goblin through a door and up a darkened corridor. Robin stopped watching. She was inspecting the creature Bob had shot, eyeing it from different angles, trying to decide if it looked familiar. The goblin's head was still the same size that Chuck's head had been, more or less; being stuck on top of that spindly, wiry, absurdly small body threw everything out of proportion, but, damn.

She looked at Bob and said: "I think you shot Chuck."

"No way," Bob said.

"Yes way," Robin said. "Come and take a closer look."

He did so. "That's not Chuck," he said. "That's a goblin." He didn't sound entirely certain, though.

"You saw the same thing I did just now." She turned to Patrick. "These goblin things … Do you know where they came from?"

"Uh-huh. It was one of the first scenes. Most of the extras got herded down to the old gym and put through the fire. They ended up like that."

"Are you fucking kidding me?" Bob said. "They're *people?*"

Patrick shrugged. "Used to be."

Bob knelt down next to the goblins. "Chuck? Chuck?"

"Bob. He has an arrow in his face." Then, to Patrick: "Who herded everybody down to the gym?"

"They did."

"Shit!" Bob said.

Robin heard a gross popping noise, which she suspected was Bob pulling the bolt out of Chuck's face. As if that would help him at this point. "Who are *they*? Collins and Baxter?"

"Uh-huh. Them, and also——"

Suddenly Bob elbowed her aside, grabbing Patrick by the collar and half-yanking him off the couch. "Damn it, why didn't you tell me that was Chuck before I shot him?"

Patrick started swatting Bob's wrists. This proved ineffectual. Robin got between them and pushed them apart. Surprised, Bob tried to shove her away, but she grabbed his hand and leaned in and said, "This won't accomplish anything. You saw how he stopped those goblins. You think he can't do the same to you? Or worse?"

Bob glared at her, then pulled free and stalked off to a far corner, muttering. Robin watched him for a moment, then sat down next to Patrick, who was shooting Bob unfriendly looks. Hoping to reset the mood, she said: "Hey, Patrick, why did Collins want that key so badly?"

"I'm not sure. Maybe you should follow him and find out what he does with it. Maybe you both should."

"Maybe we should——wait, what? What he *does* with it? How did he get it?"

"Weren't you paying attention? It was sticking right out of the teddy bear bag when your friend dropped it. Dr. Collins took it and left while he was fighting the goblins."

Bob was back, hand on his sword, his face red with anger. He might be turning into a goblin himself. "I was fighting them because you let them in."

"I let them in because you were annoying me. Besides, you wanted to fight them. You know you did. Makes for a better show, don't you think?"

"God damn it, whose side are you on?" Bob said. "Ours or theirs?"

"I'm not on anybody's side. Mostly I just watch. Mostly."

Suddenly the television got louder again. Cheesy music swelled.

"Hey, look," Patrick said. "A game show."

Robin and Bob both turned to the television, which showed something that seemed to be a parody of *Let's Make A Deal*. Collins, resplendent in Seventies leisure suit glory, was just bounding onto the stage. The camera tracked him as he moved, passing a woman—Margaret, Robin thought—who sat in a chair against the wall. Maybe *sat* wasn't the right word. She was straitjacketed, held into her seat with straps, and appeared to be unconscious. The set scrolled by until another woman came into view. The camera zoomed in on her. Myra. Apparently she was the contestant, although she didn't look very pleased with her good fortune.

Bob said: "Now what the fuck is *this*?"

"She has to pick a door. If she picks the wrong one, she loses. If she picks the right one, she gets a prize."

Robin snorted. "Yeah, like Collins would give anyone anything."

"He will if she picks right. He has to. That's how it works. Haven't you ever seen this program?"

"Where is that?" Bob said. "Is it in this building?"

"Yep. Down three floors and take a left. Follow the signs for the auditorium. You can't miss it."

Bob was gone, out the door in a flash, not even waiting for Robin to say if she wanted to go with him or not. Seconds after he had left the room, the camera panned to the audience.

The auditorium was full of goblins. Dozens of them.

"Shit," Robin whispered. "They'll tear him apart."

"Probably," Patrick said. He sounded pretty cheerful about the prospect. "I wish I had some popcorn." And just like that he had a movie theatre bucket full of fluffy white crowns with a hint of gold, sitting in his lap as if it had been there right along. He proffered the tub to her. It smelled delicious. "Want some?" he said.

Robin thanked him, grabbed a handful, stuffed it into her mouth, and took off running out the door.

~~~~

Collins stood there holding that ridiculous microphone in front of her face, waiting for Myra to respond. She just stared at him. As each second passed, his grin stretched a little wider. Finally he brought the mic back to his own mouth. "Well? What do you say?" He jabbed the microphone at her again. Myra's gaze wandered from him to the audience to the big doors at the back of the stage and, finally, back to Collins.

She said: "You have *got* to be fucking kidding me."

He pantomimed an expression of elaborate, wounded shock. As if he had never seen her before and had no idea who she was, he leaned in to peer at a name tag, which she just noticed had mysteriously appeared on her chest. "Come now, Myra. There's no need for that kind of talk. This is a family show. I would hate to have to disqualify you for bad language." He turned to the audience. "All you kids out there, swearing doesn't make you cool, it just makes you crass. So don't be a potty mouth like Myra!"

The goblins answered with a series of grunts, hisses, and cries. Collins smiled serenely and waited until the noise died down, then turned back to Myra. "Now then, let me ask you a question: Which door am I thinking of?" She opened her mouth to speak, but he cut her off. "Consider before you answer. Consider *carefully*. You could be betting your life." He looked past her, in Margaret's general direction. "Or someone else's."

So that was his game. If she said the wrong door, he would do something to Margaret. That was why he'd told her she wouldn't cheat on the test this time. And if she *did*, he would bring Bob in and put him on the line next. Such an elaborate setup, just to make her give an honest answer. What was the point, when he already knew that she knew which card he'd been looking at? What was he trying to prove, and who was he trying to prove it to?

"I'm waiting," Collins said. "We're all waiting. The audience is getting restless." On cue, the goblins started hooting and stamping their feet. Yeah, sure, he had to keep the audience entertained—not just those gremlins out there in the seats, but Patrick, too, wherever he was. Watching Collins flip cards over for an hour wasn't nearly as entertaining as a big, gaudy set with big, gaudy doors and a big, gaudy asshole in a hat to run the show.

"Time's almost up, Potty-Mouth Myra. What's your answer? Is it door number one? Door number two? Or door number three?"

He was thinking of door number three; she could just sort of tell, the same way she had been able to tell what card he was looking at. She just *knew*. But what would he do if she chose that door? Would he congratulate her and let her go? Not likely. But she had to tell him *something*, so it might as well be what he wanted to hear, buy herself and Margaret a little more time. She started to speak, then hesitated. She was picking up something else from him, something he was trying to hide. She cocked her head at him. He was trying to trick her by thinking of door number three, but that wasn't the one she was supposed to pick. More goblins waited behind that door, with orders to come out and shred them if they were released. Some monstrous version of Baxter lurked behind door number one, with the same instructions. That left door number two. Whatever awaited that choice was a secret, concealed somehow, hidden in fog. She couldn't read it. But if the other options represented certain death, she obviously couldn't pick them. She had to take her chances with the murky one.

Collins said: "Well?"

She glared at him. "Door number two. Motherfucker."

He turned to the audience. "The lady—and I use the term loosely—picked door number two. Let's see what's coming to her!" He produced a big brass key, strode to the door, inserted it into the padlock, and turned it. The padlock clicked open. Collins removed it from the latch and swung the door wide.

Patrick floated behind behind it, encased in a dull amber glow, his feet just above the floor.

"Look, folks! She's chosen Patrick!" Collins turned, a big smile on his face. "Everyone give her a big hand!"

The audience roared and clapped and hooted as Collins performed an ostentatious mic-drop and then launched into the old mime bit of pulling a rope hand over hand. Patrick drifted forward in time with the action, as if Collins were reeling him in. This Patrick seemed barely conscious as he moved across the stage, toes dragging across the old wood. Myra felt like she should be running, but couldn't. She stayed rooted to the spot, like in one of those dreams where your feet were welded to the floor.

Patrick's aura enfolded her. He seemed to wake up, raised his head. His eyes were dark pits with cyan-grey dots in the middle, like an ancient television set just before it went dark. As she stared at them the dots expanded, became snow, static on a dead channel. They seemed to be pulling her out of herself and into him. She heard a high-pitched whine, and realized she was the one making it.

Then Patrick took her hands in his, and the static exploded.

Barriers

BOB PRACTICALLY SKIED down the stairs, taking the steps four or five at a time, jumping from one landing to the next. Myra was nearby, and she was in trouble. He had to get to her before it was too late. He couldn't fuck this up. Not again.

Three floors down, he crashed through a door at the bottom of the stairwell, stumbling out into a hallway. He looked around, spotted a door labeled *Auditorium*. Patrick had told the truth. He raced over to it, kicked it down, and ran inside. The audience—dozens of goblins—turned as one to look at him, like a synchronized staring team. Down on the stage, Patrick was approaching Myra. Collins stood nearby, beaming. A hazy glow surrounded Patrick, enveloping Myra, obscuring both of them from view. Before Bob had taken more than two steps down the aisle, some kind of power wave erupted from Myra and Patrick, disrupting the air with weird ripples spreading in concentric spheres. It tore through the audience seating, sending goblins flying through the air like toys kicked by a child, starting with the rows nearest to the stage and progressing outward like a blast front. He slowed and stopped and gawked at it.

Somebody grabbed Bob's arm. Robin. She dragged him out of the room, yelling something. He couldn't make out the words, they were meaningless, slowed down so much as to be unintelligible. She hauled him down the hallway and into the stairwell, flung him into a hollow space beneath the steps, and hurled herself in after him. A moment later the shockwave hit. The cement floor rippled beneath his hands and knees. The stairs creaked and twisted overhead. The bucking floor tossed him against the back wall of the stairwell. Robin landed on top of him, the two of them lying crossways. Another wave passed, and another, and another. Concrete dust filled the space beneath the steps, choking him; he felt pressure in the sealed parts of his body, his eyes, his skull, his abdomen. He was afraid he might explode, then started wishing he would, just to put an end to it. But at last, after a few minutes, or maybe a few hours, the waves stopped coming, leaving him feeling like he'd just been run through a cement mixer and poured out into a heap.

Robin rolled off of him and sat up. He noticed she had blood on her face, from her nose and around her eyes, a thin dribble of it from the left corner of her mouth. She tried to speak, but nothing came out, just a little wheeze. She shook her head, closed her eyes, tried again. "What the hell happened in there?"

"Patrick and Myra," he said. "I don't know what he did—"

Suddenly the stairwell door, which had somehow survived the blast, blew inward off its hinges. It smashed into the back wall and clattered to the side, landing at an angle against their hiding place, partially blocking it. The two of them squeezed as far back into the shadows as they could. Footsteps entered, clattering up the stairs overhead. Bob didn't have to look to know the goblins were on the march; he'd thought the explosion might have finished them off, or at least left them stunned for a while, but no such luck. They were Patrick's creatures, tough little bastards. Something else followed, something that dribbled a liquid glow. It seeped into their little bolt-hole. Bob craned his neck so he could see through the gap between the door and the steps. Patrick. He floated by, headed up the stairs. A viscous yellow light surrounded him, leaving bits of itself behind as he drifted along. Even after he had passed from view the glow continued to drip from the steps, falling and sizzling like errant fireworks before burning out.

When the last bits of glowing goo had faded and the stairwell had been quiet for a while, Bob pushed the door out of the way and crawled out through the opening. The floor had buckled into a spider's web of cracks. He ran down the hallway. One of the auditorium doors was off its hinges; the other hung on by one or two screws. It fell off after he went inside. The interior was a shambles, seats scattered around, curtains torn down. Myra lay crumpled on the stage in approximately the same spot she'd been when the blast had struck, staring up at the ceiling, head in a pillow of hair that had gone stark white. Bob hurried to the stage and knelt beside her. He touched her still-warm throat, felt a good strong pulse, but her eyes were wide and glassy. "Myra?" He gave her a little shake, then another. "Myra?"

"How is she? Is she alive?"

He looked up. Robin had arrived. "Yeah, but she's catatonic or something."

Robin climbed onto the stage and came over. After a moment she said, "Maybe they drugged her. You weren't in much better shape when I found you."

"No. This is different." He looked at Robin. "Patrick did something to her. I'm going to kill him."

"First you have to find him," Robin said. Then her gaze moved past him, toward the other end of the stage. "Margaret's here. I'm going to go check on her." She headed off in that direction, patting him on the shoulder as she passed.

After she was out of earshot, Bob muttered: "I don't have to find him. I know *exactly* where to look."

~~~~

Robin examined the pile of wreckage that was Margaret. The blast wave had shattered the chair she'd been tied to, leaving her trussed up in a tangle of straps and buckles and pieces of wood. There were splashes of crimson on the dirty cloth, but it didn't look like she'd been impaled by any of the debris. Robin rolled her over. Given her previous condition, it was difficult to tell how much Margaret had bled from the orifices of her face. Her brain could have liquefied and oozed out her ears and she would hardly have looked any worse than she had before.

Suddenly Margaret's eyes snapped opened. The whites were stained red. Robin nearly jumped a foot. "Margaret?" she said, a little warily, remembering Bob's experience with Gwen. "Are you all right?" The response was a squeak, followed by a nod, followed by squirming. "Shh, okay, hold still," Robin said. "I'll get you loose." She fumbled with the straitjacket but failed to make much progress. "Bob?" she called. "A little help?" He blinked at her a few times, then came over and roughly cut through the straps with a dagger before turning away to examine the exits, probably plotting some lunatic assault on Patrick that would get them all killed.

Margaret got unsteadily to her feet. She eyed Bob with a certain degree of concern, as well she might given his arsenal of weaponry and general demeanor, then made a noise that sounded like an inquiry. "Oh, right. You haven't met. Margaret, this is Bob. He's Myra's husband. Bob, this is Margaret." The doctor grunted. Bob grunted back at her.

Margaret looked a question at Robin.

"Just," Robin said. "Chuck's gone, and Myra's in some kind of coma."

The next noise Margaret made sounded disappointed.

"Yeah," Robin said. "I know."

Bob turned around. He seemed to have come to a decision. "Help me get Myra into the room behind door number two, okay?"

"Uh, sure." She took Myra's ankles and Bob took her shoulders, and they carried her into the little alcove behind the open door, laying her on the floor near the back wall. It wasn't exactly protected, but at least she'd be out of the way if more bad stuff started happening on the stage. Margaret tottered in after them. Three little roaches, hiding from the light.

"Okay," Bob said. "I think that's the best we can do for now." Then: "Your friend should stay here. If she comes with us she'll only slow us down, and besides—"

"If she comes with us where?"

"—when Myra wakes up, I don't want her to be alone."

"Bob," Robin said, "where do you think we're going?"

"Back upstairs," he said.

"To do what?"

"Take out Patrick."

"I see. So if you get through the army of goblins, and Baxter, and Collins, and whatever else gets in your way, and you manage to get to Patrick, what then? Are you going to cleave him with your mighty sword?"

"Yes."

"And you think he'll just let you do that?"

Bob shrugged. "We'll find out. Here, take this." He handed her the dagger he had used to cut Margaret free. She wasn't sure what she was supposed to do with it, but took it anyway. At least now she was armed. She waved her new toy in the air a few times while he removed a small scabbard from his leg and secured it around hers, fastening the three buckles like an old pro despite his bandaged hand. As he did that, kneeling with his face to her thigh, she idly contemplated stabbing him in the back to get even with him for threatening to shoot her, but only did it in her imagination.

He straightened up. "All set."

"Thanks." She sheathed the dagger, then practiced yanking it out and putting it back a few times, just to get the hang of it. Made her feel kind of like a gunslinger.

"Don't cut yourself with that," Bob said.

"I won't." She put the weapon away. "There are a bunch of different Patricks running around, you know. Which one are we looking for?"

"We'll start with the one in the lounge. Because we know where to find him."

"Out of all the Patricks, that one seemed pretty harmless."

"I was harmless too, once," Bob said. "I got over it.

~~~~

Robin let Bob take the lead as they left the auditorium. The stairwell was dark and silent, the goblins gone, Patrick's weird oozing glow long since dissipated. Robin wondered what would happen if you could catch some of that stuff in a bottle. Would it stay in there like liquid fire? If you held it in your hand, would it burn?

At the third landing, they found the door blown out, lying bent and twisted in the hallway beyond. She and Bob exchanged a look. "Be careful," she said. "He might still be on this floor."

Bob peeked out into the hallway, looking left and right, then motioned her forward. The two of them stole into the hallway, then to the lounge. The television was on, but it was showing snow. Static emanated from the speakers. Chuck and the other dead goblins were gone, but Lounge-Lizard Patrick lay sprawled on the sofa, eyes glassy, staring at the ceiling.

"Fuck," Bob said.

Robin hurried to the young man's side, felt his wrist. His pulse was very faint. She looked at Bob. "Catatonic. Just like Myra." She stepped back. "The other Patrick got here first."

"I don't understand. They're the same person."

"Maybe they're not," Robin said. "Not here, anyway." She gestured Bob forward. "Well, there he is. Cleave away."

Bob approached Patrick and pulled out his sword, and for a moment she thought he was actually going to go through with it; but then he stopped and sheathed his weapon and said, "Fuck. I can't. Not when he's just *lying* there. Let's bring him downstairs."

"What? Why?"

"Maybe if we get him and Myra back together, they'll wake up."

"I don't know if that's a good idea, Bob."

"Do you have another one?"

She didn't answer.

"Yeah, I thought not. Come on, give me a hand."

When she didn't move to help him, Bob bent at the knees and sort of rolled Patrick up, hefted him, slung him over his shoulders, and stood, only staggering a little. The kid must have weighed next to nothing. Robin turned in place, watching him carry his unconscious passenger toward the door. "Bob, I really don't think we should do this. He doesn't go out in the hallway. He said so."

"He's out cold," Bob said, as he stepped across the threshold. "He'll never even——"

A flash of light blew through the corridor. Bob flew back into the room as if he'd been kicked by a giant. He ended up in a heap against the wall. Patrick somehow landed back on the couch, settling in right where he'd been before Bob had picked him up.

Robin hurried over and hauled Bob to his feet. "Are you okay?" she said.

"Holy shit. I think I cracked a rib." He looked at her. "I guess you were right. Patrick doesn't go out in the hallway."

"I hope you remember that the next time I tell you not to do something stupid." Then: "Is it just me, or do you hear something coming?"

"My ears are still ringing."

"Well, I think you might have set off a goblin alarm."

"Great," Bob said. He tried to draw his sword, then stopped and made a whimpering sound. "My ribs. Damn it. Here, take my sword and——"

"*No*, Bob. We can't keep hacking them up. You heard what Patrick said. They're people, or used to be. Maybe they will be again."

The echoing sounds from the hallway had resolved into something like a small horde of flipper-wearing children stampeding to see who could be first into the pool. "So what do we do, then?"

"We hide. Come on." She helped him over to the radiator, which still hung open. They ducked through, entering the dim, low, narrow space beyond. The radiator had a handle on this side, and a sliding bolt. Robin pulled it closed and shoved the bolt home. A moment later a small group of goblins entered the lounge. She could see them through a slit in the backside of the radiator; it lined up with a vent on the front, giving her a wide horizontal view of the room beyond. Like a small red CSI team, the goblins fanned out, sniffing around, on the hunt for clues and perpetrators. It wasn't long before they lined up in front of the radiator, peering at it with their bulbous yellow eyes. After a discussion that consisted of grunts and whistles, they started tugging on it. When that failed, they started scrabbling at it with their claws, and when that didn't work either, they started pounding on it with their hard little fists. Robin was fairly confident that they wouldn't be able to open it from that side without the key, but the banging was horribly loud. God knew what would show up in response.

"We have to go," Bob whispered. She nodded. They crawled away from the radiator, up the low dark passage, then emerged from a T-intersection into a tall, narrow chamber where they could stand upright. A single naked bulb burned far overhead. Robin thought they might be in an old chimney; the opening they had come through looked like the backside of a disused hearth, the walls around them consisted of crumbling, blackened brick, and a layer of ash and cinders covered the slate floor. These had been recently and thoroughly disturbed by the passage of numerous big flat feet.

"Robin," Bob said. "Check it out."

She looked where he was pointing. Someone had scratched an arrow into one of the decaying bricks. It was down low, at about the level of a goblin's shoulder, and it looked fresh, lighter than the surrounding surfaces.

"What do you think?" Bob said.

"I think Chuck is helping us out from beyond the grave." She tipped her head towards the back end of the arrow. "Let's go."

~~~~

They moved slowly so they didn't miss the signs, many of which were in shadowed places; there weren't a lot of lights back here, and the borders between them tended to get pretty dark. Robin's theory, which she explained in terse, hastily whispered sentences as they went, was that the regular goblins wouldn't need signs to guide them around back here, but Chuck did, and so he had left the arrows for himself to mark his way. She figured they would point in the direction he was going, so that was why she was following them backwards. Which made sense, Bob supposed, though they wouldn't find out if she was right until they got to the end—or, depending on your point of view, the beginning—of the trail.

After some time, they passed a corridor on their right that ran a short distance to a door that stood half-open, revealing a small room beyond. An arrow was scratched into the wall directly opposite the stubby passage. They had a hasty vote on the topic of checking out the room, which passed unanimously. Bob went first and checked it out from the shadows. It contained a table and a couple of chairs. To the left, a broken window gaped, revealing another small chamber beyond. Both rooms appeared to be empty. He moved forward, Robin close behind. A stack of thick cards sat on the table on top of a legal pad, along with a folded cardboard screen. Bob turned a couple of the cards over. They had shapes on them, stars and squares and squiggles and such. "What kind of weird game is this?" he said.

"They use those to test psychics," Robin said. "I've seen it on television." She slid the legal pad out from under the deck and showed it to him. It had Myra's name on top, then two columns of pictures that never matched and one column full of red Xs. "This is a scoring sheet, right? The symbols are the same as the ones on the cards. Somebody must have been testing her."

He took the pad and looked it over. "She didn't do very well. She got every one wrong."

"That *is* pretty bad," Robin said. "It looks like there's an elevator in that other—Oh God."

"What?" He put down the pad and joined her at the window. He could see the elevator she was talking about. The doors were stuck open, and it had a hole in the floor near the back corner.

Which was beginning to light up with an amber glow, coming from underneath the car.

Bob pointed at the exit. Robin nodded. Together, they scurried back into the labyrinth of secret passageways, no longer looking for Chuck's arrow marks. Patrick's luciferous presence lit up the hallways and intersections, sometimes behind them, sometimes in front of them, forcing them to make rapid and unexpected turns. Bob didn't understand it. If Patrick was that fast, if he could be in back of them one moment and ahead of them the next, why couldn't he catch them? Was he even trying to? Finally the chase, if it *was* a chase, came to an end; they turned a corner and Bob, in the lead, smacked into a blank wall and bounced off. He ended up on the floor with a bloody nose and pain from his injured side reverberating through his chest. After Robin helped him to his feet, he kicked the wall hard. It gave a little, shivering from the blow. He'd thought he felt it shake when he hit it the first time, and now he was sure. This wasn't a fixed barrier; this was a door. He stepped back, examining it, but the lighting was so poor he couldn't discern the mechanism that might make it open.

"What is it?" Robin said.

"I think this is a way out. Help me find a latch or something."

She stepped up and the two of them ran their hands all over the wall, testing loose bricks, pulling on nail heads, sticking their fingers into the crevices between the old lath and getting micro-stabbed by exposed ends of chicken wire. While they searched, the corridor grew lighter, as Patrick approached from around the corner of a nearby intersection. The floor began to hum with power. Bits of wood and plaster shook loose, bouncing off Bob's head, his arms, his shoulders. A small piece of the crumbling wall sloughed off, revealing the lock: A flat metal bar about the length of a ruler, tarnished black from age and moisture, with a pivot on one side. It was currently horizontal, set into a slot in the door, immobilizing it. He scrabbled at the strip with his good hand, trying to open it, but his fingers couldn't find any purchase. Robin elbowed him out of the way, worked the dagger beneath the bar, and pried it loose from the plaster, allowing her to rotate it out of the way. Bob gave the door a shove and it creaked outward, opening just wide enough for the two of them to spill through into some scraggly, prickly bushes outside.

Outside!

He dragged Robin to her feet and they ran, along the narrow space between the shrubs and the wall. Thorns and small branches plucked at them. At a thin spot in the bushes they bolted away from the Retreat and across the grounds. A cold wind had risen, stiff and bracing. The night seemed much darker than it had been when he'd entered the building, the sky full of black clouds. Dawn didn't seem to be getting any closer. If anything, it seemed to be farther away.

They reached the fence before pausing to look back at the building. Patrick hadn't come after them, but Bob could see his glow spilling from the secret door. The bushes were moving along the foundation of the Retreat; maybe it was the wind, or maybe Patrick had sent goblins out to get them. Bob's gaze traveled up to the roof of the building. He realized that the black clouds hadn't been brought by the wind; they were spewing from the chimneys, spreading *outward* from the mountain, blotting out the sky for miles around, as if it were a malign factory in the business of manufacturing darkness and pollution.

"Bob! Robin!"

Bob hadn't heard *that* voice in a while. He whirled, as he and Robin said simultaneously: "Paltruck?" Then they looked at each other. Bob felt an absurd urge to laugh and say she owed him a beer.

"You have to get out of there," Paltruck said from the other side of the chain link. The little guy looked awful, his wooden skin gone grey, like old ashes. He had lost his hat. "Climb the fence!"

"For God's sake, Paltruck, can't you just open it?" Robin said.

"No! You have to climb!"

"But I can't," Bob showing Paltruck his injured hand. "My hand. My ribs. I can't climb."

Paltruck stared at him, his little eyes flicking back and forth between the two of them. "*You* can climb," he told Robin.

Bob said: "What?"

"We can't just leave Bob in here," Robin said. "We *can't*."

"If I open the fence," Paltruck said, "I'll never be able to close it again."

"So what?" Bob said. "The gate's not closed. What difference does it make if the fence has a hole in it?"

"Paltruck, *please*," Robin said. "Let us out. I know you can do it."

The sprite looked miserable, but he squeezed his eyes shut and raised his arms, his palms pressed tightly against each other. As they watched, he turned his hands so their backs were together, then slowly pulled them apart. His arms trembled, as if fighting enormous resistance. The wrapped wires of the chain link quivered and split, creating an opening just wide enough for them to squeeze through. Bob had to slide his satchel around to the side to fit. Once they were through, Paltruck dropped his hands and fell to his knees, then got back up and, with what looked like a tremendous amount of effort, pressed his hands back together, straining against some invisible force. The fence knit itself back up, but Bob felt something coming out of it, a dribble of energy. It made him think of boiling an egg with a cracked shell, how the inside would bubble out and congeal in the hot water. But to Paltruck, he said: "See, you did it. You closed it back up."

"No," Paltruck said, "I didn't."

~~~~

It took a few minutes for Paltruck to recover from the effort of opening the fence, during which time he sort of curled himself up into a little ball, rocking back and forth and muttering. Robin couldn't make out what he was saying. She kept looking at the Retreat. There didn't seem to be any outdoor activity there right now—the bushes that had been in motion earlier had settled down—yet she felt something coming from it, prickling, crawling on her skin like tiny spiders. She was relieved when Paltruck finally unfolded himself and stood. He took Bob's injured hand in his right and Robin's hand in his left, and wordlessly led them away from the retreat, moving a little distance into the woods. They hunkered down in a cluster of boulders.

"So what are you doing up here?" Bob said. "I mean, I'm glad to see you, but I thought you couldn't come to the Retreat. The rules, you said."

"The rules are out the window," Paltruck said. "Some of it's my fault. I climbed the fence and went on the roof. I meddled. He told me not to but I did." He pressed his small hands against the sides of his head. "I shouldn't have done it. I shouldn't have come here. It was a trick."

"What was a trick?" Robin said.

"He let you escape and get to the fence. He knew you wouldn't be able to climb it. He knew I would open it for you so you could get out. Because I help. That's what I do." He looked at her and added, his voice rough as his skin: "Now there's a breach."

"A breach." Robin looked up the hill towards the fence. She couldn't see it, but she knew what he was talking about. She had felt it. Paltruck had put the fence back together, but the patch wasn't perfect. It wouldn't hold. The china cup had a hairline crack. "And that's something he can use, right?"

"Right," Paltruck said.

"Wait," Bob said. "Something *who* can use?"

"Patrick," Robin said. "I mean, you know, the *other* Patrick. Not this one."

"Not this one? What are you talking about?"

"Paltruck's another version of Patrick. Right? That's why you can do the things you do." She crouched in front of him. "So what are you supposed to be? His, like, conscience or something?"

"Or something," Paltruck said.

"If you're Patrick, tell us what he's doing," Bob said. "And no goddamn riddles this time. Give it to us straight."

"He's putting himself back together," Paltruck said. He grabbed Robin's hands with his small wooden fingers. "He's eating up all the pieces."

Bob pressed the heel of his good hand into his forehead. "What does that even *mean?*"

"I think we already saw what it means. Myra? The Patrick in the lounge? They got eaten up. Didn't they, Paltruck?"

Paltruck nodded.

"Then we need to find the hungry bastard and shove a finger down his throat," Bob said.

"Can we do that, Paltruck? Can we make him give Myra and the other Patrick back?"

"I don't know. He's using Myra's gift to make himself stronger. That's why he sent the Count after her. She's the glue that's going to bind us back together."

Bob was staring at him. "Myra is not glue," he said, sounding baffled.

"Here, she is. Reality is collapsing back into illusion. Maybe it's the other way around. I don't even know anymore, and it's too late to stop it."

"I don't accept that," Robin said. "There must be something we can do."

"But it's *spreading*. Don't you see those clouds? That's Patrick erasing the boundaries, and I made it easier for him when I opened the fence. Because I help. Right now people are looking out their windows because they thought they saw something in their yards that shouldn't be there. They're sitting up from naps, wondering what woke them Some of them will have a spark, too, like Myra, and Patrick will use them to jump farther and farther. And the farther he goes, the stronger he gets."

"Jesus Christ," Bob said. "Why didn't you just tell me all this in the first place?"

"I *tried*, I did! *Save Princess Myra*, that's what I kept saying!" Paltruck sighed. "But nobody did. And I opened the fence. Now he knows where we are. His little men are coming to get me."

"Goblins." Bob spat the word. He looked up the slope, towards the Retreat.

"They'll bring me to him. He'll eat me up too, and I'll be gone."

Bob turned around. "And what happens then?"

"Let's not find out," Robin said.

"Yeah," Bob said, "let's not."

His voice had taken on a new tone, one Robin recognized and didn't care for. "No," she hissed, moving forward. "You are *not*—"

Bob body-checked her so hard that she stumbled to the side. She tripped over something, a rock, a root. Whatever. She fell. Her skull glanced off the big boulder. Stars blossomed in her vision.

They faded just in time for her to see Bob's sword bite into Paltruck's neck.

~~~~

Chopping Paltruck's head from his shoulders felt about the same as hitting a small tree with a hatchet, at least until the electric shock hit; then a surge of power flashed up the blade and down the hilt and into Bob's hand, as if he had just sliced into a power line. The recoil flung him backwards, away from Robin and Paltruck, out of the small ring of sheltering stones. He flipped over some low rocks in the lee of the boulder and tumbled down the mountainside, arms and legs flailing, unable to stop himself. Finally he slammed shoulder-first into another big rock, a boulder with a tree growing out of the top, like a celery stalk jammed into a potato. Something snapped, sending pain screaming up his neck and down his side. Gritting his teeth against it, he sat up, stared back the way he had come. It was easy to see where he'd started; light fountained into the air from the small heap of stones, geysering into the air from Paltruck's neck. He could hear it from here, a roar like a giant waterfall. Up close, it must be deafening. How could Robin stand it? She was back on her feet; he could see her there, a black silhouette in front of the light. She seemed to be trying to stanch the eruption with something, a rock maybe, or Paltruck's severed head.

Bob slowly stood, unsteady. His right arm hung useless. Now he had no good hands at all, but he had finally accomplished something, had gotten done what needed doing.

The luminous plume lit up the slope, the thin forest. Bob saw them then, Patrick's little men, the goblins, creeping down the rubble-strewn slope among the trees, coming for him, for Robin, for Paltruck. But they were too late. Bob had gotten there first. Patrick wouldn't be able to eat Paltruck up. Lunch was canceled.

Then the tower of light bent and stretched into a ribbon that arced through the air, flowing towards the roof of the Retreat as if being pulled through an invisible siphon. Robin had given up trying to stop it. She faded into the shadows as the last of the glow departed. For a moment the night was black, no trace of the moon visible through the thick oily clouds; then the windows of the Retreat began to glow, as if someone were turning up all the lights at once. He could see the rock circle again, but Robin was no longer there. Had the goblins come and carried her off during the period of darkness? If they had, surely he would be next. He sagged back against the boulder, weaponless, exhausted, his body aching. He had nothing left. Everything he had tried to do had failed or turned out wrong.

So when the goblins started creeping out of the surrounding foliage, coming towards him with their yellow eyes and their sharp sharp teeth, it was almost a relief.

~~~~

After the last scraps of Paltruck's energy vanished into the Retreat, Robin felt a new pressure in the air, a certain deceptively light touch, as if she were being held in a fist that could, at any time, squeeze shut. She hadn't failed to notice the goblins creeping her way during the light show, and as it ended, she took the opportunity to duck and scuttle away. On her way out of the little field of stones, she spotted something, a flicker of light from between a couple of the tooth-shaped rocks on the downward slope: Bob's sword. That fucking moron had used it to cut Paltruck's head off. She detoured to grab it, because why not? She felt a little tingle from the hilt as she picked it up, as if it held a bit of a charge. Maybe it had soaked up some of Paltruck's energy, had gotten itself enchanted. That would be nice, having a magic sword in hand.

Maybe if she believed it, it would become true.

Trying very hard to convince herself she was carrying a powerful, mystical weapon, Robin made a very wide circle, down the slope and around the goblins and back up the mountain towards the fence. She paused when she got there. She couldn't climb while holding the sword, but she didn't want to let go of it either; she had a feeling she would need it, and that it would vanish if she put it down. On impulse she took a swing at the fence. The blade cut through the wire like it was butter. The fence quivered and thrummed. Go, magic sword, go! Another slice and the chain link peeled back in both directions like paper rolling up. She felt something wash over her, as if she'd just opened a dam holding back ghostly water. She hesitated. Had she just made things worse? How could they be worse? Fuck it. Ignoring the slight resistance, she darted through the opening.

As she entered the grounds, she felt the earth shivering under her feet, as if in a constant low-grade quake. A series of sharp explosions splintered the air. She covered her head with her hands as the windows of the Retreat blew out all at once, the glass pulverized, erupting like tiny diamonds sparkling in the glare from the building's interior. The wind abruptly kicked up to a fearsome level, whipping across her with the touch of icy knives. A weird ululation rose over the howling storm; she thought it might be the goblins on the mountainside. She wondered what they were ululating about. Probably nothing good.

When the wind died down, she raised her head, peering up at the Retreat. Its internal glow cast strange oblong trapezoids of light across the black grass. Damn. Here she was, hurrying up the hill, making believe she was carrying Excalibur, but what was she going to do once she got there?

She was going to rescue Princess Myra, that was what. Oh, and

also save the world.
    No pressure.

Imagination

MYRA WAS RIDING a tornado, swirling and spinning, unable to see, unable to stop, buffeted by endless winds; or maybe it was a crashing airplane, spiraling towards the ground far below, its barrel-roll pinning her to her seat while loose luggage bashed and bounced all around her; or maybe it was a whirlpool, carrying her around and around as it dragged her inexorably into its maw, where she would be pulled under and drowned like an exhausted rat. Was this a dream? It had to be a dream. She couldn't be in all those places at once. Could she?

A small voice somehow cut through the roar of the storm, the plane, the water. "You have to wake up. Take my hand. Can you take my hand?"

Nearly insensible, she dragged her right arm up and out, stretched it in the direction of the voice. Small, cool fingers closed on hers, locking tight. They seemed to be made of wood, as if she were holding hands with a puppet. The arm behind the hand pulled, but the dream held her tight. She squirmed, wriggled, kicked her feet. No good. She couldn't get free. It felt like she was had fallen into a well that was too narrow for her. She couldn't escape from it, not as she was. Not without getting smaller. Not without leaving something behind.

"Leave it behind, then. I'll try to find a way to get it back to you."

She hesitated.

The small voice, growing smaller still, said: "Please hurry. We're almost out of time."

If that was the only way to get free, then okay. She started jettisoning everything she didn't need, everything that was holding her in place, keeping her from escaping. Layers and layers of stuff, of herself, of what made her Myra, sloughing away. She felt a shift, movement. It was working. Maybe she could find a way to get it all back later.

One last piece molted, one last pull from the hand, one last kick against the grip that held her, and she popped free.

Myra opened her eyes.

What had happened? Where was she? Had she blacked out? Was she hurt? She had the sensation that she had recently been battered, and badly, but she didn't feel injured, just confused. She sat up. She was in some kind of small, dark room, a garage maybe, or a shed. The light was dim and flickering, as if provided by lightning strikes outside, but she didn't see any windows that would let such light in. There was an opening nearby, like a retracted garage door. She crawled forward and peered out into a wide, open space beyond the shadowed alcove where she had awakened. It looked like an auditorium or playhouse. What was she doing here?

Someone moved into her field of vision, a woman with missing arms and blood-crusted clothes, made even more horrible by the rollicking lights, a zombie in a discotheque. How could she even be *alive*, let alone moving around, with her arms torn off like that? The woman took a step forward, but stopped when Myra scuttled backwards against the wall. She cocked her gore-streaked head to the side and emitted a throaty squeak.

Myra said: "What?"

The woman squeaked again, twice.

"I don't understand. Can't you talk?"

A strange expression crossed the apparition's ruined face, and she backed off a step, glancing over her shoulder, as if hoping she might find someone else to squeak at. Myra scrambled to her feet and ran out of the alcove, into the wider space beyond, but came to a dead stop before she even got to the edge of the stage. The auditorium was an utter mess. Chairs were scattered all over, many smashed to pieces; wall coverings had been torn down and strewn about like velvet capes left behind after a superhero massacre. Only two or three lights were working properly; the rest were either out, hanging down and swinging, or fizzing crazily, providing the flicker she'd mistaken for lightning. She even spotted a few bodies, small ones. Children? No; they weren't kids, weren't even human. They were strange little misshapen things, creatures with claws and teeth and weirdly sculpted faces. What *were* they? Had they attacked her? Had they mauled the woman with no arms who couldn't talk?

She heard footsteps behind her. That horrible mutilated creature had come out of the alcove and was approaching Myra with an unsteady gait. After seeing these inhuman corpses, Myra wasn't inclined to have this strange squeaking ghoul anywhere near her. She jumped off the stage and ran up the steps toward the exit, whose doors looked like they had been blown outward off their hinges. There was a hallway beyond, empty and dark except for the fluorescent light that leaked in from the auditorium. She spotted a stairwell, also missing its door, not far away. The stairs only went up. She took them two at a time until she reached the first landing, then banged through into a hallway lined with doors. One, not far away, said *EMERGENCY EXIT*. She darted through it, and found herself on a landing with stairs going up and down and a door in the opposite wall that said *EMERGENCY USE ONLY* and, below that, *ALARM WILL SOUND*.

Well, if this situation didn't call for sounding an alarm, then she didn't know what would.

<center>~~~~</center>

Robin reached the Retreat and turned right. She didn't dare go in the front door, and didn't want to return to the maze of passages either, but the place had to have side entrances, right? She raced along beneath the looming walls, moving as fast as she could in the ridiculous flip-flops that still disgraced her feet. She didn't want to lose what little protection they provided against the crystals of broken glass that glistened in the grass. She rounded a corner and bounced off someone going the other way, falling hard on her ass. Somehow she managed not to slice herself open on the magic sword. She quickly got back to her feet and looked around to see who or what she had collided with. She spotted Myra lying on her side near the bushes, and paused a moment to gape. How had *she* gotten out here? Robin looked around and noticed a steel door in the wall not far away, accessible through a split in the bushes; it looked like an emergency exit, the kind you could only open from the inside. Had Myra escaped that way, or had the cleaning crew just tossed her body out into the yard?

Robin nudged the other woman with her foot. "Hey. Myra. You awake?"

Myra cracked one eye, then the other, and looked up at her. "Do you know me?"

"What? Of course I know you, Myra."

"Who are you?"

"I'm Robin."

"Who am I?"

"You're Myra. That's why I keep saying it. Myra Myra Myra. What happened in there?"

"I don't know," Myra said. She shivered. "There was a woman with no arms, and—"

"That was Margaret. I know her, too. So do you."

"Well, I don't remember her. And there were these awful dead things that weren't people. Do you know them too?"

After a moment, Robin said: "We're acquainted."

"So I ran away, but it doesn't seem any better out here. Is there a storm?"

"Oh, hell yeah, there's a storm," Robin said.

"What should we do?"

"We should go back inside."

Myra looked at the Retreat. The expression on her face said she'd rather step into a gas chamber. "In there?"

"Afraid so," Robin said. "I think you left something important behind."

"What?"

"Yourself. Come on." She took Myra's hand and pulled her to her feet, half-dragging her to the emergency exit. She eyed the door for a moment, then thrust Excalibur into it. The blade bit through the metal with a screeching sound. She wrenched the blade to one side, then the other, up, down, left, right. The door fell apart, leaving the entrance wide open.

Myra goggled. "How did you do that?"

"Magic sword. Here, take this." She unbuckled the dagger Bob had given her and strapped it to Myra's leg. "Use it to defend yourself if I'm not around."

"Why wouldn't you be around?"

"People have a way of disappearing around here."

"Where's here? Who else disappeared?"

Jesus. She really didn't remember shit. "I'll explain later. Let's go."

The door took them through a stairwell and into a long corridor, not unlike the one she had gotten trapped in earlier, except this one didn't go on forever; they had entered where it turned a corner. She could see the lobby straight ahead. The other corridor ran off into the distance. A television lounge was nearby, but it wasn't *the* television lounge. Opposite them was another stairwell. So many directions, so many doors. She looked at Myra. "Where did you come from?"

"There." Myra pointed at the other stairwell.

"Okay." Robin darted across the hall to the stairs. Myra didn't follow, even when Robin gestured her forward; she just shook her head. "Come on," Robin said.

"I don't want to go back down there. There's *things* down there."

Before Robin could remind Myra that there were *things* everywhere, the dim stairwell lit up with a neon-blue illumination. Robin jumped, then located the source of the light: A painted sign on the wall that said *ROOF ACCESS*, with an arrow pointing skyward. She hadn't noticed it until it lit up; maybe it hadn't even been there. And then, just in case she was too dense to get the message, the arrow started flashing.

Robin turned to face Myra across the hallway.

"We're not going down," she said. "We're going to the roof."

~~~~

Bob leaned against the boulder, underneath the tree, as the gang of goblins gathered around him. He felt like an exhibit. Somebody was hawking tickets. Come look at the loser, last chance to see! Why didn't they just move in and finish him off? He was no threat. He couldn't fight back. What were they waiting for?

One of the small creatures broke ranks and approached to stand in front of him. This goblin had a familiar-looking arrow sticking out of its eye; black fluid ran from the socket down its face, into its lipless mouth, then out again from both corners to drip down its cheeks and onto its thin shoulders.

Bob said: "Chuck?"

Goblin-Chuck hissed and bared bloody teeth, its remaining eye glassy and baleful. It reached up, grasped the shaft, and wrenched the bolt out of its face. Clutching the projectile the way a child might clumsily hold a pencil, it moved in closer.

"Hey, Chuck, come on," Bob said as he retreated, trying to back up around the boulder. "I didn't know who you were when I shot you, man. How could I? I was trying to protect Robin. You would have done the same thing in my place."

He bumped up against something, a person, blocking the way. Turning, he saw Toomes, leaning up against the boulder as if waiting for a bus to the underworld. He was covered in blood. It still leaked from his torn flesh. His disarticulated limbs were held in place, sort of, by fishing hooks and lengths of line, as if he'd been sewn back together by material from a tackle box.

"You." Toomes jabbed an accusatory finger into Bob's face. His voice was a gurgling rasp, horribly distorted by a gash in his throat that let the air out too soon, and he moved jerkily, like a macabre puppet. "You led me into a trap and abandoned me."

"What? No ... I mean, I didn't know. Kyle came and—"

"Don't go blaming me."

Bob looked up. Kyle was perched on one of branches of the tree that grew from the boulder. He looked even worse than the last time Bob had seen him, with a caved-in skull in addition to the stab wound in his chest. Grey matter sat among shards of bone, jiggling like some kind of grotesque gelatinous salad. Blood ran down his face and across his Cheshire Cat smile, dripped off his chin, spattered onto the boulder and trickled down the sides. "I mean, come on, Bob. How dumb do you have to be to trust a guy with one leg who's babbling about ogres?" Then Kyle looked past Bob, and said: "Hey, look. The gang's all here. Mostly."

Bob turned. Zombie Gwen had somehow made her way down the slope, dragging her ruined, mangled body towards him. His severed fingers were still sticking of her mouth.

"Jesus, Bobby," Kyle said, "how many people did you kill tonight, anyway?"

"She ... I didn't kill her. She was dead when I got there."

"Details," Kyle said.

Bob closed his eyes. "You're not here. Gwen's not here. Chuck's not—" His mantra of denial turned into a yelp when he felt a stabbing pain in his leg, slicing through the general miasma of agony. His eyes snapped open. Chuck the goblin had just jabbed him in the thigh with the point of his own arrow.

"I don't think Chuck agrees with you that he's not here," Kyle said. "I know *I* don't. Gwen ... Well, Gwen's not much for thinking in her present condition, so we'll leave her out of it. Toomes, what about you? Do you think we're not here?"

Toomes shook his head, sending blood splashing in an arc.

"I'm just hallucinating," Bob said. "I'm hallucinating you all."

"Maybe you are," Kyle said. "Maybe we're the ghosts of your guilty conscience. Some people say that's the worst punishment, you know. A guilty conscience. Hey, Toomes. Do we agree with that?"

The vampire hunter slid a long knife out of his coat.

"No," he said.

~~~~

Myra clearly didn't like the idea of going up the stairs much better than she had liked the idea of going down them, but she tagged along with Robin as they climbed one flight, then two, then three, then arrived at a door labeled *ROOF*. It was locked, but a few slashes from Excalibur showed it the error of its obstructive ways. Robin pushed what was left of it aside, and the two of them stepped out onto the pebbled rooftop of the Retreat.

Robin looked around. It mostly looked like a standard industrial-type roof. A smallish structure—a rough and misshapen parody of a geodesic dome—stood not far away. It had a weird organic lividity, as if the building had sprouted a malignant tumor. She went in that direction. Myra followed. The surface under their feet changed, pebbles giving way to cracked black tar, which then gave way to something like leather, or tough skin. They stopped a few yards short of the dome. Its lattice-like exterior was shot with rounded branching things, ordered but not symmetrical, in the manner of roots or blood vessels. The dome expanded and contracted in a gently rhythmic pattern, as if it were breathing, or had a pulse, or both. When it expanded, the spaces between the veins seemed to glow a deep red, the way your hand looked if you held it over a powerful flashlight. As she pondered what the fuck *this* was supposed to be, exactly, she heard footsteps crunching across the surface. Collins came around the dome, dressed like a G-Man who had wandered in from the set of a 1950s crime drama; he even wore a fedora, slung at a jaunty angle on his head. Robin moved to stand in front of Myra, holding Excalibur across her body like a shield.

"Nice suit," she told him. "Who are you now?"

"I'm the execution producer."

She raised an eyebrow. "Don't you mean *executive* producer?"

"That depends on you. My advice is to take your witless friend there—" Myra made an offended noise. "—and turn around and go back down the stairs."

"If you say we should go, it must mean we should stay."

"It means you should go." He spread his hands. "I'm just trying to prevent further conflict."

"Of course you are." Collins wouldn't have invited her up here just so he could order her to leave; the sign directing her to the roof must have been put there by someone else, most likely one of the

Patricks, working against the others. She was supposed to be here. She just didn't know why.

"Last chance," he said. "Leave."

Robin widened her stance and pointed Excalibur at Collins. He sighed, removed his hat, and set it down on top of a nearby ventilation pipe.

The fedora was off. It was time for Serious Business.

He moved forward, striking a ridiculously exaggerated martial arts pose with his arms. Myra retreated, watching with wide eyes. Robin backed off, blade at the ready, the two of them circling each other, just like in the painted board room, except this time there was no table between them, and less pretense of civility. Collins threw a feint, then a few more, right fist, left fist, right fist, making her waste energy trying to block blows that were never intended to land. His hands sprouted a glow every time they struck, as if they were meteors heating up in the atmosphere, making his kung fu stylings seem much less absurd.

He came at her suddenly, flinging a haymaker at her head. This punch looked real. She ducked and thrust her sword at his midsection, but he put his momentum into an upward kick of his shiny-shoed foot, connecting with her wrist. She heard small bones breaking. Excalibur shot skyward like a silver rocket. His red-hot fist came at her stomach. She tensed her abdominal muscles just before impact, but it still felt like getting shot in the gut with a cannonball. She flew backwards and hit the roof, tumbling and sliding for yards along the pebbled surface before she finally stopped, sprawled on her back. She had lost both of her flip-flops. Good Goddamn riddance.

Twenty or thirty feet overhead, she saw Excalibur hanging in mid-air, point up and quivering. The rocket had failed to achieve escape velocity. As she watched it turned and fell, point first, but not straight down like a normal object in normal gravity; it was heading for Myra, moving at an angle as if along a wire. Robin couldn't even shout a warning before the sword pierced Myra's chest. She clutched at the pommel, then went limp, slumped but upright, pinned to the rooftop, a prize butterfly with a thumbtack through its heart.

Collins seemed startled by Myra's impalement. He studied her for a moment, hands half-raised; then he shrugged, turned away, and began walking towards Robin. The pebbles crunched under his feet. Robin tried to crawl away, but didn't get far; she could barely breathe, let alone flee, and Collins easily overtook her. He stood there looking down at her, shaking his head, then raised his right foot as high as he could, preparing for the big stomp. From below, his shoe looked as huge and heavy as a cinderblock. The sole was worn nearly smooth.

A dagger flew over Robin's head and sank into his thigh. With a howl, Collins fell backwards. He crashed through the rubbery surface of the roof, which broke like a crust of ice, revealing thick, black, steaming goo underneath. He screeched and writhed, struggling to extricate himself from what seemed like at least a foot of hot tar. That was going to occupy him for a minute. Robin rolled away and looked back towards the dome. The last time she had seen that dagger, it had been in the scabbard around Myra's leg. Obviously it wasn't there anymore. Myra was on the move.

Having thrown the small blade to rescue Robin, she was now sliding herself down along the big blade until she was horizontal, but she was still pinned. She rolled her legs up, planted one foot on each side of the crossguard, and pushed. After a moment Excalibur popped loose and did a little turn in mid-air. Myra was on her feet and caught it by the hilt before it could land.

Robin glanced at Collins. While she'd been watching Myra, he had dragged himself out of the mire, pulled the dagger out of his leg, and bound the wound with his tie. He looked at Robin. She offered him the most unpleasant smile she could muster, complete, she hoped, with bloody teeth.

The Director heaved himself to his feet and tried to run towards Myra, but all he could manage was a lumbering shuffle. It wasn't just the wound in his leg slowing him down; he was trailing threads of stiffening tar, slowing his movements, sticking him to the roof, making every step an obvious and increasing effort. It reminded Robin of one of those bad dreams where you needed to run but you couldn't because your feet kept adhering to the ground. She hoped the asshole was enjoying his nightmare, because she sure was.

Myra stood her ground, waiting for him. If any ill-effects remained from being impaled, they weren't showing; aside from the bloodstained rent in her shirt, there was no sign it had even happened. She held Excalibur up in front of her face in a firm and steady grip, studying the glossy steel. Collins stopped and watched her warily. She smiled, spun in a circle, and flung the blade in his direction. It whisked past his head. His left ear fell off and fluttered to the ground, followed by a cascade of blood down his cheek. The sword hit the roof near Robin and stuck there, bobbing up and down at a lazy angle, close enough that she could see her reflection in the blade. Man, she looked like shit.

The sword kept bobbing slightly, as if beckoning her forward. *Come on in, the water's fine, no alligators, I promise.* It occurred to her that Myra might not have been throwing it at Collins, really; she might have been throwing it to her, Robin. But for what? It wasn't like she could wield the damn thing in her condition. It was a *magic* sword, though, right? It would lend her strength. She would be able to stand; she would be able to strike. She just needed a target.

Robin squirmed over to Excalibur, crawling on her stomach, trying to ignore the grinding sensation from her ribs, hoping one of them didn't shift far enough to puncture a lung. She was surprised that she actually made it that far. Go her. She reached out, then up, because reaching out and up at the same time was too much effort, and closed her fingers around the pommel. And you know what? She *did* feel better, like she might actually be able to get up off the ground. She pulled herself to her knees, then to her feet; she teetered a bit, but she didn't fall. She held the crosspiece like handlebars, bent at the knees, and straightened up. The sword slid out of the roof. It seemed to find its own way into her hand. She felt even better now that the weapon was in her grip, the blue steel up and radiating soft light into the darkness. She still didn't feel *good*, but she felt *better*. It would have to do.

Robin turned in a circle, saw that Myra was keeping Collins occupied. She didn't need to involve herself in that. Myra hadn't thrown the sword to her so she could get into another fight with the Director. Instead, she turned to the dome. She was pretty sure Collins had been guarding that thing. What might be inside? She ran her thumb along the flat of the blade. This sword had cut through the fence. It had cut through the metal doors. It had cut through the roof.

It could certainly pop a pimple.

She tottered over to the dome and circled it, looking for a door. There wasn't one. She stopped on the side opposite Collins and Myra, at a spot where the enclosing veins were thin. She lifted the sword over her head with both hands. This brought a fresh flood of pain up from her ribs, into her arms and down her legs, causing her to stumble forward as she brought the blade down on the swollen, pebbled hide. It went through the pitch and tarpaper like a needle lancing a boil. The surface split open, a zigzag crack running to the top, the sides peeling back and folding inward, leaving them hanging like two large flaps of skin. She couldn't see what lay beyond, except that there were clashing, flickering lights on the other side. Like a lot of televisions going at once. She had a pretty good idea what that might mean.

Robin set her jaw and pushed forward, though the curtains, to go meet the television man.

~~~~

Bob backed off as Toomes brandished his knife. The vampire hunter was moving more slowly than he used to, but so was Bob, and there was nowhere to run; the goblins had him surrounded, and although zombie Gwen was no threat, Chuck and Kyle were both more mobile than he was. He might be able to avoid getting filleted, but not indefinitely.

Kyle, from his perch in the tree, said: "You might as well stand still and let Toomes gut you, Bobby-boy. At least he'll be quick about it."

"Maybe," Toomes said in his guttural, damaged rasp.

"It wasn't my fault!" Bob said.

"Sure, Bob," Kyle said. He jumped off the branch to the boulder, and from the boulder to the ground, like some kind of weird giant leaping bug. "Nothing's your fault. Poor you, stumbling along, accidentally leaving a trail of bodies behind. I mean, you let the Count dismember poor Toomes. Do you know how *long* that took? And me!" He gestured at his wounds. "Poor me. Did I deserve this?"

"What? You were *working* for the Count!"

"That makes it sound like I had a choice," Kyle said. "Like I was getting *paid*. I needed help just as much as your precious Myra did. And did you help me? Did you help *her?*"

"I tried, but——"

"You *tried*. So pathetic. Poor Gwen. Not so pretty now, is she? Ripped apart and eaten by zombies. And you say you *tried*."

"I wasn't even *there* when Gwen got attacked!"

"*I wasn't even there*," Kyle said, his voice a mimic's singsong. "Yeah, you weren't there to save Gwen, but you were there to shoot poor Chuck in the face, weren't you?"

"He showed up looking like a goblin," Bob said. "How was I supposed to know who he was?"

"Face it, Bob," Kyle said. "You're a first-rate fuckup. Everything you've ever done has been a mistake. No wonder everybody abandoned you."

Bob squeezed his eyes shut. That wasn't right, it wasn't how things had happened. Kyle was trying to confuse him, mess with his mind. He wouldn't stop talking. How could he keep talking with his head all smashed in like that? Bob hadn't left him in that condition. Who had done it? Should he ask?

"Robin," Kyle said.

Bob opened his eyes. "What?"

Kyle gestured at his bashed-in skull. "You're wondering who did this to me? It was Robin. So I have just as much reason to be angry with her as you do."

Bob thought for a minute. Did he have a reason to be angry with Robin? Had she done something to him?

"Come to think of it," Kyle said, "she was there when Gwen got killed, and she was there when Chuck got killed, too. And she was with you, but as soon as you got hurt, she took your sword and left you defenseless. How do you like that, Bob? That's not very cool, is it?"

Bob had to agree that it didn't sound very cool, not when it was put like that.

"My wife cannot be trusted with that weapon," Kyle said. "God knows what she'll do with it." His filmy eyes gave Bob a significant look. "You should go and get it back."

"How am I supposed to get it back?" Bob said. "I don't know where she went. I can't even move my arm. I can barely walk."

Kyle's grin curled into a sneer. His teeth were lined with crimson. "You can always find a reason not to do something, can't you?" he said. "Toomes will patch you up. Chuck knows secret ways into the Retreat. That's where Robin went. She took your sword and went back into the Retreat to find Myra. Do you really want *her* to be the hero instead of you?"

Bob stared at him.

"Well?"

"I'm supposed to be the hero," Bob whispered.

"What did you say, Bob? The others can't hear you."

"*I'm* supposed to be the hero!" Bob shouted.

The goblins started hooting and cackling and stamping their feet, and Toomes put away his knife.

~~~~

Collins pressed a hand to his missing ear. Blood oozed between his fingers. He took it away, looked at it, looked at Myra. "You missed," he said.

She shrugged. "Only by a little."

"Why aren't you dead?"

"I don't know." She was only sort-of lying. She remembered being run through by the plummeting sword; she remembered dying. There had been a shock of pain, a rush of memories, and then, blackness. The blackness hadn't stuck, but the memories had. Her head felt swollen with thoughts and images, many of them not her own, swirling and whirling as they settled into the pathways of her brain, cluing her in to someone's plans for her, and a possible way out of this. She was pretty sure the information had been transferred via the sword. That was why it had come at her. She would've appreciated a less traumatic delivery method, but, oh well. "I could ask you the same thing, *Count*."

"I still have a role to play. You don't. Your part is over. You should die like you're supposed to."

"And I should do that because you say so?"

"Because it's in the script."

There *was* a script, or something that could be called that, tattered though it might be at this point. Competing versions existed. She had been given a revision that Collins didn't have. For instance, in her version, Robin was sneaking around behind the dome with her magic sword while Myra kept Collins occupied.

She wasn't about to tell *him* that, though.

"Script?" Myra said. "I don't know anything about a script."

"Just like the law of averages doesn't care how badly you guess, the script doesn't care if you know about it or not," he said. "We wrote it, Patrick and I, and while you're here, you have to follow it."

"Oh, please. You and Patrick are in charge? You're running the show together? You might want to think that, but we both know it's not true. Nobody is really in charge, and you're just as much of a nothing as the rest of us." And he *was* nothing; there was something hollow about him, a null space inside him where something was missing. She felt a wind blowing through him, as if she were being menaced by little more than a black cloak flapping on a line.

"Perhaps." Collins reached down and picked up his fedora, which still sat on the pipe he had put it on earlier. He turned it over, reached inside, and pulled out a single card, which had been tucked into the inner brim. "But I still have my part to play, as do we all."

"I'm not guessing any more cards for you," Myra said.

"I think we established that you never *guessed* them." He held it up, not letting her see the front. "Come on. One more time."

What the hell. Why not. "Wavy lines," she said.

"Wrong." He showed it to her. Circle.

Myra smiled at him. "But I said wavy lines. Look again."

He turned the card toward himself, frowned, glanced at her, and showed her the face again.

Wavy lines.

"Told you so." She snapped her fingers and the lines lit up, crackling with energy. The cardstock around them burned away, leaving him holding three long, luminous, whiplike tendrils. They snaked down his arm, constricting, squeezing tar out from between them. She held up her right hand and the free ends of the coruscating lines leaped across to her. She caught them. They thrummed in her grip, dribbling sparks onto the rooftop. She sent a power surge back down the wires at him. His eyes widened in the instant before the tar that coated his clothes and body ignited and turned him into a man-sized torch. The heated air made him light, and really, he already weighed next to nothing, being just an empty suit. She spun herself around a few times, bringing him with her, a flaming brand on a string. He left a comet's trail of fire and smoke behind him. Then she let go and flung him away. He rose into the sky like a huge firework, his wavy lines waggling in the air behind him like a streamer. He punched a hole through the dark clouds. Lightning roiled them for a few seconds, then faded.

"Sorry, asshole," she said. "You've been written out."

~~~~

Passing between the hanging flaps was kind of gross; they were filmy and a little sticky, and wanted to bond with Robin's skin as she pushed through. Beyond, the floor sloped downward, pink and ridged and a little spongy, like firm meat, with an organic curve that made for tricky footing, especially in her current creaky condition. Fortunately it was only a few steps to the bottom. She found herself in a shallow depression, like a combination sunken living room and planetarium. The air was moist and warm and slightly foggy, and the interior surfaces—what she could see of them—were smooth and fleshy. The fitful illumination she had seen from outside emanated not from televisions, but from a central column not far away, which projected cones of light in various directions, filling the entire underside of the dome with flickering images. It reminded her of those enormous movie screens where they showed vertigo-inducing 3D films of mountain climbers or airplanes flying through canyons or stampeding wildlife or undersea adventure. Here, though, there was no single unified experience; it showed hundreds of different videos, maybe thousands of them, flipping by so fast they barely had time to register as anything more than a blur. She couldn't retain any particular image, just a general impression, subliminal almost, of houses, yards, dogs, cats, cars, buildings, forests, people's faces young and old. It was like someone was flipping at lunatic speed through every video channel on the planet.

Robin slowly moved forward, conscious of Excalibur in her hand. It seemed to have lost its sense of intention, its gyroscopic inertia; it felt dull and heavy. Something had happened to it. She tried to convince herself it retained its uncanny sharpness, because if she stopped believing that then it would stop being true, but she wasn't sure she had that much imagination left in her. As she approached the column, she kept an eye out for Patrick, but he didn't seem to be here. No one was, except for her. The only sound was her own ragged breathing. The floor felt warm under her bare feet. Vapor condensed on her thin clothes, formed crystalline droplets on the light hair along her arms.

She stopped a few yards from the projector. It consisted of Patrick, and a few more Patricks, and Paltruck, and a few other people she didn't recognize, all of them mashed together: A face here, an arm there, a leg, another face. The faces, slack and distended, were the source of the pictures, with rays of flickering light shining out of their eyes and ears and mouths. It was like someone had dumped their bodies into a cylinder and then squeezed until they were all compressed into a neatly uniform column. She moved around it in a slow circle, until she caught sight of a bob of black hair. Fuck! Was that Myra? Robin stopped short and gasped, which devolved into a round of racking coughs that didn't end until she hacked up a gob of bloody mucous. Wonderful. She returned her attention to the face that had so shocked her, and, yes, it was definitely Myra's. Her eyes and mouth were closed, not projecting anything. Robin thought about talking to the Myra-face, but didn't, afraid it might actually answer her, and tell her things she didn't want to know.

Robin stepped back, tried to think. So. Okay. Here was a projector. Was sending out everything they were seeing? The goblins, the monsters, the black skies, all the crazy? Robin thought so, and was pretty sure that she was supposed to stop it. But she couldn't unplug it, and she couldn't switch it off; that was why she had been sent here with a sword. She only had one slash left in her, maybe two, no more. She had to hit it in the right place. What had Paltruck said? That Myra was the glue? Well, there she was, the obvious target, the spot that was different from the rest.

She aimed the point of her sword at Myra's face, drew it back, and closed her eyes.

"Sorry, Myra," she said, thrusting forward.

Something clanged into the top of her blade and drove it into the floor instead.

~~~~

One minute Bob had thought Kyle and the others were going to exact their revenge by tearing him to pieces; the next, Toomes was handing over his long knife, Chuck was sinking his claws into the big rock and hauling it out of the way to reveal a rough stairway going into the ground, and Kyle was explaining what Bob had to do once he got to where the stairs would take him. Even zombie Gwen got involved, spitting his fingers at him, which Toomes helpfully reattached by tying them on with strips of cloth. Good old Toomes. You could always count on him.

Thus armed, briefed, and repaired, Bob had stumbled down into the darkness underground, which somehow deposited him in a small, dome-shaped chamber, just as an obviously injured Robin was drawing back to thrust his stolen sword into a column full of faces. Into *Myra's* face, just like they'd told him she'd be doing. He was almost too late.

Almost.

Putting on a burst of speed, he got there just in time to bring Toomes's knife down on her weapon, putting all his weight behind it, driving her blade into the floor. Her eyes flew open, widened when they saw him. She backed off and assumed a defensive stance, as if he might come at her, not realizing he was in just as bad shape as she was. If she hadn't been so weak—the sword had been quivering in her two-handed grip even before he got there—he never would have had the strength to stop her. He certainly didn't have the strength to fight. But neither did she.

Bob interposed himself between Robin and the column as she slowly lowered the sword, finally ending up half-leaning on it, as if it were a cane. The look in her eyes was murderously fierce, almost enough to knock him over, but when she spoke her voice was tired and raspy. "What the fuck are *you* doing here, Bob?"

"They sent me here. To stop you."

"They? They who?"

"Everybody. Kyle. Gwen. Chuck. Even Toomes. They came to me and told me what's going on."

"And what's that?"

"We all just exist in Patrick's mind. If I let you do what you're trying to do, we all go away."

"And you believed that?"

"I don't know what to believe anymore. All I know is you were about to stab Myra in the face, just like they said."

"And what if I told you I had left the real Myra outside, on the roof? Would you believe that?"

Bob shook his head. "Patrick ate Myra up. That's why she's in there with him. That's the real Myra."

"Make up your mind. Did Patrick invent Myra, or did he eat her up?"

"Why can't it be both?"

Myra's voice said: "Bob?"

He turned in the direction of the voice. Myra was there, pushing her way through an opening in the dome, a dark silhouette against the darker skies beyond.

"Well, here she is," Robin said. "Maybe you should ask her."

~~~~

Myra somehow wasn't surprised to find Bob inside the dome. She approached him and Robin, the sad remnant of their little band, while looking around at the crazy show flickering across the interior. The place seemed familiar, like a half-remembered dream. "I think I've been here before," she said.

"Are you all right?" Bob said.

"Yes, I'm fine."

Robin said: "Collins?"

"Gone." Myra approached them. "What's going on? How did you get up here, Bob?"

Robin answered first. "He came special delivery, with instructions to stop me."

"Stop you from doing what?"

They both started talking at once, Bob jabbering about how they were all imaginary and Robin was going to ruin everything, Robin calling Bob a lunatic and gesturing at the column in the center of the dome. Myra was only half-listening to either of them, because of what she saw looking back at her; Bob was trying to hide it behind his body, but only partly succeeding.

"Both of you, be quiet," Myra said.

They both clammed up, silenced by her tone.

"Bob. What's that behind you?"

After a moment he said: "You don't need to see it."

"I think I do. Can you move?"

He shook his head. "Come on, Myra. Let's just go."

"Go? Go where? Back out there? No thanks." She let her voice harden along with her eyes. "I don't want to *make* you move, but I can, and I will. Step aside."

Bob glanced at Robin, but whatever he was looking for there, he didn't find it. Myra wasn't surprised. He finally shuffled out of the way, giving Myra a good look at herself. She was jammed in at a low spot, towards the bottom of the column, framed by an arm and an elbow, a leg and a foot. Unlike the other faces in the column, hers wasn't projecting anything. Her eyes were closed, her mouth slightly open. Was that what she looked like when she was asleep? Was she asleep now? She didn't think so, but who could tell?

"She was going to stab you, Myra," Bob said. "She was going to stab you in the face. Was I supposed to let her do that?"

"That's not me, though, Bob," Myra said. "Not really. Look at me. I'm standing right here."

"No you're not. You just think you are." And then Bob launched into a story about being visited by Chuck and Gwen and Kyle and somebody named Toomes, about getting dragooned into stopping Robin from bringing Patrick's world down around them, because once it went away, they would too. Robin opened her mouth once or twice as if she wanted to interrupt, but she didn't. When he had finished, she had a better understanding of what she had stepped into here, and why Bob was acting this way. They had presented him with an alternate version of the script, too, and in his version, none of them really existed. Was his script right? Was hers? Maybe they both were. But there was only one way this could play out now.

She approached the Patrick-thing in the middle of the dome. When she got there, she held out her hand, palm open; Robin gasped in surprise as the sword ripped itself out of her grip and flew into Myra's.

Bob said, "Myra, what are you doing?"

"I'm ending this," she said.

"But they said—"

"You told me what they said. Maybe it's true, maybe it's not. I don't know. What I *do* know is that we can't stay here forever. And even if we could, I wouldn't want to. Would you? Is this what you want your life to be? Shadows and monsters and nothing real?"

Bob stared at her as if not quite sure where he had seen her before, but he didn't move, not until she started getting ready to strike the blow. Then he darted forward, long knife raised. "Wait! Let me do it, okay? Let me do it."

She gently pushed his knife down with the sword.

He raised the knife again. She pushed it down again, a little less gently this time. "No, Bob," she said. "This is my job. Stand back."

Bob looked at her, then at Robin, then at the column of twisted Patricks and her face among them. Finally he dropped his knife and took a few paces back. "Okay," he said. "You win."

"This isn't winning," she said.

Putting all her weight behind the sword, Myra stabbed herself in the face.

The Real World

ROBIN OPENED HER eyes.

Where was she? She was sitting down somewhere. She tried to get up, but couldn't. Something was holding her down. Had Collins caught her and strapped her to a table or something? Wait. No. No, she was in the van, belted in next to Kyle. She unbuckled herself and leaned forward, dizzy, fighting the urge to throw up. She had a severe but fading pain in her chest, beneath her ribs; she couldn't catch her breath, and then she could. After a minute or two she felt more or less all right and sat up again and took a quick look around. The engine was still running, the air conditioner pumping out cool air. Outside, she recognized the road to Blackberry Hollow, with the day just moving on towards afternoon around her. Night was nowhere near falling yet. It looked like just about the exact same time that it had been when they'd arrived, before everything had gone sideways.

She turned to Kyle, gave him a push. "Kyle. Hey, Kyle. Wake up."

He just sat there, slumped over. It didn't look like he was breathing. She felt his wrist for a pulse, but couldn't find one. Maybe she was doing it wrong. She thumped his chest hard a couple of times but had no idea if she was trying to do CPR or if she just wanted to hit him.

Chuck and Gwen still sat in the front seats, slouching against each other, their heads touching. She grabbed each of their shoulders and shook them both. Nothing. They were still warm, too, but just as unresponsive as Kyle. She leaned forward, stretching past Chuck's body, and pushed the horn, blasting the stillness to pieces. As the sound faded she heard movement from the back of the van; Bob was stirring, as if awakening from a night's restless sleep. He opened his eyes, looked around, then pushed open the door, fell out, and lost his lunch along the roadside. She tried to ignore the sound and smell of it, lest she should contribute to the mess herself. After a little while the retching noises stopped and he reappeared. He glanced at Robin, then checked on Myra, who still hadn't moved.

"Is she alive?" Robin said.

"She's breathing," Bob said. "Why won't she wake up?"

"I don't know," Robin said. "Be thankful she's even breathing. The others aren't."

Bob nodded. He had his phone out. The screen was black. Apparently it wouldn't power up no matter how hard he pressed the button.

"Bob. We need to get them to a hospital."

"Okay." Bob pointed out the window. "How about that one?"

She looked, and saw a state historic site marker pointing the way to the Blackberry Mountain Retreat. Was there really anything up there?

Bob seemed to think there was. "I'll drive," he said. "I know the road."

~~~~

The two of them couldn't really lift Chuck, who was a big guy; Bob still felt some lingering pain and weakness in his arm and shoulder, and Robin couldn't exert herself much without getting out of breath. So they transferred Gwen into the middle row, then heaved Chuck over the center console and into the shotgun position, freeing up the driver's seat for Bob. Robin took Bob's former place next to Myra in the back as Bob settled in behind the wheel. He stomped on the gas as soon as he saw Robin sit down. He thought he heard her yell something at him, but he wasn't listening; he only had eyes for the road and ears for the engine. He made a sharp turn at the three-way intersection, coming onto a straight run of blacktop. He floored it, hitting sixty before he had to ease off for a wicked curve to the left onto the unpaved road that led to the facility. They careered up the narrow forest track—which was better than it had been in Patrick's world, but not by much—as if it were a desert highway with no speed limit, the van bouncing and rocking and hopping on the uneven surface. The seat belt strap dug into his shoulder as the momentum tried to fling him right, then left, then right again.   Finally they came to a straightaway that ended at the closed gate to the Retreat.   Instead of braking, he floored the accelerator.   The barrier loomed large.   Robin shouted, "Bob, God damn it, wait a——"

They slammed into the gate.   It bowed inward and broke.   Chunks of iron spun through the air.   The airbag deployed in Bob's face.   He lost control of the vehicle as it veered off the road and into the grass. He wrenched it back onto the driveway, heading for the front entrance. The airbag, now deflated, hung from the steering wheel like a used condom.   A steady stream of invective, flung by Robin, bounced off the back of his head.   He ignored her and kept driving.   The road didn't go all the way to the front entrance—it curved off to a parking lot around the side—but when it stopped, he didn't.   The van left the pavement and rambled up the sidewalk.   He finally skidded to a stop at the foot of the stairs, which were just like the ones in that other Retreat, only intact, and with the addition of an access ramp.

He looked over his shoulder.   "How is Myra doing?"

Robin just glared at him, and ostentatiously fastened her seat belt.

"Why are you doing that now?" Bob said.   "We're here."

~~~~

While Bob jumped out and ran around to open the side door next to Myra, Robin poured herself onto the gravel and resisted the urge to go sock him in the face.   She noticed a woman in a white coat standing at the top of the stairs, scowling down at them.   She was flanked by a couple of tall orderlies.   When the woman caught sight of Robin, her expression changed.   She hurried down the stairs.   The orderlies exchanged a glance and followed at a somewhat more cautious pace.

"Margaret!" Robin met her at the bottom of the steps and hugged her.   "Look at you.   Arms and tongue and everything."   Then she took a step back and said: "You do have a tongue now, right?"

Margaret nodded.   "Right.   I had to try a few times before I could speak, though.   And my arms are still a bit numb, like I slept on them wrong."   She looked at the van.   "When I was informed a vehicle had broken through the gate and was approaching at high speed, I didn't expect *you* to be in it."

"Yeah," Robin said.   "We were in a hurry."

"Myra is unconscious," Bob said.   "She won't wake up.   Can you help?"

"I don't know."   Margaret pulled a small two-way radio off her belt and held it up to her mouth.   "I need four stretchers at the front entrance." A responding burst of static contained something that sounded like a confirmation. Putting the radio back, she said: "Most of our patients, staff, and visitors have either recovered or aren't going to. But I also have one who won't wake up."

Robin didn't need to guess who that was. Neither, apparently, did Bob. "Can you take us to him?" he said. "Me and Myra?"

Margaret seemed surprised. "Why?"

Bob put his hand on Myra's shoulder. "If we put them together, maybe she'll wake up. Maybe they'll both wake up. We were going to try it, in there, but didn't get the chance."

Margaret's gaze drifted from him to Myra as she considered it. Finally she shook her head. "No. It's too dangerous. I'm sorry."

"Please? Just for a minute?" Then: "Come on. I know she saved you from the zombies. You would have gotten torn apart. You *owe* her."

Robin recognized his look, his tone; if he'd still had his little crossbow, he'd be aiming it at Margaret and making demands. But he didn't, thank God, and so he was reduced to wheedling. Margaret's lips had become a thin line, but finally, she said: "All right. We can try it. But if anything the *tiniest* bit strange happens, we abort immediately. Got it?"

Bob nodded, but Robin knew him well enough by now to understand that his agreement was provisional, non-binding, and not worth the paper it wasn't printed on.

The big front doors banged open and a fleet of stretchers emerged, like the cavalry arriving just in time, or maybe just too late. They swooped down the access ramp in a rattling, blue-sheeted convoy. The orderlies went to work getting the immobile passengers out of the van. Bob, of course, hovered near Myra, as if he thought he needed to personally supervise the operation, make sure they didn't drop her. Robin and Margaret stayed off to the side, out of the way.

Robin sidled up close to her newly loquacious friend. "So, uh, where is he?"

"I left him in the lounge. I didn't know what else to do."

"What about Collins?"

"He's in his office. Dead. No sign of trauma. It's the same with about a third of the people in the building."

"That many?"

"Yes. I don't know if it's cardiac arrest or something in the brain, but we were unable to resuscitate any of the victims." Margaret grimaced. "And then there's the village. A number of the camps were occupied. I sent a few people down to check. I expect them to find a similar situation."

"Have you called anyone?"

She shook her head. "Telecom's out. So is the computer network and all the cell phones. The lights and the elevators work, and the older vehicles, but anything with delicate electronics is down."

"Yeah, our cell phones are dead too. Is that all because of Patrick?"

"Seems so." Margaret tapped the walkie-talkie on her hip. "These things happened to be in an equipment box in the basement. Shielded them from it, I guess. One of the IT people called it a Faraday cage."

"Any idea how it happened? I mean, what started it?"

"I'm told Dr. Collins had started Patrick on a new drug combination, but the information isn't in his chart." The van was cleared now, the stretchers loaded. Margaret told them where to take Myra. The group moved out, back up the ramp, stretchers first, pedestrians trailing after. Bob stayed alongside Myra. "I knew what he was doing with the Zener cards. It seemed harmless enough. Passé, but harmless. I suspect he tried to speed things up. Chemically." Margaret grimaced. "If the records exist, I'll find them."

From the tone of her voice, Robin didn't doubt her.

"It seemed harmless," Margaret said again.

"Sure," Robin said.

"But it wasn't therapeutic. I could have tried to make him stop."

"Nobody's blaming you."

"Maybe *you're* not," Margaret said.

They entered the building. The lobby looked more or less like it had when Robin had been here before, except not abandoned, and with no gigantic picture of Collins looming over everything. Three of the stretchers went one way; Myra's went another, along with Bob, of course. Margaret followed Bob, and so did Robin. No way was she missing this.

Whatever *this* turned out to be.

~~~~

The corridor was long and dark and silent. Myra ran along it, her footfalls barely a whisper on the cold tile. She didn't know how she had gotten here; she remembered shoving the blade home, then a tingle, then a burst of light. She'd thought that would release them all, that she would wake up in the van, but something had gone wrong and she woke up in the Retreat instead, alone, no Robin, no Bob. Just her, and something else, something gurgling and unpleasant. She had come close to it a few times—she had heard it moving along a connecting corridor or down the stairwells as she passed—but she hadn't actually seen it, and didn't want to.

She came to an elevator. The doors opened without her pressing any buttons. Was this an invitation? A trap? She looked up and down the hallway, and stepped into the elevator just as the doors began to close. She turned to study the buttons for the floors. *B*, *1*, *2*, *3*. The button for *3* lit up on its own. The elevator started to move.

Third floor it was, then.

As the car trundled upward, Myra thought she heard people whispering. She couldn't make out any words, just sibilant, scarcely audible voices. She turned around and around in the elevator. It was a box, an empty box. Population: Her. But just because she couldn't see anyone didn't mean no one was there. She hoped her invisible companions weren't trying to tell her anything important.

The elevator stopped and the doors opened. She stepped into the hallway. It didn't look much different from the one she had left, but it *felt* different. The air up here was charged, electric. She thought Patrick might be nearby. Myra moved slowly up the corridor, in the direction that felt the least wrong. She began to hear sounds in the stillness, people murmuring, similar to the whispers in the elevator, but louder, closer. She recognized the artificial quality of voices emanating from a small, cheap television speaker.

Television.

She bet she knew who she would find watching it.

~~~~

They rolled into the lounge, Bob and Myra and a couple of orderlies, Robin and Margaret bringing up the rear. There was Patrick, curled up on the couch, eyes closed, as if he had fallen asleep watching a movie. The attendants positioned the stretcher in the middle of the room and then, at a subtle signal from Margaret that Robin noticed but Bob didn't, positioned themselves between Bob and Patrick.

Bob stood there peering into Myra's face. At length, he said: "Nothing's happening."

"It was a long shot," Robin said.

"They need to be closer. They need to be touching."

The orderlies looked at Margaret, who shook her head slightly.

Bob picked up on it this time. "Come on," he said. "Just their fingers. What could it hurt?"

Margaret sighed. "All right." To the orderlies: "Just their hands.

You do it. Not him."

"But I—"

"My people, my rules," Margaret told him. "Step back."

Bob reluctantly moved aside as one orderly took Patrick's wrist and another took Myra's, then stretched out their arms so the backs of their hands touched. Robin braced herself for a shockwave, like in the auditorium, but that didn't happen. Nothing did. Bob, hovering nearby, opened his mouth, probably to suggest hauling Patrick up onto the stretcher, but Margaret forestalled him with a raised hand and a shake of her head.

The orderly holding Myra's wrist said: "Her heart rate is accelerating."

"What does that mean?" Bob said.

Margaret approached the stretcher. Robin trailed along behind her. Myra's eyes were moving fast behind their lids, the dome of her cornea sliding around beneath the think pink skin.

"I've got the same thing here," the other orderly said. "Do we break contact?"

"Not yet," Margaret said.

"What's going on?" Bob peered into Myra's face. "Is she dreaming? Are they having the same dream?"

"I don't know," Margaret said. "There's no way to tell now that we're not in there with them anymore."

"Or maybe we just *think* we're not," Bob said.

~~~~

Myra entered the lounge. It was empty except for a couch, a television, and a Patrick. He looked at her, patted the couch. Uncertain, she sat down beside him. "What's going on?" she said.

"I don't know. I woke up here a little while ago. I've just been watching television." As before, it was showing clips of what appeared to be scenes from the nightmare world of darkness and monsters where they'd spent the night, but the screen was fuzzy, disrupted by static and ripples and oddly ghosted shadows.

"What's up with the picture?"

"I don't know. Something's wrong with the reception. We have satellite and usually the picture is good, unless there's a big storm or something."

"Has it been like that since you woke up?"

"Pretty much."

"How long ago was that?"

"Not long."

They sat in silence for a little while, and then Myra said: "Do you remember anything? From before you woke up?"

"Some. I was watching a different show. I think you were in it. The picture was better then. Do you know how to fix it?"

"No, I don't. Sorry." Then: "Patrick, where did everyone else go?"

"Everyone who?"

"Everyone else who was in the show. Robin. Bob. Margaret. Collins. Do you remember them?"

"Yes. They got written out, I guess."

"Why are we still here?"

He looked at her. The flickering light of the television played across his features. "I'm still here because I never go out. I don't know why you're still here. If you want to leave, go ahead."

"What do you mean?"

"Leave. Walk out the door."

"That's it? Just walk out the door? I can do that?"

"Uh-huh."

She eyed him for a while. "Okay," she said, "but you're coming with me."

"No, I have to stay here."

"No you don't. Look, I'll help you, okay?" She stood up and offered her hand. He didn't seem to know what to do with it, but he finally took it and let her pull him to his feet.

"I'm not sure about this," he said, as she led him into the hallway, then toward the elevator.

"It'll be fine," she said. "It'll be …" She trailed off as a tone announced the arrival of the elevator. Why was it arriving now? Why had it left the floor at all? Who had called it away?

And what was it delivering?

~~~~

Bob had his face so close to Myra's that when her eyes flew open, he practically felt her lashes brush his nose.

Startled, he jumped back, then leaned in and said, "Myra?"

She didn't answer, didn't seem to know he was there. It was like in the car, when she'd had the migraine, and had opened her eyes without seeing. It was happening again. But if he said that, Margaret would order her men to separate Myra and Patrick, and then what would happen? He looked up at the doctor and found that she was looking right at him, her eyes narrow. Whatever she saw in his face, she obviously didn't like it.

"Break contact," she told the orderlies. "Break it now."

The two men tried to pull the hands apart, but they wouldn't separate. Bob could see the skin surfaces sticking together, as if magnetized, or melded.

Robin said: "Oh, fuck."

~~~~

Myra turned around and tried to hurry Patrick back to the lounge, but he dragged his feet, looking over his shoulder. "Why are we running away?" he said. "I thought we were taking the elevator."

"Something else took it first," she said.

"What?"

"I don't want to know." But when she heard the doors slide open, she couldn't help but look back, to see what was coming. It wasn't a creature, as she had feared; it was some sort of liquid darkness, a tide boiling into the hallway. It flung pseudopods ahead of itself, ropy things that stuck to the walls and ceilings and pulled the main mass along. Faces formed and disappeared along the glimmering surface, some quiet, some screaming, some talking, some singing. They made an intolerable babble of voices, fusing together into something that sounded like radio static, but wasn't.

The two of them stumbled into the lounge. Myra kicked the door closed with her foot. It didn't have a lock. She started pushing the couch in front of it. Patrick took the other side and helped her, blocking the way in. Patrick retreated to the radiator and started scrabbling at the pipes. Myra moved over to stand next to him, back to the wall, watching the exit.

Thump!

Something hit the door hard, shifting the sofa.

Thump!

The sofa tipped over. Something fell out of the cushions, a big brass key, grey with tarnish. It looked like the one from the game show, which had opened door number two. It hit the floor and skidded across to them, stopping at Patrick's feet. He snatched it up, inserted it into a spot on the radiator pipe, turned, and pulled. The radiator swung away from the wall, revealing a black opening and a dim, lath-walled passageway. Patrick yanked the key out and started to scramble into the opening, but she caught his shoulder. "Wait!"

Thump!

Black ooze flowed in, over and around the sofa.

Patrick was looking up at her. She said: "Where does this go?"

"Secret passageways. We can hide in here. We can hide for a long time, until it goes away."

Thump!

The couch slid across the smooth tile. The black stuff poured in through the door, now fully opened. She could hear it screaming. It sounded like a hundred people jabbering at once, a thousand people, a maddening cacophony. If there were any coherent sound in there, it was lost on her.

Patrick scuttled into the passageway. She followed. He pulled the radiator shut behind them. A latch snapped into place. The boiling mass surged into the room, but it didn't seem to be able to flow through the radiator. It filled up the lounge, blotting out the lights, the television glow, leaving the passageway in utter darkness.

Patrick took her hand. "Come on," he said.

"But it's so dark."

"We don't need light," he said. "I know my way around in here."

And Myra followed him away from the lounge, into the labyrinth.

~~~~

As the orderlies struggled to pull their hands apart, both Myra and Patrick started thrashing around like they were trying to escape from something. God only knew what might be going on in their heads.

Margaret grabbed the side of the stretcher and pulled, trying to separate them that way, so Robin helped her. Bob just stood there babbling at Myra to wake up. Fucking Bob and his fucking bright ideas.

Suddenly Myra gave an enormous wheeze and stopped moving. Her hand came apart from Patrick's easily, as if they had never been stuck together. The stretcher rolled sideways and nearly tipped over, but didn't. Robin ended up on her ass, looking at Myra's dangling arm, her limp fingers.

Then Patrick coughed a few times and sat up.

Epilogue

Visiting Hours

ROBIN IS COMING to see us today. She tends to come on sunny days, because this place is less depressing when the sunlight streams in. The brightness makes the bars on the windows less noticeable. She never says that, but we can tell that she thinks it.

She doesn't know that we know she's coming; she doesn't know that we can tell when she's in the parking lot, when she's coming up the stairs, when she's getting ready to knock on the door. We usually pretend to be surprised to see her, but every once in a while we forget, and then, on her way home, she wonders.

Today we remember to act surprised.

She brings us some cookies. We knew about them; we smelled them while they were baking in her oven. She puts them on the table near the window so the sun will keep them soft.

Robin asks us how we're doing. We tell her we're doing fine. She asks if we've seen Bob lately. We tell her no, he never comes to visit us. Unlike Robin, Bob doesn't believe that Myra's in here; he thinks there's only Patrick, playing mind games with him. We can't really blame him; after all, Patrick's is the body that we wear. Still, sometimes, we send him nightmares to punish him for staying away. Robin thinks only Myra is in here. We haven't corrected her misconception. It would only upset her.

Robin mentions that Margaret wrote a paper about what happened. Robin has read the paper, although Margaret has not sent it to any of the scientific journals. We read it too, while Margaret was writing it. It's just as well that she leaves it locked in a drawer in her desk. If she made a serious effort to air such claims, she would probably end up sharing a room with us here at the Retreat, regardless of how much corroboration other victims might give.

We make some small talk with Robin. We tell her that we're hoping to leave the hospital soon. It's not like we're imprisoned—they couldn't keep us here against our will unless they could prove we were dangerous—but we aren't ready to get out. Not yet. We need a place to live, a way to support ourselves. We're arranging it. We're just not quite finished.

Robin offers to let us stay with her for a while, once we leave the Retreat. That's awfully nice of her, but we already have plans. When we walk out of here, we'll head down to the lake, knock at the door of the biggest summer house there, and present ourselves as a long-lost member of the family. They'll believe us, when the time comes. We've been working on their dreams.

And did we mention that they have a really big television?

About the Author

James V. Viscosi is the author of several horror and fantasy novels. An expatriate New Yorker, he currently resides with his wife and various finned and furry animals in sunny Southern California, where he spends most of his time hiding beneath a very large hat. Visit him at www.jamesviscosi.com.

www.ingramcontent.com/pod-product-compliance
Lightning Source LLC
Chambersburg PA
CBHW020716130726
47899CB00012B/1737